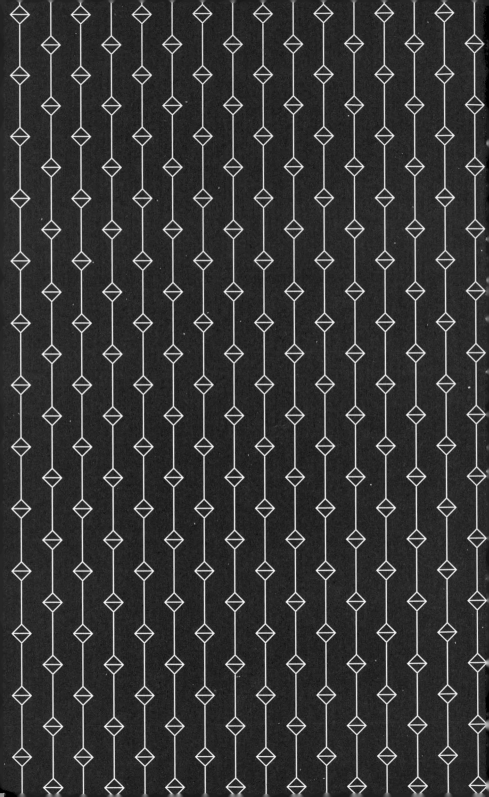

IRON CAST

DESTINY SORIA

AMULET BOOKS
NEW YORK

For my mom, who taught me to read.

And my dad, who taught me to love the stories.

And for Kara, who is golden.

Library of Congress Cataloging-in-Publication Data

Names: Soria, Destiny.
Title: Iron cast / Destiny Soria.
Description: New York : Amulet Books, 2016. | Summary: In 1919 Boston, best friends Corinne and Ada perform illegally as illusionists in an infamous gangster's nightclub, using their "afflicted" blood to con Boston's elite, until the law closes in.
Identifiers: LCCN 2016013279 | ISBN 9781419721922 (hardback)
Subjects: | CYAC: Magicians—Fiction. | Criminals—FIction. | Nightclubs—Fiction. | Gangsters—Fiction. | Prejudices—Fiction. | Boston (Mass.)—History—19th century—Fiction.
Classification: LCC PZ7.1.S678 Iro 2016 | DDC [Fic]—dc23
LC record available at https://lccn.loc.gov/2016013279

Printed and bound in U.S.A.
10 9 8 7 6 5 4 3 2 1

ABRAMS The Art of Books
115 West 18th Street, New York, NY 10011
abramsbooks.com

WE ARE THE MUSIC-MAKERS,
AND WE ARE THE DREAMERS OF DREAMS

—Arthur O'Shaughnessy, "Ode"

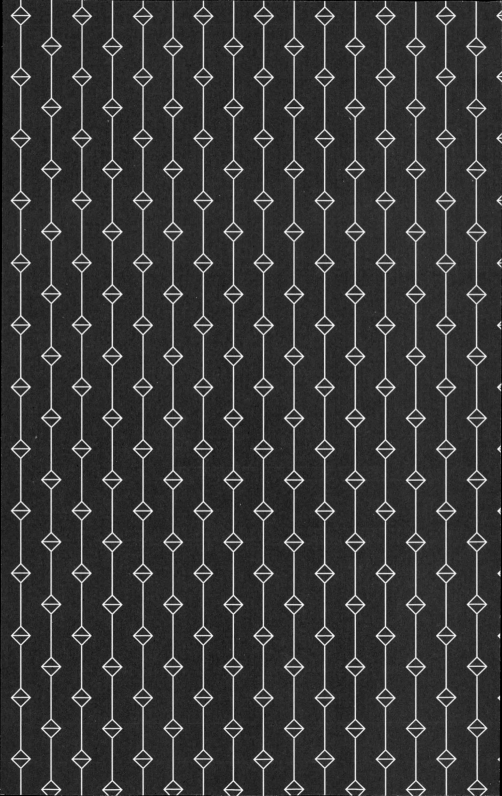

CHAPTER ONE

───── ◈ ─────

CORINNE'S FIRST DAY AS A NURSE AT THE HAVERSHAM ASYLUM for Afflictions of the Blood was a frosty Thursday. It had been a little over a week since the start of the New Year, and so far 1919 was not showing signs of promise—at least according to the head nurse. Corinne smoothed out her white starched uniform as the pale, hawkish woman clucked her tongue at the state of the world.

"Mark my words, this is the year when the Bolsheviks make themselves known," said the head nurse. "America is under siege from within."

"No doubt," Corinne said vaguely. She wasn't really paying attention. She couldn't even remember the head nurse's name, though she supposed it would come to her eventually. The corridors they walked were all the same hideous taupe, from floor to ceiling. It gave Corinne a headache, though that might have been due to the comically large ring of keys that clinked and clanked with the head nurse's every step. Over the PA system, a dreary voice told Dr. Knox that he had a visitor, and to please report to the front desk.

The buckle of Corinne's left shoe had loosened, and she hopped on one foot to fix it while the head nurse unlocked the door marked *205* in shiny black paint.

"You'll start your rounds every morning at precisely seven a.m.," she told Corinne. "Structure and punctuality are very important here. You'll have a chart that explains which patients are confined to their rooms and which are permitted to take breakfast in the dining hall."

The lock gave way with a groan, and the head nurse returned her key ring to her belt.

"Ada," she said into the dark room. "Ada, I know you're awake."

"Morning, Molls," came a voice from the corner opposite the bed. A small, barred window let in enough light for Corinne to make out the girl's warm, sepia skin and high, jutting cheekbones. She was sitting on the floor, wedged into the corner with one knee clutched to her chest. Her eyes glinted in the dim daylight as she tilted her chin upward.

"You'll address me as Nurse Heller," said the head nurse. Then she turned to Corinne. "This is Ada Navarra. She arrived here only recently and is still adjusting. There was an . . . incident when she first came, so she's confined to her room until Dr. Knox clears her."

"What sort of incident?" Corinne asked, fiddling with a strand of yellow hair that had fallen from her neat braid.

"Some lunatic tried to jab metal into me, and I politely refused," said Ada, eyeing Corinne. Her lips twitched slightly, and although her voice was weak, it held an edge. "You don't look half old enough to be playing nurse, Goldilocks. Tell 'em you were eighteen, did you?"

"Dr. Knox was trying to perform a routine examination, and Miss Navarra flipped a table on top of him," Nurse Heller said. "Ada, this is Nurse Salem. She will be assisting me on this ward."

Ada chuckled and shook her head. Her scarf was coming loose, and tight ebony coils sprang free across her smooth skin.

"I fail to see what's funny about that," said Corinne.

"Salem? You gotta be pulling my leg," Ada said, squinting at her.

"That's enough, Ada," said Nurse Heller. She rapped her knuckles against the doorframe. "You'll show Nurse Salem respect or Dr. Knox will hear of it. And cover your hair—you're indecent."

Ada tugged at the gray scarf. Her lips were still twisted into a smirk, though the lines of weariness were unmistakable in her features.

"Say, Nurse Salem, you come from a family of witches?" she asked. "Because I have this awful pain in my rear and could sure use a touch of dark magic."

"Salem is a Hellenization of the Hebrew *shalom,* which means *peace,*" said Corinne.

"Pardon me," said Ada, retying the scarf with exaggerated gusto. "I did not know I was in the presence of a scholar. You can teach me some Latin while you scrub the latrine."

"I don't expect you'd be able to handle the declensions," Corinne replied coolly.

Ada sat up a little straighter, her eyes suddenly bright.

"I can handle anything you care to throw at me, Goldilocks."

"We'll see."

Before Ada could retort, Nurse Heller slammed the door and locked it. Corinne saw that her taut jaw was trembling and her knuckles were white where she clutched her key ring.

"These are very troubled souls," Nurse Heller said after a few seconds. She straightened and patted at her coifed gray hair. "As they are hemopaths, we must pity their affliction. But as those here are also criminals, we must keep ourselves apart. If you let them under your skin, then you will be hindered in your duties. Am I perfectly clear, Nurse Salem?"

"Yes, ma'am." Corinne ducked her head obediently and followed Nurse Heller to the next door. Her shoe buckle had come undone again.

· · · · · ◆ · · · · ·

The days in the asylum had been passing more slowly than the nights. Maybe that was because Ada could watch the sunlight trace its way along the tiled floor, creeping in excruciating inches until breakfast, and then surging to a blinding line of gold at lunch. After that, it disappeared in degrees, replaced by the umber of sunset, then the deep blue of twilight. Ada had been there only two weeks, but she already knew its every station.

Tonight, when the blue finally gave way to black, she did not move to the straw-stuffed mattress across the room. She stayed where she was, her back pressed against the unyielding corner. She had tried to sleep in the bed the first night, but the inmate in the adjacent room had wept without ceasing, her wails vibrating through the wall.

The last Ada had heard from the woman on the other side was days ago. She'd screamed when they'd come for her. Ada told herself they had taken her to the infirmary wing. It was a lie, but a comforting one at least. Other than giving the nurses and doctors hell, there was no real comfort to be had in this place.

Her muscles and bones ached from her confinement, but she still did not move. If they were coming for her, she wanted to be awake. She wanted to fight back. The asylum was full of people just like her, but she still felt terribly alone.

Until today.

From outside the cell came the sound of a key sliding into the lock, jolting with force, and then the door swung open. Silhouetted by the light from the corridor, Nurse Salem leaned against the doorframe, arms crossed, smile visible even in shadow.

"Well?" said Corinne. "Are you coming?"

Ada climbed to her feet. Blood rushed to her head, and the aching of her body retreated to the back of her mind.

"Two weeks?" she asked, joining Corinne in the corridor. "My grandmother could have planned a faster rescue than this."

"I was going for a slow build to a grand finale. Like an opera."

"You've never been to an opera in your life," Ada whispered as they made their way briskly toward the stairs.

"Sure I have. I had two whole weeks of leisure while I was waiting for the suspense to build. Learned embroidery too."

At any other time, the image of Corinne trying to thread a needle would have sent Ada into fits of laughter, but tonight she could feel the walls of Haversham crowding around her. She tried to shake herself free, but some part of her was still back in that cell, watching the darkness slither in. They descended the stairs two at a time. Corinne's shoes clattered on the polished wood, while the cotton slippers they had given Ada were silent. The door in the stairwell led to another corridor on the ground level, and they crept through it.

Considering the costume and the fact that Corinne had been making rounds as a bona fide nurse that day, Ada supposed there was some kind of plan in place. Of course, there was always the possibility that Corinne had concocted an elaborate scheme to get in but hadn't bothered with an escape route, in hopes that things would sort themselves out. It wouldn't be the first time.

Ada jumped at a sound behind them, fighting the flurry of fear in her gut. There was nothing there. Corinne gave her a strange look, but as she opened her mouth to speak, there was a commotion around the corner, where the main entrance was. Doors were banging and feet were shuffling and a man was screaming. Another man snapped something to a nurse about a sedative. More scuffling. Then quiet.

Before Ada could grab her, Corinne edged along the wall until she could peek around the corner. After a few seconds of listening to the muffled voices, Ada joined her.

Two men in dark suits gripped a limp, ragged man between them. Their hats were pulled low over their features, but Ada could see that they were both unconcerned by the unconscious weight they held. One of them made a joke about the weather while the nurse on duty whispered nervously into her desk phone. The other one laughed, but it wasn't a pleasant sound.

Ada shivered and pulled Corinne back before they could be seen. It was clear enough that they were HPA.

"Dr. Knox wants to know if you have any paperwork on him," the nurse was asking.

"Miss, I know you're doing your job, but this slagger is getting heavy. Tell Knox it's another one for the basement."

The nurse relayed the information in a murmur; then there was the click of the receiver.

"Use the back stairs," she said.

There was more grunting and slamming of doors. Corinne yanked on Ada's sleeve and whispered in her ear. "What's in the basement?"

Ada shrugged, but she was thinking about the inmate in the next cell over. The one they had come for late in the night.

Corinne shook her head and pulled a brass pocket watch from her uniform. The familiar sight was comforting. In four years, Ada had never seen Corinne without that watch.

"Five fifteen," Corinne said softly. "Showtime. Stay close, and try to look contrite, will you?"

Ada didn't get a chance to demand an explanation before Corinne marched around the corner toward the front desk. Lacking a better alternative, Ada followed her. She kept her head down in what she hoped was an approximation of "contrite." Her heart was slamming against her rib cage, and she had to twine her fingers together to stop their shaking.

At their approach, the nurse jumped up.

"Nurse . . . Salem," she said, fumbling only briefly for the name. There was a magazine on her desk that she shoved neatly under a stack of papers. "What are you doing?"

"Dr. Knox prescribed Navarra a brisk walk every four hours, no exceptions," Corinne said. "Can you point me to the walking path? He said something about a pond?"

"It's dark outside," the nurse said.

Peering up through her eyelashes, Ada could see suspicion all over the nurse's face. She was reaching for her earplugs, which dangled from her neck on a fashionable necklace that was probably a protective iron alloy rather than nickel or silver. Ada had the sudden, exasperating thought that maybe Corinne really had expected to just walk out the front door.

"Nurse Salem, any particular reason you're gossiping in the hallway?" A man's voice made Ada jump, and she whirled, finding herself face-to-face with Dr. Knox.

He was lumpy in his white coat, with a bald head and thin spectacles that he must've repaired since his last encounter with Ada. He ignored her and crossed his arms.

"Sorry, Doctor," Corinne said. "I was just asking where I could find the walking path."

"Go left," he said, waving toward the front doors. "Weren't you given a tour this morning? No one here has time to draw you a map."

He cast a sympathetic glance toward the desk nurse, who seemed appeased by his scolding of Corinne. She sat back down.

"The agents are waiting for you in the basement, Doctor," she said with a preening smile.

He nodded and finally acknowledged Ada. "Miss Navarra, I trust that after our discussion about rewards and consequences, you'll be able to behave yourself on these little walks?"

Ada couldn't recall any such discussion. In fact, the last time she had seen Dr. Knox, she had just flipped a table on top of him, but she just nodded.

"Good," he said. "Remember, privileges are earned." He patted Corinne on the shoulder in a fatherly gesture and left.

Ada saw the face Corinne made but didn't dare say anything with the nurse still watching them from her chair. She kept her head down, reminding herself to look contrite, and they walked out the front door.

They didn't turn left toward the brown grassy lawn. They just kept walking down the wide gravel drive—slowly at first, but soon they were sprinting. The sharp rocks stabbed at Ada's feet, but she didn't care. Moonlight wafted across the grounds like a jazz melody, and the cold wind of January had never felt so good.

"What about the gates?" Ada asked. She had to pump her legs to keep up, even though Corinne was much shorter. Her muscles were just now remembering what it meant to move.

"Jackson will have them open."

"Jackson? He's here?" The newest hire at Johnny's club had been around for only a week before Ada was arrested.

"Cripes, don't tell me you didn't recognize him. I thought for sure he got the eyes wrong."

No wonder Doctor Knox had seemed so forgiving toward her.

"Dead ringer," Ada said, ignoring the burning in her lungs. "He's good."

"He's an ass."

A laugh burst from Ada before she could stop it. She didn't know why she was laughing, except that her best friend was beside her, and they were running so fast her feet were barely touching the ground, and up ahead she could see the open gates of the wrought-iron fence surrounding the Haversham Asylum for Afflictions of the Blood.

They breezed through with a brief twinge of pain, crossed the road, and half ran, half slid down the long embankment on the other side. They had only the moon for light, and Corinne slowed as she headed for the line of trees. Ada followed close behind her.

"We gonna walk to Boston?" Ada asked. She rubbed her arms vigorously against the cold.

Corinne glanced over her shoulder toward the empty road, then blew some warm breath into her hands. She didn't seem particularly concerned by the increasing likelihood of someone in Haversham realizing they'd been duped and chasing after them with iron-tipped billy clubs. But then Corinne never seemed *particularly* concerned about anything.

"I brought the Ford," she replied, stopping for a moment to fiddle with the buckle on her shoe. "There's an access road through here."

"I hate the Ford," Ada said.

"So sorry, Princess. I could always leave you here. Maybe your next rescue will be more to your liking."

Ada knew it was a joke, but the mere notion of going back was like a knife in her stomach. Even as they went deeper into the wood, she could feel the asylum looming over them. Suddenly every stone and fallen branch was excruciating beneath her ill-protected feet. Corinne was looking at her strangely again as they walked, no doubt confused by Ada's sudden reticence. Ada forced a tight smile.

"I'll admit," she said, "I was hoping for some explosions or at least a sleeping draft in the head nurse's tea."

"What are we, gangsters?"

"Well—"

"Never mind."

The dead trees and underbrush extended for only a few hundred yards before opening onto a dirt road, where the hulking black Ford was waiting. Ada climbed in to shield herself from the rising wind, and Corinne leaned in through the driver's side to grab some leather gloves from the seat.

"There's a coat in the back, and aspirin's under the seat," Corinne said.

Ada immediately snatched up the bottle of aspirin and swallowed three. She shook a few into Corinne's palm as well. Then she retrieved her coat from the backseat and slid into it gratefully, buttoning it all the way. The winter chill had reached her bones by now, but she felt marginally better buried under the thick gray wool.

It took Corinne almost twenty minutes to start the car, but finally it roared to life. Ada never understood how Corinne, who was small and wiry, with only five feet and a couple of inches to her name, ever found the strength to crank the pistons to life—and with only one broken thumb on her record. It wasn't an achievement many sixteen-year-olds could boast of. She suspected Corinne was just more stubborn than the engine.

Corinne eased the Ford, humming and juddering, along the dirt road until they reached the main roadway. She hit the gas, and the countryside whipped past. Behind them, the asylum receded into the distance. Ada told herself firmly that she was free, but there was still a tingling at the back of her neck, a certainty in her chest that it couldn't be this easy. No one ever made it out of Haversham.

After a few minutes of silent driving, Ada made herself speak, if only to break free from her own twisting anxiety.

"What's a declension, anyway?" she asked, because that was the first thing that popped into her head. She had to raise her voice to be heard over the rumbling wheels.

"How the hell should I know? I think I only attended one lecture that entire term."

"What a waste of a good education."

"That's funny coming from someone who thinks Walt Whitman is a brand of chocolate bar." Corinne fiddled with the mirror for a few seconds, looking at the dark, empty road behind them. "Besides, I spent that time learning the first three cantos of the *Inferno* in the original Italian. A couple lines of Dante serve a wordsmith better than a year's worth of Latin conjugations."

"Careful, Nurse Salem—we're not far from your namesake. They're probably still burning our type for being witches there."

"Then you'd better be nice to me, or I'll be tempted to drop you off."

"What could they possibly want with me?" Ada made a show of straightening her head scarf. "I'm but a simple escaped convict. You're the one taking the name of their beloved town in vain, as one of the most idiotic aliases in the history of crime."

The familiar banter was like a tonic, keeping her exhaustion at bay. Haversham was retreating slowly from her thoughts as the aspirin eased the ache of her muscles.

"It wouldn't have been nearly as transparent if you hadn't started laughing like a fool."

The car careened over a pothole, and Corinne had to hug the wheel to keep it steady. Ada braved a glance through the back window, but even in the moonlight, the road behind them disappeared almost immediately into darkness. Hidden behind hills and trees, Haversham wasn't even a distant glimmer anymore.

"You come in there with a name like Nurse Salem, and you want me to keep a straight face?" Ada asked, looking forward again.

"It really does mean *peace*," muttered Corinne.

Ada laughed for only the second time in two weeks, a reckless, helpless laugh that rang over the rumbling of the wheels and the roar of the engine. After a few seconds, Corinne laughed too. Her fair skin was flushed a rosy pink. She rolled down the window and yanked off her blond wig, revealing her short brown hair, plastered with sweat. The blond braid flapped wildly, then was rushed away by the wind. The January cold dipped into the window, nipping at Ada's skin. She didn't mind, though.

She was going home.

CHAPTER TWO

THE CAST IRON WAS A CLUB ON THE CORNER OF CLARENDON AND Appleton Streets, too close to the South End to be high-class but too close to the theater district to be disreputable. The current owner, a Mr. John Dervish, enjoyed skirting the line between the two. The building stood proud and alone, with only empty storefronts for neighbors and an abandoned bakery at its rear. A garish red door led into a dim corridor lined with mirrors. The heavy wooden door at the other end opened into the club proper, which boasted a long bar and tables of all shapes and sizes scattered around the room.

When Corinne and Ada walked in, arm in arm, just before seven, business was gearing up for the evening. There were only a few patrons scattered among the tables, nursing drinks and swaying to the sinuous melody of a lone pianist onstage. Ada reassured herself that her coat was buttoned over her Haversham-issued smock, just in case.

"Heya, kiddos," said the bartender, glancing up from the glass he was drying. He was tall and lean, with salty hair and cheeks covered in grizzled stubble.

"Heya back, Danny," said Corinne, tossing the car key onto the bar. "Be an absolute peach and get Johnny's car back to his garage?"

Danny looked down at the key, still polishing the glass with practiced flicks of his wrist. "I look like a chauffeur to you, Wells?"

Ada leaned across the bar and gave him a quick peck on the cheek. "I'll get you a cap, and you'll look mighty fine," she told him.

Danny raised an eyebrow, with the look of a man determined

not to be moved. After a few seconds his face broke into a grin, revealing two gold teeth. "Ada Navarra, you incorrigible minx."

"Five syllables, Danny? Where'd you learn that one?" Corinne asked, stretching over the counter beside Ada to nab a bottle of gin.

"Pain-in-the-ass girl I know," he said. "Steals my alcohol and has apparently decided to take up nursing. By the way, that bottle's going on your tab, not mine. If those teetotalers get their way, I'm going to need every penny for my early retirement."

"America is the land of liberty, Danny dearest," Corinne said. "She won't stand for Prohibition, mark my words."

Danny snorted and shook his head. "So you two dolls ever gonna tell me why the Cast Iron's best musician mysteriously vanished for two weeks and now you're both showing up looking like a couple of pawn shop mannequins?"

"Probably not," said Corinne.

"Figured."

Danny set down the glass on the worn wood of the counter and pocketed the key. Corinne headed toward the back, hugging the gin bottle. Ada reached over to pluck it from her arms and, ignoring Corinne's indignant protests, handed it back to Danny.

"Thanks, Ada," Danny said. "Give your ma my regards."

"Will do, Danny."

Ada saluted the bartender and tugged a still-protesting Corinne through the doorway at the other end of the hall. The narrow stairs went down half a level to the storage room, which was stacked with crates of liquor, boxes of dry goods, and anything else that had been shoved there and forgotten. That included Gordon Calloway, who was two hundred-odd pounds of sunflower seeds stuffed into a cheap suit. He spent eight hours a day sitting in a wooden chair in the storage room and was paid handsomely to do it.

"Johnny's waiting in his office," he said, spitting out a sunflower seed.

"Why yes, Gordon, my day has been swell. Thanks for asking," said Corinne.

Ada elbowed her, but Gordon just grunted. Corinne went past Gordon to the wall in the corner of the room. She pressed against the wood paneling with one hand, and a section of it swung inward, revealing a flight of rickety steps that led all the way to the basement. When Ada had first come there, it had taken her days to find the right panel with any accuracy. She was still embarrassed thinking about the number of times Gordon had watched her out of the corner of his eye while she fumbled across the wall.

The only light in the stairwell emanated from the base, but Ada knew every step instinctively. The living quarters where Johnny Dervish's chosen few hung their hats were cramped and a little musty, but no one had ever complained. There was a central common room with a ratty couch, floral armchairs, and a coffee table— usually piled with sheet music, books, and half-finished bottles of whiskey or gin.

Ada couldn't hold back a sigh of relief. For the first time since fleeing Haversham, she didn't feel the asylum's presence bearing down on her. Maybe one day, the past two weeks would become a distant memory, something she could tell as a diverting story between cigarette pulls and frenzied turns on the dance floor. Until then she was just content to be here, hidden away in the tiny kingdom that Johnny Dervish had built. The Cast Iron meant safety—it always had.

She and Corinne shared a room opposite the stairs, with a low door partially obscured by a potted plant. Not much more than two army cots and a stack of milk crates, but they had made it a home, papering the walls with magazine cutouts and draping silk scarves from the plywood ceiling.

Ada shed her shapeless asylum garb and slipped into a skirt and blouse. She yanked the scarf off her head and tossed it into the corner. Her freed hair emerged cloudlike around her face. She examined it carefully in the mirror. Two weeks without proper care had left it worse for wear, but the damage was not irreparable. Out in society, she would garner nasty glares by leaving it free like this, but if there was one place she could always walk without fear, it was the Cast Iron.

Behind her, Corinne had stripped off her uniform and left it bundled in the corner with Ada's scarf. She was dressing in a blue, low-waisted frock that appeared to have spent the majority of its life wadded in a ball. She leaned around Ada's shoulder at the mirror to twist her fingers through her limp hair for a few seconds before finally giving up.

In the reflection, Ada caught a glimpse of something on her bed that she hadn't seen before. She turned to find a small canvas painting, maybe twelve inches square, propped against the wall. It depicted a sprawling tree by a creek, ringed by the riotous glare of yellow-white sunlight. The emerald grass grew tall and wild, even in the dappled shade of the branches. There were clumps of vibrant purple wildflowers, painted with such dexterity that they seemed to have motion in the breeze. A wooden swing hung in the foreground, a picture of peaceful tranquility.

In front of the painting on the bed, tied with simple twine, was a bunch of purple wildflowers, the exact shade and shape as the ones in the painting.

"Saint left that for you." Corinne was in the corner, hopping on one foot as she tried to free herself from her shoe. "He thought you might want some springtime, after the asylum."

There was a pang in Ada's chest, and she bit her lip. For a split second she was back there again, paralyzingly alone in a prison built for people just like her.

"Is he here?" she asked, struggling to keep her voice even.

"I haven't heard from him in a while." Corinne finally gave in and sat down on her bed to unbuckle her shoes. "You should have seen him the night you were arrested, Ada. He was a wreck when he got back to the Cast Iron. Johnny almost called the doctor."

Ada pushed the painting facedown on the bed and turned her head so that Corinne couldn't see her expression.

"Everything jake?" Corinne asked after a few seconds.

"I don't want to talk about it." Ada went back to the mirror and rubbed vigorously at the dark circles under her eyes.

Beyond her own reflection, she could see Corinne eyeing her, deciding whether or not to press the issue further. Finally Corinne shrugged.

"Come on," she told Ada. "Johnny will want to know it all went without a hitch."

Ada followed her out the door, relieved the moment had passed. It was rare that she kept anything from Corinne, but this was still too fresh a wound. She arranged her face into the wry expression she knew Corinne would expect.

"Giving you the key to his Ford and sending you off to an asylum with a fake uniform and the foolproof alias of 'Nurse Salem'— how could he think anything would go wrong?"

"I'll have you know that this brilliant plan was entirely my design," Corinne said.

"Oh, I don't doubt it."

"Do I detect a hint of sarcasm?"

"You're the wordsmith around here, Cor. I just play the music and look pretty."

Corinne snorted but didn't say more.

Johnny's office was in the basement as well, at the end of a corridor by the stairs. Johnny didn't live at the Cast Iron, in the sense that he had a house and bed elsewhere, but anyone would be hard-pressed to find a time when he wasn't in his office or at his reserved table on the club floor, working through lines of visitors and petitioners like a king of old.

"There's my girls," he said, beaming at them from behind his massive oak desk.

There were a handful of people in his office, including someone Ada had never seen before. The stranger was sitting on the corner of the desk, his black shirtsleeves rolled up to his elbows. He had short, unruly brown hair, pale skin, and a look of suspicious amusement that belied his youthful features. His coal-gray trousers were neatly pressed, but Ada saw that his shoes were practical and well-worn.

The office cleared, with most of the visitors patting Ada on the shoulder. The exact circumstances of her absence weren't widely known, but it was hard to keep a tight lid on something like that. No telling what the latest rumor was. No telling how much Corinne had embroidered those rumors herself.

Only the stranger stayed behind, standing and unrolling his sleeves with slow, careful movements. He hadn't made eye contact with Ada or Corinne yet.

"Girls," said Johnny, "this is Gabriel Stone. I hired him to help with security around here. After recent events, I want to make sure all avenues are covered."

"Looks a little scrawny for a bodyguard," said Corinne. He was nearly a foot taller than her.

"I manage well enough," he said, his gaze flickering across the two of them for the first time.

"You a wordsmith?" Ada asked. He had that look about him. Perpetually smug and mildly sardonic. And he had obviously set Corinne on edge. She didn't play well with people she considered competitors.

He shook his head but didn't offer any more explanation.

"You can give him the rundown tomorrow," Johnny said. "I assume you had a clean break from your little situation, Ada? I don't expect Jackson back for another couple hours."

"They're going to take it pretty hard," Ada said. "I was their favorite inmate."

Corinne threw her arm around Ada's shoulders. "You know our Ada, making friends, respecting authority, flipping tables onto doctors."

"Sounds more like you," Johnny said.

"What can I say?" Corinne shrugged. "I'm her role model."

Ada rolled her eyes, and Johnny flashed a smile. He was striking rather than handsome, with a light, ruddy complexion, a dash of gray at the temples, and a brash grin that inspired confidence in even the wariest of business associates. Unlike some of his contemporaries, he stayed away from silk suits and flashy cuff links, opting for attire that wouldn't look out of place on a horse ranch. Ada had asked him about it once, and he'd laughed and given a vague reply that didn't really answer her question.

"Good to have you back," he told her. "Corinne is unbearable without you. All she does is mumble obscure poetry and drink."

"I can't help that she's the fun one," Corinne said.

"You really all right, kid?" Johnny asked, looking at Ada. She wondered if there was something in her expression that told the tale of her sleepless nights huddled in the corner of that godforsaken cell. Everything was so much better here, surrounded by oak and pine and the pungent scent of cloves.

But that wasn't something she would say out loud, not to Johnny. Anyway, Gabriel was watching her with his dark eyes and slightly raised eyebrows.

"Everything's copacetic, boss," she said.

Johnny's lips twisted. He was fiddling with a pocketknife on his desk, which might have been ominous in any other context, but Ada knew that Johnny only ever used it as a letter opener. It had been a gift from his predecessor.

"You two up for a set tonight?" he asked. "We haven't had a decent night's run without you, Ada."

Ada hesitated, thinking longingly of her bed. Her entire body was pulsing with exhaustion, and her violin hadn't been tuned in two weeks.

"We've got Charlie on loan from the Red Cat," Corinne said, nudging her.

Ada elbowed her back but couldn't repress a smile. "Why not?"

"Perfect," Johnny said. "You go on at nine. Gabriel, go tell Danny that I'm expecting Senator Jacobs and his wife tonight. Keep my table clear."

Gabriel nodded and stood up. He followed Ada and Corinne out of Johnny's office.

"You ever seen a show before?" Ada asked him.

"Hemopath shows are illegal," he replied.

Corinne snorted. "Someone should tell the senator that," she said. "He'll be so disappointed."

Gabriel ignored her. They had reached the common room, and he paused at the base of the stairwell, watching Ada with the wrinkle of a frown in his forehead.

"Didn't you just break out of Haversham?" he asked.

"So?" Ada crossed her arms, keeping her tone carefully neutral.

"And now you're going on stage in front of some of the city's wealthiest, most upright citizens?"

"This is the Cast Iron," Corinne said, looping her arm through Ada's again. "It's always safe here."

"Besides, if they were such upright citizens, they wouldn't be at an illegal hemopath show," Ada said.

Gabriel shrugged, though his expression gave no hint as to whether the gesture was in agreement or uninterest. He started up the stairs without further comment.

"He's going to be a killjoy," Corinne said once the panel had slid shut behind him. "I can tell."

Ada laughed and tugged her toward their bedroom to get ready.

Show nights in the Cast Iron always started the same. Seats began to fill up fast after eight o'clock, once dinner engagements had concluded and excuses had been made. Patrons ambled down Clarendon and Appleton alone and in pairs, slipping in through the red door only when the coast was clear, surrendering any iron as they arrived. The watchword for entry came at a high price and changed with every show. Usually it was the same old crowd—rich, bored regs who found hemopaths to be novelties or magicians or misunderstood souls, rather than diseased in the blood. The Cast Iron wasn't the only one of its kind, of course, but it had the best music by far. In this day and age, the music was what mattered.

In the old days the Cast Iron had been a quiet, unremarkable pub. Its patrons had been the intellectuals and idealists of Boston, men without a penny to their name but enough on their minds to keep the fire in the hearth burning well into the night. When he took over, Johnny had dragged the club into the modern era, and now its spectacular shows were the worst-kept secret in Boston.

Ada waited backstage with the other musicians, her violin on her lap and her fingers intertwined with Charlie Lewis's. They sat on a threadbare sofa, talking in hushed voices while the rest of the band pretended not to eavesdrop.

"I'm just saying that Corinne should have told me what was going on," he said. "Maybe I could have helped."

"I wouldn't have wanted you to help," she said, not meeting his eyes.

"What?" He leaned forward, tilting his head to better see her face. Charlie was lean and rangy, with close-cropped hair and eyes that caught the light like a dark prism. His sleeves were rolled to his elbows, revealing the tattoo of a twisting, leafless tree on the tawny brown skin of his left forearm.

"I meant—Corinne had it under control," Ada said.

"That's not what you said."

Ada plucked at the E string on her violin, wishing fervently that she hadn't spoken. This was not a conversation she wanted to have backstage, surrounded by their fellow songsmiths, with a severe lack of sleep draining her better judgment.

"Can't we just forget it?" she asked. "At least for tonight?"

Charlie regarded her for another few seconds, then nodded and leaned back. Ada squeezed his hand and rested her head on his shoulder in relief. She'd first met Charlie almost a year ago, when she and Corinne had attended a show at the Red Cat with Johnny. She'd never heard anyone play a French horn like Charlie could.

She figured he probably knew that, considering his cool confidence in asking her out the next day, drawling his sultry Southern accent and winking like they shared a secret.

In retrospect, she liked how effortless it had been. Being with Charlie was easy, and these days, precious few things in her life were.

The stage door opened, and Corinne stuck her head in. She had a half-empty gin and tonic in hand and was wearing her favorite evening dress. It was pale pink and shimmery with tiny beads, capped at the shoulders and fluttering around her calves. A gold-and-silver headache band glimmered over her dark hair. The entire getup was in stark contrast to her usual fare of whatever wrinkled garment she stumbled over first in the morning. Tonight she was onstage, and when Corinne put on a show, she liked to shine the brightest.

"You all ready?" she asked.

The musicians gave their assent and started filing through the door. When Ada passed Corinne, she lifted her left hand to Corinne's right for their signature handshake. They tapped their fingertips together twice. A brief touch, easily overlooked. Ada didn't know how it had been possible to miss such a simple gesture so fiercely.

She took her spot stage left, a few feet away from Corinne, who gave her a broad smile. Corinne was dazzling under the stage lights, the beads on her dress glinting with every small movement. Ada smiled back and propped her violin under her chin. Her own dress of midnight-blue silk was simple in comparison, but Ada didn't mind. Subtlety had its own distinction amid the flair of Boston's nightlife.

The faint aroma of spicy hors d'oeuvres and bittersweet

beverages filled the room, mingled with perfume and cigarette smoke. The club was packed tonight, elbow to elbow with men in black suits and women in glittering dresses. The Cast Iron was small and humble in comparison to the Red Cat, its main competitor, but that didn't stop its loyal patrons from putting on the ritz for every performance. The lights were almost blinding, and Ada could barely make out Johnny at his corner table, entertaining the nervous senator and his wife. For Johnny the evening shows were all business, though he still refused to wear a dinner jacket. Jackson, also underdressed for the occasion, was sitting by Johnny, halfway through a beer. She noticed Gabriel at a table near the stage, though he didn't have a drink in front of him.

Corinne stepped up to the microphone, which was custom-made from brass and carbon. She didn't even have to speak before the crowd fell silent.

"Welcome to the Cast Iron" was all she said.

Ada recognized her cue and sent the first mournful note into the air.

The musicians rarely rehearsed together for these shows. It was widely believed that a more spontaneous sound led to a more spectacular experience. Even though she'd played with Charlie only on the rare occasions when he wasn't needed at the Red Cat, she knew he would find an entrance and intertwine with her melody. The goal, of course, was harmony, but not just in the music—in the emotions as well.

Ada always started low, laying down loss and longing like a delicate lace. She kept her melody in the minor key, and for almost three minutes hers was the only sound in the room. Charlie's horn opened soft, for a few bars matching her tone; then he began drawing out a new thread, a vague sense of hope that Ada recognized from the first time she'd ever heard him play. She forced herself to focus, following his lead into a wistful place. The other musicians were playing too, keeping the pace, tying everything together, but it was clearly Ada and Charlie's show.

The faces in the crowd were slack with the proffered feelings. Ada could sense the emotions that her fellow songsmiths were churning out, but with a little effort she could avoid being overwhelmed by them, letting the gentle melancholy slide off her like rain. It was different for the regs, who wouldn't be able to put up more than token resistance even if they wanted to. Hemopathy for public consumption had been banned in Boston by city law six months ago, but the shows had continued behind locked doors, and attendance had barely faltered. There was something irresistible about the experience.

Corinne moved closer to the microphone, her voice a gentle, swaying murmur. She was reciting a poem that Ada didn't recognize. Something about an idle king and barren crags. The stage lights seemed to dim. Suddenly the ceiling above them was a blanket of stars, with a silver moon draped in gossamer threads of light. The audience burst into murmurs of appreciation and awe, but no one onstage broke stride.

Corinne kept reciting, her voice only a hint louder than the music that enveloped them. She spoke of sinking stars, dark broad seas, and men who strove with gods. The constellations came to life. A thunderous Leo shook the heavens in a silent roar. The Twins danced together across the captured sky. The Water Bearer poured his load, sending a river of sparkling light across the patrons.

The entire show was an intricate dance. Even the performers were never entirely sure whether Corinne was matching the music or whether Ada and Charlie were following her lead. Finally the stars began to dim. Corinne cast Ada a surreptitious glance, and

Ada dipped her head slightly in recognition. She and Corinne had never played this particular illusion before, but she had an idea where Corinne was going.

Corinne held up her hand and the other musicians fell silent. Ada drew out a long note, then slid into a new melody. Her hope wasn't as good as Charlie's, but she'd been told that her nostalgia was masterful. She pushed it into the room, shut her eyes, and envisioned the feeling like a mist, settling over each person.

Ada had never wanted to be a star. There were certain doors that would never be opened to a girl whose parents had formed what society considered an unspeakable union. She didn't believe in dreaming for the impossible, but the illusions and emotions that she and Corinne could weave together—those were more real to her than the heat of the spotlight, than the gushing of the crowd.

She let herself be consumed by the strings of her violin, the curving action of the bow. If she thought too hard about the enigmatic talent that gave her these abilities, it would elude her. Instead she focused on the mechanics of her music and let a distant part of her mind touch that indescribable place beyond. The people below her would suddenly be remembering that perfect childhood birthday party or that first sunset kiss.

She escorted them past the memory with a final keening note. Then, following a clash of cymbals behind her, she sent them spinning into frenetic, delirious bliss. People leapt to the black-and-white tiled dance floor, hooting and swinging their partners with verve. A chance to remember and a chance to forget. It was what kept people coming to the Cast Iron, night after night.

Once the dancing was well under way, Ada rested her instrument and let the other musicians take over. Corinne had already hopped off the stage at the behest of an eager partner. She was kicking up her heels and laughing wildly, drink sloshing in her hand. Ada smiled and stepped down to the floor. Her exhaustion was a distant memory now. Playing her violin always transported her well beyond her own limitations.

"You gonna pity a poor Southern boy and take him for a spin?"

Ada whirled to see Charlie, sitting on the edge of the stage behind her, his right foot swinging in time to the music. His grin was bright under the stage lights, and there was no trace of their argument in his features. Maybe tomorrow they would have to revisit it, but tonight the Cast Iron was effervescent with laughter and gleaming dresses and clinking glasses. Tomorrow was so far away.

Ada smiled and took Charlie's hand, pulling him onto the dance floor.

After a couple of hours of dancing, Corinne abandoned the floor in search of some quiet. She made her way through the gauntlet of admiration and introductions and pleas for another set. She went through the storage room, waved at Gordon, then took the back door into the alley. If she was honest with herself, she wasn't entirely surprised to find Gabriel there, leaning against the wall. She had noticed him leaving before the performance had ended. Corinne saw the red glint of cigarette embers and heard him exhale.

"You smoke?" he asked. His voice sounded husky and strange.

In the darkness, Corinne couldn't quite make out his features— just the lines of his profile, gray against the shadows. She shook her head but leaned against the wall beside him. Even though she wore heels, he was much taller than her, and she had to crane her neck to see his face.

"You didn't like the set?" she asked. The flush from her dancing was starting to wear off, and the cold was creeping along her arms.

He took another pull from the cigarette, held it for a second, then exhaled through his nose.

"It was incredible," he said.

"You left during Ada's solo."

"I've never— The way she was making me feel, it wasn't—" He hung his head.

"I understand," Corinne said.

"I don't think you do." There was a thread of anger in his voice that caught Corinne off guard. "You go into people's heads, and you root around in there and tug on strings for entertainment or profit. How can you realize what it's like for the rest of us?"

"Excuse me?" Corinne straightened and turned to confront him. "You knew what we did here when you signed on, and now you want to take me to task about it?"

Despite the chill on her arms, her cheeks flushed with heat as she glared at him. To her surprise, he didn't rise to her challenge. He didn't even move. In the shadows, his pale features were like cut glass: all sharp, unforgiving edges.

"I'm sorry," he said. "I'm not trying to fight."

Corinne considered him for a few seconds. She didn't know anything about him. He was just another hired gun who would soon tire of the low pay and bizarre company and move on. It made more sense to go back inside, to rejoin the party. Instead she leaned back against the wall.

"Ada's music affects some people more than others," she said in what she hoped was a conciliatory tone. "When she plays loss and longing, she can send people into fits of weeping."

"It wasn't the loss," he said. "It was the happiness."

Corinne tilted her head, trying to read his expression in the gloom.

He still didn't meet her gaze. He exhaled a puff of smoke like a sigh. "It reminded me of things I . . . hadn't thought about in a long time."

They were both quiet for a few minutes after that. Corinne could see puffs of her own breath in the air, mingling with the cigarette smoke. Finally Gabriel dropped the butt and ground it out with his heel.

"I have to make my rounds," he said. "They're probably missing you at the party."

"Probably," Corinne agreed.

His lips twitched in the beginnings of a smile, and Corinne couldn't help but feel the tiniest bit triumphant. They walked back to the door, but before Corinne could open it, there was a sound farther down the alley. Some garbage cans fell over and a shape rose up, lumbering toward them. Gabriel grabbed Corinne's arm and yanked her behind him. Corinne sensed his gun before she saw it. The movement of steel sent a wave of nausea through her. No wonder she felt on edge around him.

"Put that away," she said, pushing past him. "It's just Harry."

"Who the hell is Harry?" he asked.

"He's nobody. He comes around sometimes." Corinne took a few steps toward the scraggly man, who was dressed in a wrinkled suit, worn threadbare at the elbows and knees. His brown hair was matted and unkempt, and there were remains of some long-past meal in his beard.

"Johnny told you not to come back here," Corinne said.

"Corinne, is that you?" he asked, shuffling forward. "I just need a little bit. Can't you ask Ada to—"

"Ada won't play for you anymore. Go home."

"I can't." There was a snuffling sound, and Corinne realized he was crying. "Just a few bars, please. There's ghosts in my head, and she's the only one can shake them loose."

"Go home," Corinne repeated. She turned back toward the door, but then Harry was grabbing at the back of her dress. She could smell his sweat and grime and desperation.

"What about you?" He was crying. "You can give me some sunlight, some blue skies. I need to shake them loose."

Corinne swung her elbow and felt it contact bone, but the man was unfazed. Gabriel pulled her free and shoved Harry away. Harry hit the concrete with a loud sob.

"He's never been this bad before," Corinne said, retreating a few steps.

"He's drunk," Gabriel said.

She shook her head. Even from a distance, Harry stank of urine and sweat—but not alcohol.

"No. He's an edger."

"Meaning?"

"Meaning he uses hemopaths' talents as an escape, but he fell down the rabbit hole and there's no coming back." She dusted off her dress in short, jerking movements, trying to hide the trembling of her hands. She told herself it was just the cold.

"Bitch," Harry howled toward the black sky. He tried to drag himself upright, but he finally gave up and collapsed onto the concrete. "I hope the ironmongers get you. I hope you—"

He was interrupted by the rolling wail of sirens. Corinne's heart skipped a beat at the sound. They were coming closer. Too loud, too fast.

Harry was laughing. It was an unsettling sound, with barbed and bitter edges. He was still lying on his back, mindless of the alley's filth.

"Bulls are coming for you," he managed to gasp out. "Better run, slaggers."

Corinne whipped around and sprinted for the door with Gabriel at her heels. She took the half flight of stairs to the club two steps at a time, barely remembering to shout a warning to Gordon over her shoulder. Once inside, she lost track of Gabriel in the throng of people. That didn't matter, though. He would tell Johnny. She had to find Ada.

The band was still playing, and she couldn't hear the sirens over the music and clinking glasses and bursts of laughter. The patrons were still blissfully unaware. Corinne darted through the crowd to the dance floor, but she couldn't see Ada and Charlie among the whirling black jackets and sequined silk. She scrambled onto the stage to survey the entire club. Behind her, the musicians had stopped playing. She could see Johnny calmly shaking the senator's hand while Jackson waited to escort him and his wife out the back door. Some of the patrons had realized that something was wrong and were hastily gathering coats and purses. The last of the musicians had already packed up his instrument and was slipping out the back, headed for the basement to wait out the raid.

After the law had passed, Johnny made sure that his crew knew how to make themselves scarce at a moment's notice. It was illegal to perform or participate in any sort of hemopath activity, whether songsmiths' emotions, wordsmiths' illusions, or the less invasive talents, like Saint's. Technically, the regs who paid for the show were also breaking the law, but the cops never seemed interested in arresting them. The lawmakers had written the law with a vagueness that made it possible for police to arrest hemopaths for just gathering in large groups, even without evidence that they had been performing. Maybe in a court of law the charges wouldn't stick, but hemopaths were carted straight to Haversham, and no one ever left Haversham. Except Ada.

Johnny caught Corinne's eye and waved expectantly toward the microphone in front of her. He didn't seem rattled by the turn of events. But then, Corinne couldn't remember ever seeing Johnny Dervish rattled by anything. She turned on the microphone and cleared her throat. The remaining laughter and conversation died down as the unsuspecting patrons turned their attention toward her.

"That's all for tonight, ladies and gents. Don't forget to tip the band." She stepped away from the microphone, then changed her mind and leaned back. "By the way, the cops are about to break down the front door, so now would be an excellent time to start panicking."

The reaction to her words wasn't immediate. A few people even laughed. But without the band playing, the sound of encroaching sirens swept through the room. The crowd of carefree patrons quickly degenerated into a seething mess of confusion and alarm. It wasn't likely that the cops would arrest the regs, but that didn't mean they wanted to stick around for a raid. Johnny would give her hell for it later—he liked to keep his patrons happy, and purposely throwing them into a panic was not the best business practice. But Corinne wasn't worried about the regs right now. The cops would have to fight their way through the fleeing patrons in order to find any hemopaths to arrest. An extra minute or two was all she needed. Satisfied with her work, Corinne slipped backstage to continue her search for Ada.

Ada couldn't hear the sirens from the basement, but she knew what was happening as soon as the first musicians started maneuvering down the stairs with their bulky instrument cases. She'd known a raid would happen eventually. According to Charlie, the cops broke up shows at the larger, ritzier Red Cat at least once a month. So far, the Cast Iron had remained below the notice of the bulls, but the bribes Johnny paid could go only so far.

Ada had said good-bye to Charlie almost half an hour ago. He wanted to make it back to the Red Cat in time for the last set. She could have found another dance partner or asked Danny to make her a drink, but all she really wanted was some solitude. Now that the initial excitement of the evening had worn off, her fatigue had crept back, more insistent than ever.

She kept her seat on the couch as the musicians filed in. They didn't seem concerned by the ruckus upstairs. Someone pulled out a deck of cards and started dealing. Ada stood up when Johnny and Jackson emerged from the stairwell. Worry had started edging into her chest, pressing against her lungs.

"Where's Corinne?" she asked.

"Being a pain in my ass, as usual," Johnny said, with uncharacteristic shortness. He disappeared into his office with Jackson right behind. The door slammed shut.

There was a creak of footsteps on the stairs, and Ada ran to the base. Gabriel was coming down, alone.

"Have you seen Corinne?" Ada asked, aware that panic was bleeding into her voice.

Gabriel hesitated on the bottom step, his eyes darting around the room. The thin line of a frown appeared between his eyes.

"I thought she would be with you," he said.

Ada didn't need to hear more. She slid past him and ran up the stairs. He called after her, but she opened the panel and ducked out. Gordon had not left his post. He watched her with his usual air of unconcern as she closed the panel. He popped a few sunflower seeds into his mouth.

"Has Corinne come through here?" Ada asked.

Gordon pointed silently toward the door leading into the club. Ada could hear muffled shouts and banging that could only be the bulls, tearing the place apart in search of hemopaths. She swallowed the acidic fear rising in her throat. She didn't know if her escape had been reported to the local precinct yet. She did know that the next time they arrested her, they'd lock her so deep in Haversham Asylum that even Corinne would never be able to find her.

Ada sucked in a ragged breath and climbed the five steps to the door. She turned the brass handle in slow, agonizing degrees and pushed her palm against the smooth wood until the door creaked open a couple of inches. She peered through the crack, expecting any second that someone would yank it open from the other side. She could see Danny behind the bar, arguing with one of the cops.

After a few seconds, Danny caught sight of her and inclined his head toward the stage in the briefest of gestures, then resumed his vehement denial that he'd ever seen any hemopath activity in the Cast Iron. The backstage door was open, and Corinne was being prodded by a burly uniformed officer onto the stage and down the steps to the dance floor. She was loudly declaring that she'd only come here for a good time and had never so much as talked to a hemopath in her life. Ada bit her lip, thinking that they might actually be convinced. Corinne's dress was nice enough, and she knew how to carry herself like a blue blood.

Then another cop produced a burnished gray rod, no bigger than a pencil, and Ada knew it was over. She didn't let herself think anymore. There was no time for that. She was halfway to the stage when the cop pressed the iron against Corinne's neck and her gasp of pain revealed her as a hemopath. They were grabbing their earplugs as Ada reached the microphone, the melody already thrumming in her throat. She'd hummed only a few notes when the hands started lowering, earplugs forgotten. She watched their faces as they searched the room in confusion. They spotted her, but not soon enough. Their faces were already slack, eyes glazing over.

Since the law had passed six months ago, there had been a push in law enforcement to develop hemopath-resistance techniques. Given enough time, the cops would probably find ways to withstand emotions and illusions, but Ada had been honing her skill a lot longer than they had been learning to resist it.

It was a fluid melody that she offered, deceptively complex—but then trust was a complex feeling. With enough focus, she could concentrate the full force of the music on the cops in the room. Danny would still feel residual effects, but he would be able to keep his head about him at least.

Corinne looked up and met Ada's eyes. She was smiling. She extricated herself easily from the cops, who were standing in dumb fascination, ready to believe anything that Corinne wanted to tell them . . . or show them.

She patted the shoulder of the man next to her in an exaggerated show of sympathy. Then she started to speak to them in quiet tones. She was fiddling with her brass pocket watch, a habit that had become a ritual. They hung on her every word, nodding occasionally, even laughing once. Ada focused on her melody, layering trust and blurring the edges of their memory. The instinctual harmony between her and Corinne extended beyond the shows they played for regs.

Movement on the other side of the room caught her attention. Gabriel was standing in the doorway to the storage room, watching the cluster of cops around Corinne with visible unease. He was reaching for his gun when Ada caught his eye. She shook her head, careful not to drop any notes. He would be starting to feel the effects of her song now, though not with the same overwhelming intensity that she was aiming at the bulls. His hand drifted back to his side, and he blinked.

Corinne had almost finished whatever she was murmuring to her rapt audience. Ada could tell that she was building up to the big finish. Her brown eyes were bright with a triumph that Ada had learned to both relish and dread.

"Oh my stars," Corinne cried, with a sudden Southern drawl that had Danny snickering behind the bar. The policemen didn't seem to notice her abrupt theatrics.

"I think that bank down the street is on fire." Corinne flung her arm in the direction of the front door. There weren't any windows there, but the cops were falling over each other to stare at the blank wall.

"I don't—"

"Wait, I see it, there's smoke!"

"Let's go."

"And maybe just to be safe you shouldn't come back," Corinne called after them with a wave.

The door swung closed.

For a few seconds the Cast Iron was silent. Then Danny guffawed and hurled a dish towel at Corinne.

"Getting a little sloppy, don't you think, kid?" he asked. "They'll be back before long."

"Not a chance. I made sure to explain in detail how thoroughly they had searched the place," Corinne said. "Not a hemopath in sight. What a regrettable mistake."

"Still," Danny said with a shrug. "Better leave the acting to the thespians."

Corinne put her hand to her heart as if wounded.

"Why must you hurt me, Danny? I've been practicing that fire gag for weeks."

"What poem did you use?" Ada asked, hopping off the stage.

"'That Nature Is a Heraclitean Fire,'" Corinne said. "Hopkins."

"Appropriate."

"Not really—the poem is a foray into questions of transience and immortality. Also clouds."

Corinne grinned at her and lifted her hand, palm up, for their signature handshake. Ada knew it was the closest thing to gratitude Corinne would ever express, but she didn't mind. The two simple taps of their fingertips together somehow held more significance than words ever could.

"That was a close one," Ada said. "If they'd already been wearing their earplugs—"

"But they weren't," Corinne said. "Did you lay down some memory loss?"

"The past half hour should be a haze for them."

"Then we're in the clear."

"Doesn't it seem strange that they were plain old uniforms and not HPA agents?" Ada pressed. "Since when do the bulls deal with hemopaths? I think there must have been agents here we didn't know about."

"If there were agents here, then why did they let us fleece those cops?" Corinne picked her fingers through her hair, which was tangled and damp with sweat. "They probably just got bored with raiding hemo joints and decided to make the bulls do their dirty work."

Ada wasn't anywhere near appeased, but she didn't have the energy to argue with Corinne, who was still reveling in their success. Ada couldn't find the same exultation inside herself. Manipulating regs who weren't paying for it always left her feeling hollow.

"I'm just sad that Danny-boy was the only one to witness our brilliance," Corinne said.

Ada frowned and glanced toward the back door.

"What about—" But she cut herself short, because Gabriel was already gone.

Johnny's office always seemed warmer than the rest of the basement, with two lamps that cast equal amounts of golden light and muddled shadow. There were overflowing file cabinets in three corners of the room, and a coat rack in the fourth that held a moth-eaten scarf and a fedora that Johnny had never worn.

Corinne felt at ease in the cramped space, even though half her time there was spent apologizing for whatever her most recent reckless stunt had been. Ada always managed to avoid the hot seat, which Corinne thought was unfair, considering she wouldn't get into nearly as much trouble if she didn't know Ada would be there to bail her out of it. She fidgeted in the chair that was facing Johnny's desk while he shoved some paperwork into one of the overflowing file cabinets. There hadn't been time to change out of her dress, which was ripped at the back seam and still smelled of Harry's grime. She knew the black kohl lining her eyelids was smudged, and the cupid's bow of her mouth had faded. It didn't really matter in here, though. Johnny had seen her looking much worse.

"I'm not your headmaster," he said at last, dropping heavily into his chair. "Frankly, I don't feel like giving a lecture on how vital it is to keep our customers happy, and how important it is to not, say, purposely send them into a panic."

"That's good, then," Corinne said. "Because it doesn't sound like a lecture I'd pay much attention to anyway."

Johnny's expression betrayed some amusement at the quip, but mostly he just looked tired.

"The Cast Iron is losing money," he said. "We can't last on two or three shows a month, especially if they're cut short like tonight. I have no idea how Carson is keeping the Red Cat open."

Corinne fingered the shabby arm of her chair, picking at the flaking leather.

"I was trying to give the songsmiths more time," she said. "I wouldn't have done it otherwise."

"I know."

She met his eyes, trying to read his face in the dim light. She could count on one hand the people in her life she was scared of disappointing, and Johnny Dervish was first and foremost. Johnny sighed and picked up his pocketknife. Absently he chiseled into the wood of his desk with the tip.

"That mark you've been trailing—the jeweler," he said. "You said he drops off money for his mistress on the second Friday of every month? That's tomorrow."

Corinne hesitated.

"You want us to pull a job tomorrow? Ada's picture will be all over the police stations by morning."

Johnny gouged into the wood a little deeper. With the shadows darkening the circles under his eyes, he seemed more exhausted than Corinne had ever seen him. He had inherited the Cast Iron decades ago, when he was only a few years older than Corinne was now. She couldn't imagine what it was like to watch his life's work crumble from the peak of its glory. The Cast Iron had been her home for only four years, and the mere thought of its closing felt a little like dying.

"If I can't afford to pay the bills and bribe the right people, then the Cast Iron will go dark," Johnny said. He looked up from the desk and met her eyes, unblinking. Corinne knew what he wasn't saying. If the Cast Iron closed, there was nowhere for her and Ada and Saint to go. Boston was an unforgiving city, ribboned in iron and steel. There were thousands of hemopaths in Boston, but jobs for their kind were scarce. Corinne had known desperate hemopaths to swear fealty to Johnny like serfs of the Middle Ages. Unlike his predecessor, Johnny ran the club like a business instead of a social fraternity. Those who did the work earned a cut of the profits. Some of the jobs were less legal than others, but in times like these the line was blurred at best.

Others might be able to find work with Luke Carson at the Red Cat or the Witcher brothers at Down Street, but Ada and Corinne had been a part of Johnny's inner circle for years. Carson and the Witchers would never trust them. Loyalty to one of the iron-free clubs was loyalty for life. And Corinne couldn't return to the life she'd had before.

"We can do it," she said. "We know the patrol routes."

Johnny folded the blade and tossed it into an open desk drawer. "Quick and clean," he said. "I can't handle another news headline like last summer."

"So no elephants then?"

"No elephants. And stay away from the councilman."

Corinne grinned. The so-called Bengali banker scam had been run once or twice in history to moderate success, but it wasn't considered by grifters to be a tenable scheme. Corinne had modified it for her and Ada's peculiar skill set, and the resulting con was her magnum opus as far as she was concerned. She refused to apologize for it. Despite nearly popping a vein when he'd first heard about it, Johnny had since made peace. The two thousand dollars that Corinne and

Ada had scored softened the blow. It was enough to keep the Cast Iron supplied with food and booze for half a year.

"We'll go in the morning," she said, heading for the door.

"Take Gabriel along," Johnny said. "Someone's got to show him the ropes around here, and I've got my hands full."

Corinne paused with her hand on the doorknob, trying to decide the best way to dodge the responsibility. She wasn't sure what it was about Gabriel Stone that irked her so much. It might have been the way he'd spoken to her in the alley, or his refusal to argue so that she could prove herself right, or the way he seemed generally unimpressed. Possibly a mixture of the three.

"Are you sure I'm the best person for that job?" she asked.

"No, but Ada tends to be competent enough for the both of you, so I'm not concerned."

Corinne weighed the consequences of arguing further, but in the end it seemed to be more trouble than it was worth. As long as Gabriel kept a lid on the moralizing that regs were so fond of, she might be able to keep a civil tongue.

"Fine. But if he can't keep up, we aren't going to hold his hand."

"Fair enough," Johnny said, leaning back in his chair and thrumming his fingers on the desktop. "Get some sleep. You did good tonight, Corinne."

She shut the door behind her without a reply, but the rare praise suffused her as she crossed the dark common room to her bedroom, so that she barely felt the cold.

Despite the weariness deep in her bones, Corinne lay awake for a long time that night, running through the events of the day in her head, comforted by the occasional creak of Ada's bed. When she'd been cornered by the bulls tonight, it had never occurred to her to be worried, even when they'd touched the iron to her skin. She'd known that Ada wouldn't be far away. It was an incontrovertible fact of her existence that Ada would always be there for her. That was what had made the past two weeks almost unbearable. She'd felt like half of her was missing.

With a small, strangled sound, Ada sat bolt upright in bed. Corinne pulled herself up onto her elbows, squinting in the darkness. Ada panted for a few seconds, rubbing her face vigorously, then flopped backward. A nightmare. Corinne lay back down, listening to her friend's uneven breathing for a few minutes.

"We can talk about it, if you want," she said at last.

Since they'd left Haversham, she'd seen the changes in Ada— the muted fear and disquiet that Ada tried valiantly to hide. The asylum was iron-free, touted as the "humane" alternative to prison for hemopaths, but that didn't make it any less a prison. Every cell was solitary, every surface cold and unyielding. Corinne remembered seeing an old photo once, with the founders of the asylum in their Victorian garb, staring humorlessly from the shadow of the great brick structure. The camera hadn't captured the wrought-iron fence around the perimeter. Or the fact that hemopaths who were taken there never seemed to have a court date or a sentence. Once they were taken through those iron gates, they never came back out.

Ada hadn't spoken, though Corinne could tell by her breathing that she was still awake.

"I don't think we should go tomorrow," Ada said at last. "The HPA will be looking for me."

Corinne stared at the dark ceiling, trying to pick out the images from the magazines that she and Ada had pasted up there. For her side of the room, Corinne had chosen castles on the moors in Europe and poems and reviews from the *Literary Digest* and the *Atlantic*.

"Boston's a big city," Corinne said.

"Not that big." Ada's voice was soft and slurred with sleep. "I don't want to go back there, Cor."

Haversham Asylum for Afflictions of the Blood had been a looming presence at the edge of Boston since its construction thirty-six years ago, but it was only in the past year—since the new law had passed—that stories had started trickling through the hemopath clubs about what its true purpose might be. The theories ranged anywhere from lobotomies to ritualistic slaughter. Corinne chewed on the inside of her lip and thought about the man the two HPA agents had brought to the basement. She knew that there was something comforting she was supposed to say to Ada, but she also knew she had never in her life managed to say the exact right thing.

"We don't have a choice," she said. "The Cast Iron can't stay open without us. And what about your mother?"

She rolled onto her side and squinted through the darkness. The walls on Ada's half of the room were an eclectic mix of foreign landscapes and clippings from *Garden & Home Builder* of the "Picture-Perfect Kitchen!" and "A Rose Garden Fit for a Queen." Pasted in the center of it all was an old, wrinkled picture of her parents. Her mother was perched neatly on a fence, her hair wrapped in a scarf, trying to keep her skirt from blowing in the breeze, while Ada's father stood on tiptoe, one hand on his hat, leaning in for a kiss.

"And what's my mother supposed to do if we're both carted to the asylum and never seen again?" Ada asked.

"We won't get caught," Corinne said. "Not as long as we're together."

Ada didn't say anything more, and soon her breaths deepened into sleep.

Corinne tried to calm her own mind, but to no avail. She pulled her grandfather's pocket watch from the wooden crate that served as her bedside table. Clutching the cool brass to her chest, she laid her head back on the pillow. Her fingertips searched out the familiar grooves of the inscription inside the delicate timepiece, lulling her mind into a blank peace. She fell asleep still cradling it.

Ada couldn't fall back asleep. She forced a steady rhythm into her breathing, trying to trick her mind into rest. It was no use. No matter how many times she told herself that she was free, that she was home, whenever she closed her eyes, she was back there. Gray walls around her. Fear like acid in her throat.

Her first day at the asylum, she'd thought it was going to be a breeze. The corridors were dreary and the cells were cold, but there were no instruments of torture, no prisoners being dissected. The rumors must have been exaggerated by gossiping regs and paranoid hemopaths. Ada knew that Corinne would come for her. All she had to do was wait.

On the second day, they brought her into an examination room for tests. She remembered with clarity the framed diploma on the wall and the black-and-white tiles—not unlike the Cast Iron's dance floor. A porcelain washbasin sat in the corner, pristinely white and draped with a soft cotton towel. As touted to the public, the facility was iron-free, so she had succumbed to their poking and prodding. They had checked for lice, rashes, symptoms of influenza. Nothing that wouldn't happen in any ordinary doctor's office in Boston.

When the Dr. Knox who was heralded on the diploma came in, he seemed so harmless with his spectacles and warm smile that Ada found herself smiling back.

"Family?" he asked a nurse, who handed him a chart.

"Father, in prison," said the nurse. "Mother, address unknown."

Dr. Knox nodded thoughtfully, and Ada felt the first twinge of worry in her gut. She was sitting on a wooden exam table, her legs dangling. Suddenly she felt exposed. Helpless.

"She's a songsmith?" he asked as he thumbed through the chart. "Are you any good, my dear?"

Ada stared back at him, unsure how to answer.

"According to the agency, she's one of the hemopaths involved in that scam on the bridge," said the nurse. "The one with Councilman Turner and the elephants?"

Dr. Knox's eyes lit up with new interest, and he scratched his chin.

"One of Dervish's girls then?"

"Will that be a problem, sir?" the nurse asked.

Dr. Knox was studying Ada like she was a slab of meat in the butcher's shop.

"I'll need her in the basement for the second phase," he said at last. "We're still disposing of the failed subjects, so it will be a few weeks yet."

"We can keep her upstairs for now," the nurse said. She took back the chart and made a note in it.

"The second phase of what?" Ada asked.

Dr. Knox seemed surprised that she'd spoken. He frowned slightly, then turned to the nurse.

"Let's take some blood samples while she's here. Give me a syringe."

When Ada saw the gleam of metal in the nurse's hand, she scrambled off the table. She tried to run for the door, but the doctor was in the way. She shrank back into the corner. She could feel the stinging presence of the metal only with concentration, which meant it was some sort of iron alloy. Probably steel. The only thing she knew for certain was that she wouldn't let them stick that needle in her.

"No," she said, and was pleased with the vehemence in her voice. It was a strength she didn't feel.

"None of that," Dr. Knox said sharply.

He snatched the syringe from the nurse and reached for Ada's arm. Her body was tense and coursing with adrenaline. She sidestepped the doctor, leapt onto the table, and rolled to the other side. Then she flipped it on top of him.

All the rest was a blur in her mind. The nurse screaming. Others rushing in to help. Ada tried to run, but someone pushed her down. There was a lancing pain in the back of her shoulder, and then she fell unconscious. When she awoke, she was in her solitary cell, with nothing to do but await the basement. And wonder what Dr. Knox meant by "failed subjects."

She hadn't told Corinne any of that yet. She wasn't sure if she could.

Corinne would have a thousand questions. She would want to figure it out, solve the mystery. Ada didn't want to know what was happening in the basement, though. She wanted to ease back into her comfortable life and forget the asylum even existed.

After an hour or so, she did manage to drift off. But the screams of the woman from the next cell over followed her into her dreams.

CHAPTER THREE

$\diamond$

THE NEXT MORNING ADA SLIPPED OUT EARLY TO GO SEE HER mother. Corinne considered joining her but fell back asleep before she could decide. After another hour of sleep, she pulled on the first dress she could find from a pile on the floor and trudged upstairs to the bar for breakfast. The tables were populated with the morning crowd of those who worked daylight hours for Johnny. Most were groggily clutching white mugs of coffee. A few were eating from the breakfast spread on the sidebar.

Gabriel was at a corner table—alone, predictably enough. The Cast Iron crew was slow to trust and even slower to pleasant chit-chat. Corinne sighed to herself, then loaded up a plate with eggs and toast and joined him.

"Sleep well?" she asked.

He just looked at her. His short brown hair was as disheveled as it had been the night before, though every part of his attire, from his plain collared shirt to his pressed black trousers, was fastidiously neat.

"That's called a question," Corinne said when he didn't reply. "In polite society, it involves an answer."

His eyebrows shot up, and Corinne could detect a hint of what could have been a smile or a smirk around his mouth. The movement did nothing to soften the severe line of his jaw. The tousle of his hair made the angles on his face even more pronounced, and there was something etched in his features that she couldn't quite pinpoint. Like a gaunt hunger.

"I wasn't aware that I was in polite society," he said.

"You can't hold last night against us," Corinne said, turning her attention away from his jawline and back to her toast. "Not every day here involves asylum escapes and police raids."

"I'm not sure I believe that."

Corinne smiled and hid the expression with another bite of toast. Now that she'd had a few hours of sleep, she had decided to play nice with Gabriel Stone. Johnny wasn't an idiot, and he didn't let just anyone join his crew. If he'd hired Gabriel, there was a good reason for it.

"I thought we'd start with the tour," Corinne said.

"Don't you want to finish your breakfast first?"

"No need. There's the stage, the backstage door—that's where the musicians shoot the breeze when they're waiting for their set. Beside that is the kitchen door, which leads, predictably enough, to the kitchen. You've been to Johnny's office downstairs, and the other rooms down there are all private, aside from a few closets."

"Thorough," he said drily.

Corinne ignored his tone and continued. "Danny runs the bar every night, but don't believe a word he says about me because he is a bitter, bitter man, and I am a darling. I'm sure you met Gordon, our resident charmer. He's usually only on duty when the club is open, to keep drunk patrons from snooping. There used to be a show every night, but the new law complicates things."

"I'd say police raids are more than just a complication."

"Debatable. Anyway, Ada and I had it covered."

"Right," he said.

It wasn't the way he said it but his fleeting expression that gave Corinne pause. "What?" she asked.

He hesitated.

"Look," she snapped. "If you've got a problem with Ada, then—"

"I don't have a problem with Ada."

"Then is it women in general who shouldn't be handling things?"

He sat back in his chair, obviously bemused. "I didn't say anything like that," he replied.

Corinne eyed him and finished off her toast.

"Sorry," she said once she swallowed. "I guess I'll let you actually say something stupid before I berate you for it."

"Appreciate it."

Corinne stood up. "Nice chat," she said. "Now if you'll excuse me, I have to change into something more suitable. We're meeting Ada at ten. I'll explain on the way."

Corinne dropped her dishes off in the kitchen and went downstairs. She and Ada didn't have a wardrobe in their room, so finding a dress that wasn't hopelessly wrinkled was a challenge, although Ada never seemed to have a problem. Corinne dug her maroon silk out of a crate. Not the right material for the season, but with its belted waist and gold thread trim, it was her most respectable dress. She pulled on stockings and her black suede kitten heels. Ada's black felt cloche finished the ensemble, and Corinne grabbed her coat off the pile of clothes at the foot of her bed and ran out the door.

She made it two steps before running into Guy Jackson.

"Slow it down, sweetheart," he said, gripping her arms as she caught her balance.

Corinne shook him off. "You forget my name already?" she asked.

Jackson grinned at her toothily. He was of average height, with compact muscles, a shaved head, and permanent stubble on his chin. His brown eyes were always either darting or leering. Right now it was the latter. Corinne slipped her coat on and started for the stairs. He joined her.

49

"Good show last night," he said in a pleasanter tone. "Your friend all right?"

"Ada's fine."

"Glad to hear it. Haversham's a nasty place."

At the top of the stairs, something occurred to Corinne and she turned around. He was a couple of steps lower than her, making their height even.

"Did you go into the basement?" she asked. "What are they doing down there?"

His brow furrowed at the question. "I don't think you want to know what's going on down there, sweetheart," he said, scratching his stubble absently. "I think you'd be better off praying that you never have to find out."

There was something about his tone that made her feel very young all of a sudden. Maybe it was the lack of his usual smarmy self-satisfaction, as if he were talking to a child and not a fellow member of Johnny's crew. Other girls her age were sitting in classrooms right now, listening to lectures and passing secret notes. Another day she might have laughed off his uncharacteristic concern, but the sight of that hemopath dangling limply between the two HPA agents was still fresh on her mind. She and Ada had been only a hundred feet away. It could have just as easily been either of them.

Corinne backed away from the stairwell and went into the club, telling herself that Jackson probably knew as little about it as anyone else and she didn't have the time to waste.

"Be careful out there," Jackson called after her, his voice dipping again into smugness. "Ironmongers don't care who your daddy is. They'll chain and drain you same as the rest of us."

With gritted effort, Corinne managed to ignore him. She knew he was just trying to get a rise out of her, which wasn't much of a challenge, but she did enjoy deliberately disappointing him on occasion. Gabriel was waiting for her near the front door, in a black coat and brimmed hat. Corinne grabbed his sleeve and yanked him outside before Jackson could catch up.

"Everything all right?" he asked, letting her drag him along for a few steps.

Corinne released him and forced herself to take a breath. The sun was shining today, but a bitterly cold breeze pricked at her exposed skin.

"We're going to be late" was all she said. She slipped on a pair of gloves from her pocket and started walking at a more reasonable pace.

Gabriel fell into step beside her, and they headed northeast on Tremont, toward the financial district. The war in Europe had ended only two months before, and the sides of buildings were still plastered with posters, telling passersby to "Buy war bonds!" and "Help America's sons win the war!"

She and Gabriel were both quiet as they walked, and Corinne was just beginning to think that the silence had shifted from peaceful into awkward when Gabriel spoke.

"Okay, I have to know. How did you pull off the Bengali banker?"

"What?"

"I asked Johnny, but he just said that you and Ada have a knack for the ridiculous and changed the subject."

Corinne smiled at that and glanced at him. His expression was folded in deep thought.

"I mean," he went on, "obviously Ned Turner must have been a gullible idiot who lucked his way into office, but the papers said there was a crowd of people on the bridge. Someone must have seen through it."

Corinne laughed.

"Ned Turner? That suspicious son of a gun? Don't worry, our councilman is no idiot. You know he was the one who first started wearing an iron ring as a way to identify hemopaths when he shook their hands? Every jeweler in the city made a mint after that story broke."

"I don't see how you did it, then."

They passed under the tracks of the elevated railway, and a train rumbled overhead. Sunlight glinted off its windows as it passed. Corinne walked a little faster until they were free from the crushing weight of the steel and iron.

"It's not that hard to follow," she said. "The Bengali banker is a long con based on the pig in a poke. But instead of foreign banknotes, we used elephants."

"Why elephants?"

Corinne shrugged.

"Currency can be counterfeit. No one's going to pay for foreign bills without having them examined. When Ned Turner saw those elephants, he was practically throwing money at us. No one can counterfeit an elephant."

"No one except a wordsmith."

"No one except an exceptionally skilled wordsmith," Corinne said, skipping over an uneven patch of concrete. "Elephants aren't particularly subtle."

"I still don't get it."

"It's not that complicated. We pretended we were with a failing circus from Canada, selling off our attractions as we traveled south. The Franklin Park Zoo is managed by the city, and Turner was eager to make his mark as councilman. We offered to sell our elephants for an absurdly low cost—or I guess it was. I'm not entirely sure what the market value for elephants is. Honestly, I didn't expect him to make such a public spectacle of the deal."

Once the newspapers had been tipped off, Ada wanted to call it quits, but Corinne couldn't resist the challenge. If they could swindle the councilman on a bridge full of citizens and press, then they would be the talk of Boston for decades to come. Hemopaths had been running small cons in the city for as long as Corinne had been alive, but no one had ever pulled off anything like her version of the Bengali banker. The fact that the councilman was the chief proponent of the movement to illegalize hemopathy only made their success that much sweeter. She just wished she could have seen Ned Turner's face at the moment the elephants faded into nothing.

"I understand the con," Gabriel said, with only the barest hint of irritation in his voice. "I just don't see how you tricked a Columbia graduate with twenty years of politics under his belt into thinking there was an elephant on the Harvard Bridge."

"It was four elephants," Corinne said. "And in my experience, the smartest person in the room is always the easiest one to fool."

Gabriel shook his head. "Maybe if you catch them off guard. Maybe years ago before anyone knew what hemopaths could do. But as soon as I hear you start quoting Wordsworth or Keats, then I know that you're about to create an illusion. I know it's not real."

"First of all, I would never waste breath on one of the Romantics. Second of all, are you really suggesting that I couldn't fool you, right here, right now?"

Corinne stopped walking and turned to face him.

"How could you, if I know you're about to do it?" Gabriel asked.

"Take off your hat," Corinne said.

"What?"

"Let's find out if you're smarter than the councilman. Take off your hat."

"I just said—"

"If it only works on the weak brained or the gullible, then you have nothing to worry about."

Gabriel looked ready to protest further, but he removed his hat, holding it in both hands. There were a few people passing on the sidewalk, but they were all bundled in their coats, lost in their own business.

"Now, what are you holding?" Corinne asked.

With a pained expression, Gabriel tried to keep walking, but Corinne blocked him.

"I know we just met last night," she said. "So here's the first thing you should know about me: I never back down from a challenge."

"I didn't challenge you to anything."

"Two minutes," Corinne said. "That's all I need, I swear."

Gabriel glanced around them at the passersby, who weren't paying them any mind. He sighed his consent.

"What are you holding?" Corinne asked.

"My hat."

"'Twas brillig, and the slithy toves Did gyre—'"

"What the hell are—"

Corinne pressed her finger against his lips. He let out a startled breath, warm even through her glove. She forged ahead. Her left hand was in her pocket, gloved fingers wrapped around the brass timepiece. Its familiarity helped her find focus.

"'Did gyre and gimble in the wabe. All mimsy were the borogoves, And the mome raths outgrabe.' That ought to do it."

Corinne stepped back and crossed her arms in satisfaction.

"Do what?"

"What are you holding?"

"My hat."

"Are you sure?"

"Of course I—" Gabriel looked down and saw that he was holding a soft black rabbit.

He cried out and dropped it, stumbling back a few steps into a hunched old lady in a Sunday hat who whacked him across the back with her walking stick.

Corinne was laughing so hard, she gripped her stomach and doubled over. People were starting to stare now. Gabriel regained his dignity and approached the animal with the caution of a soldier approaching a land mine.

"It's not real," he said, but it came out as more of a question.

"Touch it," Corinne said. "It won't bite. Probably."

Gabriel knelt down and prodded the fur hesitantly. The rabbit looked at him and twitched its nose.

"I find Carroll especially potent for animals," Corinne said. "There are some wordsmiths who swear by Blake, but Carroll captures the *motion* best, I think."

Gabriel shook his head, still prodding at the rabbit. "I have no idea what you're talking about."

"I'm just proving that you have no idea what *you're* talking about, Mr. Stone. Now pick up your hat. You're causing a scene."

Gabriel started to protest, but before he could make a sound, the rabbit had become his hat once again. He picked it up, carefully, and put it back on his head. He stood up, watching Corinne with a new look in his eyes. Fear with a smidgen of awe. Her favorite.

"Come on," she said. "Ada will be waiting."

Corinne tucked her hand into the crook of his elbow and tugged him gently along. The brick and stone businesses of the financial district dominated the cityscape, casting vast shadows across the lines of sleek black Oldsmobiles and low-riding roadsters in the street. As they got closer to the heart of the district, the car horns and sputtering exhaust fumes drowned out all memory of the Cast Iron's sleepy neighborhood.

"I don't get it," Gabriel said after a few minutes, his hand drifting again to his hat. "I *knew* it was an illusion. How did it feel so real?"

"You've heard the phrase *mind over matter*?" she asked. "Well, that doesn't apply here. When I recite, I give you whatever image I want, but I don't have to convince you it's real. Your own imagination does it for me. It's a rare person who can overcome their own mind, and the better your brain works, the stronger the illusion."

"Making the smartest person in the room the easiest one to fool."

"Now you're on the trolley."

Gabriel just shook his head.

"What?" Corinne looked up at him.

"It's bizarre. Poetry of all things."

"Why not poetry? Makes perfect sense to me," Corinne said. "When a reg quotes Lewis Carroll at you, what happens?"

"I think they're off their rocker."

"You might imagine the gyring and gimbling of the slivy toves or the mimsy borogoves, and as the poem progresses you might start to feel the Jabberwock coming closer, picture the vorpal blade in the hero's hand."

"I suppose."

"When I quote Lewis Carroll at you, I can make you see so much more than that. I can make you see anything I want."

His brow was wrinkled in concentration. Corinne imagined he probably tackled most problems in his life with that exact same expression.

"So Ada is a songsmith?" he asked.

"Probably the best in Boston. She's the only reason we can pull off any con."

"Why's that?"

"I can make you see all the rabbits I want, but you said it yourself—I can't make you trust me."

Gabriel's thoughtful frown deepened, but before he could formulate a question, they had reached their destination. Corinne led the way down a side street, away from the busiest thoroughfares. Ada was waiting for them in front of an empty storefront, buttoned into her navy blue coat and adjusting the satin lining in her cream-colored cloche. Her hair was styled into flat twists, protected against the dry winter. When she saw them, she replaced her hat and picked up her violin case from the sidewalk.

"How's your mother?" Corinne asked.

"Angry that I disappeared for two weeks," Ada said. "She yelled at me for ten minutes in Swahili, then another five in Portuguese. It was a lovely visit."

She cast Gabriel a curious glance.

"He's playing tourist," Corinne said. "Johnny asked us to show him the ropes."

"Well, have a seat," Ada told him, pointing to a bench just across the street. "We don't have a lot of time. Corinne—the jeweler will be here any minute."

"I'm ready. You're the one who hasn't tuned yet."

"Wait," Gabriel said as Ada knelt to open the case and retrieve her instrument. "Are you two pulling a job right now?"

"We have to hit him today," Corinne said. "He only carries cash every second Friday."

"You might have told me," Gabriel said.

"What, did you think this getup was all for you, Mr. Stone?" Corinne twirled to show off the flounce of her dress under her coat.

Gabriel glanced briefly heavenward. "It never occurred to me to assume anything about your wardrobe, Miss Wells."

Ada laughed and plucked at the strings of her violin.

"Could you drop a few coins in there?" she asked Gabriel, nodding toward the case at her feet. "I'm trying to look like a busker."

Gabriel obliged, though he was still watching them both warily.

"There he is," Corinne said, whirling to face them. "Gabriel, go sit down. For cripes' sake, you look about as inconspicuous as a smoking gun."

Gabriel frowned at her, but Ada started playing, and he seemed to forget what he was going to say. He crossed the street and sat down on the bench. Corinne patted her hat down and then started to pace up and down the sidewalk. This street was emptier than most in the district, with only a few businesses and negligible traffic. Corinne had seen their mark turning the corner up ahead, his brimmed hat low over his ears, his chin tucked into his collar against the cold. There was no one else in sight. It was now or never.

"Help me out with a little tragedy, won't you?" she murmured to Ada. "I'm no thespian."

Ada obligingly sailed through a few minor chords. Corinne felt the wave of sorrow almost instantly. She had no trouble summoning tears after that. Provided they were focused, hemopaths could generally remain unaffected by other hemopaths, but if they were caught off guard—or wanted to be—they were just as susceptible as regs.

By the time the man had reached them, Corinne's eyes were red and swollen. She paced more quickly, wringing her hands and making short, intermediate sobs. As the man tried to pass, she bumped into him and sprawled backward to the concrete.

"Sorry about that, miss," the man said, tucking his newspaper under one arm and offering her a hand.

Corinne took it and immediately felt the iron of his ring, even through her glove. She jerked her hand away and made a show of dusting herself off. She hoped her weeping was enough to hide her wince.

"Oh," she said, between gasps. "Oh, he's going to be so *angry*."

The man watched her for a moment, hesitant. Ada changed her tune, very slightly, and his expression changed with it.

"Is there something the matter?" he asked Corinne. He was a short man in a fine black suit, gripping a brown leather briefcase in his left hand.

"Oh," she said. "I don't want to trouble you, sir, only—only—I wonder if perhaps you could help me."

He shifted his weight from one foot to the other, glancing past her down the street. Ada slowed her song to a leisurely pace, drawing out each note with ringing clarity. The man set down his briefcase.

"Perhaps I can," he said to Corinne.

"I've lost a huge sum in a bet—nearly a year's worth of savings! My beau is going to be furious with me. The money was set aside for when we're married, and I promised him I wouldn't gamble any-more—only I thought for sure that this would pay out."

"Gambling is a terrible vice for a young lady," the man said.

Corinne started sobbing again. "I know," she wailed. "If he finds out, he'll leave me. I know he will."

The man was starting to look impatient again. "Miss, I'm sorry, but I don't see how I can help."

"That's just it," Corinne said. She grabbed his sleeve, careful to avoid the hand with the ring. "That's why I'm here. I've been in that pawn shop all morning trying to make the clerk see reason, but he

doesn't believe me. He thinks I'm a . . . a . . . woman of the night."
She spoke the last in an exaggerated whisper.

Ada sniggered and dropped a few notes but quickly righted herself.

The man scratched his head beneath his hat, revealing a receding hairline.

"I'm still not sure how I can help," he said.

"Can I tell you something first?" Corinne asked, her voice softer.

The notes of Ada's violin wafted above and around them. The man's face was lax, and Corinne could see a familiar blurriness in his eyes. She had learned to recognize it a long time ago. Clear eyes were a warning sign—there were those rare few who weren't as receptive to Ada's gentle nudging.

Corinne's hand moved to his lapel, and she tugged him closer. She whispered in his ear for almost thirty seconds. When he stepped back, he blinked at her, expression even more dazed. She had opted for a few lines from a volume of poetry that Ada had given her a couple of years ago. Edna St. Vincent Millay hadn't gained much renown yet, but Corinne was betting on a Pulitzer by the time she turned forty.

"I'm not sure I catch your meaning, miss," the man said, still blinking.

If Ada hadn't been churning out a healthy dose of trust mingled with confusion, he would no doubt have fled after the first couplet. Or garroted her with the thin iron chain she could see peeking out from beneath his collar. There was no truth in the belief that pure forged iron made the wearer immune to hemopathy, but it didn't stop regs from paying through the nose for it.

"Look at what I have here," Corinne said, holding up her cupped hands. "Do you see it?"

The man nodded fervently.

"It's a golden brooch," she said, firming the illusion. "Studded with real diamonds. Have you ever seen the like?"

He shook his head.

"That's a mighty fine trinket, miss," he said. "Where did you get such a thing?"

"My grandmother gave it to me. I'm sure it must be worth at least a hundred dollars. That's all I need—only I can't get the clerk to buy it from me. He keeps threatening to call the police."

She sniffled and watched the befuddled man through her eyelashes. She and Ada had been keeping tabs on him for two months. He was one of the jewelers in Boston who had made a small fortune selling iron jewelry to regs as a ward against hemopaths, but it was what he sold under the counter that caught their attention. Iron knuckles, iron-braced clubs, and iron barbs, no bigger than a needle, that were designed to break off in the skin—a special kind of torture for hemopaths, whose blood had a visceral aversion to iron that science had yet to explain. They were the sorts of weapons that would appeal only to ironmongers, those citizens who had decided in the past year that the surest way to stop hemopaths from scamming them was to grab any hemopaths they could find—criminal or not— and string them up in straitjackets of iron chains.

Corinne thought it was only fair to exact a tax on the profits he made at the expense of hemopaths. The only question was whether his lack of scruples extended to taking advantage of a wide-eyed, desperate girl. The brooch he could see in her hands would be worth three or four times what she was asking. She could practically read the thoughts flashing across his face in quick succession. He wasn't a particularly subtle man.

She knew that they had him.

"Maybe I can help," he said. "I've been looking for an anniversary present for my wife. What if I bought it from you?"

"You would do that for me?" she asked. Ada would tell her later that she was laying on the innocent doe act a little thick, but the jeweler was too entranced by his own greedy imagination to notice.

"You said it was worth a hundred dollars, right?" He knelt down to open his briefcase and pulled out a fat envelope. "I was just on my way to the bank."

"Oh, I can't do that," Corinne said, clutching her hand to her chest. "What if it's worth much less than that? I don't want to cheat you. Maybe this was all a mistake. I'll just find another pawn shop."

"My wife will love the brooch," the man said. "That's worth the money to me."

He spoke with such gentle reassurance that Corinne had to bite her lip to keep from laughing.

"Only if you're sure," she said, hesitantly extending her hand.

The illusion might not hold much longer—it depended on how well the poem stuck in his mind. He was thinking so hard about the profit he would make selling the brooch that the verses were probably being crowded out with every passing moment.

He counted out five twenty-dollar bills and pressed them into her palm.

"My wife will be so pleased," he said, tucking the envelope and the brooch into his briefcase. Before he could snap it shut, Corinne let out a small gasp as the breeze caught one of the bills in her hand. It swirled into the road.

"Oh no," she cried, trying to sound as helpless as possible.

"I'll get it," he told her, checking for oncoming traffic and then ducking into the street. While he stooped to pick up the bill, back turned, Corinne opened the briefcase and pulled the rest of the bills out of the envelope. She shoved them into her coat pocket and straightened right as he turned around.

"You're too kind." She summoned a few more tears for effect. "I can't thank you enough."

"It's my pleasure, miss," he said, beaming. "We've both had a run of good luck today."

"No more luck for me, sir," she said. "I'll never place another bet in my life."

Ada's violin trilled, and the jeweler smiled blandly. Corinne knew the music was scattering his memories of the past few minutes. Ada couldn't make him forget completely, but she could blur Corinne's face in his mind and make the details of their conversation impossible to recall with any accuracy.

Corinne recognized her cue and bade the man a hurried farewell. She went the opposite way down the sidewalk, quickening her pace until she turned the corner, where she broke into a run. Hopefully Gabriel had enough sense to follow Ada to their rendezvous point. Corinne twisted and turned through the streets without slowing to check her direction. When she made it to the Central Burying Ground, she stayed across the road from the weathered gravestones, a safe distance from the iron fence encircling them. She knew that somewhere among those stones lay the bones of several of her more illustrious ancestors. She wondered what the stodgy old men would think about their descendant running cons a few blocks away from their final resting place.

Ada and Gabriel arrived before she even had a chance to catch her breath. The three of them took the path leading through the frostbitten grass and bare-branched trees of the Common.

"There's at least four hundred here," she told Ada, patting her coat pocket.

"His mistress is a lucky woman," Ada said.

"Mistress? But didn't you hear? He was going to the *bank*." Corinne had regained enough breath to laugh. "That's why he just happened to have an exorbitant amount of cash on him."

Gabriel was looking between them, eyebrow raised slightly.

"I don't suppose it's even worth asking what just happened back there," he said.

"Probably not," Corinne agreed.

"You two seem to have everything under control."

"We've been at this for years," Ada said.

"Then you won't be at all concerned about the beat cop who's about to catch up with us."

Both girls stopped and whirled. Corinne cursed. "Ada," she said.

But Ada was already yanking her violin free from its case. She threw the case at Corinne and tucked the instrument beneath her chin. She had barely coaxed out a few notes before the policeman roared into earshot, shouting at them to stop. Ada kept playing, the sound barely carrying above his cries. He started to slow. The expression on his face grew lax. He was almost upon them now.

Ada closed her eyes and played on.

The policeman kept walking, brushing elbows with Corinne and Gabriel. He didn't turn around. Ada played until he was out of sight, then with Corinne's help repacked the violin. The three of them ducked down another path. They took the long way back to the club, slipping through side streets with eyes always cast backward, alert for followers.

There weren't any patrons in the Cast Iron this early in the day, and Danny was busying himself polishing glasses.

"Little early to be raising hell, isn't it?" he said by way of greeting.

"Some of us work for a living," Corinne said, and ducked the rag he threw at her.

Danny retrieved another cloth from under the bar and cast Gabriel a glance.

"Don't let these two scare you off," Danny said. "Johnny never lets them torture the regs for long."

"I resent that," said Corinne.

"Don't care," said Danny.

"I resent it too," said Ada.

"In that case, I'm sorry to have offended," said Danny.

Corinne made a face at Ada, who smiled innocently.

"If you have any questions, you can ask me," Danny said to Gabriel. "We regs have to stick together."

"Too late," Corinne said. "I already warned him that you don't have two pennies' worth of brains to rub together."

"Next thing I throw at you won't be a dishrag," Danny said mildly.

"See you later, Danny," Ada said, giving Corinne a nudge.

The three of them went downstairs. Corinne angled toward Johnny's door first but saw that it was shut. At this hour, that meant he was not to be disturbed. She unbuttoned her coat and plopped down in an armchair. Ada and Gabriel sat on the couch.

"There aren't usually cops on that beat before noon." Ada was picking at a loose thread on her sleeve, but her expression was far from nonchalant.

"They've been edging into our territory ever since the Harvard Bridge," Corinne said.

"I told you it was too big."

"We pulled it off, didn't we?" Corinne leaned back in the chair, crossing her arms. "Johnny will handle the bulls."

Ada didn't look appeased, but something else caught her attention, and she leapt to her feet.

"What the hell are you doing here?" she asked, her normally mild voice ringing through the room.

Corinne twisted in her seat to see the redheaded young man who had just come out of Johnny's office.

He looked from Ada to Corinne and swallowed. His eyes were widened slightly.

"I'm glad you're back, Ada," he said. He had a soft voice, all smooth edges and warm timbre.

Ada started around the coffee table, spitting out a string of curses. Corinne grabbed her arm as she passed and yanked her to a stop.

"It's not Saint's fault," she whispered.

The look Ada gave her was pure and righteous fury. "The bastard flipped on me," she said.

In the quiet room, her words carried. Johnny had come out of his office during the racket and was leaning in his doorway, watching them in silence.

"What do you mean?" Corinne asked.

"I mean that they didn't have enough to arrest either of us, and he let the bulls scare him into confessing. They promised him if he told them everything, he could walk."

Corinne couldn't find any words.

"Ada," said Saint. "Ada, please, you don't understand."

"*You* don't understand," Ada shouted, pushing past Corinne and shoving him backward. "Two weeks I rotted in that hole, all because you couldn't take the heat."

"I didn't know what else to do," he said, pleading. "You have to understand—"

"You should go, Saint," said Corinne.

He looked at her, his gray eyes begging her to intervene.

"Go," Corinne repeated.

He left, and Corinne laid her hand on Ada's arm, but she shook her off.

"I didn't know," Corinne said. "You should have told me."

She thought of the painting Saint had given her and the wild-flowers, both shoved unceremoniously under Ada's bed. She realized that Ada had told her, and she just hadn't been paying attention.

"I didn't think it mattered," Ada said. "I didn't think the little snake would ever show his face here again."

"Ada." It was Johnny, still standing in the doorway of his office. "Come in here for a minute."

Corinne pulled the cash from her coat pocket and started to join her, but Johnny shook his head.

"Just Ada."

Ada and Corinne exchanged a glance. Then Ada took the money from Corinne and followed Johnny into his office. Corinne sat down on the couch and massaged her temples. She had the beginnings of an awful headache. She needed a drink.

"Who was that?" Gabriel asked.

"Sebastian Temple," Corinne said. "We all call him Saint. He's lived here about five years, but he's known Johnny for longer than that."

"I gather he was with Ada when she got arrested."

"I haven't seen him since that night. Johnny said he was lying low." Corinne glanced toward the closed office door. "I wonder if Johnny knew the whole story."

She drummed her fingers on her knee, thinking. Then she shook her head and jumped up. "I'll be right back," she said.

She went to Saint's door and entered without knocking. The pungent smell of oil paint greeted her. Saint's room, though not any bigger than hers, doubled as his studio. Every inch of wall was covered with a canvas, and every inch of floor space held an easel or a can of paint or a bucket of brushes. There was only the slenderest of paths from the door to the cot. Saint was sitting there, slouched with his back against the wall.

Corinne toed her way through the chaos and sat down on the foot of the bed. Leaning against the wall, stacked against several other paintings, was one of the larger canvases she'd seen Saint work on. It was only broad strokes right now, but she could already see that it was the Mythic Theatre, which was odd. Saint usually spent time only on paintings he could pull an object from.

A reg looking around the room would assume the brass candlestick in the corner was the model for the painting above it, but Corinne had been there the day he pulled the candlestick from the canvas. It was one of his first successful pulls, and she could remember Johnny slapping him on the back. She remembered how happy Saint had looked.

Tucked among the painting supplies was evidence of other practice pulls. A milk can, a vase of wilting flowers, even a bowl of eggs. Johnny had been pressuring him in the last year to paint items of value that they could sell, but no matter how much time Saint spent on the painting, the objects he pulled were never quite perfect. Precious gems were declared worthless by jewelers. Gold bars were little more than gilded lead. Even the candlestick, which was brass by all appearances, was pliable to the touch, like modeling clay.

Johnny never said much to Saint about these attempts, but somehow that only made the failures more cutting. Corinne knew their talents had always been intertwined with their duty to the Cast

Iron, but the stakes hadn't always been so high. She remembered a night, years ago, not long after she and Ada had moved to the club.

The three of them had sat on the floor of Saint's room, legs crossed, breath bated, while he pulled out a plate of steaming cookies from a fresh painting. The treats hadn't tasted quite right, but that didn't stop them from devouring the lot until their stomachs ached.

"I'm sorry about Ada," Saint said suddenly, not looking at her. "That's all I can say, all right?"

His soft eyes and the freckles across his pale face always made him look much younger than seventeen. Normally that was something Corinne teased him about, but now it just made her feel worse. She drove her fingernails into her palms until they stung. She knew she owed it to Ada to say what needed to be said.

"You've always been a good friend to me," she said at last.

"But?"

"But Ada is much more than that, and I saw where she spent the past two weeks."

Saint buried his head in his hands. "I didn't know what else to do," he murmured.

"I believe you," Corinne said. "But I'll always stand by Ada. You know that."

He didn't reply. Corinne sat beside him for a few more minutes, thinking more about the night with the cookies, how those three children never once suspected what the ensuing years would bring. Finally she shook herself free from the memories. She patted Saint on the back and left without saying anything more.

In Johnny's office, Ada dropped the money on his desk. She refused the seat he offered her. Johnny counted the cash and began dividing it bill by bill. The only sound in the room was the shuffle of paper.

The smell of cloves and pine that had been so comforting the night before was suffocating now. Finally Ada couldn't stand the silence.

"What did Saint tell you happened?" she asked.

"He told me everything," Johnny replied, still counting.

"Then when will he be gone?"

Johnny stopped counting. He folded his hands and looked at her.

"He's not going anywhere, Ada. He's one of us. You know that."

She shook her head. "He sold me out to save his skin. He's not one of us, not anymore."

Two weeks ago, Ada had run a simple—if slightly illegal—errand for Johnny. With Corinne home for Christmas break, Saint went as the lookout. Ada knew he wasn't quite comfortable on the street, but he had played the role before without incident. No one could expect to live at the Cast Iron without paying their dues, even Saint—whose father had served in the same regiment as Johnny.

When things went awry, she'd kept her mouth shut at the police station. It never once occurred to her to flip on Saint, or to doubt that Johnny would bail them out before they were sent to Haversham. It also never occurred to her that Saint would fold under their bluff, that he would betray her for the chance to walk free.

Johnny closed his eyes briefly. He always had such a calmness about him. Ada could never figure out where that kind of serenity came from.

"I can't turn him out," he said.

Ada stared at him, incredulous. "Johnny, loyalty is the only thing that's ever mattered to you."

"I've got bigger concerns than that right now. If Prohibition passes next week, the Cast Iron's days are numbered." His tone had a grim edge to it.

"Do you really think it will pass?" Ada asked.

The movement to ban the sale of alcohol had been quietly fuming for as long as she could remember. Alcohol was a huge part of the Cast Iron's income, especially now that they could host hemopath shows only every couple of weeks. If alcohol was banned too, then the club would be sunk for good.

Johnny shrugged. He pulled out his pocketknife and slit open an envelope on his desk. Whatever was inside must have been unimportant, because he tossed it away. He rammed the tip of the knife into the wood and looked at her.

"Saint isn't going anywhere. I'm not asking you to forgive him, or to even speak to him. But he's staying." Johnny glanced down at the bills stacked on his desk. With a single finger, he straightened an errant note until the pile was perfectly even. "I've got debts to pay. Same as anyone else."

"What's that supposed to mean?"

He sat erect in his chair, and the expression that had crept across his face vanished, replaced by his usual genial smile.

"I'll have your cut for you in a couple of hours."

He turned his attention back to the money, and Ada realized she had been dismissed. She left and shut the door quietly behind her. The anger was still there, a tiny, persistent flame, but Ada was too tired to fan it right now. Corinne would make sure Saint kept his distance, but there wasn't much else to be done. Whatever his reasons, Johnny had made his decision.

Saint had broken the number one rule of the Cast Iron: trust. But Ada knew better than to break the second, which was to never cross Johnny Dervish.

That evening, Ada took advantage of the empty common room to tend to her violin. The instrument had been a gift from Johnny a couple of months after she'd first found her way to the Cast Iron. A sympathetic doctor had whispered Johnny Dervish's name to Ada's parents, who were wretched with worry when their daughter suddenly fell ill, racked with pain from the inside out. Hemopath manifestation was a gruesome process, usually lasting at least a week, and Ada's blood had turned when she was relatively young—only ten. She had blocked out most of that horrific time and remembered only how sweet the iron-free relief of the Cast Iron was. Johnny had offered to let her stay there as long as she needed, and her parents had relented, because they didn't know what else to do. Young hemopaths needed years to adjust to the city's plethora of iron sources, and the ones who couldn't find or make an iron-free refuge either fled to the countryside, committed themselves at Haversham, or turned to more grisly, permanent means of escape.

Ada had always intended to move back home, once she could cope with the ever-present ache of the outside world, but somehow it had never happened. The closest she'd ever come was when Corinne had first moved in—Ada had decided she would rather live in an iron box than deal with the petulant, demanding, blue-blooded twit Johnny was making her share a room with. Sometimes she thought about how different her life would have been if she had followed through with the decision, but in four years she had never once wished she had.

Ada slid the hair of her violin bow across a block of rosin, coating it to the right density. Then she systematically tuned her violin, tweaking the pegs until every note sang with perfect pitch. Once she was satisfied, she sat on the edge of the couch and sailed through the first few measures of "Amazing Grace." It was one of the songs her father had taught her. When she was small, he'd bought her a cheap violin from a pawn shop. It had a seam down the back and a bridge that never seemed to stay in place, but none of that had mattered to Ada. She practiced every spare moment she had. Her father called her a natural, but that was generously ignoring the late nights she spent drilling herself over and over again, no doubt driving every resident of their run-down tenement insane.

The violin Johnny had given her was seamless, with superior sound and strings that were exquisitely responsive to her touch. Even away from her father's tutelage, she had excelled, improving her technique and learning new ones from the violinists Johnny paid for shows. The first time she had played an emotion, it had been an accident. Johnny had explained the nature of hemopathy to her, of course, and she knew that somewhere inside her lurked the ability to make people feel anything she wanted them to feel. But it had still come as a surprise when a sonata she was playing made Danny start to cry, right in the middle of pouring a drink.

She'd started practicing emotions with the same vigor as she had practiced her father's lessons, and soon Johnny was letting her play with the house band. The shows had been bigger back then, before the law. There were usually several bands in one night and performances four or five times a week. Ada had loved the unbridled thrill of it, the knowledge that she was giving people exactly what they wanted, what they paid for. Back then it had all been so simple.

Ada had played through nearly to the end of "Amazing Grace" without thinking about it when Corinne bounded down the stairs.

"There you are," she said. She collapsed on the couch beside Ada in exaggerated relief. "Danny just made me help him mop the club, and it was terrible. Why don't you ever have to help?"

"I help Danny all the time," Ada said, lowering her violin. "You're the one who's always conveniently absent. Serves you right."

Corinne rolled her eyes at her. "I can't help that I'm better at being unproductive than you." She twisted to face Ada, crossing her legs on the couch.

"Let's play a few rounds. We haven't in ages."

"You may have forgotten, but I've been indisposed for the past couple of weeks."

Corinne poked her on the knee. "That means you're rusty. You need the practice."

Ada wrinkled her nose in consideration but shook her head.

"I was going to straighten up our room and go to bed early tonight."

"That is possibly the saddest thing I've ever heard." Corinne grabbed her upper arm with both hands. "Please? I'm bored, Ada."

She dragged Ada's name into a whine, giving her best puppy eyes, which Ada never had the heart to tell her weren't persuasive in the least.

"Fine," Ada said. "One round, and only because you're so pathetic."

"I'll take it," Corinne replied, scooting back so that Ada had room to pull up her legs and mirror Corinne's posture. They sat face-to-face, Ada still holding her violin.

"You start," Ada said. "Someplace warm."

Corinne nodded, her face screwed up in concentration. Then she began to speak in measured rhythm.

> "I found you and I lost you,
> All on a gleaming day.
> The day was filled with sunshine,
> And the land was full of May."

Ada released a breath and let herself succumb to the illusion. It was less like opening her mind and more like jumping into a rushing

74

current. The room began to change around her. The ratty armchairs and cluttered coffee table dissolved like burning paper, crumbling into nothing. Suddenly they were sitting on a beach. Ada could feel the coarse sand tickling her legs and taste the salt in the air. The sun was scorching overhead, raising a sweat on her arms. She looked out over the cerulean sea and watched the white-capped waves. She could hear their rise and fall, a steady pulse beneath the cawing birds.

When Corinne created illusions, she usually only gave the broadest strokes, letting her audience's mind fill in the details. She had told Ada once it was easier that way, and she still had control over the illusion as a whole. But with more effort, Corinne could draw every detail from her own mind, shaping it with precision so that every aspect was her own design.

Corinne grinned at her, and Ada realized it was her turn. She raised her violin and let the bow hover over the strings for a few seconds while she racked her mind for the perfect melody. Then she started to play, letting the emotion carry through the whole room, since there was no one but Corinne to feel it. Corinne softened as she let it wash over her.

Ada began with simple joy, then built in layers around it. Love. Wistfulness. The tiniest hint of fear at the inevitability of such joy fading.

Ada couldn't read people's minds to know their memories, but she could harmonize emotions to call forth specific types of recollections. Usually she just knew whether the listener would be remembering their childhood or thinking of a past love or mourning a loss. With Corinne it was different, because she knew so many of her memories so well. Ada had tailored her song to evoke the Wellses' summer vacations on Martha's Vineyard when Corinne was a child.

She could tell by Corinne's expression—nostalgia chased by irritation—that she had succeeded. Corinne didn't like being reminded of her family.

"Not fair," Corinne told her.

Ada smiled and kept playing, but she slid into a new melody, drawing inspiration from the ocean that still stretched beyond the horizon. She summoned only emotions this time, no accompanying memories. Freedom. Power. A boundless, howling rage.

It was Corinne's turn.

Corinne closed her eyes as the emotions filled her. She licked her lips and began to recite.

> "Oh, a hidden power is in my breast,
> A power that none can fathom;
> I call the tides from seas of rest,
> They rise, they fall, at my behest. . . ."

As she spoke, the tide began to rise. The sun fell behind roiling gray clouds, and the ocean boiled with the oncoming storm. Ada blinked, and they were no longer on the beach but on the edge of a towering cliff. The wind beat around them, pelting icy rain. A crash of thunder shook the rocky ground, reverberating in her chest. Then came the lightning, a jagged gash so bright that it seared the insides of Ada's eyelids.

Corinne was grinning again, looking far too pleased with herself.

"Lightning comes before thunder," Ada said.

Corinne scowled at her, and the illusion dropped. They were suddenly back in the common room, knee to knee on the couch. The rain that had been dripping down Ada's face just a moment earlier had vanished without a trace.

"Best two out of three?" Corinne asked.

Ada laughed. Years ago, when they had first started this game, it had been a way to practice, with Corinne holding the illusions of everyday objects in her hands and Ada coaxing the simplest emotions from her violin. The harder they had pushed each other, the more complex the exercise had become, until it was less like practice and more like a conversation—a call and response with an intimacy that was lacking during onstage performances.

"I told you, I'm going to bed early," Ada said.

"Wait." Corinne grabbed her wrist before she could get up. "Don't you want to talk about Saint?"

The feeling of contentment Ada had managed to cultivate shattered. She slid her legs off the couch and started wiping down her violin with the felt cloth she kept in her case.

"He's a coward and a snitch," Ada said. "What else is there to talk about?"

"He's been our friend for years."

"That's what I thought too, but friends don't push your head onto the chopping block to save their own neck." She shoved her violin into the case, a little more roughly than she intended.

"He was scared," Corinne said. "I'm not defending him, Ada, but can't you—"

"If it were you instead of him, would you have sold me out?" Ada asked. She snapped the case shut and faced Corinne. "If you were scared and alone in a room with the HPA threatening to send you to lockup, would you have turned on me?"

Corinne shook her head. She didn't even hesitate.

When they were twelve years old, the day that Ada had decided to move out of the Cast Iron and away from her insufferable new roommate, a member of Johnny's crew had muttered a racial slur within earshot. Ada had ignored it, as she always had, because it was easier that way. But Corinne, who had not managed a kind word for Ada since the moment they'd met, called the man out in a room full of people and demanded an apology.

He had begrudgingly given one, but only after Johnny had come into the room to see what the commotion was. The incident accomplished nothing but to make the man hate both of them equally. Ada never forgot it, though—not because she had needed Corinne's help, but because she knew that Corinne's strange brand of loyalty was not to be taken lightly. Something had changed between them that day, and though it wasn't something that Ada could readily identify, she had not left the Cast Iron after all.

"I know Saint was scared," Ada said. "So was I. But I kept my mouth shut, and he didn't, so how am I supposed to ever trust him again?"

It was not a question with an answer. Ada stood and picked up her case. She knew it wasn't fair to ask Corinne to stop being friends with Saint, but she also knew she didn't have to. Corinne would have already made that decision herself.

And, deep down, there was a part of Ada that just wanted to punish him.

She didn't want to examine that part of herself too closely. It was easier to lock it away like her violin in its case. It was easier to just forget about Saint and the wildflower painting and all the other gifts and jokes and small comforts throughout the past several years. Remembering only made the nightmares about the asylum worse, because it meant that her incarceration hadn't been bad luck or even justice for her crimes. The terror and the sleepless nights had been done to her by someone she trusted and loved.

Ada didn't think she could live with that.

CHAPTER FOUR

―――――― ◇ ――――――

Pᴵᴄᴷᴵɴɢꜱ ᴡᴇʀᴇ ꜱʟᴵᴍ ᴀᴛ ʙʀᴇᴀᴋꜰᴀꜱᴛ ᴛʜᴇ ɴᴇxᴛ ᴍᴏʀɴᴵɴɢ. Apparently the cook had decided to take the day off. Saint was sitting alone at one of the tables in the club, staring into a coffee cup. Corinne and Ada ignored him, sitting on the opposite side of the room. It was a surreal experience for Corinne. Just a few weeks ago the three of them had been sitting at this same table, cutting up about something inconsequential. Ada was teasing Saint about one of the new delivery boys, and Saint was blushing to the tips of his ears. Corinne remembered laughing until she couldn't breathe.

Today she and Ada ate their breakfast without saying much. Ada was sitting with her back to Saint, but Corinne could see that his presence had stiffened her shoulders and tightened the corners of her mouth. Corinne couldn't help but peek past her to gauge how Saint was doing. She had never gone this long without speaking to him before. His expression wasn't as forlorn as she expected, and he was staring hard across the room. She followed his line of sight to the stage, which was empty except for a couple of chairs and a forgotten microphone stand. There was also something white in the center of it that looked like an egg, of all things. It was still too early in the morning for Corinne to wrap her mind around that particular oddity, and when Ada noticed her staring, she looked back at her food without a word.

Gabriel came in at precisely half past ten, looking more awake than anyone else. Corinne couldn't understand how he managed to be clean-shaven at this hour, with his slacks and shirt neatly pressed. He nodded at Corinne and Ada but went straight downstairs, no doubt headed for Johnny's office.

Jackson sauntered in a few minutes later, trailed by Tom Glenn, a drifter whom Johnny had hired a few years back to help with the shipments at the wharf, when they had started coming nightly. Glenn and Jackson were laughing raucously about something. Jackson tipped his cap to Corinne, but she ignored him. He didn't take the hint and came over to their table, resting both his hands on the wood.

"Morning, ladies."

"Morning," Ada said, managing a smile.

Corinne chose to maintain her stubborn silence.

"You look like you've recovered from your stint at the asylum," he said to Ada. "I accept gratitude in cash or check."

He winked at her, and Corinne coughed loudly.

"Gratitude for what?" she said. "I recall being the one in the ridiculous nurse getup, pulling off all the stealth and subterfuge. You just waltzed in at the last minute with your vaudeville imitation of Knox."

Jackson shrugged, unaffected. "Ada was fooled."

Corinne gave Ada an expectant look, and her lips twitched.

"The eyes were wrong," Ada said.

"Exactly," said Corinne.

Jackson looked between them, but both were stone-faced. A united front.

"You two are hard ones to crack," he said at last, moving away from the table.

"That might be the first real compliment you've ever given," Corinne told him.

"My pleasure." Jackson flashed his toothy grin and gave a parting wave.

"I still don't like him," Corinne said to Ada, once he and Glenn were gone.

"I'm not sure you've ever really liked anybody," Ada said, taking a sip of coffee.

"That's not fair. I like you. I like your mother. I like—" Corinne barely stopped herself from saying Saint. Old habits. "I like that baker who gave me a free cupcake that one time."

"He gave *me* that cupcake, and you stole it." Ada was smiling, giving no indication she'd noticed Corinne's near slip. "Jackson doesn't seem all that bad. Kind of reminds me of you, actually."

Corinne searched for something to throw at her, but she wasn't willing to part with her biscuit. She took a bite of it instead.

"Let's go uptown today," she said around her mouthful. "I've got an idea that might be worth some aces. It's like an abbreviated Carraway coal mine, but with scarves."

Ada looked at her strangely, and Corinne wiped her face, expecting it to be smeared with food. "What?" she asked.

Ada let out a short laugh.

"You've forgotten."

"Forgotten what?"

"You're due at the train station today. It's still school holidays, and your parents are expecting you."

Corinne groaned and dropped her head onto her arms.

"Can't I just telephone them and tell them I fell off a horse during equestrian lessons and the school nurse demands I stay in bed?"

"And risk your parents' driving to Billings Academy to visit you?" Ada raised an eyebrow at her, unmoved by her distress. "You pay the headmistress to send home good reports, but not nearly enough to deal with your parents in person."

Corinne moaned and did not raise her head.

"There, there," Ada said, patting her arm with faint sympathy. "It's better than actually having to attend Billings. Posh food and unparalleled academia. The horrors."

"Snotty debs and itchy uniforms and not a single drop of booze for miles," Corinne corrected. She stood up. "Fine, but I'll be visiting Aunt Maude first thing tomorrow, so I'll meet you here around ten."

"One day you might consider spending more than a few minutes with your aunt Maude."

"You wouldn't say that if you'd ever actually met the woman."

Corinne took her dishes to the kitchen and headed to their room to change. She kept her school uniform folded in a suitcase under her bed. The leather-and-brass case was by far the nicest possession she had, but she touched it only during the holidays. She had been at home for Christmas still when Johnny called to tell her that Ada had been taken into custody. She couldn't even remember the details of the barely coherent lie she'd concocted to convince her parents that she had to leave the next day to return to school. Something about a national Latin competition and the Billings contestant having the flu. If they hadn't been immersed in preparations for their New Year's party, they never would have bought it. Corinne was skilled at taking advantage of her parents' inattention, though. She'd promised to catch the train home in two weeks and escaped before they could come to their senses.

The uniform was a white pleated skirt, white blouse, white stockings, and white Mary Janes. Billings had an obsession with the color. The school motto, *Super Omnia Puritatis*, "Purity Above All," was emblazoned in various strategic places across the sprawling campus. Since it was located in Pennsylvania, Corinne didn't have to worry about her parents stopping by for a surprise visit, and she used almost all of the money she earned running cons to compensate the headmistress for her role in the elaborate deception that was Corinne's life.

She didn't particularly enjoy lying constantly to her family, but she didn't have any other choice. When her hemopathy had manifested, she had been starting her second year at the academy. She grew too ill to function, barely able to leave her room. A nurse had recognized the symptoms almost immediately, but she hadn't told the headmistress, or Corinne's parents, or even the Hemopath Protection Agency, which was supposed to be notified of all hemopaths so that they could be properly registered. Corinne learned later that the nurse's younger brother was a hemopath, living in seclusion in the countryside, safe from society's fear and hatred.

The nurse had heard the stories of the club owner in Boston who took hemopaths under his wing. She wrote to Johnny Dervish, and a week later there he was: a man dressed like a farmhand who had pockets full of cash that he handed around the ward, buying allies, buying silence. He didn't try to buy Corinne. He explained to her, very simply, what her choices were. She could register as a hemopath, weather her family's disappointment, and spend the rest of her life wearing her *affliction* as a public brand of shame. Or she could go with him to Boston, to a safe haven where she could develop her talent, where the only rules were loyalty and trust, where she could thrive among her peers.

She had chosen Boston, without hesitation. Her only acts of penance were the occasional visits to her parents' home. A small price to pay for a life of bliss.

She lugged her suitcase up the stairs and went out the front door of the club, rather than risk dirtying her Mary Janes in the alley. After walking a couple of blocks with the suitcase banging against her leg and the cold gnawing through her coat, she started to consider swallowing her aversion to the giant steel traps that were taxicabs, at least for the ten-minute ride to the train station. By the next block, her left shoe had started to rub a blister, and she gave up.

As she searched the street for a taxi, she saw two men at the corner of the block, both in nondescript suits, hats, and overcoats. She might not have noticed them at all except that they were both staring in her direction. Neither was moving. They just stood there. The hairs on the back of her neck stood on end, and Corinne strengthened her grip on the suitcase. Even at this distance there was something unsettlingly familiar about them. Every instinct inside her screamed that she should run, but she took only a single step back. The men still didn't move. They also didn't look away.

A taxicab cruised around the corner, and Corinne flung out her arm so quickly that her shoulder popped. The cab screeched to a stop beside her, and she shoved her suitcase into the backseat before the driver could even climb out to help her. She followed her suitcase and slammed the door shut. The effort to block out the instant throbbing from the steel and iron cost her dearly, but she told the driver her destination and sat back with a forced air of comfort. There was a sign prominently displayed in the front passenger window: NO NEGROES, NO HEMOPATHS. Corinne gritted her teeth against the headache clawing at her skull and peered through the window as they passed the corner where the two men were standing.

They were gone.

Corinne dug her pocket watch from her coat and gripped it in her right hand, like an anchor to her own sanity. She shut her eyes and didn't open them until the cab reached the train station.

The Wellses were expecting Corinne on the twelve o'clock train. The cab dropped her off with only a few minutes to spare, and she ran through the station with her suitcase banging against her thighs. A few people gave her strange glances when she ran to the arrival platform. The train hadn't come yet, and she could see her parents at the opposite end of the platform. She cursed and stepped behind a potted plant. When the train pulled in, she waited until the rush of people disembarking had flooded the station; then she wended her way through the crowd and tapped her father on the shoulder.

"Corinne!" he said. "You always sneak up on us."

"Very light feet," she said. "Those dancing lessons at school have their practical applications."

She dearly hoped her parents would never call on her to display her so-called skills, which the headmistress of Billings detailed in quarterly letters to the Wellses. Corinne embraced them each in turn. Her mother asked about the Latin competition, and Corinne gave purposely vague answers to all her questions, until finally her mother gave up and started telling her excitedly about some fete that had gone better than anyone expected. Corinne tried to listen, but she couldn't stop thinking about the two men outside the club, why they looked so familiar, and Ada's insistence that the Hemopath Protection Agency wouldn't trust the bulls to deal with the Cast Iron. The HPA had been formed by special appointment from the mayor less than a week after hemopathy had been declared illegal. Supposedly the agency's purpose was to ease the integration of hemopaths into society through mandatory registration, but in the past six months, it had become obvious that the HPA was more interested in sweeping hemopaths off the streets for any imagined offense than in helping them integrate into society. Corinne had never come face-to-face with any agents, but if tales were true, they were ruthlessly efficient and handpicked for their heightened resistance to hemopathy.

It was hard to focus on anything with her mother rattling on, and finally Corinne pushed her anxious thoughts aside. She would tell Johnny tomorrow about the incident. He would know what to do.

Her father had driven the Mercedes, and Corinne rode in the backseat, popping three aspirin when her parents weren't watching and trying not to grimace. The taxi and the train station were bad enough without having to ride in the family's metal deathtrap all the way to their estate in the countryside. Perry and Constance Wells lived close enough to society to be involved, but distant enough to still seem important. Corinne had asked her mother once where the money came from, since her father's job as a banker didn't seem lucrative enough for their style of living. Her mother had said it wasn't polite to ask about finances, though Corinne later overheard phrases like "family money" and "old blood." She didn't care enough to ask more, which was something her brother, Phillip, found disgraceful.

"Our name means something around here," he'd told her once. "You should be grateful to be a part of it."

The Wells name didn't mean anything around the Cast Iron or the other clubs—other than the reputation Corinne herself had built. That was all that mattered to her anymore. These holidays at the family estate were just bumps in the road.

Her mother had lunch served promptly at half past one, and Corinne sat down with her parents in the sunroom for sandwiches, fresh tomatoes from the hothouse, and a cucumber drink that she actually quite liked. The Latin competition was not mentioned again, to her relief.

"Where's Phillip?" she asked, once she felt recovered enough to actually engage in her mother's one-sided conversation.

"He's with Angela and her family today," Mrs. Wells said. "I was just saying in the car that he'll be driving back tomorrow morning."

"Sorry, I must have been distracted." At least she would be gone when he returned. She loved her brother, as a sister ought, but that was the only feeling she could conjure. "Like" was not something she'd felt toward him in years.

"I expect you'll give a speech at the rehearsal dinner on Tuesday," her father said. "You've always been good at that sort of thing, Corinne."

Corinne nodded absently before dropping her fork. Rehearsal dinner.

"His wedding is next week," Corinne said.

Her parents exchanged a glance.

"Of course it is, darling," her mother said.

"Don't tell me you forgot," said Mr. Wells. "What sort of environment is that school, if you're too busy to remember your own brother's wedding?"

"I didn't forget," Corinne said, though of course she had. "It just . . . sneaked up on me."

"Me too," said her mother. "Just yesterday I was remembering that no one has even bothered to ask the caterers if they can come early, because of course we can't expect the florists to set up at the same time, and Phillip is absolutely useless, but he doesn't want Angela being bothered with the arrangements."

Her mother kept talking, but Corinne shared a look with

her father and gleaned from his glazed expression that it was all right to tune her out. The rest of the afternoon passed in a dreary, familiar monotony. Corinne refused to let the maid help her unpack, because then her mother would find out that the entirety of her suitcase was a hairbrush and a brick wrapped in a blanket to add weight. She'd sold all her school possessions after moving to the Cast Iron. There were always a few dresses in her closet at her parents' estate to tide her over.

She took a walk with her mother through the rose garden, but after half an hour the winter chill forced them inside. Fortunately her mother was too preoccupied with the wedding to insist on more quality time. Her father had already sequestered himself away in his office, so Corinne had free rein of the house. She headed straight for the study in the oldest part of the house, where most of the construction was wood and brick. It had been her grandfather's when he was alive. He was her mother's father and had come to live with them after his wife had died.

As a child, Corinne would sneak in while he worked and finger the knickknacks on the shelves. Sometimes, when he wasn't busy, he would tell her where they came from. There were wine corks from France, a dagger from Spain, and a crimson quill from the village where Shakespeare was born. Then there was the brass pocket watch from nowhere special, with its simple engraving: *Love, Alice.* Corinne never knew why it captured her imagination as it did, but she would spend hours sitting at his desk, watching him clean it, learning how to wind it, trying to convince him to tell her who Alice was. Her grandmother's name had been Dolores.

Her grandfather told her many times who Alice was, but every time she was someone different. Sometimes she was a lion tamer he'd met at a circus in Romania, or a fearsome pirate who had boarded his ship in the Adriatic Sea, or an opera singer in Venice who could shatter glass with only her voice. Corinne had never particularly cared to hear the truth. What she loved best were the stories.

All her grandfather's possessions were gone now, packed away or given to relatives. The study was kept furnished but empty. After his funeral, Corinne's visits to her parents' home had dwindled to only holidays and very special occasions. She didn't see the point in coming more often than that, not when he was gone.

Corinne sat in the chair behind the desk and took out the pocket watch. She wanted to clean it, but she didn't have the right supplies. Instead she set it on the desk and traced the etched swirls on the back with her fingernail. She recited a poem by Christina Rossetti, even though there was no one around to see an illusion. She liked the way the words felt on her tongue without artifice. Beautiful and poignant and rhythmic, like the ticking of the watch beneath her fingertips.

Even though Ada knew that it was smarter to stick around the Cast Iron, she didn't want to while away the day doing nothing. Besides, she wasn't about to eat soggy leftovers for lunch when her mother lived only five blocks away.

She pulled on her coat, gloves, and a warm cloche hat. The common room was empty—she, Corinne, and Saint were the only ones living down here right now. Other members of Johnny's trusted circle drifted in and out on the current of their erratic lives. There had been one memorable summer when every inch of floor space was filled with blankets, pillows, and dirty socks.

Today everything was peaceful. The seating area was cluttered as usual, with books and sheet music and half-cleaned instruments.

As she walked past Saint's open door, she caught a glimpse of his red hair, but she didn't slow down. The sharp scent of paint and brush cleaner followed her all the way to the stairs.

She knew that someday, somehow, she would have to find a way to at least acknowledge his presence, but not yet. She was still having nightmares about Haversham.

At the top of the stairs, Gordon was in conversation with someone, which was strange enough by itself. What was stranger was that the visitor was Charlie.

"What are you doing here?" she asked him, leaning in for a peck on the lips. Charlie never showed up at the Cast Iron during the day. It wasn't that he wasn't welcome exactly, just that the rivalry between the Red Cat and the Cast Iron hovered between friendly competition and something much more caustic. Several years ago Luke Carson had tried unsuccessfully to edge Johnny out of business. It had escalated from mudslinging to violence in less than a month, ending only when Johnny had shown up at the Red Cat during a performance, sat down right at Carson's table, and calmly promised to burn the club to the ground if Carson didn't back off. That was how the story went, anyway. It was one of Corinne's favorites. Supposedly the two club owners had buried the hatchet since then, but Ada was still careful not to spend a lot of time with Charlie when Johnny was around. Just in case.

"Good morning to you too," he said, his mouth working into a smile. He looked dapper in a brown coat and slacks, holding his hat in his hands.

"Morning," Ada said, heading for the back door. "Did we have plans?"

"Not as such." He skipped ahead of her to open the door. "Hold on—you take care, Gordon, you hear?"

He waved farewell before shutting the door. Gordon returned the wave, which was another first.

"Why does Gordon like you?" Ada asked.

"We've been together for nine months now," Charlie said. "Haven't you figured out that everybody likes me?"

Being best friends with Corinne meant being practiced at looking unimpressed. Ada put on that expression now and crossed her arms. Charlie chuckled and offered her his arm. She wanted to be annoyed at him, but his expression was so earnest and genuine that she tucked her hand under his elbow and walked with him to the street. The alleyway wasn't the most pleasant place to have a conversation, what with the stench of garbage lingering.

"You hear about the raid the other night?" she asked.

"Why do you think I came?" He slipped his right hand over her fingers on his arm.

"We're all fine," she said.

She wanted to tell him about the close call with the cops, but the words curdled in her throat when she remembered the dead look in their eyes as she'd played them into oblivion. Charlie didn't have any family to support, and he made enough money at the Red Cat that he never had to run cons with Carson's crew. Charlie was a songsmith who played hope and joy better than any other feeling. Ada, on the other hand, could make a grown man forget his own mother's face with only a few bars. She could play loss so keen that regs would sometimes fall to their knees and weep. What did that say about her?

"I wish I'd been there," Charlie said.

"I'm glad you weren't," she told him. She coughed around the lump in her throat and realized that she had inadvertently brought them back to the argument they had started and never finished before the show. She worried her lip between her teeth and waited for him to speak.

The street was quiet today, with a crisp cold breeze and a sky the color of a troubled sea. Ada could smell the bakery around the corner, and somewhere distant a child was laughing.

"If you'll tell me why you're mad at me, I'll apologize," Charlie said. "I just don't know what I did."

It took Ada a few seconds to figure out that he wasn't joking.

"You didn't do anything," she said. "I'm not mad."

Charlie pulled her gently to a stop and turned to face her, holding her hand between them. He studied her face intently, as if he couldn't quite bring himself to believe her.

"I never know exactly what you're thinking, Ada," he said at last. "I love that about you, but I also can't help but feel that there's something you aren't telling me. Something you don't want me to know."

Ada wanted to deny it, but she couldn't get the words out. The truth was that there were a thousand things she didn't want him to know. Things that scared her about herself. Things that shamed her. Things she didn't trust to anyone but Corinne. Being with Charlie was easy, and she was terrified of losing that.

"I just want to be with you," she managed to say. That was true, at least. "The rest doesn't matter."

"You told me you wouldn't have wanted my help at the asylum." The accusation in his voice was gentle, but it was there.

"Because I don't want you to get hurt." Because if he risked that much for her, she could no longer pretend that whatever was between them was simple and uncomplicated.

"I want to be there when you need me," he said, gripping her hand more tightly. His brown eyes were golden bright in the daylight. He moved a half step closer, just close enough that she could feel his warmth pressing up against her. "I love you, Ada."

The words were somehow both a succor and a crushing blow. Love had never been on the table before. Love wasn't simple and uncomplicated. Ada wanted to slide her hands around his neck and feel his lips against hers. She also wanted to run away.

She took a step back.

"I have to go see my mother," she said. The heat rising in her cheeks was almost unbearable. She tugged her hand free and shoved it into her coat pocket so that he wouldn't see the trembling. She took another step back, finally daring to meet his eyes. The wound she had inflicted was manifest in his features. Her chest was aching so fiercely that she couldn't breathe.

"Ada," he said, but he couldn't seem to find more words.

"I meant what I said," she told him. "I want to be with you. I just . . . I have to go."

She walked away from him, her hands deep in her pockets, her eyes to the ground. She counted her steps until tears blurred her feet past recognition.

The Wellses hosted a dinner party for a few neighbors that evening. Corinne wasn't in the mood for high society, but she knew her mother liked to show her off to their friends. Corinne was usually able to fib her way through the awkward conversations, though most of the time she was longing for Ada to be there, playing a song on her violin that would make everyone crave utter silence.

One thing she did enjoy about the parties was that it inevitably meant a new dress. Tonight's number was already hanging in her closet when she arrived. It was midnight blue with silver trim, with sleeves falling well past her elbows and a skirt falling well past her knees, but the cut was so flattering that Corinne didn't mind. She paired it with some black shoes and a long silver chain dotted with pearls. Her short haircut had flabbergasted her parents when she'd first arrived with it; but since then her mother had made peace and even on occasion mentioned how well it suited her round face.

When Corinne went downstairs to greet the guests, she had to remind herself with every step to keep the smile plastered on her face, lest her expression give way to a grimace. The house was old enough that it was predominantly stone and wood. Sometime after Corinne had left for school, her mother had gone on a redecorating rampage and replaced all the old fixtures with the latest styles. Thankfully the latest styles all happened to be brass. Corinne didn't like to think about what stepping inside the house would have been like with its original iron hinges, knobs, and latches. She still had to avoid the kitchen at all costs.

With the guests' arrival, she could sense the iron alloys in their jewelry and cuff links like an ache niggling at the base of her neck. Apparently not all of her parents' friends could afford to wear pure gold and silver to cocktail parties. She could handle a little iron, though. It was the small talk that drained her. After twenty minutes of exchanging inane pleasantries, she was exhausted.

She was trying to decide if it would be worth the effort to fake a fainting spell when her mother grabbed her by the arm and dragged her to greet the newest arrivals. The young couple was only a little older than Corinne, arm in arm, with smiles that had probably taken years of practice to look so genuine.

"James, Madeline, we're so pleased you could make it," Mrs. Wells said, taking each of their hands in turn. She was flustered from all the preparations, and her complexion was splotched with uneven red. If she'd known about the stain on the silk of her dress, she would have been mortified. Corinne decided not to mention it.

"How could we miss our dearest Corinne's homecoming?" Madeline asked.

Madeline Gretsky was tall and proportioned like a catalogue model, with dark curls and cherry-red lipstick that somehow didn't look cheap against her pale face. The Wellses had known Madeline's family since Corinne was in diapers and Madeline was dressing her up in homemade costumes and reenacting scenes from her favorite fairy tales. Madeline's husband, James, had come along a few years ago, wooing high society with his charm despite his solidly middle-class upbringing. James was Madeline's perfect complement, with golden hair, sleepy blue eyes, and a face like poetry. He offered Corinne a languid smile.

"We never see you around the Mythic," he said.

"I go to school in Pennsylvania, remember?"

"Right, right." He wrapped his arm around Madeline's shoulder with lazy ease and kept smiling.

"I'm so sorry that Perry and I haven't made it down to your little theater yet," Mrs. Wells said, her hands fluttering uselessly, as if she couldn't decide what to do with them. "We're so terribly busy, you know. With the wedding."

Corinne snorted. Her parents' refusal to attend a play at the Mythic Theatre had nothing to do with their schedules and everything to do with its less-than-grand premises and reputation for attracting uncouth artistic types.

Madeline's smile was beatific, making a matching set with her husband's.

"It's perfectly all right, Mrs. Wells," she said. "We understand."

"Thank you so much for the invitation," James said.

"Of course," Mrs. Wells said, waving her hands in a way that

Corinne thought resembled a frenetic bird. "But you'll have to excuse me. I think the maid mixed up the place settings."

Mrs. Wells glanced toward the dining room in distraction and moved off.

"So wonderful to see you," Madeline said with a dainty wave. She waited until Mrs. Wells was out of earshot, then smacked Corinne on the shoulder.

"What was that for?" Corinne asked, rubbing her arm reflexively.

"Why didn't you come to *Glass Staircase* in November? You promised you would."

"No I didn't!"

"You said you would try, at least."

"I believe my exact words were: I'd rather jump off the Custom House tower."

"She's right, Maddy," James said musingly, resting his chin on top of her dark hair. "Those were her exact words."

"Oh, hush," Madeline said. She batted him away. "I'm trying to win an argument here. I was a positively thrilling Lucinda."

"I don't know who Lucinda is," Corinne said. "No one has ever heard of your ghastly plays."

Madeline's lip puckered into a pout, and she crossed her arms. She glanced around, but none of the other guests showed any interest in eavesdropping on their conversation.

"James and I are good enough to keep your secret, Cor," Madeline said, dropping her voice to a forceful whisper. "The least you could do is support our theater."

"No," Corinne said as the dinner bell rang. "The least I can do is not tell anyone *your* secret."

"Another excellent point," James said, still unperturbed.

Madeline rolled her eyes but didn't seem to have a retort.

Corinne took that as a victory and led the way into the dining room with a smile.

The dinner portion of the evening was more or less predictable. Corinne was an expert at having food in her mouth every time someone asked her a question about school. Madeline was called upon to regale the table with tales of her studies in Paris, which Corinne was grateful for. Not only did it distract the guests, but it kept Madeline from provoking her—one of the older girl's favorite pastimes. James did lean over at one point during a particularly flamboyant segment of Madeline's story and ask Corinne about Ada and Saint.

"Ada's fine," Corinne said, and frowned. "I thought Saint would have been spending his time at the Mythic. He hasn't been around much since—"

She cut herself short, and James raised an eyebrow. Before he could ask anything further, Madeline called on him to do his impression of the French prime minister.

"He's better at being Clemenceau than Clemenceau is," she told the table, eyes bright with laughter.

James winked at Corinne and obliged, donning a ridiculous French accent and somehow capturing the essence of a walrus mustache with just his expression. Their conversation was quickly swept away by the merriment of the guests.

Once the party had adjourned to the parlor, Corinne took her usual spot in the northwest corner, which was the farthest from any iron and kept her headache to a dull roar, easily silenced with some aspirin and a few swigs from her hip flask when no one was looking. She was in the middle of a furtive sip when someone slapped her back roughly.

"Please tell me that's medicinal," came the booming voice.

"Phillip," she said through her coughing. She barely had time to stash the flask before her mother breezed across the room, arms wide to embrace her son.

"Phil, when did you get here?" Mrs. Wells cried. "You slip in without even a word? Where's Angela?"

Her questions went unanswered for a few minutes as the other guests noticed the new arrival. There were handshakes all around and congratulations on his upcoming nuptials. Corinne was trapped in the corner behind the tall bulk of her brother, and she eventually just sank onto an ottoman to wait it out. After declining dinner and wine and cheese and everything else their mother tried to shove at him, Phillip finally took a seat. He shared their mother's brown hair, though his eyes were blue like their father's. He'd inherited all the height in the family as well, towering even over Mr. Wells. When she was younger, Corinne had started a game with herself, trying to keep count of the number of times people told the Wellses how dashing their son was. She'd lost count somewhere in the hundreds.

"Angela's staying with her parents until tomorrow," Phillip said, completely comfortable under the weight of the entire party's attention. "She wanted me to come early to help Mother with the final preparations."

Corinne couldn't suppress a snort of laughter at that.

"And to spend time with family that's coming in," he continued. He leaned over to muss Corinne's hair with just a little too much force to be tenderly affectionate. She jerked away from him and almost fell off the ottoman. He knew how much she hated when he did that.

"She's so considerate," Mrs. Wells said, beaming with pride at her son's choice of bride.

Corinne ran her fingers through her hair and thought it much more likely that Phillip was tired of Angela's family, but she wasn't keen on being pulled into the tedium of wedding preparations. As far as Corinne could tell, Angela was much more comfortable dictating her preferences from a tea table at a country club.

The conversation ran swiftly toward the stress on young brides and from there on to the economy and which neighborhoods were going downhill. Corinne lost its thread for a while, so she was caught off guard when the discussion suddenly turned to hemopaths and the Harvard Bridge.

"Are the police even trying to find them? Surely out of all the people on that bridge, someone remembers them."

"It'll be the Hemopath Protection Agency that's after them, not the regular police."

"Charlotte Dower said her cousin was there, and he barely remembers a thing. Still swears up and down those elephants must've been real."

"I've been saying for years that hemopaths are a danger to us. If they know how to get inside your head like that, what's to stop them from doing it all the time?"

"Is the law even enough to stop them? I've heard they still host those parties in secret. The police can't shut them all down."

"Maybe the ironmongers have the right idea."

The man who said that was one of her father's business partners. An uneasy silence fell over the room at the suggestion. The masked vigilantes who kidnapped hemopaths from their beds were hardly a topic for civilized conversation. Corinne squeezed her hand into a fist and concentrated on the pain of her nails cutting into her palm.

"There's no need for anything like that when there's Haversham Asylum," said one of the women from her mother's bridge club.

"Did you hear that some hemopaths are petitioning the governor to shut it down?"

That set off a new flurry of titters. Corinne had to hold her breath to keep herself in check. She knew where the conversation would go. She'd heard it so many times, it was like a hated song on a phonograph that she'd memorized completely but never learned not to despise.

"They say there's torture going on there. Some kind of experimentation." The man speaking was trying to sound informational, but he obviously just wanted to scandalize everyone.

"Torture? In *Boston*? We're not the Bolsheviks."

"Can you imagine the nerve, petitioning against a prison that was built solely for their comfort?"

"Judging from the crime rates, they should be expanding the asylum. Phillip, maybe you can talk to Angela's father about that."

"Yes, I've told him as much," Perry Wells said, placing a hand on his son's shoulder. "If you're serious about running for office, that's your campaign platform right there."

Her father was not a man of many words, so each one of those cut Corinne to the quick. Her father had no idea that she was a hemopath, of course. That didn't make it hurt any less to hear him talk about the asylum in such generous terms.

Her brother just shook his head, his lips turned up in a slight smile. Corinne watched him closely, though part of her wanted to find an excuse to leave the room.

"It's an interesting situation, that's for sure," Phillip said. A standard answer for polite society. "Seems like a better platform might just be reminding voters that our esteemed Councilman Turner paid twenty-five hundred in taxpayer dollars to a couple of hemos for a poem and a song."

"Twenty-*five* hundred?" Corinne echoed before she could stop herself.

Phillip cocked his head at her, his eyes bespeaking a hidden amusement. "To the penny," he said. "I play golf with one of the city accountants, and he saw the requisition."

"A disgrace," said her father, shaking his head.

"Indeed." Corinne pressed her hand to her lips to conceal a smile. She and Ada had conned Councilman Turner out of only two thousand, meaning that five hundred dollars had mysteriously vanished. Johnny would be interested to know that the councilman was skimming off the top. That kind of information had value.

"Well, surely that's enough of this topic," Mrs. Wells said, her hands twitching nervously in her lap. She hated anything that verged on controversy, so touching hemopathy and politics in the same conversation was a social catastrophe.

Corinne had never been so grateful for her mother's delicate sensibilities.

"Mother's right," she said. "Next thing you know, we'll be talking about anarchism and women's suffrage and racial equality, and then the gates of hell might open up right in this parlor."

There were a few titters at that, but most people looked at their feet in awkward silence. Corinne wasn't sure why she felt quite so pleased about that. Only Madeline was still looking at her, lips quirked in amusement. James was shaking his head, perplexed either by her manners or by his wife's tacit approval of her manners. Suddenly Phillip laughed, a thunderous sound that always made Corinne jump. He probably would have tousled her hair again if she hadn't been subtly scooting the ottoman farther and farther away from him.

"You'd think a school like Billings would be able to train the sarcasm out of you," he said. "I thought Father was paying for a proper young lady."

"All the tuition goes to bleach for the uniforms," Corinne said.

A few people laughed at that, and the conversation moved on. Corinne stared defiantly at Phillip until he looked away. She hated how he always wore that smug expression, even when she had clearly bested him.

Though the party had been about to break up, Phillip's arrival had given it new life. Corinne stopped trying to appear engaged and started fantasizing about giving a poetry recital and making everyone think that the house had been overrun with badgers. She couldn't, of course. Without Ada here to lay down a fog on their memories, they would realize she was a wordsmith immediately. The scandal of the Wells girl being a hemopath would hit the papers by morning, and by the next evening there would be no place left on the Eastern Seaboard for her to live in peace.

When a maid slipped into the room to tell her she had a phone call, Corinne leapt off the ottoman so fast that she almost tripped and landed face-first on the Persian rug. She took the call in the hallway and was surprised to hear Ada's voice on the other end. No one from the Cast Iron ever contacted her at home.

"You'd better get back here fast" was all Ada said. She hung up.

Corinne stood dumbly for a few seconds before dropping the receiver in the cradle and sprinting toward the chauffeur's cottage behind of the house. He answered the banging on the door after a couple of minutes and promised to have the car around front in ten minutes.

Corinne didn't know what she was supposed to tell her parents. There was a sick feeling in her gut that she couldn't shake. In the end she cornered her father, who was less apt to ask questions, and told him that her friend in the city was grieving the loss of a dear cousin and needed her support. He was confused but didn't try to stop her from leaving. She didn't bother saying good-bye to anyone, even though Madeline was eyeing her suspiciously, and she slipped out the door before her mother noticed.

Ada's mother was baking *pão*, filling the apartment with the warm aroma that reminded Ada of the birthdays and holidays of her childhood. Ada liked sitting at the table, kneading dough while her mother kept an eye on the bread in the oven and told stories about Mozambique. Her mother was tall and graceful, with high smooth cheekbones and lips made for softly whispered bedtime stories. When Ada was young, she would sleep on the sofa in their tiny one-bedroom apartment. She loved her mother's stories, but what she loved most was looking past her mother into the darkness of the bedroom doorway, where her father would stand, his face pale in the moonlight as he swayed gently to the cadence of her voice.

The day her father was convicted for a crime he didn't commit, Ada had gone to Johnny Dervish and asked to join Corinne on one of her cons. Even though she'd been living in the Cast Iron and playing shows for two years, she'd always refused to be a part of the club's less-than-legal side operations. But when she and Corinne worked together, it was magic, and it took her only six months to move her mother to a nice flat and fill it with stylish furniture and colorful drapes and ornamental figurines. None of it could make her mother happy, but that didn't stop Ada from trying. Even with Johnny's connections, she couldn't free her father from prison, and she couldn't bring herself to leave the Cast Iron.

So instead she visited her mother once a week, sometimes more, and helped bake and listened to stories about a beautiful African queen named Nyah and the scrawny prince named António who sailed to her lands from a faraway country. She told how the prince was afraid of snakes, though he pretended he wasn't, and how he would sing to her, though he couldn't carry a tune. She told how he fell in love with her, and she with him, and how they decided to run away together to a new country, full of promises.

Sometimes she told about the beautiful princess they had in this new country, a princess who could evoke purest joy or deepest sorrow with just her violin, a princess who could crumble kingdoms with a song.

The stories always stopped there. Ada never asked her to go on. She knew how the real story ended.

"And how is Corinne?" her mother asked, leaning over her shoulder to prod the dough.

"Still getting me into trouble every chance she gets," Ada said.

Her mother smiled. She liked Corinne, who always devoured her bread and stories alike.

"She is a very strange girl," said Nyah. "Strange and clever."

It was the same epithet she always gave Corinne. Ada had relayed that to Corinne once, and Corinne had laughed so hard she fell off the bed. That night she had introduced herself onstage as Corinne the Strange and Clever, Master of Illusory Delights. Johnny had snorted his drink out his nose.

When the phone rang, Ada was on her second hot *pão* roll, which she ate by itself despite her mother's insistence that it wasn't a proper meal. Her mother was elbow-deep in suds, washing dishes, so Ada reluctantly abandoned her food and snatched the phone off the cradle on the fifth ring.

"Ada, I need you and Corinne. Get here as soon as you can."

"Johnny? Johnny, what's wrong?"

"As soon as you can," he repeated. "Be careful." He hung up. Ada grabbed her coat and hugged her mother good-bye.

"Wait—I wanted to talk to you about something," Nyah said, grabbing her wrist with a soapy hand.

"I can't, Mama. I have to go."

"You have time for your mother." Her voice was sharp, which was distinct enough that Ada hesitated. The rare times when Nyah was angry, she bellowed Swahili and threw dish towels across the room. The rest of the time she was all grace and tenderness. There was no in-between.

"What's wrong?" Ada asked.

"You told me months ago that you were going to come back home. You cannot live in that . . . place for your whole life."

Ada hesitated. She'd told her mother that to appease her, thinking she would forget about it. This apartment that she'd rented and carefully filled with tiny luxuries for her mother was not Ada's home. Once her home had been a tiny one-bedroom, with her mother baking and her father coming in late from his clerking job, bearing fresh flowers and a sheepish smile as an apology, but those memories were distant and hazy now.

One day almost four years ago, Nyah had called her at the club, frantic because the police had dragged her husband away in handcuffs. What came next was a haze of meetings with a lawyer and trips to the courthouse. Ada knew her father hadn't stolen any money from his employer, but she also knew that whoever had was probably long gone by now, and the police weren't interested in digging further. The jurors had heard her father's accent, still stubbornly strong after so many years, and they had studied Ada and her mother with varying expressions of suspicion, confusion, and disgust. Then they had declared António Navarra guilty.

She hadn't seen her father since that day in court. She had tried visiting him in prison with her mother, but there was too much iron. She couldn't even make it through the front doors. Two different appeals had been overturned, and even though Corinne had offered on multiple occasions to help Ada mastermind an escape, Ada knew her father would never agree to such drastic measures. He was a law-abiding man, even when the law had betrayed him.

There was only a year left to his sentence. Ada sometimes felt guilty at how fast the time had flown—she was sure that the years had not been as kind to her father. Her mother brought letters from him regularly, and Ada responded as often as she could, but there was only so much she could tell him about her life. Ada's home was the Cast Iron now, and she'd promised to keep its secrets.

"I can't leave the club now," she told her mother. "It's the only place that's safe."

Nyah snapped something in Swahili that Ada suspected was a curse. Her parents had spoken Portuguese to each other when she was growing up, so the only words she knew in her mother's native tongue were from the bedtime stories.

"I read the newspaper stories about the police raids," Nyah said. *"Eu sei o que se passa ali."*

"Não te preocupes, Mama. Johnny knows what he's doing." Ada slipped her arms into her coat and started toward the door.

Her mother said something else, this time in Swahili. Ada paused with her hand on the doorknob.

"What?" she asked, trying to keep the impatience from her voice.

"I said you put too much faith in that man."

"He's never let us down."

More Swahili. Ada left and slammed the door behind her.

CHAPTER FIVE

CORINNE COULD SENSE THE CHAOS AS SHE ENTERED THE CAST Iron. Danny was shooing all the customers out of the bar, claiming a family emergency. Gordon had abandoned his chair and was standing in front of the back door, arms crossed, face clouded.

Corinne hurried downstairs. The door to Johnny's office was cracked open, and she went inside without knocking. Ada was in there with Johnny and Gabriel. At first Corinne couldn't figure out what was wrong. Johnny was pacing in front of the desk, and Gabriel was sitting in his chair, shirtless, with Ada kneeling beside him. Then Corinne saw the bright-red blood on the towel Ada was pressing against Gabriel's ribs.

"Cripes," Corinne said, rushing forward. "What the hell happened?"

"It's just a graze," said Gabriel.

"Then why's it still bleeding?" Ada demanded. "Stop moving, or I'll get another songsmith in here to play you into a coma."

Gabriel grimaced at her but stopped trying to push her away.

"There was an ambush at the docks," Ada told Corinne. "Glenn is dead. Maybe Jackson too. We can't find him."

Corinne grabbed the corner of the desk. "Who did it?" she asked.

"It had to be Messina or the Gustin gang," Johnny said.

Gabriel shook his head. "One of them was . . . like you." He gave a vague wave of his hand.

"You mean a hemopath?" Corinne asked.

Johnny stopped pacing beside her and looked at Gabriel.

"Jackson wasn't there when we arrived," Gabriel began, but Johnny interrupted him.

"If he wasn't there to signal, then why did you—"

"He *was* there," Gabriel said. "That is, he gave the signal, and when we got close, even Glenn didn't see anything off. Then he shot Glenn, and suddenly he wasn't Jackson anymore."

"A thespian," said Ada.

"Which means Jackson is probably at the bottom of the harbor," Corinne said quietly.

Johnny slowed a little in his pacing, his expression taut, but he didn't disagree.

Gabriel had closed his eyes. "He fired at me, but I got away. He didn't follow."

"The doctor will be here soon," Ada said. There was a sheen of sweat on her forehead and a frown etched between her eyes.

"Ada," said Johnny, "when the doc's finished patching up Gabriel, I want you to make him forget he was ever here."

Ada frowned. "Doc Reeves has been coming here for years. Surely he's not—"

"No chances," said Johnny. He turned to Corinne. "I want everyone who doesn't live here to leave—even Danny. Close the bar."

Corinne nodded. Johnny was grabbing his coat and hat from the rack.

"On second thought," he said, pausing in the doorway, "you'd better tell Gordon to stick to his post. No telling who will be nosing around."

"Where are you going?" Corinne asked.

He was out the door without answering. The three of them were quiet for a few moments; then Ada sprang into motion.

"I'll talk to Danny and wait upstairs for Doc Reeves," said Ada, gesturing toward Corinne. "Come here and keep pressure on this."

"Why me?" Corinne protested.

"I'm fine," Gabriel said at the same time.

"I've been playing nursemaid for half an hour now, and it's your turn," Ada said to Corinne. "And Gabriel, there's a lot of blood here, so stop pretending you're not going to faint in the next ten minutes."

Begrudgingly, Corinne moved around the desk and took up Ada's post.

"What am I supposed to do if he does faint?" she called out, but Ada had already whisked out of the office.

"I'm not going to faint," Gabriel told her. "And I can hold pressure myself."

He pressed his hand over the top of hers. Corinne hesitated, considering Ada's reaction if Gabriel *did* collapse and bleed to death. Finally she slipped her hand free from his and stood up. He had closed his eyes again, but she was fairly certain he was still conscious, so she didn't panic. She pulled herself up to sit on the edge of Johnny's desk, her feet dangling. There was a smear of blood on her palm, but she didn't want Gabriel to see her wipe it off.

"It almost always takes a thespian to spot another," Corinne said. "That's why Johnny hired Jackson in the first place. Anyway, you'd only met Jackson once or twice, and it was dark. There's no way you could have known."

Gabriel's eyes sprang open, and he gave her a wary look. Corinne couldn't blame him. She wasn't sure why she was trying to reassure him either.

"I'm just saying it could have happened to any of us," she said. Had the conversation with Jackson really been that morning? It felt more distant than that. She couldn't even remember the last thing she'd said to him. She hadn't known Glenn that well, but he had been around for years. She hoped Johnny was going to make sure his body made its way to a proper burial.

"Thank you," Gabriel said, still slightly skeptical, as if he thought her consolation was some sort of trap.

"You ever been shot before?"

He shook his head. That didn't surprise her. She didn't think he could be any older than eighteen. He'd most likely been hired by virtue of a steady gun hand and the ability to keep his mouth shut. What he probably didn't have were years of experience running in a gangster's crew.

"I took a bullet in the leg once," she told him.

He watched her for a couple of seconds, then shook his head again. "Bullshit."

"Dammit," she said. "Usually Ada's the only one who can tell when I'm lying."

"High stakes are the key to a good bluff."

"Well, there's my problem," she said. "I don't care enough to try to impress you."

He shifted in the chair and winced. The wiry muscles in his shoulders were strained in sharp definition, and his entire torso was slick with sweat.

"Why lie, then?" he asked, his voice labored.

Corinne leaned forward on her perch, suddenly certain that he was about to pass out. He didn't, though, and after a few seconds his breathing evened out. When Corinne pulled her gaze away from his chest, she realized he was watching her expectantly. Warmth crept up the back of her neck, but she told herself he hadn't noticed. Probably.

"To see who I'm dealing with," Corinne said, resting her forearms on her knees. "It takes a good liar to spot another."

"That why Johnny hired you?"

She laughed shortly. "Johnny didn't hire me. He saved me."

Gabriel raised an eyebrow. "From what?"

The lamp on Johnny's desk cast twin glows in the centers of Gabriel's pupils, and Corinne realized for the first time how dark his irises were. Almost black. Briefly, seduced by the deceptive intimacy of the moment, she wanted to tell him everything. About Billings and her parents and her brother and the entire life that she could never quite leave behind, that was still waiting for her even now.

Then the moment passed, and she slid off the desk.

"Never mind," she said. "I'm going to change out of this dress. Try to stay conscious for that long."

He no doubt had a retort to that, but Corinne didn't stick around to hear it.

Once Corinne had changed into something less flashy and more comfortable, she went back to the office and resumed pacing where Johnny had left off. Doctor Reeves had arrived finally and was stitching the gash across Gabriel's rib cage. Despite the doctor's cajoling, Gabriel had declined to let a songsmith ease the pain. Corinne suspected that his staunch refusal had something to do with the memory of Harry, frothing in the alleyway, desperate for one more hit.

Just as the doctor was finishing, Ada came in, her violin in hand.

"Come on, Doc," she said. "I'll walk you upstairs. How're the kids?"

Doctor Reeves talked happily of his youngest, who had just lost her first tooth, and followed Ada out of the office. Gabriel watched them go, a strange expression on his face.

"What?" Corinne asked, pausing briefly in her pacing.

"She can just . . . make him forget? Take an entire chunk out of his life?"

"Cripes, you make it sound so dramatic. She'll just blur the past hour or so in his mind. There's no harm done."

Gabriel didn't say anything, which Corinne didn't like.

"What?" she demanded.

"If it's so easy to just do what you like with people's minds, why bother conning anyone? Why doesn't Ada just play a little ditty and have them hand over their life's savings?"

Corinne leaned in, resting her palms on the top of the desk. "You're pretty self-righteous for someone who's carrying a gun."

Gabriel shrugged, then grimaced at the motion. "I'm not passing judgment. Just making an observation."

Corinne snorted. "Well, maybe it will aid you in your observation to know that Ada can make people more trusting and susceptible to suggestion, but she can't just make them do anything she wants. And we don't take people's life's savings. Our marks are always regs who had it coming. You can't con an honest john."

"So you're Robin Hood."

"And you're a smug prick."

Gabriel leaned back in the chair and closed his eyes again. "Why do you turn everything into an argument?" he asked.

"I'm not going to dignify that with a response."

"Am I going to have to separate you two?" Ada asked, coming into the room.

"Forget it," Corinne said. "What's the plan here?"

"The plan is to stay put, like Johnny said," Ada replied.

"I hate that plan," Corinne said.

"At the risk of being called more names, I have to agree with Ada," Gabriel said.

"Shut up," Corinne said without heat. "And put on a shirt."

He raised an eyebrow at that. Now that the blood was mostly gone, his bare chest was even more distracting, but Corinne wasn't going to admit to that. She just glared at him until he reached for the clean shirt that Johnny had left on the desk, then resumed her pacing. It was making her dizzy, but her blood was pumping too fast to stand still.

"We have to do something," she said. "Where do you think Johnny went?"

"Probably to the Red Cat or Down Street," Ada said.

"You think he'd really just walk in like that? No protection or anything?" Corinne asked. "I'd say it's pretty obvious that either Carson or the Witcher brothers are responsible for this."

"We don't know that," Ada said. "Carson and Johnny called a truce. And the Witcher brothers don't care about anything but their cause."

It was true that the Down Street saloon, though it was iron-free, had very little to do with the competition between the Red Cat and the Cast Iron. The Witchers didn't put on hemopath shows, even though the meetings they held in their secret back rooms were just as illegal. Corinne had met the Witchers only once, and it was clear that neither of them particularly liked Johnny, but that didn't mean they wanted to hurt him.

Corinne sighed. "So there's a rogue bunch of hemopaths, roaming Boston and shooting up the crew of one the most powerful men in the northeast?"

"Could've been ironmongers," Ada said.

"They would never work with a thespian. Besides, their brand of vigilante lunacy is more of the 'drag you out of your bed in the middle of the night' type."

"Maybe Messina then. He's hired hemopaths before."

"How would he even know that they would be there tonight?" Corinne asked. "Johnny keeps the warehouse close to the vest. I've never even been there before."

"Me neither," Ada said. "But there are shipments there almost every night. Anyone could have figured it out."

Corinne shook her head and sat down heavily in a chair.

"We need to know who the thespian is," she said. She glanced at Gabriel. "Would you recognize him? His real face, I mean?"

Gabriel considered for a moment, then nodded.

"Better yet, could you describe him?" Corinne asked, suddenly sitting up straight.

"Why?"

"Cor, what are you thinking?" Ada asked, an edge to her voice.

"I'll get Saint," Corinne said, jumping to her feet. "He can sketch whomever Gabriel saw."

"Corinne, no," Ada said. "I am not—"

"Then go tune your violin or something, Ada," Corinne snapped. "Don't we have bigger things to worry about than your hurt feelings?"

She regretted it as soon as the words left her mouth. The damage was written all over Ada's face as she stiffened. Ada shoved past Corinne and left.

Corinne kicked Johnny's coat rack and cursed.

"Shut up," she said preemptively to Gabriel. "Stay here while I find Saint."

Gabriel lifted his hands in mute surrender. Corinne crossed the common room and banged on Saint's door until he answered. He was wearing his smock, and his fingertips were smudged with paint. A single gash of blue sliced across his forehead, brilliant against his pale skin.

"What?" he asked, peering suspiciously past her, as if expecting an ambush.

"In case you haven't noticed, all hell has broken loose. Get your sketchbook and come on."

Saint didn't move.

"Don't worry," Corinne said. "Ada's not there."

He considered her for a few moments, then slipped off his smock. He took up a pencil and a pad of paper and followed her to Johnny's office. When she introduced him, Gabriel shook his hand, not giving any indication that he knew about Saint's transgressions. Corinne was oddly grateful for that. Saint seemed more relaxed once she shut the office door, which was good. His art suffered when he was pressured or upset.

Corinne explained what she needed him to do, and he nodded.

"I've done it before for Johnny," he said, and looked at Gabriel. "I'll just ask some questions and make some sketches, and you tell me what looks right."

He pulled the chair around to sit beside him and they started working. Corinne paced again, thinking that she should go and find Ada but still unsure how to make amends. She hadn't entirely meant what she'd said, but then she hadn't necessarily *not* meant it either. Corinne didn't like apologizing for things that weren't her fault.

In the end, she didn't leave the office, reasoning that Ada would come around eventually. Their fights never lasted long. It took almost an hour before Gabriel agreed that the likeness Saint had created was the man who had shot at him. He was a middle-aged white man, round-faced, with a meaty nose and drooping ears.

"I don't recognize him," Corinne said, frowning at the portrait. "Do you?"

Saint shook his head. "Johnny probably will," he said. "Ask him when he gets back."

Corinne scowled at the thought of waiting, but she knew that the others were right. They couldn't leave tonight, after Johnny had expressly forbidden it. Maybe this was some sort of misunderstanding, and he would smooth it out by morning. Even as the thought occurred to her, she inwardly berated herself. Misunderstandings didn't end in two men dead. Whatever had happened tonight, it wasn't going to end quietly.

Normally Ada was the motherly one, but since she was still missing, Corinne found a room with a cot that Gabriel could use for the night. It was technically a closet with a cot stored inside, but she figured it was homey enough, considering there weren't any obvious spiders or rats.

"I can probably find some spare blankets around here," she said as Gabriel eased himself onto the cot and leaned his back against the wall.

"I'm fine."

Corinne hesitated in the doorway. "I can get your coat."

"I'm fine," he repeated. He had closed his eyes.

Corinne was already feeling the chill in the tiny room, but she wasn't entirely sure where his coat was, and she didn't particularly want to search for it.

She was debating whether or not to say good night, and

whether or not she had already lingered too long in his doorway like an idiot, when he spoke again.

"Do your parents know about you?" he asked. "I mean, that you're a hemopath?"

Corinne was caught off guard by the question but shook her head. Then she realized his eyes were still closed. "No," she said.

"Do you ever wonder what they would say? What they would do?" His words were growing soft and slurred.

"No," Corinne said, even though she did. Her brother would disown her and possibly call the police. Her father would start contacting hospitals and universities in search of a cure. And her mother would melt into hysterics of the collapsing-on-floors, begging-God-to-take-her-now variety.

Gabriel was obviously falling asleep, still propped against the wall. Corinne glanced behind her, but the common room was deserted. She maneuvered past a mop and bucket into the room and put her hand on his shoulder. He jerked awake, his dark eyes wide for a second before he focused on her face.

"You need to lie down," she said. "Or you're going to fall over and rip your stitches."

"I'll go to sleep when Johnny gets back," he said.

"Don't be stupid," she said, even though she had been planning on doing the exact same thing. "It could be hours."

"You know, you're not very good at this whole nursing thing," he said. He had rested his head back against the wall, and there was a definite smile playing on his lips.

Corinne told herself to leave, but her feet didn't move. All that was waiting for her in her room was a cold bed and an angry Ada. She didn't want to face either right now. She sat down gingerly beside him on the cot, half expecting a snide comment, but he didn't say anything.

"What about your parents?" she asked. "Do they know how you spend your time?"

His smile twisted into something sadder.

"My father died when I was a kid. My mother thinks I drive a grocery truck."

"Impressive."

"She wants me to run my own store one day. She likes the idea of not having to buy groceries anymore."

"You could do the grocery shopping for her, you know."

"I tried once, but I came home with cornstarch instead of corn-meal and a carton full of broken eggs. She never trusted me with the grocery money again."

Corinne laughed. "The first time I ever saw a carton of eggs," she said, "I thought there were live chicks trapped inside, and I broke every one trying to free them."

Gabriel laughed with her this time, and the cot creaked beneath them. Corinne was surprised at how comfortable she felt beside him, with her bare arm brushing against the crisp cotton of his shirt sleeve. He smelled of smoke and blood and something else that she couldn't identify. Something sharp but earthy, like concrete after rain.

"Can I ask you something?" he said.

He had turned his head and was looking at her. She met his gaze, suddenly conscious that his face was only a few inches from hers. She could feel his breath on her cheek.

"Sure," she said when she had caught her own breath.

"Don't you feel guilty at all? When you swindle unsuspecting regs—people like the doctor?"

His tone was cautious, and his eyes had a kind of regretful determination about them. He obviously was expecting her to react poorly. Corinne decided to keep her temper, just for the sake of being contrary.

"Before I answer, can I ask you something?" She kept her voice even.

Gabriel nodded, not breaking from her gaze.

"Have you asked Johnny if he feels guilty? Or Jackson?"

A hint of a frown flickered across his face, and he shook his head.

"Then why are you asking me?" Corinne said.

"Because I'm trying to figure you out," he replied.

"And because I'm a girl, so my tender, feminine feelings ought to make me feel sorry for the marks that Johnny gives us? Is that why?"

His frown deepened, and he actually seemed to be considering the point. "Maybe," he admitted.

"You know, we don't pull jobs for the hell of it—well, maybe once or twice—and we just take enough to keep the Cast Iron open. It's the only way we're safe."

"That doesn't really answer the question," he said softly.

Corinne had leaned closer, without really meaning to, and her shoulder was pressed hard into his. She wondered if he noticed, and if he could feel the uneven thudding of her pulse.

"No, I don't feel guilty," she said at last. "I'm not a nice person. Ada is, but not me, so the sooner you wrap your head around that, the better. I don't like people expecting me to be something I'm not."

His eyes searched her face for a few seconds. She desperately wanted to read his expression, but he didn't give anything away.

"Okay," he said, in a frustratingly neutral tone.

He faced forward again, and after a moment of studying his profile, willing it to give up his thoughts, Corinne did too.

"Why did you come here, anyway?" she asked. "Surely a job as a grocer would have been less complicated."

He was quiet for a while, and she wondered if she'd somehow offended him, or if he had just fallen asleep. She stole a quick glance. He was staring straight ahead, a slight crease in his forehead.

"There are things I want to accomplish," he said at last. "And being a grocer wasn't going to help me accomplish them."

Corinne nodded, knowing there was no use in pressing for details. Secrets were a dime a dozen around the Cast Iron. They fell into a peaceful silence. She let her eyes close, thinking that she needed to stand up and leave.

She woke up what must have been hours later, still sitting beside him with her head rested on his shoulder and the weight of his head on hers. Their hands on the bed were touching, just slightly. Hers was stiff with cold, but his was warm. After a long while, she tried to ease off the bed without waking him, but he was a light sleeper and woke with her first movement. His right hand moved toward his back, toward his gun, before he remembered where he was.

Corinne didn't know what to say, but she didn't want to leave without saying anything.

"See you tomorrow," she said in the doorway, and shut the door before he could reply.

The common room was dark and cool and quiet. She crossed the floor to her and Ada's bedroom. Ada was asleep, curled on her side. Corinne dropped onto her cot and stared at the ceiling. She wasn't sure why she'd lied to Gabriel. The truth was that she did feel guilty sometimes, when she forced regs to see something that wasn't there, when she traipsed over the sanctity of their free will for whatever cash was in their wallet. She refused to let the guilt fester like Ada did, though. She didn't see the point, when there wasn't any other choice. Without Johnny and the Cast Iron, she and Ada and Saint had nowhere to go.

Corinne instinctively shied away from the thought. The chill of the room was starting to settle over her. She breathed in deeply and caught the scent of the grape-seed oil that Ada used in her hair, as well as a lingering hint of smoke and copper. She pulled the blanket over her head and recited poems to herself until she drifted off.

CHAPTER SIX

THE RESIDENTS OF THE CAST IRON SLEPT UNTIL ALMOST NOON the next day. When Ada woke up, Johnny was still gone. She knew that it would be futile to try to keep Corinne indoors all day. She was still sore at her for the comment last night, but it was hard to stay angry with Corinne, who was rude almost as often as she was witty. Ada had decided long ago that it came with the territory. She did make a point of banging around her compact mirror and cosmetics loudly until Corinne finally woke up and muttered a bleary apology.

"Accepted," Ada said.

"Good. Can I go back to sleep now?"

"Where were you last night?"

"Waiting for Johnny." Corinne groaned and sat up halfway before falling back down to her pillow. "With Gabriel."

The way she said it made Ada turn around. "And?"

"Don't get too excited," Corinne said, pulling her blanket over her head. "We just talked. And slept."

"Together?"

Corinne threw off her blanket and sat up.

"I am a lady of *class*, Miss Navarra. I don't appreciate your insinuations."

Ada smiled and went back to her morning routine. After some coaxing, Corinne climbed out of bed and wiped away last night's powder and kohl. Her frock was a wrinkled mess, but that wasn't out of the ordinary.

"Have you called your parents?" Ada asked her.

"Do I have to?" was the immediate reply.

Ada didn't bother responding. She knew Corinne would do it rather than risk her parents' starting a citywide search for her.

"What are the chances of us sitting quietly today and practicing our embroidery?" she asked, once Corinne had struggled into something halfway presentable.

"Is Johnny back yet?" Corinne asked.

"No."

"Then the chances are exactly zero," Corinne said.

"I figured," Ada said, pulling her hat onto her head. "What's the plan?"

"The Gretskys. We have a sketch of the shooter from last night, and they know every thespian in town."

"You sure they'll want to talk to us? You know they steer clear of the Cast Iron's problems."

"I happen to have something that Madeline wants."

"And that is?"

"A warm body to fill a seat in her precious theater. Apparently, their insurance agent told their accountant who told Madeline's mother who told my mother that attendance is perilously low."

"Listen to you," Ada said, jabbing a comb in Corinne's direction. "Picking up society gossip and using it against your friends like a true lady. Your mother must be so proud."

Corinne made a face and snatched the comb away.

"Curtain's up at seven."

"I'll be back by six. I have to visit my mother."

Ada left Corinne wrestling the comb through her tangled hair. She could hear her cursing all the way up the stairs. At the top she nearly ran into Saint, who was holding what looked like an egg in his hand. He wisely ducked his head and stepped aside so she could pass. She knew Gordon was watching them, even as he feigned interest in his bag of sunflower seeds. Corinne had told her there was a bet going around the Cast Iron as to how long it would take Ada to break one of Saint's bones.

Ada didn't find it as funny as Corinne did. She and Saint had been friends. They had shared drinks and swapped stories and rolled eyes when Corinne was being incorrigible. Not long ago, Ada had comforted him at his father's funeral, holding his hand as the gunshots of the three-volley salute ripped through the summer air.

Ada was so preoccupied that she arrived at her mother's apartment building with very little recollection of the trip there. She climbed the interior steps slowly to the second floor, trying to arrange her features into remorse and brace herself for the oncoming wrath. Her mother was sitting on the couch, her back ramrod straight, her hands folded in her lap.

"Hi, Mama," Ada said tentatively, shutting and locking the front door behind her.

"What did you do, Ada?" Nyah asked. Her voice was quiet and precise.

"What do you mean?" Ada sat down beside her, noting the worry lines etched into her forehead.

"There were men here this morning. They told me that my daughter is a wanted criminal."

Hearing the word *criminal* from her mother's mouth made Ada wince. Her mother had an idea of what she did, of course. Nyah was no fool. But the topic had never been broached before.

"Were they police?" Ada asked.

Nyah shook her head. "They wore suits. Their badges said Hemopath Protection."

Ada's stomach turned over. How had they found her mother? Were they following her? She stood up and crossed to the window, half expecting their black cars to be on the street waiting. The street was empty.

"What did they ask you?" she demanded.

"Do not speak to your mother like that," Nyah said. She went into the kitchen and pulled a brass pan from the cupboard with a loud clatter.

Ada's mother knew she was a songsmith. She knew what she was capable of, and that iron was anathema to her, but they never talked about it. It was just something that existed wordlessly between them. When Nyah had moved from their old one-bedroom apartment to the newly furnished one that Ada had rented, she did not once ask where the new wealth had come from. Without a word of discussion, she had left behind everything she owned that contained even a speck of iron—including her cast-iron pans and the iron-hinged trunk that had carried all of her and her husband's possessions into this new country.

Ada had seen the loss like a shadow on her mother's features, one that had faded over the years but never dissipated completely.

"Mama, please. What did you tell them?" Ada tried to keep her voice reasonable, but she couldn't fight the rising panic.

"Nothing." She banged open a drawer and pulled out a spatula, then seemed to change her mind and threw it back. "I told them I know nothing."

"Did they threaten you?"

Nyah shook her head. Her frown deepened. "They asked about Corinne. They did not know her name, but they described her."

Ada's heart stuttered. "Did you tell them her name?"

Nyah shook her head again.

"I told them that you had left Boston, but they only laughed at me." Her mother swiped a damp rag across the counter in fretful strokes, then flung it into the sink. "The short one—he had a serpent smile—said that they knew exactly where to find you. Then the tall one said they were patient. That they wanted the . . . the whole set."

"They mean Corinne," Ada said. And who else? Johnny? Saint? The rest of Johnny's crew?

Her mother's hands were hovering at waist level, as if she were torn between pulling out more cookware and pulling Ada into an embrace.

"I should not have let you go to that club," she said softly. Her eyes were fixed on a distant point over Ada's head. "Now it is too late. Now your life is ruined."

"Cor and I will find a way to fix this." Ada rounded the counter, reaching for her mother's hands. "We always do."

Nyah's expression hardened. "So your father and I must always be afraid for you? We must pretend we don't know what you are doing at that club? António is in prison for a crime he didn't commit, while our daughter uses her talent to be a criminal. We tried to raise you to give more than you take. I see now that we failed."

Ada recoiled and dropped her hands. Her mother began to furiously scrub the pan she had just retrieved, even though it was already clean.

"I'm trying to help you." Ada's voice, when she finally found it, was feeble and wavering. "I've done all this for you."

But she wasn't sure that was true.

"It is not your place to protect us," her mother said. "We should have been protecting you—from that club, and from Johnny Dervish."

"Johnny saved us, Mama." Unexpected heat chased her words. "When they took Papa away, Johnny was the only reason we didn't starve."

"You do not think I could have provided for us?"

"I didn't say—"

"I am lonely, and I miss my husband, but I am not weak," said her mother, throwing down the dishrag. *"Sina hofu."*

Ada didn't recognize the words in her mother's native tongue. She was quiet, waiting, but Nyah didn't translate for her. Ada wondered if her mother was tired of translating for a child who never learned, for a daughter who listened to stories and sang lullabies in Swahili but knew nothing else about the world her mother had given up. For the first time, she wondered if she missed more than just her husband.

Nyah turned her head to look at Ada, her palms planted firmly on the edge of the sink, her shoulders hunched like she was a lioness preparing to leap.

"I love you," she said. "I love you so much, but this is not how things were meant to be."

Ada wasn't an idiot. She knew that the tale of the queen from the beautiful, wild lands of northern Mozambique and the foreign prince who fell in love with her was a romanticized version of the truth, removed from the context of four hundred years of colonization, but her mother had taken such care in preserving the tale that Ada couldn't bring herself to imagine anything different. And this wasn't how that story was supposed to end.

"I'm sorry," Ada said.

"Go back to the Cast Iron," Nyah said, waving her hand. She was not looking at Ada now. "Maybe you are safer there, and that is where you want to be."

The words were blows that only her mother was capable of delivering. Ada closed her eyes briefly. She knew she should stay, apologize more, make things right somehow. But she was hurt and angry and the apartment suddenly felt very small.

She gave her mother a hug and left without another word.

The walk back to the Cast Iron was bitingly cold, and Ada concentrated on her icy nose to avoid dwelling on anything that had just happened. She didn't think she was being followed, but it was hard to know for sure.

It should never have gone this far. She and Corinne had lived and worked for years in peace, pulling the occasional con when business was slow without the regs being any wiser. But the Harvard Bridge had tipped the scales. Councilman Turner's proposed bill for banning hemopathic activity had suddenly gained unprecedented support, and it had passed two months to the day after the Bengali banker job. Corinne insisted that the law would have passed anyway, but Ada knew it was their fault. They had reached too high and brought a storm down on the hemopaths of Boston. There would be no peace for them anymore.

Ada cupped her hands over her mouth and nose and blew into them. Her mind still turned in queasy circles as she opened the alley door and stepped into the relative warmth of the Cast Iron's storage room. When she saw Charlie there, leaning against the wall and chatting with Gordon like it was any old day, her mind went blank.

"Morning," he said.

Ada blinked.

"Morning," she said, after a few seconds' delay.

"Can we take a walk?" he asked.

Ada studied his features in the dusky light, the crinkling at the corners of his eyes from his habitual grin, the crooked length of his nose, though he swore he'd never broken it. He didn't look like he wanted to argue with her. He looked relaxed. She nodded.

"You kids be careful," Gordon said, spitting out a sunflower seed.

It was the first time Ada had seen Gordon express concern about any of the Cast Iron's goings-on. She wasn't sure how to respond to him. Charlie gave him a cheerful wave and opened the door.

"See you later, Gordon, old pal," he said.

Gordon made a sound somewhere between a snort and a grunt and spat out another seed. It was the closest to a farewell that Ada had ever received from him. When she told that to Charlie, he just laughed.

"Gordon? He's a big softie. Just ask him about his cat sometime. He'll melt like butter in June."

Ada hadn't known that Gordon owned a cat. She stared at Charlie's profile, trying to detect some hint of sarcasm, but it wasn't there.

"What?" he asked, looking at her. "I got something in my teeth?"

She shook her head. They walked toward the street, elbows brushing every few steps. Ada wanted to take his hand, but she wasn't sure how he would react to that. Their last conversation still hung between them, barbed and broken.

"I didn't expect to see you today," Ada said at last, unable to stand the silence.

"I heard about what happened last night. I was worried about you."

Ada hugged herself against the rising wind. Across the street a nun was leading a gaggle of orphans down the sidewalk. Trailing a block behind was an elderly couple, both with canes. The man was chuckling and clutching his hat in the wind. The woman reached out with a shaky hand and brushed something invisible from his shoulder. Ada looked away from the simple intimacy of the moment and sucked in a short breath. She stopped walking and pulled Charlie to face her. The question burned her throat, but she had to ask it.

"Charlie, was it—was it Carson? At the docks?" She searched his face. Corinne swore that deception was always in the eyebrows, but Ada wasn't sure what to look for.

Charlie shook his head. She didn't know if he meant that it wasn't Carson or that he didn't know.

"There's a lot they don't tell us, Ada," he said.

"They?"

"Carson. Johnny Dervish. I know it feels like a family sometimes, but it's not. You can't think that."

"What do you mean?"

He broke away from her gaze and stared down the sidewalk for a few seconds. His chapped lips were parted slightly as he gathered his thoughts. The sky today was a pale blue. The sun gave no warmth but glistened on windows and lampposts in sparks of pure white. A couple of blocks away, a trolley rolled along the track, its bell clanging as it passed through the intersection.

"Come out with me today," Charlie said. He grabbed her hand with a suddenness that startled her.

"Today?" she echoed. "Where?"

"We'll figure it out," he said. "Don't you want to get away from this—just for a while?"

Ada hesitated.

"We don't have to talk about anything important," Charlie

said, rubbing his thumb across her palm. "I just want to be with you, Ada."

She wanted to be with him too. She wanted everything to be easy again, like it was before the asylum, before the Bengali banker. Maybe it could be, just for tonight.

"Okay," she said. "Let's go."

Corinne ended up spending most of the morning on the phone with her mother, trying to convince her that this unnamed friend Mrs. Wells had never heard of was in dire need of Corinne's tender ministrations and could not be abandoned for another day at least. In retrospect it was the "tender ministrations" that made the story difficult to believe. Constance Wells knew her daughter too well for that.

With her mother finally appeased enough to not come after her, Corinne spent the rest of the day ranging around the basement of the Cast Iron, picking up books that she could barely concentrate on and pretending to straighten up the common room, though she really just shifted the mess and rearranged the piles. All this occurred under Gabriel's vaguely amused watch from his seat on the couch. She noticed that he hadn't moved much since making his way there from the closet with the cot, though he swore that his wound didn't hurt that badly.

Corinne wanted to go out and do something, but there was nowhere to go. She also felt strangely guilty at the thought of abandoning Gabriel, even though she was under no obligation to tend to him, and he probably wouldn't have let her if she'd tried.

She had told him about her plan to go to the theater tonight with Ada, mostly because she figured that being able to disapprove of something would aid his convalescing. Gabriel disapproved, but he didn't bother trying to dissuade her. And when he calmly insisted that he was coming along, she put up only a token amount of resistance. "You probably won't be able to walk that far anyway. And I hate taxis."

In reply, Gabriel struggled to his feet. Corinne forced herself not to jump out of her chair to help him. She concentrated on glaring at him in a way that might convey how stupid she thought he was.

"I'm fine," he told her, for the eighth time that day. "I need to go check on my mother."

"I'll go with you."

"No."

His voice was even, but the word had a finality to it that gave Corinne pause. She remembered how carefully Ada guarded her mother's home. Gabriel walked to the stairs with only the slightest hitch in his gait, and Corinne decided he was probably okay to hobble home on his own. The wound on his side didn't have that many stitches, after all.

"We leave at six," she called after him. "Wear a suit."

He lifted a hand in acknowledgment and disappeared, slowly, up the stairs.

"And try not to look armed," Corinne shouted as an afterthought.

Gabriel responded by slamming the panel shut. Corinne picked up the book she'd been trying to read, but even in solitude she couldn't focus on the words. When Saint crept out of his room, she was glad for the distraction. He kept to himself these days, which made him easy to forget about. Saint didn't say anything to her, just slipped past her chair to the coffee table and snatched up an egg that she didn't remember seeing during her attempt at tidying.

"Where did that come from?" she asked.

He looked at her like a preying wolf had just spoken to him, and he cupped the egg protectively.

"It's for a painting," he said, not really answering her question. "The—the composition is wrong."

Corinne wanted to say more, like how odd it was that eggs seemed to be turning up all over the Cast Iron, as if there were a stealthy chicken on the loose. But she remembered she was supposed to hate him and looked back at her book. Saint scurried away. Once he was gone, Corinne twisted in her chair and leaned over the back as far as she could. She could just barely see past the doorframe into Saint's room. He was pulling a painting from the easel and replacing it with a blank canvas. Stretching over the chair back a couple more inches, Corinne saw that the finished painting was of the common room, rendered in perfect detail, down to the rips in the couches and the clutter on the coffee table.

Saint shut the door—possibly he had noticed her not-so-subtle spying. Corinne dropped back down in her chair and made herself dutifully turn the pages of her book until half past five, when the phone in Johnny's office began to ring. She sprang free from the chair and ran to grab it. Maybe Johnny was calling with news.

It was Ada.

"Hey, Cor. Don't be mad."

"Something wrong?"

"No, nothing."

There were muffled voices in the background. Corinne thought she heard music.

"We just lost track of time," Ada continued. "I'm not going to make it to the play tonight."

"Who's we? Where are you?"

"Charlie and I are in the South End. You don't need me, do you?"

Corinne wanted to tell her that she *did* need her, even though that wasn't strictly true. Mostly she just didn't understand why Ada would rather go to what sounded like a party with Charlie than help them figure out who was behind the shooting at the docks.

"I'll live," Corinne said. "You sure you're okay?"

"Everything's copacetic. Don't go alone, though. Take Gabriel."

"I hope you realize that making me attend a play alone with Gabriel is cruel and unusual punishment."

"I owe you one, Cor. Gotta run."

The line went dead, and Corinne dropped the receiver into its cradle with a sigh. She returned to the common room, trying to convince herself that she wasn't upset. Ada had begged off things before, and Corinne understood that. The theater district was a welcoming place relative to the rest of Boston, but society could stomach only so much progressiveness before it revolted. A girl who was both black and a hemopath could not expect a carefree evening on the town, which was something Ada had to remind Corinne of occasionally, as Corinne preferred to forget the ugly truth of it.

This was different, though. Two members of Johnny's crew were dead, another wounded, and Johnny still hadn't returned. Why did Ada insist on pretending that everything wasn't falling apart? Corinne kept telling herself she wasn't angry all the way across the common room and to Saint's doorway. She knocked on the door twice, and after a few seconds he creaked it open, dripping paintbrush in hand.

"You're coming to the Mythic with us tonight," she said. "Find a suit."

Ada hung up the phone right as the musicians in the other room roared into a new song. It was all staccato horns and plucked strings and rolling piano. She couldn't help but smile at the sound.

"Hey," Charlie said, sticking his head into the room. "You need to go back?"

Ada shook her head. She took his hand, and he led her back into the parlor, which had once been a quaint sitting room, decked with floral wallpaper and matching chartreuse curtains. Now the room was hot and packed with bodies. Everyone moved together, sharing cigarettes and passing bottles of liquor. The glossy china plates displayed on the walls quivered with the pounding percussion and shaking floors. The ambience was overwhelming and powerful, and Ada felt closer to the music than she ever had before—even when she coaxed it herself from the violin.

Corinne didn't need her at the theater to talk to the Gretskys. And if Ada was honest with herself, she didn't really want to go. Even if they figured out who the thespian at the docks was, there was nothing they could do about it until Johnny came back. She would rather be standing here, leaning slightly into Charlie, letting him sprawl his fingers over her left shoulder. His index finger tapped an absent rhythm into her collarbone.

He hadn't told her much about the party on the way here, just that he knew the band that was playing and it was not to be missed. There were enough iron fixtures in the house that Ada knew the hosts, at least, weren't hemopaths. When she'd asked Charlie if they knew about him, he had just shrugged and told her that those who knew didn't care, and those who didn't know didn't care to.

When the music started, Ada began to suspect that she and Charlie were the only hemopaths present. There were no emotions being forged by the instruments. The sound was fully organic, offered with no agenda. It had been so long that Ada had forgotten what it felt like to just listen to the music, to feel whatever she wanted to feel about it, to think about other things while she listened, like how reassuring Charlie's touch was and how well she fit against his chest.

"Dance with me?" he asked, his voice rumbling against her back.

"All right," she said.

She took his hand, and they slipped into the crowd of dancing couples. The song was slow for dancing, and much of the crowd thinned while the pianist crooned a ballad about a moonlit night and a lovers' rendezvous. Ada and Charlie stayed pressed together, her arms around his neck, his around her waist. As they swayed to the rhythm, Ada rested her cheek against his chest and breathed deeply. He smelled like freshly laundered cotton, and for a moment the Cast Iron and Haversham felt so far away that she thought maybe they had happened to someone else. Maybe this was the only life she'd ever had, dancing here with Charlie Lewis.

When she opened her eyes, she realized they were the only ones still dancing. How long had the music been stopped? Charlie hadn't noticed either, and Ada blushed hotly at the whistles and cheers they garnered. Charlie just laughed.

"Come on," he said to the band, eyes bright. "Help me out, won't you?"

The pianist chuckled and obligingly leapt into a new, faster melody, followed closely by the trumpets and drums. Ada grinned and let Charlie spin her into the new dance. They were rejoined by the other couples, and soon the party had climbed to a new frenzied height.

Once they had exhausted themselves, they took a break to mingle with the other guests. Ada met more people than she could possibly remember, and all of them shook her hand joyfully and assured her that any friend of Charlie's was a friend of theirs. Ada liked the way he moved around the room, effervescent and artless. He hugged people because he was happy to see them. He smiled because he felt like smiling.

More than anything, she liked being the one at his side.

"Heya, Charlie," said one man, throwing a wink in Ada's direction. "Who's your friend?"

"Not his friend," Ada said. "His girl."

"Aw, you sure about that, honey?" the man asked with a good-natured grin.

In reply, Ada had wrapped her hand around Charlie's neck and planted a firm kiss on his mouth, catching his startled laugh. The man laughed too, bowing out gracefully.

"Damn, I like the sound of that," Charlie said to her.

Ada smiled and kissed him again.

They stayed for hours, dancing more and sampling the host's collection of spirits and food. She was so happy that she even found it easy to ignore the headache from the iron sources in the house. When Charlie took her hand and asked if she was ready to leave, Ada wasn't at all. But it was getting late, and she was still hoping to beat Corinne home. It took fifteen minutes of farewells before they were allowed to depart, and Ada was sorry when the door shut on the music and they were left in the cold, quiet street.

"What did you think?" he asked. He hadn't let go of her hand.

She was thinking a thousand things. Like how handsome he looked in the moonlight, the sheen of sweat on his forehead drying rapidly in the cold. Like how he'd never once made her feel guilty for not telling him she loved him too. Like how much she wanted to kiss him again.

"I'm glad we came," she said at last. "I don't think the Cast Iron or the Red Cat have ever thrown a party half as good."

"The secret ingredient is Carrie Greene's chitlins and cornbread. Best I've had since I came up north."

When she'd first met Charlie, he'd told her he was from down Birmingham way. The only reason he'd given for why he'd left was a few bars from an old blues song about his gal leaving him for a railway man. She hadn't brought it up since. She'd always been afraid to ask.

Tonight, with her hand in his and the music from the party still singing through her veins, she felt brave.

"I hear it's pretty bad down South," she said.

Charlie was quiet for a few seconds, then lifted his shoulder in a half shrug. His free hand drifted absently to his left forearm, and she wondered if he was fingering the tattoo of the tree. Something else she'd never asked him about.

"Most of the white folk out on their plantations haven't gotten the news that slavery was abolished. No better in the cities either. Soon as my mama passed, God rest her soul, I hopped the first northbound train I could find."

They crossed over some trolley tracks, and Ada flinched as her heel struck the steel embedded in the pavement. Charlie squeezed her hand, and they hurried the rest of the way across the intersection to the safety of the sidewalk.

"I didn't know about your mother," Ada said. "I'm sorry."

Charlie shook his head, his eyes fixed ahead. He didn't reply.

Ada still wasn't brave enough to ask about the other stories she'd heard about the South, stories of black men being burned alive, of boys barely out of the school yard being strung up in trees. She knew he probably didn't want to talk about them either. Sometimes she felt like her only choice in life was between the ironmongers' chains or the lynch mob's ropes.

"They have some fine music down there, though," Charlie said, a hint of wistfulness in his tone. "In August, even when the air is so thick and humid that the crickets are in a frenzy, you can still hear them songs for miles. Nothing more beautiful than a summer night in Alabama."

He turned his head, and Ada felt his eyes on her profile.

"Well, almost nothing," he said.

Ada's lips quirked, and she nudged him with her shoulder.

"That the best you can do? Little sappy, don't you think?"

"Give me some credit—I'm trying here."

His mouth cracked into a grin as he looked at her. For a fleeting second, everything was easy again. The rest of Boston felt faraway. Ada slipped her hands around his neck again and pulled him down for another kiss. She let this one linger, her tongue tangled with his, her heart tangled in knots.

When she released him, the white clouds of their breaths blended between them in the lamplight.

"Tell me more about the South," she whispered. She slid her hand into his, and they started walking again.

"Hot as hell," he told her. "There's mosquitoes big as birds, and so many hills and trees, you can go your whole life without seeing the true horizon."

Ada smiled to herself and listened to him go on about the fifty-odd-foot cast-iron statue at the state fairgrounds, ostensibly a god but with crooked arms and a giant Coca-Cola bottle in his hand. Their steps became aimless, and neither of them mentioned, or cared, that they were circling the same three blocks over and over.

At a quarter past six, Saint still wasn't ready, which wasn't typical of him. Corinne had never once convinced him to go with her to a party or a cabaret, but when it came to the Mythic's plays, he was a stickler for punctuality. Gabriel was running late too, which didn't strike Corinne as something that would be typical either, considering how fastidious he was about everything else. She hovered outside Saint's bedroom doorway, making generally unhelpful comments as he struggled with his tie in front of the low, paint-splattered mirror.

"I can't get the Windsor knot right," he said. "If Ada were here—" He bit his lip.

"Don't worry," Corinne said, trying to glaze over the moment. "I'm sure James will still be happy to see you with a half Windsor. A quarter even."

Saint leaned over to slam the door on her, though not fast enough to hide the flush of his freckled cheeks. Corinne laughed.

"I'm going upstairs to wait for Gabriel," she said through the door. "Hurry up."

She pulled on her coat and gloves and went through the club. She didn't like the way the bar looked when it was deserted, so even though it was cold outside, she didn't linger. She stepped out the front door into a burst of frigid wind that stole the breath from her lungs. She was just reconsidering waiting at the bar when she caught sight of Gabriel a little farther down the sidewalk.

The sun had set, but he was standing under a streetlight with an older woman. She was much shorter than him, wearing a long plain coat, with her hair tied in a kerchief and a ratty handbag over her arm. She had her hand at the back of his head, pulling him closer to her, her fingers clutching with something closer to desperation than control. She was speaking fiercely to him in a language that Corinne didn't understand. Corinne strained to hear the last word, and it was one that she did recognize: *myshka*.

When the woman saw Corinne, she let out a small noise of surprise. She kissed Gabriel firmly on the forehead and rushed down the sidewalk away from the Cast Iron, her head ducked low. Gabriel's expression when he turned to see Corinne was not one that she could identify. She had the urge to go back inside and pretend she hadn't seen anything, but words slipped out of their own accord.

"Was that your mother?" she asked, taking a few steps closer to him.

Gabriel was very still, watching her like she was either prey or predator—she couldn't decide which. She told herself to go inside, to leave it alone. As usual, she did not listen to herself.

"You're Russian," she said.

He blinked at her, still tense, still unmoving.

"*Myshka*," she repeated. "It's a Russian term of endearment, right?"

He glanced around them. The street was peppered with people hurrying home from work or hurrying out to dinner. He ran his hand through his hair and shook his head.

"I'm not talking about this here. It's none of your business."

"It's a little bit my business," Corinne said. "You're part of Johnny's crew now."

Gabriel started to shake his head again, but Corinne lunged forward to grab his arm and drag him into the club's entry corridor. They were alone in the cramped space, except for the countless hazy reflections in the mirrors lining the walls.

"What the hell are you doing?" Gabriel demanded, trying to extricate his arm from her grip with little success.

"You said you didn't want to talk about it out there. Now we're here."

Even though the mirrors created the illusion of boundless space, the air between them was stifling. Corinne shifted her weight back to her heels, silently cursing him for being so tall. He was glancing toward the door as if trying to weigh his chances of escape. Corinne tightened her grip on his coat sleeve.

"Corinne—" he began.

"I don't care if you're Russian," she said. His face registered surprise at that. "I only care that you're loyal to Johnny—to us. If you're keeping secrets, then it's hard for me to know that."

He regarded her in silence for a long while, his gaze searching. The light from the dusty fake-crystal chandelier overhead reflected in the mirrors and in his dark eyes. He seemed suddenly surreal, like a figment echoing into infinity.

"My real name is Gavriil Strelkov," he said at last. "I immigrated with my mother when I was seven, after my father died."

"Is that all?"

"What else were you expecting?" he asked.

"If you're not hiding anything, then why—"

"My mother is innocent. She knows enough English to survive, but it's hard for her, and lonely. Surely it hasn't escaped your notice that the deportation officers have been especially vigilant the past couple of years when it comes to immigrants from a certain part of the world."

Corinne had heard the gossip at her parents' dinner parties, and she'd read the opinion columns in the newspapers about the foreign anarchists who were trying to dismantle the American way of life, but she'd never given the subject much thought beyond that. She said nothing.

"If they take me from her, she won't make it," Gabriel said. "And neither of us would make it back in Russia. We have no friends there anymore. No family."

"I understand." She realized her hand was still on his arm, and she dropped it. "Your mother looked upset. Is she starting to suspect that you aren't earning your money driving a grocery truck?"

He grimaced, and his hand hovered briefly at his side, where his stitches were. The slight movement was amplified in the mirrors, spiraling into perpetuity.

"She saw my gun this afternoon, and she knows that I got hurt. She's worried."

"Well, I would be too, if my son the hired gunman was walking around with the words *I'm armed, arrest me* practically written on his forehead." Her voice shook a little with the forced joke.

He scowled at her, but without malice. "How about you do your job and I'll do mine," he said.

"Only if you'll admit that I do mine so much better than you do yours."

He rolled his eyes and reached past her for the doorknob.

"I won't tell anyone," Corinne said before he turned it. "I won't lie for you, if Ada or Johnny asks, but I won't tell anyone."

Her statement gave him pause, though she couldn't decipher whether he had expected more or less from her. They were toe-to-toe, and she could practically feel the tension coiled inside him. His expression was inscrutable in the dusky light.

"Thank you," he said at last. He opened the door, and they both went inside to wait for Saint.

CHAPTER SEVEN

THE MYTHIC THEATRE WAS A NEWER THEATER IN BOSTON, though it didn't look it. On the outside it was borderline derelict, with a marquee that dropped letters during the lightest breeze and glass doors that had long since been painted over, because the Gretskys couldn't be bothered washing them. On performance nights the crowd was inevitably thin, dissuaded by the shabby carpets and distinct smell of mildew that clung around the place. For the most part it was overlooked. The Colonial had a grander, more palatable interior, and the Orpheum put on more exciting shows. No one was very interested in plays even critics had never heard of, with titles like *Darkness in a Candle Shop* or *Star-Crossed and Long-Lost,* especially when the Colonial was running a new musical revue and the Orpheum had a brand-new cast of vaudeville girls.

The Mythic's current production was apparently entitled *Once in a Red Moon,* though a recent wind had changed it to *Once in a Red Moo.*

"You know, I've never seen a show here," Corinne said.

"Can't imagine why not," Gabriel said behind her.

"I've read this script before," Saint said. "It's good. You should give it a chance."

"How have you read it?" Corinne said, casting him a suspicious glance. "I can't even get you to read a sonnet."

Saint ducked his head and rubbed the back of his neck. "James gave it to me," he muttered.

Corinne laughed. "Well then, excuse me if I don't exactly trust your judgment on the matter."

The Mythic box office entailed a lockbox on the counter with a slot in the top for money, accompanied by a handwritten sign that read:

Admission: $3.50
God is watching.

There was a roll of blue tear-off tickets beside the box. Corinne stood at the window for a while, pondering whether or not God was truly interested in the financial security of the Mythic Theatre. Finally Saint made a sound of exasperation and shoved enough cash for all three of them into the slot.

"For an artist you are not very supportive of the arts," Saint told her.

"I don't see how pretending to be someone else on a stage is art," Corinne said. "It's not as if they write the plays themselves."

"You probably shouldn't mention that to Madeline or James," he said.

The theater had a better audience than Corinne would have expected, which wasn't to say that it was a particularly large turnout. They took their seats as the curtain rose—a slow, juddering affair. Madeline was alone center stage. She flung her arms open and cried toward the rafters about her woebegone state. With her eyelids painted a dramatic purple and her lips a bright red, she stood out against the dark backdrop like an exaggerated flower.

Madeline was soon joined by her forbidden lover, who wore a midnight-blue doublet that Corinne was pretty sure was anachronistic to the vaguely Victorian setting. His golden hair was like a halo under the stage lights.

"That's James," Corinne whispered to Gabriel.

The paramours talked for a while of their ill-fated romance, her upcoming wedding, and other clichéd plot devices that Corinne didn't bother remembering. Eventually the lover, spurned by his lady, exited the stage with a flourish. The lady had time to bemoan her loss for only a few seconds before her fiancé appeared, paunchy and black bearded and stomping a lot. Madeline widened her eyes in a show of terror that was glaringly obvious for those in the farthest row of the audience.

Gabriel shifted in his seat to whisper to Corinne, his breath tickling her earlobe. "This is absurd."

Corinne wanted to agree wholeheartedly, but she could see Saint watching them from the corner of his eye.

"Don't let their stage demeanor and this awful script fool you," Corinne whispered back. "James and Madeline are two of the best thespians Boston has ever seen."

Gabriel didn't reply, but his expression stated clearly that he didn't see how that was possible. Corinne gestured furtively toward the stage, where the lady's dastardly fiancé was bellowing about the cost of virtue or some such nonsense.

"Does he look a bit like James to you?" Corinne asked, leaning into Gabriel.

"What? No."

"Silly me. You're right, of course. They look nothing alike. He's obviously a completely different person."

She watched Gabriel's eyes narrow as he stared at the thundering fiancé, whose soon-to-be wife wilted like a womanly flower in the corner of the stage. After a minute he leaned toward her again.

"Are you saying—?"

"I'm saying that Madeline and James always put on obscure

plays because they have to find scripts that never feature more than two actors on the stage at the same time."

There weren't many thespians with enough skill to withstand glaring stage lights and a captive audience. The ones who could project anything better than a fair likeness of their subject depended mostly on confidence and poor lighting to fool people. When James and Madeline performed onstage, the real show was the one the audience didn't know about.

Gabriel's expression had turned slightly incredulous, and he didn't offer further comment about the travesty of a love story that was unfolding. Hemopaths who manifested with a thespian talent were considered the most dangerous by regs—and even by their fellow hemopaths. If the thespian was skilled enough, only another thespian could see through the impersonation. Madeline and James both cycled through a plethora of characters throughout the play, but even when she concentrated, Corinne couldn't see any resemblance. There was no evidence that the Mythic employed only two actors rather than ten. She might not care for the Gretskys' productions, but she had to give credit where credit was due. Johnny had tried to hire the couple countless times throughout the years, offering generous cuts of any con they helped run, but they always refused. Neither of them cared for Boston's seedy underworld. The Mythic was their only stage.

The play went on for almost three hours, with a brief intermission. It ended with Madeline's character jumping into a river offstage—either to drown herself or to swim to freedom. Corinne had lost track of what was happening by that point. There was no final bow, and the audience was left applauding at the lowered curtain.

Corinne led the way through the threadbare lobby and the

dilapidated front doors, around to the theater's rear alley, where a few crates rotted alongside piles of debris. Some rats scattered at their approach. Corinne banged on the huge wooden door. After a few minutes, interspersed with more banging from Corinne and the occasional comment from Saint that annoying them wasn't going to make them more likely to help, an eye-level panel in the door slid open.

Two brown eyes appeared, paired with dark eyebrows and a delicate nose.

"No autographs," she said.

"Madeline, this is important. Let us in," Corinne said.

"You know the rules," she said, eyes narrowing. "No one is allowed backstage. No one."

She started to slide the panel shut.

"Wait!" Corinne said, and dragged Saint over. Despite his protestations, she shoved his face toward Madeline's. "Look who I brought."

"Sebastian!" Madeline cried warmly. "How are you? I know someone who's been dying to see you." She seemed to catch herself and frown. "But rules are rules. No one is allowed back here."

"I've been backstage loads of times," Saint said.

"Shh," she hissed.

"It really is important," he said. "Please, Maddy?"

She considered for a few moments, then threw open the door. She was radiant in a white silk robe, even with her gaudy stage makeup still plastered on her face.

"You might have at least brought flowers," she said, propping her hand on her hip.

"It's the middle of winter," Corinne told her.

Madeline sighed dramatically and said something about the

secrets within being a great and terrible burden that they must bear in silence for all their days, and then she stepped aside to let them pass.

Corinne didn't see anything particularly burdensome in the backstage area. It was mostly creaky, splintery wood and dark drapes. There were chests full of costumes and props lining the walls, and a few half-finished sets were leaning against walls and doorways. Madeline squeezed beneath one backdrop of a starry night and led them into a room that was furnished with dressing tables and a blue velvet sofa. James was reclining on the sofa, still in costume, with his feet propped on one arm and a stack of papers resting over his face.

"Aren't you supposed to be making notes?" Madeline asked.

He didn't move.

"I'm contemplating my character's intonation," he replied, his voice muffled by the pages.

"Well, stop it. We have guests."

He sat up, letting the script slide into his lap. He'd mopped most of the powder from his face, leaving only a smudge of red at the corner of his mouth where Madeline's character had kissed him in tragic farewell.

"So much for the unbreakable rule," he said, his languorous gaze moving across the company. When he saw Saint, his lips curled into a smile. "Hey there."

"Hey there," Madeline mimicked, and shoved his legs off the sofa so that she could sit down. "You might at least put some effort into it, James. You're not nearly as irresistible as you think you are, you know."

"The charm is more in the presentation than the actual words, I think," he said, still smiling at Saint, who was by now flushed bright pink.

"Well, go on, sit down," Madeline said to the others, waving at the dressing-table chairs and a second sofa.

"Aren't we going to have introductions?" James asked, leaning back and stretching out his long legs. He was looking at Gabriel, who had just sat down next to Corinne on the sofa. "Has anyone ever told you that you would make a perfect Cassius?"

"I can't say they have," Gabriel replied.

"He just means you look likely to stab someone," Corinne said.

James smiled serenely but did not contradict her. "I'm James Gretsky. Madeline's husband."

Gabriel quirked an eyebrow. "Gabriel Stone" was all he said.

"Well, now that the tedium is over," Madeline said, "is someone going to tell us what's so damned important you have to interrupt our extremely crucial post-performance session?"

Corinne explained the situation to them as succinctly as possible, though she neglected the fact that Johnny had left the night before and still hadn't returned. She nudged Saint, who took the sketch out of his pocket, unfolded it, and handed it across to James. The pair hunched over it, their fair and dark heads touching.

"I don't recognize him," James said.

"I do," said Madeline. "Can't put my finger on it, though."

"Think harder," Corinne suggested.

Madeline shot her a glare, and James leaned over to study the picture again.

"Oh," he said. "I see it now. Looks just like—"

"Exactly," Madeline said.

"Care to share with the rest of us?" Corinne asked.

"Babe Ruth," Madeline said with a smug smile.

Gabriel laughed shortly.

"Who's that?" Corinne asked.

"Pitcher for the Red Sox," Gabriel said. "The resemblance is uncanny, now that you mention it."

"What are the chances he's given up baseball in favor of crime?" James said musingly.

Corinne stood up. "I'm glad you can all laugh about it," she said. "Meanwhile two men are dead."

"No need to be a wet blanket," Madeline said, fanning herself idly with the sketch. "If we knew who it was, we would tell you."

"Sorry," James added. "Maybe he's new around here."

"Good to know we sat through three hours of drivel for that gem of information," Corinne said. "Between that and Babe Ruth maybe we can find this bastard before he shoots someone else."

"We should go," Gabriel said, standing up beside her. "That's all we came for."

"And quite a production you made of it," Madeline said.

Corinne resented Gabriel's attempt to end the conversation before she was finished being cross, but she had run out of cross things to say, so she stalked to the door. Saint didn't move from his seat.

"I think I'll stay a while longer," he said, managing to remain within three shades of his natural color. "We still have to talk about the backdrop you need me to paint for the next production."

"Yes, the backdrop," Madeline said. "Very important business. I'll just shut myself in my room, shall I? Leave the backdrop discussion to the men."

James leaned his head back on the sofa. He smiled languidly and did not say a word.

It was a mild winter for Boston. There hadn't been any snow since before Christmas, and without any real discussion, Corinne and

Gabriel found themselves looping through the Common. They passed the white granite Soldiers and Sailors Monument, its victory column luminous in the moonlight. The fountain in the Frog Pond was off, and a murky layer of ice had formed across the top.

Corinne sank down on a park bench beside the pond. The heels she had worn were not the best walking shoes, and her feet were starting to protest. Without the warmth of exertion, goose bumps rose on her legs. She shivered under her coat.

Gabriel sat down beside her and lit a cigarette.

"Are Madeline and James really married?" he asked.

"Only technically," Corinne said. "It's a long story. Madeline's father was pretty well off, but he stipulated in his will that she could only inherit his money—and the theater building, which was her lifelong dream—if she was married. James was her business partner, and people already assumed they were romantically involved because apparently people are blind as well as stupid, so they figured it would be a tidy arrangement."

"Seems the opposite of tidy to me," he said.

Corinne plucked the cigarette from his fingers and stole a pull, savoring the warmth of the smoke as she drew it into her lungs. She gave him back the cigarette and exhaled toward the pond, watching the smoke dissipate in the golden glow of the streetlight. She hated the taste of cigarettes, but she was too cold right now to care.

"She got the theater, didn't she?" she said.

"And the money."

"Well, she gave all the money to the National American Woman Suffrage Association, in loving memory of her father."

Gabriel smiled. "I'm surprised you're not better friends."

"Who says we aren't friends?"

"Just a guess," he said, leaning back and draping his left arm across the back of the bench. "Based on the less-than-warm welcome she gave you."

"For your information, we grew up together. She's a couple of years older than me, but our parents were members of the same country club."

"Country club?" Gabriel echoed.

Something in his tone made Corinne turn to look at him. "What?" she asked.

He was quiet, examining her with an expression she hadn't seen before. There was a rigidity in his demeanor that she didn't like.

"What?" she demanded again.

"I didn't say anything," he said.

"No, but your eyebrows are doing the talking thing."

"My eyebrows are not— Never mind. I was just surprised. That's all."

Corinne tried to study his face for truth, but he turned away and blew a stream of smoke. A breeze carried it into the night. She hadn't meant to reveal anything about her background, even though the crew at the Cast Iron had all either been told or guessed for themselves. The precarious nature of the secret had never concerned Corinne overly much. No one dared to cross Johnny, and he'd made it clear that Corinne was one of them. Even Madeline and James knew better than to let on what they knew.

Corinne just didn't like to talk about it. She didn't like the looks it garnered. The whispers behind her back.

"You might as well say it and get it over with," she told Gabriel.

"Say what?"

"Accuse me of slumming. Of being a rich little girl, playing in the mud before she runs home to wash up and put on a pretty dress. Trust me, I've heard it all before."

He ground out his cigarette and didn't reply. Corinne surged forward.

"Not that anyone cares, but I can't stay at home for more than a few days before I start to go mad."

Gabriel was staring out over the pond. A hard wind rushed through the trees and across the ice, brushing his hair back from his forehead and bringing stinging tears to Corinne's eyes.

"You can think whatever you want," Corinne said to his silence. She was shivering nonstop now, and it was growing difficult to maintain the steady, righteous tone. "I don't care. You don't know the first thing about me. My life is the Cast Iron. None of it has anything to do with my parents or their damned country club."

She lowered her head, trying to shield her eyes from the wind. Gabriel was fidgeting beside her, and she guessed he was about to leave, but after a few seconds something warm dropped around her shoulders. His coat.

"If you're done arguing with yourself, we can head back," he said.

That made Corinne want to argue more, on principle, but she was suddenly very tired. She slipped her arms into his coat and stood up. She knew he must be freezing in just his jacket, but she doubted he would take his coat back, even if she insisted. She was too tired for that argument as well.

"You can pretend to be strong and silent and unaffected, but I know it bothers you that my parents are wealthy," Corinne said after they had been walking for a few minutes. "I could see it in your face."

"You're very smart, but you're also very tedious," he told her. "And you know a lot less about me than you think you do."

His tone, though not malicious, was final. Corinne took the

hint and let the subject drop. They walked in silence the rest of the way back to the Cast Iron.

Ada refused to let Charlie walk her back to the club. She didn't want the Cast Iron looming over them as they said good night. True to his word, Charlie didn't bring up their conversation from the day before. He just kissed her softly and asked her to be careful. Ada hadn't wanted to break away from his arms, but it was almost ten, and her troubles were waiting for her in the club.

The bar was still closed, and Ada went through the back door. Gordon was gone from his post in the storage room, which was unlike him. Maybe he'd figured that without any drunk patrons to keep from snooping around, he could take the night off. Or maybe he needed to feed his cat.

She was about to push open the wall panel when the alley door opened and Gordon came in. He was wheezing with exertion, and his coat was misbuttoned, as if he had left in a hurry.

"Ada," he said, leaning against the doorframe. "I tried to rush back."

"That's okay," she said. "Is something wrong?"

He didn't move from the doorway, and for a few seconds the only sound was his labored breathing. The silver winter air drifted past him, bringing the sharp scent of frost and nighttime into the storage room. Ada saw that he was shaking. She took a step forward. "What is it?"

"Ada, it's . . . it's Johnny." Gordon pulled off his cap and squeezed it between his hands. He took a few hesitant steps forward. "The police called earlier and asked me to come down. I thought it was some kind of ruse at first, but it was Rick Dalton on the phone. He's been a paying customer for years."

"I don't understand," Ada said. "Has Johnny been arrested?"

"Ada, they wanted me to come to the morgue. Johnny's dead."

There was something strange about hearing the words from Gordon, who had spent so many years sitting in this room, resolutely saying nothing of importance. At first Ada couldn't grasp the full meaning of what he was saying—just that it was odd to see him standing there, hat in hand, trembling like a schoolboy.

Johnny's dead.

Ada sat down hard in Gordon's chair.

"They found him somewhere on the wharves," Gordon said. "Someone shot him four times in the chest."

There were tears in Ada's eyes, but she didn't know what to do with them. She opened her mouth, but words wouldn't come.

"I have to go," Gordon said. There was a hitch in his voice, and he was backing toward the door. "I've been here for seven years, Ada. I never thought—I never—I have to go."

He tossed her the keys, and Ada caught them in numb reflex. Gordon shut the door behind him. Ada had never noticed how dark the storage room was at night. She stumbled into the basement and curled up on one of the couches, listening to the electric lights buzzing overhead. Corinne would be home soon. When she was here, Ada would be able to think straight.

She squeezed her eyes shut, but in that moment she was back in Haversham, the walls cold around her, the screams echoing down the corridor as they dragged her fellow prisoner away. Down to the basement. Down to whatever hell had been created for hemopaths by a society convinced of its own rectitude. Ada had been the first hemopath to ever escape Haversham, but sooner or later she would end up back there. Maybe they all would. Without Johnny the Cast Iron would go dark. The other hemopath clubs in the city had no reason to shelter their rival's crew. The HPA would catch up with her and Corinne easily, and this time they wouldn't have Johnny or his resources to bail them out.

Despite the creeping, crushing fear, Ada kept her eyes closed and began to hum. The song tasted of salt and sorrow, but it was easier than crying. It was easier than remembering how Johnny Dervish had been the one to offer her hope when her world had collapsed, how Johnny had been something untouchable and unbreakable in a city of broken, soiled dreams. It was easier than knowing that if Johnny was gone, then the rest of them didn't stand a chance.

CHAPTER EIGHT

Snow fell the next morning from a white sky, just enough to dust the treetops and windowpanes. Ice hardened on the sidewalks, and Boston was quiet.

The bar of the Cast Iron was packed with people, with everyone who needed to know the news. Corinne was the one who told them that Johnny was dead. She was still in her dress from the night before. The pale-blue satin trembled as she spoke, but her voice never broke. She bit off each word with deliberate asperity. She sat on the stage with her legs dangling, answering questions until she had run out of answers. Then she dropped into a chair beside Ada. She laid her head on Ada's shoulder and closed her eyes. No one had slept the night before.

"That's it, then," Corinne said.

For a while no one moved. No one spoke. Corinne didn't open her eyes. Finally people started to trickle toward the door. They were members of Johnny's crew, his inner circle. Some had known him for years, some only for months.

"Wait, stop," Ada said, jarring Corinne as she jumped to her feet.

The group looked at her.

"It's not safe out there," Ada said. "First the docks and now Johnny—we don't know who's gunning for us."

A couple of people shook their heads and left. The others looked uncertain, shuffling their feet.

"What else can we do?" someone asked.

"Stay," Ada said. "We're better off together."

"Johnny's gone," someone else said. "The Cast Iron isn't safe anymore either."

"We can make it safe," Ada said.

"You're just kids."

"Johnny trusted us well enough," Corinne snapped, standing up beside Ada.

But they were already leaving. Danny lingered by the door for a long time, clutching his hat. "I'm sorry," he said at last. "I've got to get back to my family."

When the hinges creaked with his departure, Corinne sank back into her chair.

She was surprised to find that James and Madeline were still there, sitting at the next table over. They had come with Saint when she'd phoned at midnight. Madeline was sitting very straight, her lips pursed, staring into the middle distance. James was leaning forward with his elbows on his knees, eyes following Saint as he paced behind Corinne and Ada. Corinne knew that Gabriel was behind her too, against the bar, outside the circle.

It had been the six of them since midnight. Mostly they had sat in silence in the common room downstairs, trying to grapple with the idea of Johnny being gone, trying to explain it away.

"It's some kind of trick," Corinne had insisted. "It was a thespian Gordon saw."

"Thespians can't stay in character if they're dead," James said.

"Then Gordon was mistaken."

"He's known Johnny for years," Ada told her. Her voice was calmer than Corinne's, but the restraint cost her. She had to use the back of the couch for support.

"I'm going to the morgue," Corinne said.

"Brilliant idea," Madeline said. "And what exactly do you think is going to happen when the daughter of Perry and Constance Wells shows up at the morgue at one in the morning and demands to see the body of a dead gangster?"

"What do you suggest, Maddy?" Corinne had cried. "Why are you even here? You and James have been hiding away in the Mythic for years. You aren't one of us, not really."

The look that crossed Madeline's face promised a nasty retort, but she stopped herself. "I'm just trying to help" was all she said, dropping her eyes.

"Johnny's *not*—"

"Cor," Ada said, her voice cutting through Corinne's fury instantly. "Cor, sit down. He's gone."

The rest of the hours before dawn dragged on. There were drinks and speculations and plans made just to be discarded a few minutes later. No one mentioned sleep. Around six they had started making phone calls. Even though she was exhausted, Corinne had preferred the movement to sitting still. As long as she was busy, she wasn't thinking about Johnny on a slab with four bullet holes in his chest.

Now that it was just the six of them again, Corinne had run out of tasks. She sat with her head in her hands, thinking about Johnny behind his desk, smiling at her latest idea for a con. Or Johnny at his regular table in the club, raising his glass to the stage. Or Johnny at Billings Academy when she was twelve years old, offering her the chance of a lifetime.

When her mind strayed again to the morgue and four bullet holes, she stood up. "We're going to the Red Cat tonight," she announced.

Everyone roused slowly from their own thoughts.

"The Red Cat?" Gabriel echoed. "Why?"

"Carson knows something about this," Corinne said. "And if he doesn't, then we'll go to the Witcher brothers at Down Street. We'll tear Boston apart if we have to. Someone's going to pay."

"We can't just walk into the Red Cat and accuse Luke Carson of murder," Ada said. Her voice was so soft that Corinne could barely hear her.

"I just have to talk to him," Corinne insisted. "If he's behind it, I'll know."

"I'm sure you will," Gabriel said, "because he'll probably try to kill you too."

"This is a terrible idea," Saint said, halting his pacing.

"I've had worse," Corinne said. "There's a show tonight at the Red Cat. Carson won't try anything while his club is full of guests."

"So he'll drag you outside before he shoots you," Gabriel said. "Saint's right. It's a terrible idea."

"I won't let the Cast Iron fall apart." Corinne whirled on Gabriel, her voice nearing a shout. "If someone is trying to destroy the club, then I'm going to find out who it is, and I'm going to find a way to stop them."

"We might have bigger problems to worry about," Ada said. Her voice was low and steady, a perfect contrast to Corinne's. "HPA agents were at my mother's apartment yesterday morning."

Everyone's attention swiveled to her.

"What?" Corinne asked. "Why didn't you say anything?"

Ada frowned down at her hands.

"I haven't exactly had a chance," she said. "They told my mother they knew where to find me, but that they wanted the whole set."

"What does that mean?" Saint asked.

"It means they want to throw us all into Haversham," Corinne said.

Madeline exchanged a glance with James. "Maybe that's our cue to go," she said, rising to her feet.

"No one expects you to stay," Corinne said. There was no anger in her tone, but there was no kindness either.

Madeline pulled James by his wrist toward the back door.

"Wait—you're just going to leave?" Saint asked. He was staring at them, a wrinkle in his pale brow.

"Corinne is right," James said, ostensibly to the group, but he was looking at Saint. "We're not one of you. It's not our fight."

"You mean it's not your problem," Saint said.

James looked like he wanted to reply, but Madeline tugged him through to the storage room. When the door shut behind them, a heaviness settled over the room. Corinne turned to Gabriel, who was still leaning against the bar, his arms crossed.

"What about you?" she asked. "It's not your problem either. You won't be getting a paycheck anytime soon."

His eyes on her were cool and inscrutable.

"Do I look like I'm going anywhere?" he asked.

When the afternoon settled into evening, Corinne was curled up on her bed, under every blanket she could find, staring hard at a crack in the wall. Ada had slept for a few hours that morning and left. She came back in occasionally, pretending to busy herself, but Corinne knew she was just checking on her. Corinne ignored her each time. She was too exhausted to move, too miserable to sleep. Her grandfather's watch was loose between her fingers, but it gave her no comfort. Instead of the sweet memories of her grandfather in his study, telling her of Alice the adventurer or Alice the enchantress, her head was fogged with a rainy spring day four years ago, with her grandfather sitting behind his desk, running his fingers over and over the engraving while tears streamed down his pocked cheeks. *She was someone I couldn't save,* he had told Corinne in a moment of such pure vulnerability that she hadn't known how to respond. And when he had pressed the beloved watch into her hands and told her that Alice would have wanted her to have it, Corinne hadn't felt anything but a sadness that she couldn't understand.

Less than a month later, her grandfather was dead.

Corinne pulled her knees tighter to her chest, unable in that moment to separate the loss of Johnny from the loss of her grandfather, and she couldn't separate either from the aching certainty in her chest that nothing could ever be the same. That everything beautiful they had built here was gone.

This time when the door opened, Ada stood in the doorway for a long time. Then she rustled around on her side of the room for a few minutes before sitting cross-legged at the foot of Corinne's bed.

"Let's play a round," she said.

Corinne turned her head just enough to see that Ada was holding her violin. She pulled the covers over her head.

"No," she mumbled into the blankets.

"It'll make you feel better."

"I don't want to feel better."

Ada tugged at the blankets until Corinne was exposed again to the chilly air.

"One round, then I'll leave you alone," she said.

"Fine," Corinne snapped, jerking upright.

> "Break, break, break
> At the foot of thy crags, O Sea!
> But the tender grace of a day that is dead
> Will never come back to me."

Instantly they were back on the towering cliffs by the raging, boiling sea. The sky was a maelstrom of blood-red clouds, scarred with lightning. Normally when Corinne tried to create an all-encompassing illusion, it took immense concentration to maintain every detail, to hold each piece together. But this one seemed to erupt from deep inside her, feeding on her grief and fury. Corinne couldn't see her own illusions the way others could. They existed only as images in her mind to be sculpted and offered into the world.

This landscape, shaped as it was by her own turmoil, felt more real than anything she'd ever created before.

Ada lifted her violin and began to play. At first the song matched the intensity of the illusion, buffeting against the rocks and spiraling upward with the howling wind. Ada's bow flew so fast against the strings that Corinne thought for sure she would lose control of the song, but each note landed with fierce precision. Corinne could feel the pain and anger finding new life as the music filled her. Her illusion responded to her rising torment. The storm hurled dagger-sharp rain against them, and the wind shrieked and spiraled, threatening to tear the world apart.

Then the music began to shift, guiding Corinne down from the terrible height. She shook her head and closed herself off to the emotions that Ada offered. She didn't want to leave behind the fury of her grief. Johnny Dervish had found her when she was broken and scared. He had given her a place to call home. Now he was dead, and it didn't seem fair that they had to go on. It didn't seem fair that without him, they might not be able to.

"What if we never find out who killed him?" Corinne asked. Her voice seemed too soft to carry over the punishing storm, but she knew Ada could hear her. "What if we can't save the Cast Iron?"

It wasn't a fear she could entrust to anyone but Ada. It wasn't even something she had admitted to herself until this moment. She was supposed to be the fearless one, the one with no qualms and no limits. Yet somehow she always ended up right here, trying to break into pieces while Ada calmly refused to let her.

Ada set down her violin, but Corinne's illusion remained, unyielding in its furor.

"Do you remember the first fight we had?" Ada asked.

"You mean five minutes after I moved in?"

"You asked me if I was in charge of the laundry."

"In my defense," Corinne said, "I was a complete and utter bonehead back then."

"Just back then?"

Corinne tried to kick her, but she couldn't disentangle her legs from the blankets. At some point—Corinne couldn't remember exactly when—she had dropped the illusion, and the comforting familiarity of their cluttered bedroom surrounded them again. The petty provocations during their first few months together seemed almost like a dream now. They hadn't hated each other exactly, but Ada would practice her violin late into the night, and Corinne would say ignorant, unfeeling things almost every time she opened her mouth, and it hadn't seemed possible for them to do anything but coexist.

Corinne couldn't pinpoint the moment they had become an inseparable, unstoppable force. She did remember the day of her grandfather's funeral, when she had wept alone on this same bed for almost two straight days, and instead of leaving her to break apart, Ada had played a song so beautiful on her violin that Corinne had felt for the first time that she might be able to go on.

"Despite your appalling first impression, we've been at this for years," Ada said. "We've never come across anything we can't crack."

"What about the HPA?" Corinne asked. Her grief was muted for now, but the fear still remained. "We can't hide from them forever."

Ada plucked at one of the violin strings, her expression tense with thought. Then she dug through the blankets until she found Corinne's hand. She gripped it tightly and looked her in the eye.

"This is you and me we're talking about, remember?" she said. "If we're in this together, then they don't stand a chance."

CHAPTER NINE

THE RED CAT WAS IN A NICER PART OF TOWN THAN THE CAST Iron, surrounded by hotels and banks and ritzy restaurants with cloth napkins and French waiters. Luke Carson liked things big, bold, and gilded. The front entrance had a uniformed doorman and a sign encircled by buzzing electric lights. Inside there were gold chandeliers, champagne, and tablecloths the color of blood.

Ada, Corinne, and Gabriel went to the back entrance, which was considerably less classy but much more private. Corinne had wanted it to just be her and Ada, since they had both performed at the Red Cat before and might be able to talk their way in. Saint hadn't argued about being left behind, but Gabriel had flatly refused. In the end, it had seemed like less trouble to bring him along.

Corinne knocked on the back door until a man cracked it open. He narrowed his eyes at them in recognition but shook his head.

"Your lot ain't coming in here tonight. Carson's orders." He spat a wad of tobacco toward their feet.

"We don't want to come in," Ada told him.

"We don't?" Corinne asked.

"Fetch Charlie Lewis," Ada said. "He asked me to meet him here."

"He did?" Corinne asked. Gabriel nudged her.

The man was staring at Ada hard, as if trying to find a reason to call her a liar.

"If you don't get him, and he finds out I had to stand out here in the cold all night, you're going to be in a heap of trouble," Ada told him.

From what Corinne knew about Charlie, she couldn't imagine him causing trouble for anyone, but she dutifully kept her mouth shut. The man was obviously at war with himself, but after a few seconds he told her to wait a minute, then slammed the door shut and locked it.

"Well, that was easier than I expected," Corinne said.

"I figured if we waited on you to sweet-talk him, we'd be out here all night," Ada replied.

Corinne jabbed her with an elbow, and Ada ignored her with the long-suffering air of a mother whose toddler was misbehaving. After a few minutes the door creaked open again, and Charlie slipped into the alley with them, hollering over his shoulder at the man to stop being such a dictator.

"Hey, Ada," he said, barely nodding toward the others. "I'm going on in fifteen minutes—I can't—"

"You've got to let us in," Ada said.

"What?" He looked around the alley, then lowered his voice. "You know I can't. Not tonight."

"Why not tonight? Charlie if you know something about Johnny, I swear—"

"What's going on with Johnny?" Charlie asked.

Ada hesitated.

"Nothing," Corinne said. "Something's ruffled his feathers, and we think Carson might be able to help. Why can't we come in?"

"Tensions are high, is all," he said, scratching the back of his head. "After what happened at the docks—well, you just need to go."

"Please, Charlie," Ada said. "We're not here to cause trouble. We just need ten minutes."

"You can't really think that Luke is going to talk to you. You'll be thrown out the second he sees you."

"Let us worry about that."

Charlie regarded them for a few seconds, his expression flickering in the moonlight. Finally he nodded.

"You two," he said to Ada and Corinne, then nodded toward Gabriel. "Not him. He looks armed."

Gabriel made a noise of protest, and Corinne elbowed him.

"There's a door around the side," Charlie said, gesturing. "It's the stage door. I'll meet you there in five minutes."

He went back inside and shut the door behind him. They could hear his muffled conversation with the other man before there was quiet.

"You two are not going in there by yourselves," Gabriel said.

"We'll probably only have a couple of minutes with Carson," Ada said to Corinne.

"So how do you want to play it?" Corinne asked.

"The same way we always do, I guess."

Ada was loosening her neck scarf, her smooth forehead creased with a slight frown. She seemed distracted, and Corinne had the sudden thought that she was upset about lying to Charlie. She wasn't sure how to address that, and before she could, Ada had started toward the stage door.

"Excuse me," Gabriel said. "Am I just going to be ignored all night?"

"Probably," Corinne said. "Unless you add something worthwhile to the conversation."

She turned to follow Ada, but Gabriel grabbed her hand and

pulled her back. Corinne was disconcerted by the sudden nearness of him. His grip was firm but gentle, and she found herself wondering how his hands were always warm. The minimal space between them felt charged, like the air before a storm. Then Gabriel spoke and ruined the moment.

"There's no way I'm letting you two go in there alone."

"Fortunately, we don't need your permission," Corinne said, extricating her hand from his. "Ada and I have been a team since before you knew how to pull a trigger, and we are capable of more than you can fathom. Kindly shut up and let us handle this."

She moved back a step but refused to break away from his dark stare.

"Even though your idea of handling it is to storm in blindly and accuse one of the most dangerous men in Boston of murder?" Gabriel asked. There was a stitch in his brow, and his fingers had curled into tight fists at his sides.

"We know what we're doing," Corinne said, turning her back. "No one asked you to come."

She rounded the corner to wait with Ada at the stage door. Gabriel trailed behind her but didn't say more. Ada caught Corinne's eye with a questioning look, and Corinne answered with a shake of her head. After a few minutes passed, Gabriel cleared his throat.

"Is there a point when I should be concerned?" he asked quietly. His tone had lost its bite. "Or shall I just sit out here all night, twiddling my thumbs?"

"Give us twenty minutes," Ada said.

"Then you can do something stupid," Corinne added.

Gabriel didn't reply. The door opened, and Ada and Corinne slipped in, tapping fingertips as they went. The inside of the Red

Cat was heady with smoke and liquor. Ada whispered something to Charlie that Corinne couldn't hear and touched his shoulder lightly, but she stayed at Corinne's side.

Together they ducked through the bustle of the backstage crowd, a cacophony of laughter and tuning instruments in their ears. Corinne led the way blindly through a door that seemed to be in the direction of the main floor. It let out at floor level, stage left. Ada shut the door behind them, and they waited a moment for their eyes to adjust.

Where the Cast Iron was all wood paneling and simple framed photographs, the Red Cat was sheer extravagance. The bar was a massive square structure in the center of the floor, roofed with intricately carved mahogany and glistening with rows of hanging bottles and champagne flutes. Crystal chandeliers hung at intervals along the ceiling, with the grandest centered over the white marble dance floor. The waterfall of shimmering crystal teardrops was three tiers deep and cast every gilded and marbled surface in the club into sharp relief.

The waitresses were in a flurry around the crowded tables, their heels clacking on the floor, their faces a sheen of perspiration beneath caked powder. Corinne saw a few people she recognized from the Cast Iron or the newspapers, mostly politicians and lawyers. She kept her head down, praying no one who knew her parents would recognize her. Those who came into the Cast Iron knew to keep their mouths shut about whom they might see around the club, but she didn't know if Carson's patrons would have the same consideration for the daughter of an influential family like the Wellses. She usually counted on the fact that important people didn't want to draw attention to their patronage of places like the Red Cat or the Cast Iron.

The girls picked their way between the rows of tables toward the bar, where Corinne ordered a gin and tonic. She and Ada had played here a few times, so she knew which side of the bar was nearest Luke Carson's table. He was sitting with his wife, Eva. There were two men in suits and coats in conversation with him. One of them was built like an athlete, and had his suit not been impeccably tailored, it no doubt would have strained at the seams. He was leaning forward with both hands resting on the table. Beneath one of his palms was a thick white envelope. The man's partner had his back to Carson and was observing the action of the club with a lazy, distant smile. He was shorter, with a receding hairline and bland, pudgy features.

When Corinne got a good look at his face, she spun on her barstool so that her back was to him, jerking Ada along with her. Her pulse was pounding so hard, she could feel it against the glass she clutched in her hands. They were the HPA agents from the asylum. She was sure of it, though she had no idea what they would be doing here.

"Did they see us?" Ada whispered, and Corinne knew she had recognized them too. Her hand was shaking as she peeled Corinne's hand from her glass to take a sip.

Corinne stole another glance over her shoulder. The massive agent was slapping Carson on the shoulder and pushing the white envelope toward him. It gapped open, and Corinne caught sight of the green inside. Carson's expression was grim, but he slid the envelope into his jacket.

Corinne turned back to the bar. "I don't think so," she whispered.

They both watched in the mirror as the two agents walked past, toward the door. Then Corinne downed the rest of her drink in a single gulp, told the bartender to put it on Charlie's tab, and went straight for Carson's table. Ada stayed at the bar long enough to pay for the drinks, then caught up with her. Ada slid in beside Eva in the semicircular booth, and Corinne plopped down beside Luke. She exchanged a glance with Ada—barely the length of a heartbeat—but it was enough to say everything that needed to be said. This was a game that the Carsons had no chance of winning.

"Hello there," Corinne said. "I imagine you probably remember us."

"Corinne Wells and Ada Navarra," Luke said. "Hard to forget a couple of broads like you."

"Usually I'm all for flattery, but let's keep it short and sweet tonight."

"You know why we're here," Ada said.

"I can guess," Carson said, disentangling his hand from his wife's hair in order to give a dismissive wave at the two brawny gentlemen who were sidling toward them. Corinne had to admit that Gabriel was at least better at pretending to be unarmed than they were.

"What I can't guess," Carson continued, "is how you managed to get in here. Care to tell me so I know who to fire?"

"Your mother," Corinne said with a smile. "Lovely woman. Not all there, but then she did have to deal with you for the better part of her life."

Carson's lips twitched, and Corinne could see his grip on his glass tightening. His wife laughed suddenly, a lilting sound like morning birds.

"Quite a mouth on such a little thing," said Eva, putting her hand on her husband's arm and rubbing it slowly. Her gaze moved between them in lazy amusement. "What a funny pair you make."

"We do tricks too," said Ada.

"Sure do," Corinne said. "Have you ever wondered what it would look like if your skin were turned inside out? Because I've got a poem for that."

Luke Carson made a small, jerking movement, as if he were ready to throw something.

Eva laughed again. "Cute," she said, and leaned to speak into her husband's ear, though she wasn't exactly whispering. "I like them. Let's hear what they have to say."

Carson's face twisted through a few expressions before finally settling into one of calm composure.

"Let's hear it then," he said to Corinne.

But it was Ada who spoke, while Corinne focused on Carson's face through the smoke and candlelight.

"Do you know where Johnny is?"

"Not the slightest idea," Carson said. He leaned back and swirled the amber liquid in his glass. "People are so hard to keep up with these days."

Corinne didn't take her eyes off him. She was watching his eyebrows. A lie was always in the eyebrows.

"Was it your people at the wharf the other night?" Ada asked.

Carson's eyebrows moved upward, only slightly. He was quiet for a few seconds, considering her.

Around them, the club echoed with movement and conversation. Someone onstage was striking the first few notes on a piano. Eva Carson's hand was still on her husband's arm, her fingertips moving in slow, soothing circles.

"No," Luke Carson said.

"Can you swear on your mother's eyes?" Corinne asked, jumping into the conversation to throw him off balance. "And while you're at it, can you swear that you didn't just accept a bribe from Agent Mammoth and Agent Slick who were just here?"

"Kid, you don't know what you're talking about," Carson said, his voice heating despite his wife's consoling touch.

"She rarely does," Ada said, propping her chin on her hands. "I'm sure the Hemopath Protection Agency is just collecting for charity."

"Maybe it's time for you both to go. The show's about to start."

"You two should play another set for us sometime," Eva said, tapping her manicured red nails against her Manhattan.

"Certainly," Corinne said, forcing a smile that more closely resembled bared fangs. "I'll save that poem for you."

"We'll see ourselves out," Ada said, standing.

"I think you won't," Carson said, waving again to his armed lurkers.

In an effort to remain dignified and avoid unnecessary bruising, the girls let the bodyguards lead them out the front door by the elbows. Once they were deposited outside, they started walking with purpose in the direction of the Cast Iron. When she heard the door shut, Corinne nudged Ada's arm and they doubled back toward the stage door. Gabriel was waiting for them.

"Well, Carson denied everything, predictably enough," Corinne told him.

"Do you think he was lying?" Ada asked.

Corinne shook her head. "It's hard to tell. He's hiding something for sure. What do you think?"

"Those HPA agents were there for a reason," Ada said after a few thoughtful seconds. "But I don't think he knew anything about Johnny."

"That settles it, then," Corinne said, linking arms with both of them to start walking back to the street. The slushy gray snow crunched underfoot. "We'll pay a visit to Down Street, see if the Witcher brothers have anything to say for themselves."

"Not tonight," Ada said. "You know they don't let anyone into the back room after ten."

"Why do you think the Witchers are involved?" Gabriel asked. "I didn't think they were part of Johnny and Carson's rivalry. Down Street doesn't even host shows."

"It's the only other iron-free joint in town," Ada said.

"The Witchers don't party like we do, but they still have their fingers in a lot of pies," Corinne said. "Illegal sorts of pies. The Witchers may not be involved, but I'll bet they know who is."

Gabriel didn't say anything. Corinne wondered how long he was going to pout about being left out of all the heroics. The three of them were walking in the direction of the club, with Corinne still linked between them. The hotels and restaurants they passed were bright with activity, as women in furs and men in silk hats cavorted between their nightly entertainments. Competing music drifted from establishments as doors swung open. Corinne was overwhelmed by the carefree nature of it all. Johnny was dead and her world was ripping at the seams, and somehow these people could go about their lives without noticing.

"We'll want to come back to the Red Cat at some point, I guess," Ada said, breaking into Corinne's reverie.

Corinne quickly pushed away the troubled thoughts and grinned at her.

"You saw it too?"

"It was hard to miss. I can't believe we never noticed before."

"What are you two talking about?" Gabriel asked. He managed to keep the irritation in his tone to a minimum, though it obviously cost him some effort. "And why do you think you'll learn any more from Carson by barging into his club a second time?"

"It's not Luke we want to talk to again," Ada said.

"His name might be on the deed for the Red Cat, but he's not the head of their crew," Corinne said. "His wife, Eva, is."

By half past one, Corinne had fallen asleep on her cot, her grandfather's watch cradled in her hands. Ada wrapped herself in her blanket and sat with her back against the wall for almost an hour before she gave up. She was exhausted, but sleep wouldn't come. Corinne was convinced that if they just asked enough dangerous people enough dangerous questions, then they could somehow make sense of Johnny's murder. That if they found answers, then they could somehow stop the HPA from inching ever closer. That they could prevent the Cast Iron from closing its doors for good.

Ada had told Corinne that together they could do it, because that's what she was supposed to say. That was always the way of things between them. Ada made the promises, and Corinne found a way to keep them. But this time Ada wasn't so sure. Ever since Johnny's death she hadn't been able to shake the feeling that Haversham was somehow inevitable.

Eventually she climbed off her cot, dragging her blanket like a cape into the common room. When she saw Saint sitting on the couch, working in his sketchbook, she almost turned around. He glanced up, and his face colored. He hunched back over his work.

Ada decided she didn't care and curled up in an armchair. For half an hour they were silent. Ada laid her head on her arm and tried to doze off, but sleep didn't come any easier than it had in her bed. She gave up and stared at Saint until he met her eye.

"Do you want me to leave?" he asked.

His freckles were still drowning in blotchy red. One of the things Ada had always liked about Saint was how his emotions always flared on his face. In the Cast Iron it was usually impossible to tell what anyone was feeling.

"I want to know what you were thinking," Ada said.

Saint's throat worked with a swallow. He looked back down at his sketch.

"I'm serious," Ada said.

"What does it matter now?" he murmured.

"I'm trying to figure out how I'm supposed to live with you. How I'm supposed to ever trust you again." Ada straightened in the chair and put her feet on the ground.

"They were going to put me in lockup," Saint said. "All that iron and steel. It's worse than the asylum."

"The bulls didn't have enough to arrest us."

"That's never stopped them before," he said. "Not when it comes to hemopaths."

"Even if they did, Johnny would've gotten you out."

"You don't know that."

"He got me out of the asylum, didn't he?"

Saint's mouth quirked with the start of a reply, but he just pressed his lips together.

"What?" Ada asked.

Saint placed his pencil on the top of his sketchbook and watched it roll down the incline into his lap.

"Just because he got you out doesn't mean he would've helped me."

"Don't be stupid. Why wouldn't he?"

Saint adjusted the sketchbook and dropped the pencil again. It rolled more slowly this time. He waited until it hit his lap to reply.

"Bad blood."

Ada instinctively looked for something to throw at him. Saint had never been one to talk riddles before. Maybe Corinne had rubbed off on him. Finding no suitable projectile, she pressed forward.

"What have you ever done to Johnny?"

Saint held the pencil in both hands, pushing his thumbs against the middle as if to snap it in half.

"Not me. My dad."

"Your father died saving Johnny's life—and half the troop. And you told me they'd been friends for years before the war."

Saint's eyes flickered to hers. There was a crinkle between his eyebrows, but Ada couldn't tell if it was anger or determination or something else altogether.

"They were friends, but my dad didn't save anyone."

Ada frowned. The priest had told the story at the funeral: how the small Allied troop had come across a German squadron. Seeing that they had stumbled into a slaughter, Temple had drawn fire to himself, giving eleven soldiers—including Johnny—enough time to retreat. Johnny had been one of the pallbearers at the graveside.

"Johnny got drunk at the wake," Saint said. "He told me what really happened."

The color had faded from his cheeks, and his shoulders were hunched. Before she could convince herself otherwise, Ada moved to sit next to him on the sofa.

"Tell me," she said softly.

"They did run into a German squadron on the highway, but the troop hid in some trees before they were seen. Johnny said it wasn't the best position, but chances were good that the Germans would just pass them by." The pencil snapped in Saint's hands.

"My dad lost it and ran. The Germans heard him, and that's when they opened fire."

Saint turned his head toward Ada, his eyes damp.

"Johnny was the only one who saw what really happened. He told the survivors that my dad had been trying to draw fire. Everyone believed him. My mother, my sisters, everyone. I'm the only one he told."

He had the jagged end of the broken pencil against his thigh and was driving it downward. Wordlessly, Ada pried it from his grip. It felt irreverent, talking about Johnny like this, like he couldn't at any moment throw open the door to his office and holler at them to keep it down.

"I asked him why he lied," Saint said. It came out like a gasp. He was struggling against tears. "He told me that debts have a way of being paid, in time."

Ada retrieved the other half of the pencil from the floor and set them both on the coffee table.

"If Johnny was holding it against you, then why has he let you stay?" Ada asked. "The bad blood was between him and your father. It doesn't have anything to do with you. Johnny would never have left you to the bulls."

"Haven't you ever wondered about that day?" Saint asked, turning to face her. "You and Cor have run that money a hundred times before without a problem."

Ada bit her lip. She'd had plenty of time to wonder while in the asylum, but she'd spent most of it wondering why Saint had betrayed her, and when Corinne was going to show up. It was true that the errand had been routine. Once a month, she and Corinne would drop off money on the Common for one of the clerks at Johnny's bank. It wasn't a large sum—just some grease money to ensure that whenever the Bureau of Internal Revenue got nosy, they wouldn't find anything amiss with Johnny's accounts.

But two weeks ago, three cops with earplugs had shown up instead of the clerk. Ada and Saint never even had a chance to run.

"The clerk ratted on us for reward money or something," Ada said. "Johnny didn't have anything to do with it. Why would he?"

Saint didn't have an answer for that. He lowered his head again. Ada could see the lines of a building taking shape in his sketchbook, but there wasn't enough detail yet to identify it. She thrust her palms together in her lap, trying to relieve the frustration in her chest.

"If you didn't trust Johnny, couldn't you have at least trusted me and Cor?" she asked at last.

He was quiet for a while, running his fingers across the page, smudging the lines slightly.

"I was scared," he said. "Just like my dad. I'm sorry, Ada."

Ada considered standing up and leaving him there. She considered letting those words be the last between them. In some ways, maybe it would have been easier. But she couldn't stop thinking about his father's funeral, how she had held his hand, and how he had trembled during the three-volley salute. She couldn't walk away now.

"I forgive you," she said.

Saint looked at her through his shaggy auburn bangs.

"Really?"

"Only because I need help reining in Corinne. After cracking Haversham, she thinks she's some kind of mastermind."

After a moment of hesitation, a smile crept across Saint's face. Ada smiled back.

CHAPTER TEN

WHEN CORINNE WOKE UP, SHE WAS SHIVERING SO HARD THAT SHE almost couldn't make it to her feet. The pocket watch clutched in her hand had no warmth, and her toes ached. She got dressed in as many layers as possible, including her coat and ankle boots. Ada's bed was empty, her blanket gone. Bleary-eyed, Corinne stared at the space above the bed, where Saint's painting of the tree and wildflowers now hung in pride of place. Despite her discomfort, she couldn't help but smile.

She stumbled into the common room, where the furnace was fuming. Even so, it was only marginally warmer.

"Another few inches of snow since last night," Ada said.

She was on the couch, her legs curled beneath her, her blanket around her shoulders. Her hair was still wrapped in the silk scarf she wore to bed. She had a damp newspaper in her lap, and there was a mug of something hot on the table. Corinne stared at it enviously for a few seconds, then went to stand by the furnace, willing the warmth to seep through her layers.

"Where's Saint?" she asked.

"The Mythic. He left a few minutes ago."

Corinne didn't have anything nice to say about the Mythic or its inhabitants at present, so she adhered to the old adage and said nothing at all.

"A hemo went missing last night," Ada said. "Apparently he was snatched right off the street."

"Ironmongers?"

"I don't know. There's not much to the article. His name was Stuart Delaney. A musician at the Red Cat."

"Never met him."

"Me neither. I wonder if those HPA agents had anything to do with it," Ada said. There was a frown etched between her eyebrows as she took a sip of her coffee.

"If Carson is taking money from the agency, then he must be up to his eyeballs in something," Corinne said.

She moved reluctantly away from the furnace and huddled onto the couch beside Ada.

Ada handed Corinne the mug and flipped the paper open to the back page.

"There was nothing in the obits about Johnny. Do you—do you think we're supposed to write one?"

Ada's voice was thin and wavering at the edges, and she didn't look up from the paper. Corinne shrugged and took a long sip, not caring that the bitter drink scalded her tongue and throat. Discussing Johnny's obituary wasn't something she could handle this early in the morning.

"When Gabriel gets here, we need to talk about tonight."

"Tonight?"

"If we want to see the Witchers, we'll have to leave here by eight. We'll sweet-talk our way into the back rooms and get them to tell us what they know."

The details of the plan were still fuzzy, but Corinne knew she would find a way. If Carson was in the dark, then the Witcher brothers had to know something about Johnny's death—or maybe the Witchers were behind it all. Either way, after tonight the Cast Iron crew would know who killed him. Then they could start planning their revenge.

Ada hadn't replied. She was giving her the look she always gave when Corinne had forgotten something she shouldn't have.

"What?" Corinne asked, already feeling a headache coming on.

"It's Tuesday."

"So?"

"Tonight is your brother's rehearsal dinner."

"Oh for cripes' sake," Corinne said, plunking the mug onto the table. "Don't we have more important things to worry about?"

"If you miss the rehearsal dinner, your parents will have every bull in the city looking for you."

Corinne scowled at her. "I could call and—"

"What excuse could you possibly give that your mother will accept, Cor?"

"What's going on?" Gabriel was coming down the stairs, unwinding his gray scarf. His coat was still covered in flecks of white. Ada had given him the keys last night, when he had insisted on going home.

"Corinne is trying to dodge her sisterly duties," Ada said.

"This is ridiculous," Corinne said. "I can't waste all night at my stupid brother's rehearsal dinner. We need to talk to the Witchers and find out what they know."

"We could go without you," Gabriel pointed out.

"No we can't," Ada said.

"Don't even think about it," Corinne said.

Gabriel shrugged out of his coat and sank into an armchair. Corinne groaned and struggled to climb to her feet without sacrificing the warmth of her blanket. She shuffled to her room, sighing indignantly all the while. She left the door open as she dug through the trunk at the foot of her bed, searching for the dress her mother had given her for the occasion months ago.

"You don't understand. I'm never going to get out of there," Corinne shouted to them.

"The dress is hanging on the doorknob," Ada said.

"No it's not."

"Yes it is."

"I'm looking at the doorknob right now and I'm telling you, it's not— Oh." Corinne pulled off a few scarves and uncovered the cream-colored dress. "My mother will keep me there all night. Unless—"

She had an epiphany and poked her head out the doorway. Gabriel and Ada were both watching her expectantly.

"We need to get you a tuxedo," she said to Gabriel.

"Excuse me?" he asked.

"It's perfect. The dinner is at the Lenox. You'll be my escort; then I'll pretend to fall ill and we'll tell my parents that you're driving me home."

"Brilliant plan, except that there's no way in hell that I'm—"

Corinne shut the door before he finished. Thirty seconds later Ada came in, still wrapped in her blanket. Corinne was on her knees by her cot, trying to see if the shoes her mother had provided were hiding in one of the shadowy corners.

"You know," Ada said, shedding her blanket, "Gabriel doesn't have to help us. He's not getting paid or anything."

"Is this the speech about how if I want to have a friend, I have to be a friend?" Corinne craned her neck to look at Ada, then sneezed when a cloud of dust fluttered past her nose.

"I thought it might be overdue."

Ada was laying out her outfit on the bed—a ritual that always awed Corinne somewhat. When Corinne was getting dressed, it usually entailed digging through piles of clothes for a frock without any noticeable stains and rolling around the floor with stockings. There was often cursing involved.

"For your information, I have not insulted Gabriel in at least twelve hours," Corinne said.

"In the past twelve hours, you've been in the same room with him for about one minute."

"No one likes a know-it-all, Ada."

"Yes, I've been trying to tell you that for years."

Corinne considered throwing a pillow at her, but that seemed like too much work at this hour. It wasn't exactly an insult anyway. Corinne enjoyed knowing it all. And she was already aware that most people didn't like her. After a few more minutes of crawling around the room, tossing their belongings from one pile to another, she gave up her search for the shoes. If she sat on the cot and looked useless enough, Ada would find them for her.

Once she had dressed, Ada found the shoes without trouble and placed them neatly beside Corinne.

"This room isn't much bigger than a closet," Ada told her. "How have you managed to lose everything you've ever owned at least once?"

"But you always know where things are, so they aren't really lost."

With Ada's help, she found the other pieces of the evening's attire and assembled them on the bed in a somewhat orderly fashion. Then Corinne shed a few layers of clothes to make herself presentable for the day. When they rejoined Gabriel in the common room, he was still sitting in the armchair, which Corinne considered his tacit acceptance of the inevitable.

"You in?" Corinne asked, trying to sound friendly for Ada's sake.

"You're both impossible," he said.

"Thank you. You can get a rental tux from Maury's at Pleasant and Piedmont. He outfits the musicians. I'm sure he'll have—"

Corinne paused at the faint sound drifting down from above. Someone was knocking on the alley door. Gabriel was out of his chair in an instant, gun drawn.

"We should stay here," Ada said. "What if it's the HPA or the bulls?"

"Why would they be knocking?" Corinne asked. "It's probably a delivery."

Gabriel, ignoring both of them, was already halfway up the stairs. Corinne followed him. Ada made a noise of protest but stayed at Corinne's heels. The stale air of the storage room was achingly cold, and Corinne immediately regretted shedding her extra layers. The knocking had stopped, and Corinne was about to suggest that Gabriel go out the front and take a look around when the new arrival called out, his voice easily recognizable through the door.

"Gordon? You in there? It's Charlie Lewis."

"Put that away," Ada said, nudging Gabriel's arm. She unlocked the door and yanked it open.

Charlie was dusted in snow, the flakes gleaming wetly on his black hat and coat. When Ada moved back to let him in, he stomped his shoes on the threshold and shivered.

"Morning," he said, his demeanor less chipper than usual.

He pulled off his hat and looked at the three of them. He paused, eyebrows raised, when he saw Gabriel's gun, still aimed at him.

"Well," Charlie said.

"Ada, you can't just throw open doors like that," Corinne said, pushing Gabriel's wrist down so that the gun was at least pointed at the floor and not Charlie's heart. "What if it had been a thespian?"

"It could still be a thespian," Gabriel said. He gave Corinne an irritated look but kept the gun lowered.

"Are you serious?" Charlie asked.

No one replied. Even Ada was regarding him with a sudden unease. Charlie looked at her, perplexed, then shook his head.

"Our first kiss was the day after we met, by the fountain on the Common."

Ada winced, and Corinne shot an accusatory glare at her. "You told me that was weeks later!"

"It was an . . . accident," Ada said.

Charlie grinned at her, but before he could say anything, Ada reached up and grabbed his chin.

"What happened to your face?"

Charlie's hand went to his left eye. Corinne hadn't noticed before, but it was swollen and darkly bruised.

"It's nothing," he said. "I just came to make sure you made it back okay last night." He very generously included all of them in the statement, but his eyes flicked toward Ada.

"Why wouldn't we be okay?" Corinne asked.

Gabriel had put away his gun, but a part of her suddenly wished he hadn't. They had no way of knowing if Charlie had come alone. He'd never given them any reason not to trust him, but Corinne couldn't stop thinking about those HPA agents, about how at ease they had been in the Red Cat, like they owned the place.

"Let's go downstairs," Ada said.

"I don't think that's a good idea," Corinne said, but it was a useless protest as Ada was already pushing open the panel.

Charlie didn't seem surprised by the secret door, which meant that Ada had already told him about it at some point. Something Corinne intended to berate her about later. She glanced at Gabriel, who seemed uninterested in helping her dissuade Ada.

"I'm going to circle the club," he said. "Just in case."

It was a prudent precaution, but Corinne suspected he just didn't want to be involved. He went up the half-flight of stairs to exit through the club. Corinne locked the back door and followed Ada and Charlie into the basement.

Downstairs, once Charlie had convinced Ada he didn't need a cold compress, Corinne was finally able to cut in. "Charlie, what happened last night after we left?"

"I don't— I'm not sure," he said.

He was sitting on the sofa, his shoulders hunched over. Ada sat near him, her eyebrows drawn together as she studied his face. Her hands were tight fists in her lap.

"Was it Stuart Delaney?" Ada asked.

Charlie nodded.

"Friend of yours?" Corinne asked.

He nodded again. "I was there when they took him," he said. "We were leaving for the night, out the stage door, and they were there, waiting."

"Ironmongers?" Corinne pressed.

"I don't think so. It was two men in suits. No masks. One of them had iron knuckles."

His hand floated halfway toward his shiner in reflex, then fell limp.

"I blacked out," he said. "I don't know how long. When I woke up, Stuart was gone. He's not—"

Charlie cut himself off and looked between them, his expression torn.

"He's not the first," he said at last. "Carson's kept it quiet, but there have been others in the past couple of months."

Corinne met Ada's eye. She had to be thinking the same thing.

"It had to be the two agents we saw last night," Corinne said.

Ada nodded, her fists tightening.

"You saw agents at the Red Cat?" Charlie asked, lifting his face. "Luke doesn't let the agency anywhere near his club."

"Has anyone told Carson that?" Corinne asked. "Because he seemed pretty chummy with them when he was taking their money."

"You saw him take money from them?" Confusion and disbelief swirled in Charlie's expression.

"Yes."

"I have to go." Charlie stood up and reached for his hat.

"You can't go by yourself," Ada said, standing with him. "Not if they're just grabbing people off the street."

Charlie was poised to argue, and Corinne was prepared to agree with him, because he certainly wasn't going to camp out in the Cast Iron indefinitely. Gabriel interrupted from the stairs.

"I'll go with you. It's on my way home." He looked at Corinne. "I'll stop by Maury's and be back in time for the dinner."

Ada seemed satisfied, which Corinne thought was a little hypocritical.

"Wait a minute," she said. "So Charlie isn't allowed to go by himself, but it's okay if Gabriel gets himself snatched?"

"I'm not a hemopath," Gabriel said.

Before Corinne could formulate a reply, he and Charlie were already halfway up the stairs.

"He'll be fine," Ada said once the door had shut behind them.

Corinne wanted to reply that she didn't care whether Gabriel

Stone lived or died, but that seemed unfairly harsh. It was also patently untrue. "Boys can't manage anything themselves," she said. "Least of all staying alive."

Ada's expression twitched, but it passed so quickly that Corinne couldn't tell if she was appreciative or unamused.

"Speaking of which," Corinne went on. "Where the hell is Saint? Why does he think he can run all over Boston while there are killers and kidnappers and God knows what else on the loose?"

"I told you, he's at the Mythic. He's helping with the set."

"That's hardly a priority right now, is it?" Corinne flopped onto the sofa, stretching out her legs and resting her head on the arm. "Besides, we're mad at James and Maddy."

"Just because you're mad at someone doesn't mean the rest of the world is," Ada said. She seemed to come to a decision and jumped to her feet. She disappeared into their room and reemerged seconds later with her coat and cloche.

"Where are you going?" Corinne asked, scrambling to her feet.

"I need to check on my mother. The HPA knows where she lives."

"Yes, because they're trying to catch *you*." Corinne was already headed to their room to grab her coat. She knew she wasn't going to dissuade Ada, and she couldn't let her go alone.

"We'll be careful," Ada said, pulling her hat onto her head. "I just have to make sure she's all right."

"It's too bad Gabriel isn't here to tell us how reckless we are," Corinne said. She slipped into her coat and was pleased to find some kid gloves in the pocket. "I might actually agree with him this time."

· · · · · ◆ · · · · ·

At Corinne's insistence, they took the long way to the apartment, staying off the more trafficked streets. Ada didn't argue, but she thought the measure was unnecessary. All the white-slick roads were empty this morning. The snow was falling faster now, sticking to her eyelashes and blurring her vision.

Corinne was hugging herself and skipping to avoid the denser patches of snow. She had always been better suited for sunshine and springtime. Ada kept her hands buried in her pockets. Melting snow was thick on her wool coat; and despite her hat, she was beginning to feel the dampness on her scalp. An umbrella probably would have been a useful thing to bring along.

"I haven't seen your mother in ages," Corinne said. "You think there will be any of that bread waiting? I can't ever remember what it's called—pan?"

"Pão." Ada hunched her shoulders, trying in vain to protect her neck from the chill. She had forgotten a scarf. "Cor, my mom's pretty angry at me. She might be mad at you too—I don't know."

"Why?"

"We had another fight. About Johnny and the Cast Iron. About what we do for a living."

Corinne's lips were a grim line. Her hair was stringy with the melting snow, and thin rivulets ran down the contours of her face.

"We're just doing the best we can," Corinne said. "You've done all this for her."

"That doesn't make any of it right." Ada's voice was so soft that the fluttering snow drowned it out.

Shawmut Avenue emptied onto her mother's street, and she could see the apartment building a block down on the right. Corinne started to cross the street, but an unfamiliar shape caught Ada's eye and she grabbed her arm. The black, hulking car was parked across the road from the apartments. There was a man leaning against the driver's side door, puffing on a cigarette. Ada didn't see his face, but the hairs on her neck prickled. Corinne saw him too and cursed. She backed up and threw open the door of the nearest shop. Ada ducked in behind her.

The shop had wall-to-floor windows, mostly obscured by artfully displayed bolts of cloth. Ada and Corinne huddled behind a violently magenta drapery and peered through the window. Once the man had finished his cigarette, he stayed where he was. He did open the car door at one point, but he only stuck his head in for a moment, then straightened back up.

"It's one of the agents from the club," Corinne whispered. "His partner must be in the car."

They were definitely waiting for someone, Ada realized. She could see it in the casual sweeps of his gaze up and down the street. They were waiting for *her*. If she had come by her usual route from the Cast Iron, she would have turned the corner and walked right into them.

"What are you doing in here?"

Ada and Corinne turned to face the clerk, a pale woman with a pinched face. Her hands were balled into tight fists at her sides.

"Good morning, ma'am," Corinne said, with all the genteel manners her aborted boarding-school education afforded her. "We were just—"

"You're not welcome in here," the clerk said, but she was looking directly at Ada. "Get out."

Ada's cheeks burned. It was a shame that never really got easier, burred as it was with anger and sorrow. The shop clerk's hostility was the least of her worries, though. If she went back onto the sidewalk, the agents might see her.

"Please," Ada began.

"Go on, before I call the cops."

Ada thought about the Haversham Asylum, about the basement, about the screaming inmate who had never returned. She wasn't going back there.

She glanced at Corinne, who nodded once.

Ada started to hum, gently at first so that the melody wrapped around the woman and held her fast before she even realized what was happening. The clerk trembled, trying to fight it, but her face was already slackening. Ada eased smoothly into a song, a lullaby her mother used to sing. The words didn't matter as much as the melody and the way her voice shaped and sharpened it.

The disdain was gone from the woman's eyes, replaced with a doleful weariness. Ada's song guided her to the corner, where she sank to the floor and rested her head against the wall, half concealed by a cabinet of gaudy buttons and spools of thread. She looked for all the world like a child, curled up for a nap in the midst of a trying day.

"Let's go," Corinne said once the clerk had started to snore.

Ada followed her through the door behind the counter. The corridor in the back had only three doors. The first was a closet, the second was locked, and the third let out into an alley. The cold air tasted heavenly. They ran down the alley in the direction they had come, slipping and sliding on the accumulating ice. Corinne was laughing breathlessly.

"That was the fastest you've ever managed it," she cried. "Soon you'll only need a few bars before they're out like a light."

Ada didn't reply. The woman's hate, the fright from their narrow escape, and her own guilt roiled in her chest. Every time she used her talent on an unsuspecting reg, she told herself that she didn't have a choice. Or that they deserved it. But it never seemed enough, somehow. She couldn't get her mother's words out of her head.

I love you so much, but this is not how things were meant to be.

Ada had always thought it was the justice system's fault, for taking her father away from them. But what if Ada had been the one to ruin everything? What if the day she shook hands with Johnny Dervish was the day that the lives they wanted had been irrevocably lost?

They ran all the way back to the Cast Iron, constantly searching for signs of the agents or their car, but the road and sidewalks remained empty. The snow had stopped, leaving the air peculiarly sharp and dry. The sky overhead was a blinding sheet of white. Other than the snow crunching beneath their feet, all of Boston felt like a silent, cavernous tomb.

When they were a block away, Ada slowed down, pulling Corinne's arm.

"What?" Corinne asked, looking around anxiously.

"Can we even go back to the club?" Ada asked, her own breath coming in ragged gasps. "What if it's not safe?"

"The Cast Iron is always safe," Corinne said.

"They won't sit outside my mother's house forever," Ada said, sidestepping to avoid a slick pool of ice. "They'll try the Cast Iron next. The lock on the door isn't going to keep them out, and eventually they'll find the entrance to the basement."

"They wouldn't dare," Corinne said.

"Why not? The rest of the crew is gone. Johnny's gone. Any protection the Cast Iron had is probably dead with him."

Ada could see how her words affected Corinne. She hadn't wanted to say them, but there was no use ignoring it any longer.

With Johnny gone, there was no one on their side. Corinne's pace slowed further. Then she stopped. She turned to face Ada. Her hair was wet and matted, and there was a high color in her cheeks. Her brown eyes were harder than usual.

"Where else is there to go?" Corinne asked. "The Red Cat? Down Street? All we have is the Cast Iron. It's *ours*."

Ada had the urge to hug her, to comfort her, because she knew that Corinne's ferocity was the only way she knew how to be brave. But Ada was thinking about Haversham. It was always waiting in her thoughts. In the snow it would be deceptively beautiful, the window ledges lined with white, the iron gates bold against the pale sky. Maybe all they were doing was delaying the inevitable.

"You're right," Ada said. "There's nowhere else that's safe for us."

Corinne was either relieved or triumphant. She turned before Ada could tell. They walked the rest of the way back to the Cast Iron without speaking.

CHAPTER ELEVEN

———— ◈ ————

GABRIEL ARRIVED AT THE CAST IRON AT FIVE O'CLOCK ON THE nose, lugging a garment bag with a rented tuxedo. Ada was the only one in the common room to greet him, as Saint still had not returned from the Mythic and Corinne had just decided only a few minutes earlier that maybe she should start getting dressed. He went to Johnny's office to change. When he reemerged, Ada was surprised at how well the rental fit him. With the clean black lines and starched tails, Ada could almost believe that Gabriel was the sort of person who would be invited to a Wells party. The rental had even included a pair of shoes, polished so that the toes each reflected a pinpoint of light.

Gabriel was pulling at the sleeves, his eyes downcast, and Ada realized with some amusement that he was self-conscious.

"You look perfect," she told him, though she wasn't sure if that would make it better or worse. "Well, almost."

He had knotted the necktie with a four-in-hand, which Ada knew Corinne wouldn't stand for, even though Corinne had never once managed to tie any kind of proper knot. Ada climbed off the couch and gestured wordlessly for permission. Gabriel shrugged, closer to helpless than Ada had seen him before. She loosened the tie nimbly.

She had learned the skill from her mother when she was a little girl. Every morning Nyah had tied her husband's tie, teasing him with the names of the knots, stealing kisses. Eventually Ada took over, standing on the edge of the bed, trying to sing along with her father in Portuguese. Sometimes her mother would sit beside her. She would hum and watch them both with her soft brown eyes, and Ada would wonder if she was studying them in the way she studied recipes, parceling out all the individual ingredients and trying to see how they made the whole.

Ada tied a Windsor and straightened it with a touch of pride. She was feeling a strange sense of camaraderie with Gabriel tonight, maybe because of his assistance with Charlie earlier, or maybe because he was so blessedly stoic in the face of Corinne's peculiar brand of temerity. Corinne didn't tend to keep friends long, which meant that Ada didn't either. She didn't mind usually, but it was nice to know there were other people in the world who were, if not a match, then at least a challenge for her best friend.

"I'll bet your mother would have liked to see you in this," Ada said, brushing off his shoulders.

Gabriel's lips wrinkled in a rueful smile. "I doubt it. She would say that my father and my father's father were workingmen, and that was always good enough for them, so why isn't it good enough for me?" He hooked two fingers under the collar and tugged absently. "She'd probably also ask why I felt the need to dress like a penguin."

Gabriel handed her two cuff links, and she palmed them, admiring the flourishes etched into the silver.

"My mother thinks tuxedos are dashing," she said while she pinned the cuff links in place. "She won't admit it, though."

Gabriel smiled in return, a small, unfamiliar action. Corinne was making a racket in the bedroom, but there were no cries for help or breaking glass, so Ada assumed she was all right. She moved to perch on the arm of the sofa and cast an appraising eye over Gabriel.

"Can I ask you something?"

Gabriel said nothing, which as far as Ada could tell was as close to assent as he ever gave.

"Why are you helping us? Why do you care?"

It had been gnawing at her since the night they had found out about Johnny, when everyone else had left. Corinne took it for granted that Gabriel had remained, because the Cast Iron was everything to her and she couldn't imagine that the same wouldn't be true for everyone who passed under its roof. But Ada knew that few people loved this place like Corinne did, with her impossible, unquestioning tenacity. Sometimes Ada thought that even Johnny couldn't be as devoted. For Corinne, it was something deep-rooted, stretching far beyond the Cast Iron's role as safe haven, farther than its history in Boston, when the city's artists—hemopath and reg alike—would gather around crackling fires upstairs and speak of Titian and Mozart and Kant, spinning ideas like golden thread, tearing down kings and sparking revolutions. For Corinne the Cast Iron was an unbreakable fact. Something that had always existed and always would.

Sometimes Ada felt the same way. And sometimes she felt like the Cast Iron was her second choice, except she had never really been given a chance at her first.

Gabriel didn't seem caught off guard by her question, though he took a long time answering it. For a few moments he considered the couch, but maybe the impeccable press of his suit dissuaded him, because he didn't sit down.

"I didn't know him for very long, but Johnny didn't deserve to die. Especially not like that."

"Justice, then? That's why you're staying?"

He did look caught off guard by that. Perhaps he'd thought that she would be satisfied with his initial answer. Ada wasn't, though. It wasn't a reason, just a statement of fact.

Gabriel crossed his arms and uncrossed them. He was so uncomfortable in the tuxedo that Ada almost felt bad for hounding him. He ran his hands through his dark hair, leaving it disheveled and in stark contrast to the rest of his person.

"My father died when I was seven," he said at last. "He was killed right in the middle of the day, and my mother found out from our busybody neighbor, who she hated. I don't think she ever forgave him for that."

His musing tone belied the weight of his words. He finally dropped onto the couch, heedless of his attire for the first time since putting it on.

"I don't even remember how I found out—whether I overheard the conversation or my mother told me herself. I just remember her kissing my forehead and telling me that I was safe, because she loved me, and we must always protect what we love."

Ada was so still that she could hear the sizzling of the furnace, the thrumming of her own pulse. Gabriel's brow was furrowed and his lips were slightly apart. His eyes focused by slow degrees as his mind skipped forward across the years, until he blinked and was present again. He looked at Ada.

"Johnny never did anything but try to protect what he loved," he said. "I don't think I can just leave, not when you're all still here, not when I can help."

His hands squeezed into fists, only briefly, and Ada got the feeling that only moments earlier they had been trembling. He jumped to his feet without warning.

Ada followed his gaze to where Corinne stood, leaning in the doorway of the bedroom. In her gauzy evening gown, with her hair curled and her lips yet undone, she looked just like her mother. Not that Ada would dare tell her that.

From Corinne's expression, Ada could tell exactly how long she had been standing there. Corinne didn't say anything, though. She just straightened and touched her gloved hand to the back of her head, as if she were afraid her curls had escaped.

Gabriel coughed. "You look—" But he seemed to have lost whatever words he had in mind. "Are you ready to go?"

"Almost." Corinne must have been having trouble with words too, because her mouth wavered for several seconds, her eyes still on Gabriel. "Ada, can you help me with my necklace? It took me forever to get these gloves on, and I'm not about to take them off."

Ada, whose amusement had her in sudden good humor, slid off the chair and followed Corinne into their room. Corinne dug around on the vanity until she found a string of pearls. She handed it to Ada and turned around. Ada fiddled with the clasp, waiting to hear what Corinne had to say, but apparently Corinne had decided against it. For once she was silent.

"You should kiss him tonight," Ada told her.

Corinne jerked, and Ada almost dropped the necklace.

"Very funny," Corinne said, but her voice was breathy and a higher pitch than normal.

Ada smiled and adjusted the necklace. The pearls were milky against the flushed pink of Corinne's neck. Ada patted her on the back, a conciliatory gesture. "Just a suggestion," she said.

The Lenox Hotel was a fortress of red and white brick. Its hundreds of windows glistened so perfectly with frost that Corinne's first absurd thought was that someone must have hand-painted each of them. She craned her neck to see the roof, but it disappeared into the darkness. She had stayed here once with her mother, the night before she took the train to Billings Academy. Corinne was five years older now, but the hotel might as well have grown with her. She had never seen anything so vast.

Gabriel handed the Ford off to the waiting valet and took the ticket. Although she was dreading the dinner, Corinne was grateful to go inside. Her head already ached from the ride in the car, and the Lenox's sheer height was starting to give her vertigo.

They entered the grand foyer and were instantly assaulted by warmth and light and clouds of ladies' perfume. The marble floor glared with reflections, and overhead crystal chandeliers tinkled delicately as gusts of outside air blew in. There was a sign to the left pointing them toward the Wells-Haversham Party in the Washington Ballroom.

"Haversham?" Gabriel asked. "Like the hemopath asylum?"

"Dearest Angela's grandfather built it," she said to Gabriel, through a plastered-on smile.

"Why? Was he a hemopath?"

"I don't know, but I doubt it. Can you imagine the scandal of a hemopath in the Haversham family?"

"Worse than one in the Wells family?"

"Much worse," she said. "The Havershams have been anti-hemopath since before it was fashionable. About ten years ago, Angela's father published a bunch of essays arguing that the hemopath affliction should be studied further, and the bodies of dead hemopaths should become government property for scientific experimentation."

Corinne paused as a footman in a smart uniform jacket way-laid them to take their coats.

"No one paid him much attention," she continued once he had

gone. "But no one actively disagreed with him either—other than hemopaths, of course."

"Are the rumors about the asylum true, then?" Gabriel asked, his voice low. "Jackson said the basement is being used for something other than storage."

His expression was strangely conflicted, like the topic wasn't something he wanted to broach at all but he felt he had to. A far cry from the scandal-mongering at her parents' party. Corinne wasn't sure how to reply. She'd asked Ada about the basement, but Ada didn't know any more than anyone else. Just gossip and tall tales. There was something happening down there, though. That was where the HPA agents had taken their prisoner. *Another one for the basement,* they'd said.

"We're late," she said, instead of answering him. "Let's just get this over with."

Even the looming promise of hours of brutal small talk and pointed questions sounded better right now than continuing to dwell on Haversham and its mysteries. Corinne leaned momentarily on Gabriel's arm. Her feet ached in her new shoes, and one of the tiny silver buckles was biting into her ankle. She managed to loosen it slightly, and she breathed a sigh of relief.

Gabriel was watching her with an eyebrow raised, and Corinne couldn't understand why her face prickled with warmth, despite the goose bumps on her arms. The dress her mother had bought her was nothing but cream silk and frothy lace, embroidered with pale blue and pink roses. The low waist and capped sleeves were stylish, at least, but there was little to protect her from the chill.

"Shall I carry you, then?" he asked.

She realized she was still gripping his arm. She released him and ran her fingers down his sleeve to smooth the wrinkles.

"It might come to that— Wait." She looked him over with narrowed eyes. Then she leaned in and whispered, "Are you *armed*?"

"How can you always tell?"

"You fidget," Corinne said.

"I'm not fidgeting."

"I can also feel the iron in it."

That explained the tingling under her skin when she touched him. She felt strangely vindicated.

"I'm not going anywhere near a ritzy hotel full of the degenerately wealthy without a weapon."

Corinne rolled her eyes and took his arm again, this time so they could enter the ballroom in proper fashion.

"Yes," she said. "I'm sure Aunt Maude will be a real threat, what with her rheumatism and trick hip."

The ballroom was brighter than the foyer, if that was possible. The crowd was already thick, threaded with waiters in white jackets serving champagne and dainty hors d'oeuvres. Corinne could feel the body heat and furtive stares and, as always, the sources of iron in the room. A hundred pinpricks of pain, scattered across her consciousness.

"You're the one who wanted me to come," Gabriel said.

He was surveying the room with a grim expression that wouldn't have been out of place at an executioner's block—not that Corinne could blame him. This event was a rehearsal dinner only in name. It was really an excuse for the Wellses and the Havershams to rub elbows and revel in their status.

Corinne wondered idly what it meant to gird one's loins and whether she should do so now.

"Just because I— Oh cripes, here comes my mother. Shut up."

"I didn't say anything."

"Go get me a drink," she said.

"Shouldn't I—"

"*Go.*" She shoved him away just as her mother arrived. She was flushed a pretty pink from excitement and looked after Gabriel with her mouth slightly ajar.

"Corinne, aren't you going to introduce me to your friend?"

"He's just fetching me a drink, Mother."

"You didn't say you were bringing someone." She studied Corinne with shrewd eyes, and Corinne had the oddest feeling that she suspected something was amiss. Or maybe her mind had already drifted to a separate crisis, like the color of the roses or the quality of the crystal. It was hard to tell with Mrs. Wells.

"Hamish Everett will be so disappointed," her mother said. "He was looking forward to being your escort when we go in for dinner."

"He'll survive, I'm sure. Gabriel is just a . . . friend."

Her mother, predictably enough, seized on the hesitation. "Where is he from, then? Do I know his parents? Corinne, you really can't just show up with a stranger to your brother's rehearsal dinner. I'm not sure if I—"

She cut off when Gabriel arrived with the drinks. His was already half empty.

"Mother, this is Gabriel Stone," Corinne said. "Gabriel, this is my mother, Constance Wells."

Gabriel took her hand in what Corinne thought was a more than passable greeting for polite society, but her mother's face had gone white.

"The pleasure is all mine," she managed to say before jerking her hand away. "I beg your pardon, but I just remembered I forgot to tell the caterers that my aunt is allergic to sage."

She whisked away before Corinne or Gabriel could reply.

"What did you do to her?" Corinne demanded.

"I didn't do anything to her. I just got here."

"She acted like she knew you. Like she'd seen you kill a puppy or something."

She expected Gabriel to be flippant with her, but he was studying her mother's retreating figure carefully, his brows knitted in concentration. Finally he shook his head.

"Honest, I don't think I've ever seen her before," he said.

Corinne couldn't read anything but truth in his face. She shrugged. "My mother does tend toward exaggeration, and my great-aunt really is allergic to sage."

As they made it through the gauntlet of elderly relatives, the matter didn't come up again. No one seemed to recognize Gabriel, and those who treated him with suspicion did so only because they trusted no one without a country club membership. One half-deaf distant cousin with bluish-gray hair and an oversized fur stole thought he was a film star and congratulated Corinne in what she probably thought was a whisper on bagging herself a sheik.

By the time they finally had a few minutes alone, Corinne had made it through three glasses of champagne and Gabriel wasn't far behind.

"Is it time for you to fall ill yet?" he asked her.

"Not until after my toast," Corinne said, patting his arm. She was feeling much more congenial toward him now that her head was fizzy with champagne bubbles. He also hadn't shot anyone yet.

"Shouldn't there be a wedding rehearsal at some point during this rehearsal dinner?"

He must've felt the champagne too, because he wasn't stiff and wary anymore. There was an unguarded leisure about him, even in the tuxedo, that Corinne liked better than his usual intensity. The memory of him on the sofa, speaking softly of his parents, sprang unbidden to her mind. She knew hardly anything about Gabriel Stone, but the way his mother had grasped him close, pressing her lips to his forehead like he was the last thing she had left to love, was somehow enough.

"I'm sure there was a rehearsal," Corinne said, "but as I'm not part of the wedding, my presence wasn't necessary."

"Bride doesn't like you?"

"Why do you say that as if it's the obvious conclusion?" Corinne asked.

His eyebrows arched.

"I'll have you know that she asked me to be a bridesmaid, but I talked my way out of it," Corinne said. "I don't like the man she's marrying."

"You mean your brother."

"Yes."

Gabriel took a sip of champagne.

"Shut up," Corinne said, though she couldn't summon any malice.

"Yet again, I didn't say anything."

"How can I be expected to play nice with someone who married into Boston's foremost anti-hemopath family just to advance his political career?"

"Still not saying anything."

"Well, I wish you would, every once in a while."

"What?" He stopped examining his cuff link and looked at her.

"You never say what you're thinking. It's tiring," she told him, and snatched a napkin from the tray of a passing waiter. "Also you still have some of Aunt Maude's lipstick on your face."

She wiped at the smudge with short, angry strokes, avoiding his eyes.

"I don't say what I'm thinking because my opinion doesn't change anything," he said, his voice low.

"It matters, though," she said.

"That so?"

Corinne realized she was still wiping his cheek, even though the lipstick was gone. She lowered her hand, risking a glance into his eyes. His gaze didn't flinch away from hers, and Corinne tried to remember why she had been so determined not to kiss him tonight.

When the dinner bell rang, she couldn't decide if she was irritated or relieved.

Ada practiced her violin for a while, trying to pass the time, but her heart wasn't in it. She gave up and rested it in her lap, fingering the polished spruce and taut strings. Even though she'd played the old violin her father gave her for longer than this one, she still felt that this violin had always been hers. It was hard to remember a time before she'd known it better than her own two hands.

She placed it back in its case on the coffee table right as the door at the top of the stairs slid open. Saint had returned from the Mythic, and he was more chipper than Ada had seen him in a long time. He was humming a tune as he peeled off his coat and retrieved his sketchbook from his room. From the couch, Ada watched him with a raised eyebrow. He sat in the armchair and gnawed thoughtfully on his pencil for a few seconds before he noticed her.

"Hi," he said.

"Nice night?"

He shrugged. "Just painting the set for James and Maddy's next show," he said. He hunched over his sketchbook, but Ada could see his smile.

"You'd think that being around Corinne for four years would make you a better liar," she said.

"I don't want to be a good liar," he replied, his pencil scratching away.

Ada smiled at the top of his head. His auburn hair was burnished by the warm lamplight and flecked with dried blue paint. She wasn't sure she'd ever seen Saint without some trace of paint on his person. There was something comforting about curling up on the sofa, watching as he sketched. She could almost forget how much everything had changed since her arrest. Almost.

"We're going to Down Street tonight," she said.

Saint was quiet for a while, and she began to wonder if he'd even heard her.

"I know," he said at last, glancing up. "But I still don't understand why."

"If Carson doesn't know anything about Johnny's murder, then maybe the Witcher brothers do."

Saint tapped his pencil on his knee, frowning in thought. After a few seconds he went back to his sketch without a reply.

"Corinne thinks it's our best option," Ada said.

"She's usually right about these things," he said absently.

"Usually. You can come with us if you want."

Saint looked strangely amused at the invitation. "The last time I tagged along, it didn't end so well."

Despite the subject still being tender, Ada felt the urge to giggle. Maybe she was more tired than she thought.

"I guess you're right," she said. "But doesn't it drive you mad, waiting around here alone?"

For as long as she'd known him, Saint had spent most of his time in the Cast Iron. He left only when Johnny had a job for him, or when he was visiting James at the Mythic. The rest of the time he was perfectly content to stay home with paintbrush or pencil in hand.

"I like it here," Saint said, returning to his sketch. "It's safe."

He spoke the last so softly that Ada wasn't sure if she'd heard him right. She waited, but he didn't say more. He was lost again in his work. After a couple of minutes, the silence got the better of Ada and she stood up. There was a phone call she had been putting off, and she was running out of time to do it.

She went down the hall to Johnny's office. The electric light buzzed and flickered when she turned it on, before it settled into a dull hum. She sat down in the chair across from the desk and pulled the phone toward her. She told the operator her mother's number and waited for the line to connect. Her mother answered in a polite, if wary, tone. She wasn't accustomed to using the phone.

"It's me, Mama."

"Ada, what is wrong?"

"Nothing. Nothing. I just . . . wanted to talk to you."

Ada bit her lip because she didn't know what else to say. She needed to ask if the two agents were still parked out front, but she didn't want to frighten her mother.

"I am sorry I was angry at you, Ada," Nyah said, after a few moments of silence. "I wish we had not fought."

"It's my fault," Ada said. "I wanted to come see you, but I can't—I can't get away."

"I know."

The way she said it was so solemn and resigned that tears pricked suddenly at Ada's eyes.

"I have to go," she said before they could spill. "I love you."

"Good night, Ada."

Ada hung up with more force than she intended. She hadn't even asked about the agents, or if the police had come by. She hadn't said anything she meant to say.

She swiped her hand across her eyes and picked up the receiver again. She asked the operator to connect her to the Red Cat. A gruff voice answered. Ada could hear the sounds of musicians warming up their instruments in the background. Someone was laughing raucously. It was a normal night there, with music and patrons and clinking glasses. In that moment, it seemed so far away from the deathly silence of the Cast Iron that Ada was disoriented. The voice spoke again, even gruffer this time.

"Is Charlie Lewis there?" she asked before he could hang up.

The sounds became muffled, like he was covering the mouthpiece with his hand. Ada held the receiver away from her ear during the ensuing scrapes and clatters and muted shouts. When Charlie answered, he was out of breath.

"Hello?"

"Hello."

"Hey there, Ada."

Ada leaned forward in her chair and rested her elbows on the desk. The knot in her chest loosened, if only slightly.

"Are you busy?" she asked.

"Got a set in a few minutes, but they can wait."

"You sure?"

"Not like they can start without me."

She heard his grin through the phone, and she smiled too. She could picture him in his shirtsleeves and suspenders, with his hat tilted at a rakish angle. The tattoo on his arm would be visible, with the inked tree branching like veins. Somehow, the night felt less empty. She wished she could see him in person. It wasn't safe for her to leave the club, though, and she would never ask him to come here, not after what had happened to Stuart Delaney. She had just wanted to hear his voice.

"I wanted to make sure everything was okay," she said.

He was quiet for a few seconds. "Sure, I guess so," he said. "You sound different. Is something wrong?"

Johnny was dead, and the Hemopath Protection Agency was lying in wait. Everything was wrong.

"No, nothing's wrong," she said. "You sound different too."

Another pause.

"I can't stop thinking about Stuart Delaney," he said.

His voice was low, and Ada thought she heard a tremor.

"There was nothing you could do," she said.

"Maybe."

Ada listened to his breathing. She wound the telephone cord around her finger, counting the seconds that passed.

"None of us are safe anymore," she said at last. She was thinking about the agents in her mother's home. "We can't go back to the way things were."

"I don't know," Charlie said. He hesitated. "I think—I think if anyone can manage it, you and Corinne can."

Someone called Charlie's name, and he hollered at them to hold their horses.

"Sorry," he said to her.

"No, I'm sorry," Ada said. "I knew you had a show. I shouldn't have called."

"I'm glad you did."

Ada's heart skittered at the simple honesty in his voice, and she squeezed the receiver until her fingers hurt. Three days ago he'd told her he loved her. She still didn't know how to say it back, or if she even could. The words were a precipice, and she was too afraid to leap.

"Go play your set," she told him. "And stop flirting with me."

She could hear the grin again, like music through the line.

"You're the one who called me."

"Good-bye, Charlie."

"Good-bye, Ada."

She hung up the receiver and slumped back in the chair. Her heart was still pounding an uneven rhythm, echoing in her ears and fingertips. She wondered if this was what it was like for patrons at the club, listening to music that filled them with unfamiliar emotions, letting that music carry them to places they could never reach on their own but always, always trusting that it would lead them safely home.

Giant double doors at the end of the ballroom opened onto an adjacent room with two parallel dining tables. Between shoulders and elbows, Corinne caught a glimpse of ornate candelabras and flower arrangements. The bride and groom, whom Corinne had been avoiding all night, entered first, followed by their parents. Corinne grabbed Gabriel's arm.

"My mother is going to try to seat us at different tables," Corinne said. "If you let that happen, I will possibly never forgive you."

"I'm not sure what you expect me to do about it," he said, but he was smiling.

Corinne's name placard was near the head of the larger table, across from her parents. Gabriel thoughtfully pulled her chair out

for her, then took the placard beside her and tossed it unceremoniously away.

"Someone named Hamish Everett," he said as he sat down
beside her.

Corinne snorted. Her mother, who had been saying something
to Mr. Wells, eyed Corinne and Gabriel but apparently decided not
to raise a fuss. After some shuffling at the lesser table to accommo-
date a miffed Hamish, the dinner was under way.

Mr. Wells wasn't at his best during parties and focused mainly
on his food. Corinne's mother kept shifting in her seat, her smiles
brief and fluttery, her eyes constantly darting. Corinne finally realized she was avoiding looking at Gabriel. He hadn't said a word
and wasn't shoveling food with his hands or anything, so Corinne
couldn't figure out her mother's problem. Maybe she was just angry
that he wasn't Hamish Everett, who was supposedly Boston's most
eligible bachelor now that Angela Haversham had snatched up
Corinne's brother.

Phillip and Angela were in fine form, holding hands under the
table and sneaking kisses when they thought no one was looking.
To please her mother, Corinne exchanged a few polite words with
them, but she couldn't look at Angela's expensive gown or multi-
tude of diamonds without thinking that the entire ensemble had
been funded by Haversham Asylum. And now her brother was a
part of it. If her father had his way, Phillip's upcoming political
campaign would revolve around an expansion of the asylum.

When it came time for Corinne's toast, she was two glasses of
red wine deep and having trouble picking up her fork. Finally she
managed to clink it against the side of her glass. Gabriel stood up,
ostensibly to pull out her chair, but he ended up holding her elbows
as she found her feet.

"You're drunk," he whispered in her ear.

"Only a little. It's when I do my best work," she said.

He shook his head and sat back down.

"Thank you all for coming tonight," Corinne said, keeping both hands on the table edge to steady herself. "As most of you know, I've only just come back from school, and I'm afraid there's not enough time between studies to write a meaningful speech."

She chanced a look at Phillip and Angela, who were holding hands again. Their smiles were bland and practiced. Corinne was surprised that Phillip hadn't interrupted yet to say something patronizing.

"Instead," she continued, "I'd like to offer a poem I came across recently, by Lewis Carroll. I thought of my brother and soon-to-be sister when I read it."

She conjured a sweet smile for the bride and groom. She'd actually memorized the poem years ago, and her brother had been the last person on her mind.

> "A boat, beneath a sunny sky
> Lingering onward dreamily
> In an evening of July . . ."

Corinne kept a gentle cadence as she quoted. Despite its cheery beginning and lyrical rhythm, the poem wasn't a romantic one. It was about golden memories and the inevitability of their fading.

Under her left hand, Corinne brushed her thumb across the brass of her grandfather's watch, using the familiarity of it to center herself. If her grandfather had been here, he would be the one making the speech, telling some anecdote about his travels, sneaking a wink at Corinne. Maybe after it was all over, she would join him in the quiet warmth of his study and he would tell her about Alice the acrobat or Alice the fortune-teller.

Corinne had to blink away the memories to get through the last lines of the poem. She hadn't meant to drink *quite* so much before dinner, but between the relatives and her mother and the iron in Gabriel's damn gun, itching at the edge of her sanity, she didn't see how she'd had much choice.

She lifted her glass with her right hand, letting her focus fall away from the room, into the abstract. It was a delicate art, finding the balance between the minds of the people she was trying to deceive and the deception itself, which she had to draw from her own mind. She'd spent years perfecting it. Trying and failing. There weren't very many wordsmiths who could conjure a tiny, detailed, lifelike illusion—one that would appear in the eyes of a room full of people. It was the movement that was the hardest. The trick was giving them the first glimpse and letting their minds fill in the details. Once they thought they saw something, then it might as well be real.

Everyone raised their glasses. Corinne brought hers to her lips. Then a gray, twittering rat ran down the length of the table, inciting uproar as it went, before finally leaping into the bride's lap. She thrashed and screamed, falling out of her chair and kicking Phillip in the chest multiple times as he dove to help her.

Ignoring the panic, Corinne calmly set down her glass and leaned across the table to catch her father's wide eyes.

"I don't feel well," she told him. "Gabriel is going to take me home. Good night."

She and Gabriel slipped out right as the serving staff arrived with brooms and mops to go in search of the culprit. They had to wait in the lobby for the footman to fetch their coats, and then wait again outside for the valet to bring the car around. Corinne hopped impatiently from one foot to the other. Her feet had gone numb in her shoes, which was preferable to the aching of before. The snow hadn't started again, but the night was still bitter with cold.

The Ford was just pulling around the corner when Phillip came outside. "Corinne, wait," he said. "Where are you going?"

He hadn't put on his coat and stood with his hands crammed into his jacket pockets. Corinne remembered when he had been a gangly teenager, with pimples and hunched shoulders. He used to stand the exact same way, even though military school was supposed to train that sort of posture out of its students.

"Gabriel's taking me home," she said. "I'm sick."

She didn't bother pretending to be sick. They had already escaped. It wasn't like he could drag her back in.

"You were just going to leave?" he asked. "You've been avoiding me all night."

The valet had opened her door. Gabriel was hovering uncertainly beside her, and she waved for him to get into the car. Phillip wore an expression that Corinne hadn't seen on him before. He looked wounded.

"I told you, I'm sick," she said. She didn't know what else he wanted from her. She had been on her best behavior all night—the rat incident aside, but he didn't know that was her.

"I told Mother not to invite Hamish."

"I don't give a fig about Hamish," she said. "Go back to your party. I'll see you at the wedding."

She climbed into the car, thinking only afterward that maybe she should have hugged him or congratulated him or something. Then the valet shut the door, Gabriel kicked the car into gear, and she'd lost her chance.

CHAPTER TWELVE

Despite the hardened, graying snow on the sidewalks, the city was bustling with pedestrians wrapped in warm coats. Corinne cracked the window for some fresh air and could hear them laughing as the car rumbled past. She dug under the seat for the aspirin bottle and shook a few into her hand.

"I hate this rattling death trap," she murmured.

"Does that help?" Gabriel asked, nodding toward the pills.

Corinne swallowed them dry and considered. "Not really," she said. She pressed her forehead against the cool glass of the window. The jolting worsened her headache, but her face was so hot she couldn't stand it. The night rolled by in a blur of golden light and shadow.

"What does it feel like?"

Gabriel's voice was barely audible over the engine, and for a second Corinne wasn't sure she'd heard him correctly. No one had ever asked her that before. The doctors and scientists who studied hemopaths' blood hadn't found a satisfactory explanation for their aversion to the iron element—or for anything else. In the eighteenth century, when the terms *witchcraft* and *magic* were replaced with *hemopathy*, it was generally agreed that there was something different—and therefore diseased—in hemopath blood. There was never any further consensus reached about the exact nature of the difference.

Iron was painful to be near and excruciating to touch. Alloys like the steel in the Ford were less severe but still unpleasant. Corinne never thought much about the cause that was hiding somewhere in her blood. Her body's reaction to iron was just a natural part of her life. She couldn't touch fire or drink arsenic either.

"You know when you put two magnets together and they repel?" she asked.

Gabriel didn't say anything, but his gaze slid away from the road and onto her for a moment. Corinne decided that was his way of saying yes.

"It feels like that," she said, closing her eyes. "As if every drop of blood in your body were one magnet, and the iron were another. Or like holding a red-hot brand half an inch from your skin. Except the pain is waiting everywhere. It's in the ceilings and the walls and the floors. It's in the simplest objects that no one else ever thinks twice about. The whole city is a minefield."

Gabriel's reply was a long time coming. "I'm sorry."

Corinne wondered if he was sorry for his gun or for the car or just for her in general. She would gladly accept apology for the first, but the second he couldn't help, and even the notion of the last infuriated her.

"I wouldn't trade it," she said. "Not for anything."

His eyes met hers again. Corinne could feel her heartbeat in her head, pounding once, twice, thrice. Gabriel looked forward again. He had to keep the car at a crawl on the slick road, and Corinne watched the passing streets through the frosty window.

They were only a few blocks from the Cast Iron when Gabriel spoke again.

"I wish you and Ada would reconsider going to Down Street."

He didn't look at Corinne this time. She studied his profile, but she couldn't read him in the uneven shadows. She could see that his hands were white-knuckled on the steering wheel.

"Johnny wouldn't want us to give up," she said. "We have to figure out who's responsible."

"And what about when the HPA catches up with you? Or the ironmongers? Dammit, Cor, it's not a—"

He had to swerve to miss a car that was backing into the street. Corinne slid across the seat and into him. He turned his head, and for a split second their lips were a hairbreadth apart. He smelled of champagne and cigarettes, and she could feel the hard line of his shoulder against her chest.

Outside, a car horn rang out, and Corinne blinked out of her daze. She dragged herself back to her side. Gabriel swore again under his breath and straightened the car. Corinne saw the storm brewing in his expression, but he was silent now. She'd never seen his temper crack before. It was almost a relief to know that his control wasn't as perfect as it always seemed.

"Johnny gave me everything," Corinne said. "I was sick and alone, and he was there for me. Without him I would never have become a wordsmith. I would never have met Ada. There's nothing I wouldn't do for him, even now that he's dead."

Neither of them said anything more until Gabriel braked the car in front of the Cast Iron.

"I don't know what to think about you," Gabriel said.

The way he said it was like a confession. His grip on the wheel had loosened. The amber glow of a streetlight through the window softened his features, until all the angles and severity were faded, and he seemed suddenly unguarded.

"Think the worst," Corinne said. "I don't like expectations."

She was watching him closely, so she caught the smile that brushed his lips. It felt strangely like a victory.

· · · · · ◆ · · · · ·

At nine thirty, Ada was waiting in the common room, with her coat already buttoned and her hat firmly in place. Corinne and Gabriel were supposed to be back an hour ago, and telling herself not to worry wasn't doing any good. Her heart was still clenched tightly, and nerves burned at the base of her throat. Saint was still in the armchair with his sketchbook. Occasionally he would squint toward the ceiling, trying to visualize, then hunch over again. The sound of pencil on paper was soothing, but not enough to ease the ache in her chest.

When the panel slid open and Corinne skipped down the stairs, Ada didn't know whether to hug her or smack her.

"What took you so long?" she asked.

Corinne raised an eyebrow at her and headed for their room. She was barefoot and held a shoe in each hand. "Well, after the party we had to catch a show," she said over her shoulder.

Ada heard some scrambling, and then Corinne reemerged wearing her ankle boots. More suitable for the weather, but not for the evening gown she still wore under her coat.

"Then we had to get a nightcap," Corinne continued. "And of course there was some passionate necking in the back of the Ford."

Saint looked up with a start, just becoming aware of their conversation.

"Wait, what?" he said, blinking.

Corinne laughed.

"If you'd been here earlier, you could have been my date," she said. "You missed a night of champagne, caviar, and my relatives trying to outdo the Havershams in snobbery."

Saint actually looked a little sick at the notion. "I honestly can't think of a worse way to spend an evening," he said.

"Me neither."

"Aren't you going to change?" Ada asked her. "And where's Gabriel?"

"No time for that," Corinne said. "Gabriel kept the car running. If we don't make it to Down Street before ten, we won't get in to see the Witchers. We need to know what they know about Johnny."

Corinne motioned with both hands in an attempt to herd Ada up the stairs. Ada, who was just starting to realize that Corinne was a little drunk, paid her no heed.

"Are you okay here?" she asked Saint.

"Better than I would be out there," he replied, returning to his sketchbook. "Call if you need me."

Ada allowed herself to be tugged up the steps. They went through the bar and out the front door, where the Ford sat, puffing exhaust. Ada took the front seat and sneaked a few long looks at Gabriel. If there had been any truth in Corinne's jab about passionate necking, Ada didn't see any evidence in Gabriel's demeanor. He was as poised and inscrutable as ever.

The saloon on Down Street didn't have a true name, and Down Street wasn't a true street, just a slanting alleyway in the heart of the West End. It wasn't easy to find, but Gabriel seemed to know the way. He parked a block away, and they all climbed out of the car in silence. There weren't many cars in the West End, or parties. The streets around them were dark and shivering with wind.

Ada kept an eye on Corinne as they walked. She seemed to be managing a straight line, which was a relief. No one had ever accused her of not being able to hold her liquor. Ada wished they'd had a chance to talk earlier. She knew there was no way to talk Corinne out of it, but she wasn't keen on the idea of meeting the Witchers on their own turf, even in peace. Down Street was a different sort of place from the Red Cat, and Ada was glad that

Gabriel had come. Even though the iron in his gun was like an itch she couldn't scratch, it made her feel safer. Corinne didn't like guns as much as she liked wit, but Ada had learned to appreciate how the presence of a weapon could make even the most hardened criminal think twice.

"What's the plan here?" Ada asked Corinne.

They were across the street from the saloon now. There were lights in the windows, and a couple of men were stumbling out, popping their ratty coat collars against the cold.

"The usual, I suppose," Corinne said. "You and I will be daring and clever. Gabriel will complain and be generally useless."

Gabriel didn't give any indication that he'd noticed the casual insult. His eyes were steady on the front door of the saloon. When they passed under a flickering streetlight, Ada could see the lines of a frown on his face.

"I meant how we'll get in to talk to the Witchers," Ada said. "They don't have any reason to see us, or trust us."

"I suppose we'll start by asking," Corinne said.

Ada grabbed a handful of Corinne's coat and yanked her to a stop. Corinne stumbled backward but kept her feet. Her expression was peeved, but even in the dark Ada could see something harder that she didn't like. It was less determined and more fatalistic. She leaned closer to Corinne.

"How much have you had to drink?" she whispered.

"There's nothing wrong with a little liquid courage."

"Maybe a little. But you're drunk."

"I suppose that makes me extra courageous then."

"No, it makes you reckless and stupid."

Corinne jerked away from her, but not before Ada saw the hurt cross her face.

"If you want to wait in the car, then go," Corinne said. "I'm not leaving until I talk to the Witchers."

It was Ada's turn to be hurt. "I'm not going anywhere," she said. "But if we just march in there, they'll throw us out. The back rooms are private for a reason. You know what goes on in there."

"The Witchers know who we are," Corinne said. "Surely that can get us through the door."

It was true that they had been here a couple of times before, but always with Johnny, and Ada didn't remember those visits ever ending with anything but tense words and veiled threats. The Red Cat and the Cast Iron had their old rivalry, but at the end of the day Johnny and Luke Carson were both businessmen. If they let the bad blood spill into the public eye, then the patrons might think twice about coming. The Witchers were outliers, though, and more invested in their cause than in anything else.

"Silas is probably the only one here," Gabriel said. "George usually travels after Christmas."

He was so matter-of-fact that it didn't occur to Ada to doubt him, even though she had no idea why he would know the Witcher brothers' itineraries. Maybe Johnny had mentioned it. Gabriel was still looking at the front door of the saloon, his brow furrowed. Ada expected Corinne to say something, but she was studying Gabriel with a dissecting gaze.

"He'll meet with us," Gabriel said at last, sounding strangely resigned. "Let's go." He crossed the street, hands in pockets, not waiting to see if they would follow.

The Down Street saloon was possibly Corinne's least favorite place in Boston. It stank of sweat and fish. There was no music here, no poetry. The men who came here worked long hours for little pay, and they were worn thin and jagged from laboring around iron and steel. The liquor was dark and flowed fast. The saloon was iron-free, but that was mostly because both the Witchers were wordsmiths. Even though it sported no entertainment, Down Street was a haven for all the blue-collar workers of the West End, not just hemopaths.

Corinne could feel the stares as they passed through. Even with their coats on, she and Gabriel weren't exactly subtle in their party attire. Most of the patrons were indifferent toward them, but one man spat toward her feet, and there were a couple of catcalls behind them that raised the hairs on her neck. She found Ada's hand and squeezed it once, more to comfort herself than for Ada.

Wine still sang in her blood, and if she wasn't careful to focus, the room would start to slip sideways. She kept her eyes on the tense line of Gabriel's shoulders as they neared the back. She didn't know why he was so confident that Silas Witcher would see them, but she was relieved that he wasn't fighting her anymore. It was hard enough trying to bring Ada on board without him brooding over his logical, but ultimately irrelevant, concerns.

Gabriel knocked on the door that led into the back rooms of the saloon. The door cracked open.

"No admittance after ten," a voice barked.

"It's five till," Gabriel replied evenly.

It was actually ten minutes past, but the man on the other side of the door didn't say anything. After a few seconds, he pushed it open a few more inches and waved at them to come in. Corinne didn't like how easy it was, because *easy* never boded well in their business. She glanced back to catch Ada's eye and could see that she harbored the same disquiet. Corinne knew that if they were going to turn back, now was their last chance. She couldn't do that, though, no matter what waited on the other side of the door. She followed Gabriel inside.

There was a meeting happening in a room to their left. Men, and some women, sat in rows of chairs, their backs to the door. At the front, pacing in a frenzy, a man was shouting about the greedy pig of capitalism. The energy was palpable, even from the hall.

There were a few other doors along the corridor, but the Witchers' office was at the very end. Gabriel hesitated for the first time since they had entered the saloon. Corinne slipped past him to knock on the door. A reedy voice answered, and she went in.

Silas Witcher was bent over his desk, scribbling furiously in a journal. He was a slight man with a dark mustache who was rumored to subsist on a diet of bread, water, and books by foreign writers. His brother, George, a retired minister, wasn't as averse to nourishment, but he spent most of his time out of town, preaching the evils of alcohol. Neither abided the frivolity and excess of the Red Cat or the Cast Iron. Corinne had asked Johnny once how a teetotaler justified ownership of a saloon, and he'd only smiled wryly and said that they had to pay for the sackcloth and ashes somehow. Corinne suspected that the Witchers' asceticism was only a means to an end. What they really believed in was a new society, a revolutionary class, an equal brotherhood, and other things that Corinne couldn't remember because she had used the pamphlet they gave her as a fly swatter.

"What are you doing here?" Silas demanded, barely glancing up.

"We just came to talk," Corinne said. Her voice felt strange, like it was coming from somewhere distant and not her own throat. She was starting to regret those last two glasses of wine.

"Not you," Silas said, waving his pen in a silencing motion. "Stone. They told me you had blinked out on us."

Corinne and Ada both stared at Gabriel, who was very deliberately avoiding their eyes.

"I didn't," he said. "Well, I did."

"Which is it?" Silas asked.

"I found work over at the Cast Iron."

"Ah. Well, that explains your new choice of company." Silas regarded Ada and Corinne with a critical eye. There had been a special emphasis on the word *company*.

"What is he talking about, Gabriel?" Corinne asked quietly.

"Gabriel used to be a regular at our weekly meetings," Silas said, going back to his work. "He's got some very interesting theories on the integration of socialism that I've been begging him for years to publish."

"I told you, I'm no writer," Gabriel said.

"You're a communist?" Ada asked.

"Socialist," he said. "There's a difference."

"Are you sure you're not a Bolshevik?" Corinne asked.

He looked at her sharply, and she could see a muted panic in his eyes. So she was the only one who knew about his Russian origins. She couldn't remember why it was so important that she keep it a secret. Her brain was bubbly, and every coherent thought was oscillating out of her reach. Something about his mother.

"A Bolshevik?" Ada echoed.

Even Silas had looked up from his writing.

"Never mind," Corinne said, unable to pull her eyes from Gabriel's, even though his face came in and out of focus with the rhythm of her pulse. "I'm drunk, remember?"

Ada's glare had switched to her, half frustrated, half concerned. Corinne shook her head, hoping to indicate that she was fine, but the movement made her dizzy. She had felt fine outside, in the frigid, open air. In here, where everything was cramped and dark and warm, she was suffocating.

"Johnny is dead," she said. They hadn't told Luke Carson that because it made more sense to draw him out and figure out what he already knew, without announcing that his business rival was dead and the Cast Iron had gone dark. The same logic probably applied here, but she wasn't equipped for that kind of subtlety tonight.

Silas's pen was scratching on paper again, his head bowed over the page.

"I know," he said.

"Did you kill him?"

Ada and Gabriel both elbowed Corinne simultaneously, which she thought was a bit excessive. She hadn't accused Witcher of anything, per se.

"Dervish and Carson built themselves kingdoms on the backs of the working class, and kingdoms always crumble," Silas said.

"You're a pretentious ass," Corinne said. "And that's not an answer."

Silas didn't lay down his pen, but his eyes drifted upward, gauging her. Corinne couldn't tell what his verdict was.

"I don't care enough about Dervish to kill him," he said. "And before you ask, I don't care enough about Carson to drive him out of town either."

"What do you mean?" Ada asked. "Carson's gone?"

"Apparently he was turning over his own people to the HPA in exchange for a tidy little sum," Silas said. He set down his pen and closed the journal. "His crew found out today, and from what I hear, he barely made it out of Boston in one piece."

Corinne struggled to make sense of what Silas was telling her. Had what she'd said to Charlie about the agents at the club been that inflammatory? And if Carson was really gone, what did that mean for the Red Cat?

She dug her nails into her palms, hoping the pinch would clear her vision. The Red Cat wasn't their concern.

"Do you know anything about the shooting at the docks?" she asked. "Anything that might help us figure out who killed Johnny?"

Silas leaned back in his chair, interlocking his fingers behind his head.

"I find it amusing that you think I would help you," he said. "You only got in here because Gabriel knew the watchword. I have no interest in your feuds."

Corinne slammed her hands onto his desk, both for effect and to steady herself.

"It's not just our feud," she said. "The Cast Iron and the Red Cat are the only other iron-free places in Boston. Ironmongers and now the HPA are snatching hemos off the street. Meanwhile, you're tucked in your little office, theorizing about taking over the government or whatever it is you want. But that's not going to help the people out there when the HPA gets even bolder, when there's nowhere else for hemopaths to hide."

Silas hadn't flinched from her gaze. When she finished, he straightened in his chair, hands resting on the desk to mirror hers.

"But that's where you're wrong," he said. His tone was silk. "Our work here is the only thing that can help us. 'The ruling ideas of each age have ever been the ideas of its ruling class.'"

He tilted his head slightly and smiled at her. Corinne's vision went black. For a moment, she thought the lights had gone out, but the darkness was absolute, and no one was saying anything. She stumbled backward, blinking wildly, but it made no difference.

"Cor, what's wrong?" Ada's voice by her ear made her jump. There were hands on her back.

"Stop it, Silas." Gabriel's voice came from her right. There was an edge to it.

"Don't tell me you've lost your zeal, Stone."

"I said stop it."

Corinne's sight flooded back, and she pressed her palms into her forehead, trying to orient herself. Silas still sat calmly behind his desk, his fingers tapping rhythmically on the wood. He smiled at her again.

"Don't take it too hard," he said. "Marx isn't for the faint of heart."

Heat rushed down Corinne's back, and she balled her hands into fists. Silas was a more skilled wordsmith than she'd thought. Before she could decide on a retort, the wail of police sirens trickled into the room. The sound was soft at first, but soon it was bouncing off the walls. Silas jumped to his feet and peered through the window, then wrenched the curtains closed.

"You did this," Silas shouted at them.

"Don't be an idiot," Corinne shouted back.

"There's a warrant out for me," Ada said. "Why would we call the cops?"

"You made some kind of deal," said Silas, rounding the desk toward Corinne.

"They didn't do this." Gabriel intercepted him and shoved him back.

"Please tell me you have an escape route," Ada said to Silas.

"In the meeting room. There's a cellar that connects to a sewer drain."

They flew down the corridor, arriving in time to be the last people through the cellar door. It was pitch-black below, but someone had a flashlight. Overhead, footsteps and shouts echoed through the room. The cellar was lined with mostly empty shelves. There was barely enough floor space for everyone, and Corinne was pressed tightly between Ada and Gabriel. The trapdoor in the corner was painted to match the concrete, and the crowd thinned slowly as people dropped down one by one. No one said anything, and Silas was the last one through. He shut the trapdoor above them only seconds before they heard the cellar door burst open.

They all waited in breathless silence, listening to the muffled sound of trampling feet overhead.

"Go," Silas said at last.

They followed the sewage drain in single file, hunched over and gagging. Corinne was woozy in the dank, putrid air and kept stumbling. She thought for sure she was going to pitch headfirst into whatever muck they were tramping through, but whoever was behind her kept her upright. She was certain it was Gabriel, but she didn't want to turn and acknowledge his help. She knew the radical politics the Witchers harbored in their back rooms weren't as violent and treasonous as headlines made them out to be, but she still couldn't shake the feeling of betrayal. Gabriel had this whole secret life that he had never hinted at, even though she'd opened up to him about her family, about the debt she felt she owed Johnny.

She remembered his reaction when he'd found out about her wealthy upbringing. She'd seen the disgust all over his face, however much he'd denied it.

You know a lot less about me than you think you do.

The three of them and Silas were the last ones up the ladder at the end. Corinne could see the silver of moonlight overhead and feel the icy breeze on her face. She took the rungs two at a time.

Someone at the top took her hands and pulled her free. She swallowed a gulp of fresh air, and then a hand clamped over her mouth.

She bit down, tasting salty skin and then blood. There was cursing in her ear, and the hand dropped. She cried a warning, but it was in vain. Gabriel and Ada were already being dragged out of the manhole and cuffed. Now that her eyes were adjusting, she could see that they were surrounded by black police cars and several wagons that were being loaded with the other detainees.

Other than calmly asking for his lawyer, Silas didn't say anything as they apprehended him. He shot Ada and Corinne a glare as he passed, which clearly indicated he thought they were to blame. When the cuffs clasped onto Corinne's wrists, she could feel the iron in the steel, a dull pain that slithered up her arms and into her head. She thought she might be sick.

"Please," she said to the officer behind her. "No cuffs."

He ignored her and grabbed her chin, forcing her jaw open. Before she could struggle, another cop had shoved a flat metal plate into her mouth. There were leather straps that cinched behind her head, so tight that the plate pressed against the back of her tongue. It worked like a depressor—or a bit. Crude, but effective in preventing hemopaths from talking or singing. Corinne had to concentrate on breathing through her nose to keep from gagging. The cold steel on her tongue was almost unbearable.

Her knees weakened, but she kept her feet as they searched her pockets, removing her grandfather's watch. She didn't even have the strength to protest. The world was spiraling in her vision, and she couldn't focus on anything until a man in a suit stepped in front of her. He was shorter than average, and his smile puckered the corners of his round cheeks.

"It's a privilege to finally meet you," he said. His voice was warm and pleasant, completely at odds with the madness unfurling around him.

Something brushed Corinne's arm, and she looked to her right into Ada's eyes, where she saw her same pain and disorientation reflected. The man who had deposited Ada beside her was also in a suit. He was much taller than his partner, with a large square jaw and not a hint of warmth about him.

"The two perpetrators of the Bengali banker," said the shorter one. "What a catch. You know the odds were five to one against that we would ever find you."

Corinne shuddered with another wave of nausea and stared at the two HPA agents without blinking. She couldn't figure out how they'd known to find them here. She couldn't figure out much of anything through her blinding headache.

"I'm Agent Wilkey," he said, then gestured at his massive counterpart. "My partner, Agent Pierce, and I will be your escorts this evening. I believe you are both already acquainted with Haversham Asylum for Afflictions of the Blood."

"This time around, you'll find the accommodations to be less . . . comfortable," Agent Pierce said, his flinty blue gaze resting on Ada.

Corinne pressed her arm against Ada's, trying to reassure her somehow, even though she couldn't think how they would find their way out of this. The police wagons were starting to pull away. Corinne caught sight of Gabriel standing at the rear of one, his hands cuffed behind his back. His eyes met hers, and his expression shifted from hard composure to something softer and more vulnerable. A policeman pressed an iron rod against his neck. Gabriel didn't flinch, and he didn't break from her gaze. They pushed him into a different police car, and then he was gone.

CHAPTER THIRTEEN

THE RIDE TO HAVERSHAM WAS LONGER THAN ADA REMEMBERED. She imagined she could feel every droplet of blood in her body, writhing in protest to the iron of the car, to the steel in her mouth. Everything was a blinding, pulsing blur as the car jolted through the city. The lights outside the window streaked past her vision like paint on canvas. Distantly, she registered that it had begun to sleet.

Agents Pierce and Wilkey spoke occasionally in the front seat, but never to her and Corinne. Pierce was driving, and every once in a while Ada would see his eyes in the mirror. There was an utter dispassion in them that frightened her. She closed her own eyes and didn't open them until she felt the jolt of pain as they passed through the iron gates of Haversham. The car shuddered to a stop, and Agent Pierce half dragged her out of the car. She craned her neck to keep sight of Corinne, who was solidly in Wilkey's grasp. Panic at the thought of being separated rose in her chest.

The agents led them into the linoleum-tiled front lobby. The familiar sharp scent of antiseptic met Ada's nose. Behind the front desk the same nurse from the night of Ada's escape peered at them through the reading glasses perched on her nose. She moved the spectacles to her head, and scorn twisted her features.

"I almost lost my job because of these two," she said.

"Fortunately for you," said Wilkey, "these two have taken a lot more than that—and from much more important people."

Pierce laughed. It was an unpleasant sound.

The nurse's upper lip was still curled slightly. She moved her finger to the intercom button on her desk. "Shall I fetch Dr. Knox?"

"No need," Pierce said.

"We know where the basement is," said Wilkey.

The nurse frowned and made a show of shuffling through her papers. "Dr. Knox is expecting three of them," she said. She ran her finger down a page, then tapped it when she found what she was looking for. "You're missing Sebastian Temple."

Ada jerked at the mention of Saint's name, and Pierce shifted his grip on her arm.

"We'll have him before the night's over," Pierce said.

"We have a few other matters to attend to first." Wilkey smiled at the nurse, revealing the dimples in his chin.

The nurse looked between them, her disdain replaced by something more wary, but she nodded. She made a show of busying herself with the contents of her desk, although Ada saw her cast them one furtive glance as the agents led them through a door at the edge of the lobby. Ada quickly lost all sense of direction as they moved through a maze of taupe corridors that all looked the same. She couldn't catch her breath. A part of her had known that Haversham was inevitable, but that didn't mean she was prepared. This was different from last time. Before, she had known that Corinne would come for her, that if anyone could plot an escape from Haversham Asylum, it was Corinne Wells. All the terror she had repressed came back to Ada in waves. Every whispered rumor, every remembered scream.

Then they turned a corner, and at the intersection of two halls was a thick wooden door with dual dead bolts. Ada had the sickening thought that it locked from the outside—clearly meant to keep people in rather than out. When Wilkey opened it, the hinges made no sound, as if they were well-oiled with use. Corinne turned her head to catch Ada's eye over her shoulder. The look was fleeting, lasting only the length of a heartbeat, before Wilkey moved between them to prod Corinne first down the stairs into the basement, but Ada saw everything there was to see. Corinne was afraid.

Ada took a short breath through her nose, trying to find some courage, some equilibrium. Then Pierce pushed her toward the stairs, where shadows enveloped her, and it was too late.

Corinne stumbled blindly down the steps, knowing that if she tripped with her hands cuffed behind her back, she would tumble headlong down the entire flight. Agent Wilkey probably wouldn't bother to catch her. As her eyes adjusted, she could see that there were a few dim electric bulbs, hanging from wires along the wall to her right. There was no banister, only faded brick that glistened faintly with moisture. The smell of mildew trickled into Corinne's nostrils, and she had to gasp in a few breaths through her mouth to fight the nausea rising in her throat. Choking on her own vomit in this godforsaken hole was not how she intended to die.

Accompanying her descent was a growing ache from iron somewhere below. She tried to quote Dante in her head, to distract herself from the pain, but it was no use. Even Dante could never have imagined the hell that Haversham had created here. By the time she reached the bottom of the steps, she was trembling uncontrollably. The stairs emptied into a long, narrow corridor lined with metal doors. Pain lanced through her legs with every footstep, and she looked down to see that the floor of the corridor was iron.

"Clever, eh?" Wilkey asked, giving her a little shove forward. "You wouldn't believe how much effort was put into this place. Just enough iron to keep the slaggers quiet, but not enough to render them useless. It really is an art."

Corinne's vision slanted sideways, and she thought she might collapse, but Wilkey was propelling her forcefully down the corridor now. The doors on either side went by in aching streaks of gray, blurring as her eyes filled with tears. They twisted through corridors and doors that led to more corridors. She told herself that Ada was still behind her, that they were still together, that Haversham and the HPA didn't stand a chance. She repeated it again and again in her head. A mantra punctuated by every agonizing footfall.

They went through a doorway at the end of a long corridor that opened into a large, low-ceilinged room. The sharp smell of disinfectant assaulted her nostrils. This room was brighter than the corridors, with bright medical lamps that glared off the white tile and stainless steel surfaces. The brilliance temporarily blinded Corinne, and they were several steps into the room before she recovered. Once she did, the only thing she could really see was the man a few feet away from her. His face was so skeletal that for a split second she thought he was dead—but no, his gray smock moved barely with the slow rise and fall of his chest. He was strapped to a hospital bed, the buckles cutting into his skin. There was a tube inserted in his bruised arm, bright red with flowing blood. In a bed next to his, strapped down in the same manner, was a woman. Her chest heaved with rattling breaths, and her damp, tangled hair covered most of her ashen face. The tube in the woman's pallid arm was connected somehow to the man's via a small machine between their beds that whirred and hummed like a phonograph with no record. A second tube in the woman's thigh trailed down beside the bed, draining crimson into a metal canister.

The woman's eyes opened suddenly, and she let out a scream that reverberated through Corinne's bones. She held the cry so long that Wilkey stomped over to her bed, still dragging Corinne by the arm. He took a rag, spotted with blood, from a nearby table and shoved it into the woman's mouth. Her strangled scream continued, even through the gag, and her wild gaze met Corinne's. The madness in her eyes, birthed of pain and terror and rage, made Corinne feel weak at the knees. She was perversely grateful when Wilkey pulled her away, continuing their trek through the room. There were at least two dozen beds, but the rest had sheets pulled over their occupants. This wasn't a hospital. It was a graveyard.

Corinne felt she owed it to them, somehow, to not look away, but her eyes fluttered downward of their own accord. Her shoes clomped on the floor, and she could almost see her reflection in the scrubbed white tiles.

When they finally passed through a doorway into a smaller room, it was a strange relief to be pushed inside, where there was blessed concrete under her feet. She didn't know exactly what she had expected to find, but the empty table with its four wooden chairs was not it. Overhead, a single bulb gave off a dull yellow glow, flickering intermittently. Corinne thought vaguely of Dante and his inferno again. They had traded one circle of hell for the next. Very faintly, she could still hear the woman's muffled screams.

Agent Wilkey made her sit in one of the chairs facing the door. Ada dropped into the chair beside her and laid her head down on the rough grain of the wood. Though she was trying to hide it, Corinne could see that she was flushed and shaking. Corinne wasn't in much better shape herself. She wished she could reach out and take Ada's hand, give some comfort, draw some in return. Agent Pierce left the room, and Agent Wilkey stood in the corner, arms crossed, humming to himself. Corinne briefly tried to summon an illusion for him—something clawed and bloodthirsty—but it was an impossible task and she knew it. If she didn't speak any words first to prepare his mind, then she couldn't make him see anything. The attempt made her feel slightly better, though.

After a few minutes that might as well have been decades, the door opened again. Corinne recognized Dr. Knox from Jackson's imitation of him. The squat, spectacled man in his pristine white coat seemed out of place in the dank room. He wiped a handkerchief across his shiny bald head and shut the door behind him. The room still held the barest scent of disinfectant. Agent Pierce had not come back.

"This is disappointing," Knox said to Wilkey, tucking the handkerchief into his pocket and sitting down across from Ada and Corinne. "I expressly instructed you to bring Temple too. I've been told he's showing signs of abilities well outside the norm of his affliction. I *need* him for the next phase."

"We'll pick him up later, when the streets are quieter," Wilkey said from the corner. "We know exactly where he is."

Corinne caught Ada's eye as she straightened suddenly. Agent Wilkey saw the movement and smiled blithely at both of them.

"Interesting setup you have at the Cast Iron," he said. "I'm assuming that basement was part of the Underground Railroad?"

Corinne's chest was tight. No one outside the Cast Iron was supposed to know that the basement even existed. The blueprints gave no indication. City inspectors had no records of it.

"Take off the gags," Dr. Knox said. "We can get started with these two, at least."

Out of the breast pocket of his coat he retrieved a pencil and pad of paper. He flipped to a clean sheet and set it on the table.

Agent Wilkey unbuckled Corinne's gag first, dropping it on the table in front of her. When he freed Ada from hers, she let loose a string of Portuguese on him so fierce and fluid that Corinne was a little in awe. She hadn't understood a word of it, but judging from the tone, there was plenty of cursing involved.

"That's enough of that," Dr. Knox said. He took something else from his pocket and set it on the table between them. It was a piece of metal, the size and shape of a nickel. Despite the assault on her senses from the other sources in the basement, Corinne could tell that it was pure iron.

"You should probably work on your intimidation tactics, Doc," Corinne said.

Without the gag she felt more like herself. Not being able to speak—and give derisive commentary—was like missing all her limbs. With effort, she pushed all that she had just seen to the back of her mind. From the corner of her eye, Corinne saw Ada raise her chin slightly.

"A gun might be more effective," Ada said. "Or a knife."

"Hell, even a pair of pliers will do," Corinne said. She turned to Ada. "I liked the Portuguese, by the way. Very incisive."

"Thank you," Ada said, falling easily into the rhythm of their familiar banter.

It was as if they'd made the decision together. Dr. Knox and his HPA cohorts clearly wanted them terrified and compliant—a pleasure that she and Ada would deny them.

"You going to teach me some of those curses anytime soon?" Corinne asked.

"Not a chance."

"How about just the translation for 'Thou art a boil, a plague sore, an embossed carbuncle in my corrupted blood.'?" She looked at Dr. Knox and smiled innocently. "I have a feeling I might need it tonight."

Dr. Knox did not appear to be perturbed by their exchange. He only scratched the tip of his nose, checked his watch, and sighed.

"If you're quite through," he said, "I would like to get started."

"By all means," Corinne said.

"There's only one simple rule," Dr. Knox said. "You do exactly as I tell you, or Agent Wilkey will hold you down and shove this iron down your throat."

Corinne's breath caught in her lungs despite herself. Suddenly the small iron coin on the table seemed enormous, crowding every corner of her vision. When she was thirteen, only a year after she had manifested as a hemopath, she had taken a dare from one of Carson's boys to hold an iron fishing sinker in her closed fist for five minutes. She'd made it forty-seven seconds before the pain became unbearable, radiating through her body until she lost touch with the world around her, until she had dissolved completely and nothing but the pain existed.

When she tried to imagine what it would feel like to have the iron inside her, she couldn't help but think that she would rather die.

In the corner, Agent Wilkey was chuckling. "We had a slagger once try to claw open his own chest. What a mess."

Dr. Knox cleared his throat. "Yes, well, he brought it on himself." He eyed Corinne and Ada. "And if you have any ideas of escaping, you should know that Agent Pierce is on the other side of the door, wearing earplugs, and he does have a gun."

Corinne wanted to look at Ada, but she was afraid of what she would see in her best friend's eyes. If Ada had given up, then Corinne wasn't sure that she could go on.

Dr. Knox nodded to himself, seemingly satisfied that they had grasped the gravity of the situation.

"Now that we have that nasty business out of the way, we can begin." He waved Agent Wilkey over. "You can take your seat."

Wilkey moved from the corner to sit next to the doctor. His expression was benign, almost bored.

"Some of the methods for conducting our research are unfortunately crude," Dr. Knox said, taking up his pencil. "But I assure you it's for the greater good."

"That's what they said when they mutilated slaves in the name of science," Ada said. Her voice was low and trembling.

Dr. Knox ignored her and continued. "Tonight will be a very straightforward experiment. You'll simply be using your hemopathy on Agent Wilkey here, who is one of our best natural-born resisters. We'll determine exactly how long he is able to resist each of you. Once we have a workable measure of the hemopathic pathogens in your blood, we'll be able to move into the next phase of experimentation."

"Is that what you're calling your torture chamber out there?" Corinne asked, concentrating on keeping the tremor out of her voice. She almost succeeded.

Dr. Knox waved his pencil dismissively. "We're winding down that phase. None of the subjects have survived the process, and I don't have high hopes for this latest round either. There's a cerebral component we're missing that interacts with the pathogen somehow. A full transfusion is not a viable cure. We need to isolate the lobe of the brain that is accelerated by the pathogen. I believe that is what gives you the power to manipulate others and to resist manipulation yourselves."

"God, you're boring," Corinne said, but inside she was reeling.

What she'd seen outside was starting to make more sense. The lunatic had been trying to replace hemopaths' blood completely, which meant there were regs being used too. Drifters, probably. People with no families to miss them. She turned her head slightly, trying to catch Ada's eye, but Ada was staring straight ahead, her shoulders squared, her jaw locked.

Dr. Knox sighed like a professor disappointed in his students.

"I wouldn't expect you to grasp the full importance of what we're doing here," he said, pushing his glasses up his nose. "If we can isolate a cure for hemopathy or an antidote to make non-hemopaths immune, then the scientific benefits will be immeasurable."

"Don't you mean the paycheck will be immeasurable?" Ada asked. She was still staring straight past him, her chin raised slightly in residual defiance. In that moment she looked so much like her mother that Corinne's heart ached.

Dr. Knox actually reddened at her words. He tugged his collar.

"Well, of course there are certain monetary considerations," he mumbled. "This has become my life's work. I've had my eye on you two since that incident on the Harvard Bridge, and I suspect that your skill may be more potent than our other subjects'. That, coupled with your youth, makes you prime candidates for my new study."

"And what does this study entail exactly?" Ada asked.

Agent Wilkey bared his teeth in a gesture that only vaguely resembled a smile. "You'll find out soon enough."

Ada flinched, and Corinne swallowed hard, her mind still echoing with the woman's screams. They had quieted now. Maybe she had run out of strength. Maybe she was dead.

Dr. Knox cleared his throat again.

"There's no need to concern ourselves with that at this juncture. First we need to ensure that you both are up to par, so to speak. Shall we begin?"

The longer Dr. Knox's test dragged on, the more outside herself Ada felt. There was something surreal about sitting in this chair, staring at an HPA agent as he sweat in intense concentration. Beside her Corinne was quoting her way through Christina Rossetti's "Goblin Market," her pace lagging only slightly as she glared at Agent Wilkey in equal concentration. They had been at it for almost an hour now, by Ada's estimation. Thankfully, their cuffs had been removed earlier, at Corinne's insistence that she couldn't concentrate with the steel against her skin.

At the beginning, Corinne had attacked the task with vicious precision, using Poe to conjure a creature so hideously fierce that even Ada was taken aback. Wilkey had resisted for almost two minutes before frowning and informing Dr. Knox that he could see the illusion. When Corinne knew that he was seeing it, she had it jump at him, claws outstretched and fanged mouth gaping. Despite his attempts to remain unruffled, Wilkey had jerked back in his chair.

Beneath the table, Ada had turned her hand palm up, so that Corinne could tap her fingertips twice. Dr. Knox had barely glanced up from his notes. He checked the time, then told Corinne to do it again.

That was sixteen poems ago. Ada knew that Corinne was running out of steam. She was slurring the words to "Goblin Market," and though Ada was just passingly familiar with the text, she was fairly sure that Corinne had skipped a few stanzas. Under normal circumstances, she needed only a few lines before she could conjure an illusion for someone, and she could keep creating the illusions for several minutes after—as long as the poem was still swimming in the hearer's brain. Wilkey proved tougher to crack, and Corinne had to quote continuously in order to break through his concentration. Her voice was starting to give out.

"A goblin?" Wilkey asked when he finally saw the illusion. "That's the best you can do?"

Corinne sat back heavily in her chair and didn't reply.

"She can't do another," Ada said. "She's too tired."

She half expected Corinne to protest the insinuation that she had any such limitations, but she was silent, which meant she was even more exhausted than Ada thought. Dr. Knox looked up from his data and frowned. The gleam from the lightbulb flashed in his spectacles.

"I'll decide when we're finished here," he said. He reached out and slid the iron coin half an inch closer, as a reminder.

Ada bit her lip and clenched her fists in her lap. Dr. Knox tapped his pencil against his chin in absent thought, studying Corinne.

"Fine," he said. "I think the data is sufficient for an accurate average. Do you need a break before we move on to the songsmith, Agent Wilkey?"

Wilkey shook his head and smiled leisurely at Ada. "I'm ready," he said.

"I play the violin," Ada told them.

"I've been told that your voice serves you just as well," Dr. Knox said with a dismissive wave. "Agent, if you'll be so kind as to nudge me when you start to feel something. I need these in order to focus fully on the data."

He fished some earplugs out of his pocket and pushed them

firmly into his ears. Ada guessed that he had been able to disregard Corinne's illusions because he knew they weren't real, but Ada's talent wasn't so easily ignored. Agent Wilkey leaned back in his chair, arms crossed. Ada glared at him and took stock of her own emotions, which were dwarfed by a single, overwhelming feeling. Hate.

She started to hum a funeral dirge, directing the full force of it at Wilkey. It took more effort to angle emotions at one person rather than let them blanket the room, but she doubted Corinne would have enough focus right now to block it out. This particular emotion was something she wanted only Wilkey to feel.

Utter, impossible, complete desolation.

In less than a minute his expression began to change. It was subtle at first. He was still trying to block her out. She didn't increase her volume. The song's quality was more important than anything else. Ada pushed the desolation into every single note. Wilkey would find himself spiraling through every hurt and heartache and loss that he had ever experienced. She played loss for the patrons at the Cast Iron sometimes, in order to sweeten the joy that would come later. This was different, though.

She didn't want to manipulate Wilkey's emotions. She wanted to use them to annihilate him.

When he felt the first wave of it, Wilkey smacked Dr. Knox's arm with a reflexive jerk. The doctor nodded and wrote down the time, but Ada didn't stop. She layered on the grief and despair, twisting them together with every ounce of guilt and shame she had ever felt. She had never purposefully used her own emotions in a song, but tonight it came naturally to her.

"That's enough," Agent Wilkey said through gritted teeth.

Ada still didn't stop. Her voice was the only weapon she had in this hell they'd created. She would inflict as much damage as she could before it was over.

"I said that's enough," Wilkey shouted.

He jumped to his feet, chair skittering backward. In one fluid motion, he snatched up the iron coin, rounded the table, and grabbed Ada around the neck. Her vision exploded red as he lifted her and thrust her against the wall. He wasn't a big man, but he was deceptively strong. She clawed at his wrist but couldn't find purchase. Her lungs screamed for air, racking her head with pain. With his left hand, Wilkey shoved the iron coin into her mouth. She didn't think it was possible, but the pain expanded, filling her completely, pouring out of her in waves.

"You want to know what the new study entails, slagger?" he hissed in her ear. She could barely make out his words. "The good doctor is going to ram metal spikes into your head and pump you full of electricity. And when your body finally does give out, he'll drain every drop of your diseased blood. I'll make sure we ship your corpse back to your mother."

He might have had more to say, but he didn't get the chance. Corinne chose that moment to smash her chair into his back. There was a crack—Ada couldn't tell if it was Wilkey or the wood. He howled, and his grip loosened. Ada fell to the floor, spitting out the coin and gasping for breath. She dove out of his reach, but not before aiming a kick at his kneecap.

"Stop!" Dr. Knox was shouting.

Wilkey didn't seem inclined to listen. He had rounded on Corinne, and she backed away until she was against the wall. Ada managed to drag herself to her knees, but her legs wouldn't cooperate. Spotty vision. Splitting headache. But she had to get up. She had to help Corinne.

The door opened, and Pierce came in. He took in the scene with a stony expression, gun in hand. The sight of his partner seemed to bring Wilkey back to himself.

"Get the cuffs," Pierce said.

"This is unacceptable," Dr. Knox said, waving his notebook with fervor. "The agency promised me the highest degree of professionalism."

Pierce ignored him and crossed the room. He yanked Ada up by her arm and deposited her back in her chair. She tried to struggle, but her failing strength ended the attempt quickly. He righted Corinne's chair and gestured at her wordlessly with the gun. She looked at him with undisguised fury and cast a glance toward Ada.

Ada shook her head fiercely. She would never forgive Corinne if she got herself shot right in front of her. Corinne set her jaw, but she sat down without protest. Ada saw that one of the chair legs wobbled now, and she felt the strangest urge to smile. The urge was fleeting.

Wilkey handcuffed their hands behind their backs again, just as a buzz of static made Ada jump in her seat. She looked toward the source to see a beige loudspeaker mounted in the corner of the room.

"Dr. Knox," came the voice of the desk nurse, "we need you upstairs."

Dr. Knox muttered something to himself and gathered his notebook and pencil.

"You two come with me," he said to the agents. "I don't trust either of you with my test subjects."

Neither Wilkey nor Pierce objected, though Wilkey cast a deathly glance over his shoulder on the way out. They left the metal gags where they were on the table, and Ada could still feel the angry pulse of the iron coin somewhere on the floor behind her. Dr. Knox shut the door behind them. The lock clicked into place.

She and Corinne were both silent for a while, readjusting to the sting of the steel on their wrists. Ada's head pounded with Wilkey's words, but she fought them back. She wouldn't give him what he wanted. He could hurt her, but he wasn't stronger than her. She'd watched him crumple beneath the weight of her music.

When she finally gathered herself enough to speak, her voice came out scratchy and soft. "I'm sorry if you felt any of that song," she said. "I tried to aim it at Wilkey."

Corinne shook her head slowly. She was staring hard at the tabletop. Ada could see her hands were shaking behind her back.

"I've never heard you play anything like that before," she said. "I didn't—I didn't know you could."

Ada hadn't known she could either. She'd had no idea that she even had the capacity to hate someone as much as she'd hated Wilkey in that moment. It wasn't really Wilkey she hated, though. It was everything he stood for. It was the atrocities they were committing in the next room. It was this world that these men were forging in their underground lair. A world where she was just a test subject, where she had no choices, no recourse, no power.

Johnny had given her those things when he'd given her the Cast Iron. She wasn't willing to surrender it, not to Haversham Asylum or to the Hemopath Protection Agency or to anyone else.

Corinne had felt only a sliver of the emotions that Ada had unleashed on Agent Wilkey, and even that was enough to make her heart clench and her head swim. She didn't pity the man in the least. After the sight of him with his hand around Ada's neck, she wished that Ada had given him much worse. She was worried, though. Ada felt guilty about using her skill to con even the most corrupt, cruel, deceitful john out of his money. What kind of pain was she feeling if she was willing to wreak such devastation now?

"They're the ones who asked for it," Ada said.

"I know."

With slow, painful movements, Corinne edged her chair closer to Ada's, until their shoulders touched. They sat in silence like that for several minutes. When the lock on the door turned, neither of them moved. Corinne told herself that whatever came next, she and Ada could handle it. She only wished she could believe herself.

It wasn't Dr. Knox or the agents who came through the door.

It was her brother.

"Come on, Corinne," he said, taking in the room with an expression of pure disgust. "We're leaving."

It took Corinne another few seconds to even register that she wasn't hallucinating, that her brother, Phillip Wells, military academy graduate with honors, aspiring politician, and fiancé to one of the wealthiest women in Boston, really was standing in the room with them, still wearing his tuxedo from the rehearsal dinner.

"What are you doing here?" she asked.

"One of the nurses called Angela's father when she heard that you were here," Phillip said. He was eyeing the metal gags on the table with obvious disquiet. "Thank God he came to me instead of Father. How did you even— Never mind, let's go. Mother's in the car."

"You brought our *mother*?" Corinne demanded. Somehow that seemed like it warranted immediate discussion.

"I didn't have much of a choice when she overheard Mr. Haversham. As far as she knows, this is all a terrible misunderstanding, and we're going to keep it that way. Now let's go." He crossed the room and grabbed her arm, but Corinne yanked herself free.

"Not without Ada," she said.

"Absolutely not." Dr. Knox had come into the room, handkerchief in hand. "Miss Navarra is a dangerous criminal, and I cannot allow her to leave this facility. I'm sorry, Mr. Wells, but your influence doesn't reach far enough to pardon convicted felons."

"There was never even a trial," Corinne protested.

Phillip stared at Dr. Knox for a while, sizing him up. The doctor wiped at his forehead with the handkerchief but did not back down.

"Come on, Corinne," Phillip said at last. "Angela called in a few favors to get me down here, but she's not going to call in any more."

"I'm not leaving without Ada."

"Cor," Ada said sharply.

"No," Corinne said, looking straight at her.

"Corinne, I swear I will carry you out of here kicking and screaming." Phillip took a step forward.

"Are you sure, Phil?" Corinne sat back in her chair. "Think of what that headline would do to the Wells name. Just go. You can tell everyone that I died of Spanish influenza. That way I won't be a smear on any future campaigns."

Phillip was taken aback by her words. He was wearing the same expression he'd had outside the Lenox only hours ago. Wounded and uncertain. Two things she had never thought that the mighty Phillip Wells, soon-to-be heir to both the Wells and Haversham fortunes, could ever be.

"Do you really think I came here for my political career?" he asked her.

"Phillip," Ada said, not taking her eyes off Corinne, "would you give us a couple of seconds?"

Phillip looked between them, at a loss for possibly the first time in his life, and nodded.

"I really must protest—this is highly irregular," Dr. Knox said.

"What's highly irregular is the fact that the basement of this facility is supposed to just be for storage." Phillip put a massive hand on the back of Dr. Knox's shoulder and propelled him toward the door.

Dr. Knox's mouth worked like a fish's as he tried to come up with a reply. He hadn't found one by the time Phillip shut the door. Corinne stared resolutely anywhere but at Ada. She had never accepted help from her arrogant, grandstanding brother in her life, and she wasn't going to start tonight. No matter what Ada had to say about it.

Ada knew the look in Corinne's eye. She'd seen it earlier that night outside Down Street. Corinne had always been stubborn, but this was more fatalistic than that. In the dim, unsteady light, with her hair plastered with sweat to her forehead and her eye makeup running down her cheeks and her shoulders hunched from the pain of the handcuffs, Ada almost didn't recognize her. That scared her more than anything else.

"You have to go with him," she said to Corinne. "This is your only chance."

"I won't go without you."

Ada nudged her arm and stared at her until Corinne finally met her eye.

"They're going after Saint," Ada said. "You have to get to him before they do."

Corinne hesitated at that. She had obviously forgotten. She shook her head again. "If I go with Phillip, he'll never let me out of his sight. I'll be trapped in that house until I die."

"Not if he thinks you just want to go home," Ada insisted. "As soon as he lets his guard down, you can get away. Please, Corinne. You know Saint. He's not like us. You know what this place would do to him."

"Those things that Wilkey said—" Corinne's voice broke. "As soon as we leave, that's what they're going to do to you."

Ada's breath caught in her throat, and fear lanced through her chest. But she fought it. She was stronger. She had to be.

"So you want to stay here so they can do the same to you? Now is not the time to be noble, Cor."

"I'm not leaving."

"You've broken me out before, and you can do it again," Ada said.

"You don't know that! I'm not leaving."

"Dammit, Cor. Why not?"

"Because I've seen what leaving you behind did to Saint, and I can't do it."

Corinne laid her head down on the table, her cheek pressed against the wood. Ada rested her cheek on it as well, so that they were eye to eye.

Corinne's eyes were red, though she wasn't crying. "I can't live with that," she whispered.

"Saint was afraid, and he made a mistake," Ada said. "I'm telling you this is the best way—this is the only way."

"It's not fair for you."

"You think this is the first time life hasn't been fair for me? Don't be an idiot, Corinne."

"You're being an idiot. You're the one being noble." There was a fever in her tone. "As long as we're together, we can figure this out. There's another way. There has to be."

"There's not," Ada said. "Please, just go. They'll be back any second."

The girls' faces were still only inches apart, their cheeks pressed into the comforting wood, their eyes locked.

"I won't," said Corinne. "I have to do what I think is right."

Corinne was still trembling. Ada could see the burn of the iron written all over her face. She could see how much Corinne wanted to leave, wanted to be free of this place. And she could see that she would never admit that to herself. Ada loved her for it, and hated it too.

"I know you do," she whispered. "I'm sorry, Cor."

Ada squeezed her eyes shut, found focus deep inside herself, far away from the pain and the anger and the guilt that had already begun to take root. She found a melody from her childhood and started to hum.

"Don't." Corinne's voice was a strangled gasp.

Ada made herself look at her. Tears had sprung into Corinne's eyes. Corinne straightened up, shaking her head violently, but Ada kept humming. The melody had already begun to take hold. Ada knew she was too weak now to resist the full force of the song.

"Please" was the last thing Corinne said before her eyes began to glaze.

Ada felt tears well in her own eyes. Her heart ached inside her. It was worse than iron. It was a kind of betrayal.

It was the only way.

She hummed, weaving the music like a net over Corinne, trapping her best friend into her will. She could make people feel any emotion she wanted. She could make them trust her implicitly and even blur their memories, but she'd never been able to make people *do* anything but the simplest of actions. She could make a rowdy patron sit down or a cop walk past on the street, but nothing more.

With Corinne it was different. She knew her so well, every twist and turn of her mind. Convincing Corinne that she had to leave was easier than convincing herself that it had to be done. Somehow that only made it worse.

When Phillip and Dr. Knox reentered the room, Ada stopped humming and closed her eyes.

"I'll go," Corinne said. Her voice sounded distant, mechanical.

"Thank God," said Phillip.

Ada heard Dr. Knox fumbling with Corinne's handcuffs. She heard the scrape of the chair against wood and the shuffle of footsteps. When she opened her eyes, she was alone with Dr. Knox.

"Strange," he said. He didn't say more.

Ada was surprised that he didn't consider all this data for his little notebook. She wouldn't let herself think about what was coming next. Corinne was safe, and Saint would be too. Maybe down here she didn't have any choices or recourse or power, but she could still protect the people she loved.

"There you are," Dr. Knox said as Agent Pierce appeared in the doorway. Dr. Knox stepped into the other room, pulling the door behind him, but it didn't latch. Through the narrow gap, Ada could see the white of Dr. Knox's sleeve and catch scattered fragments of what he was saying.

"—tell him—I want her back—Temple—" Dr. Knox's voice was low and frenetic.

Agent Pierce said something, but all Ada could hear was Phillip's name.

"We'll move them all if we have to." Dr. Knox was speaking louder now, more agitated. "We finally have subjects who might survive the tests. I won't let all this work go to waste."

Pierce said something else, and the door slammed shut. Ada heard the lock slide into place. Once she was sure they had left, she inched her chair sideways until she was as far from the iron coin as possible. She leaned her head against the concrete wall and sang a lullaby that her mother had taught her. Even though she couldn't manipulate her own emotions the way she could others', the familiar melody gave her a small amount of comfort. Music was easier than thinking about the renewed screams outside the door, or the gnawing fear that she had just seen her best friend for the last time.

CHAPTER FOURTEEN

CORINNE'S WORLD WAS A HAZE OF COLORS AND SOUNDS AND THE grip of her brother's hand on her arm. Her thoughts were wraiths. Her emotions were blank. All she knew was that she had to leave. She had to leave this place.

The beds full of bodies in various stages of dying evoked no grief anymore. That same woman, screaming, screaming, was only a distant idea now. A vague notion of horror. Phillip was pulling her faster now, and her footsteps on the tiles seemed to drum out the only thing she knew for certain. She had to leave this place.

The corridors with their iron floors pricked at her consciousness, but even that felt irrelevant. Phillip hesitated at a junction and tried the door on the left. Cool air flooded Corinne's senses, and for a moment her mind cleared. The room was some kind of cold storage. And it was stacked with corpses.

Phillip cursed and backed out. Corinne stumbled with him. She fell to her hands and knees. The iron rose up to meet her. Scalding pain and nausea rose in her chest, and she retched. Her mind was fogging again. There was a fading melody inside her, telling her she had to leave this place. But she couldn't move.

Her brother picked her up, cradling her, and pushed through the other door. The stairs were in sight now. Beyond them the lobby. Beyond that the outside world. She had to leave this place. Phillip was saying something, softly.

"I can't believe we let this happen."

Corinne tried to reply, but her mouth wouldn't form the words.

She rested her cheek against her brother's shoulder and recited poetry in her head until the haze dissolved, until the melody was gone.

Corinne didn't regain her full faculties until she was at the car and buried in her mother's arms, breathing deeply of her perfume. She swore.

"Corinne," her mother snapped. "Watch your language."

Corinne looked back to see the asylum waiting behind her, its brick facade unperturbed by the icicles along its eaves, by the frigid wind whipping around them. The cold cleared Corinne's mind even further.

"Dammit, Ada," she exclaimed into the open air. "Mother, I have to go back. My friend—"

"We're going home," said Mrs. Wells. "And we'll never speak of this to anyone."

She was gripping Corinne's upper arm, her lips pursed tightly. Her fur coat gaped open in the front, revealing her silk dress from the party. Corinne was suddenly aware of her own pitiful state. The hem of her dress had dried from their tromp through the sewers, but there was a rip in it, past her knee. She'd been too distracted in the asylum to think much about it, but even in the fresh air the smell was appalling. And she still had the taste of vomit in her mouth.

Phillip was cranking the car, and Mrs. Wells herded Corinne into the backseat. She climbed in beside her. Corinne's mind was reeling with the suddenness of everything. She barely felt the metal of the car around her. All she could think was that she was leaving Ada behind.

And Ada had made her do it.

The car roared to life, and before Corinne could decide what to do next, Phillip was steering them down the gravel driveway. The iron gates flew past with a fleeting ache, and then Haversham was lost in the distance. Corinne pressed her face into her hands, trying to shake the last vestiges of Ada's melody from her head. Vaguely, she remembered Agent Wilkey in the lobby, while her brother was browbeating the desk nurse into opening the front gate. Wilkey had leaned against the wall beside the door, smiling. All trace of the damage from Ada's song was gone from his features.

"Don't worry," he told her with a wink. "You'll be back soon."

Corinne drove her fingernails into her skin, trying to find control of her own fear. Ada wouldn't have been able to manipulate her will so easily if a part of her hadn't already wanted desperately to leave. Corinne hated herself for that.

"This is my fault," her mother said. Her wavering voice was barely audible over the jolting wheels.

"Don't be ridiculous, Mother," Phillip said. "Corinne got mixed up in bad company. She was in the wrong place at the wrong time. That's all there is to it."

Corinne looked up from her hands to see Phillip's pointed glare in the mirror. He hadn't so much as mentioned the word *hemopath*, but he must have figured it out by now. The HPA didn't accidentally cart regs off to Haversham. That was why the iron test had been introduced in the first place.

"That's all there is to it," Corinne echoed, not sure what else Phillip wanted her to say.

She knew he'd seen what was happening in the basement. Even in the murky memory of the past ten minutes, the room full of corpses stood out sharply in her mind, turning her stomach.

Phillip showed no signs of distress, though. He was his normal, mildly officious self.

Her mother was shaking her head with a mournful expression.

"I knew you were getting yourself into some kind of trouble when you showed up at the dinner with Gabriel Stone. I should have gone straight to your father. I just don't even know how you met someone like him."

"What are you talking about?" Corinne asked. "How do *you* know him?" And why had her family decided tonight of all nights to stop being unfailingly predictable?

Her mother faltered. She picked nervously at the furred cuff of her sleeve. "I . . . I've seen him at certain . . . meetings. On Down Street."

Corinne's mouth fell open slightly. "Are you . . . a socialist?"

The car swerved slightly as Phillip looked back in alarm. "Mother, what is she talking about?" he asked.

Mrs. Wells turned her face toward the window, where Boston's outer edges rolled past. The tenements and scattered storefronts were dark, with only the silver of the moon to illuminate their icy rooftops.

"I'm not a socialist," she said.

"A *communist*?" Corinne asked.

"No, Corinne, I'm— It started as curiosity, that's all. You and Phillip were both off at school. A friend of a friend told me about these meetings, of people who just enjoyed sharing ideas. She said it was powerful."

"So you went to one?"

Again her mother faltered. "I've been to several."

The car swerved again. Mrs. Wells leaned forward to grasp her son's shoulder. Her eyebrows were drawn together in consternation.

"Please, Phil, you have to believe that I would never do anything to hurt your campaign. I always stay in the back of the room so that no one will recognize me. When you announce your candidacy, I promise I'll stop."

Phillip didn't say anything. His gaze remained locked resolutely on the road.

"Does Father know?" he asked at last.

Mrs. Wells sat back in her seat and nodded. "He doesn't like it, but he's never stopped me."

Phillip shook his head in disbelief. Corinne laughed shortly.

"An arrest scandal and socialist propaganda," she said. "My, how the mighty Wellses have fallen."

"Don't talk like that," her mother said, grabbing her hand. "I don't think Gabriel recognized me, but you can't go near him again. I'm not a socialist, but I think that he must be."

"I know."

"You're not listening to me, he's— Wait." Her mother reached out and turned Corinne's chin, so that they were eye to eye. "You know?"

"It's not as if he murders puppies or anything. Obviously you don't find the ideas all that terrible, if you keep going back for more."

Her mother's forehead creased, but she didn't deny it. Corinne had never seen her mother in this light before. She had never thought of her as someone with ideas—other than ideas for the next dinner party. She also wasn't particularly pleased with the notion of her mother under the same roof as Silas Witcher, perhaps even speaking with him or shaking his hand. But that was a concern for another day.

"What will people say if they find out?" Mrs. Wells said softly.

"They won't," Corinne said. "You said it yourself. We'll never speak of this to anyone."

"She's right," Phillip said.

Mrs. Wells looked between her two children and nodded to herself, relief settling visibly over her. "I'll just be glad when we're all home," she said.

Corinne stared at the passing streetlights through the window. She recognized the neighborhood they were in.

"Unfortunately, the night's not over for me yet," she said.

"What's that supposed to mean?" Phillip asked.

Corinne turned back to her mother and clasped her hand. "I'm so sorry for what I'm about to do. It's the only way, and if you don't want me to end up back in Haversham, you won't call the cops."

Her mother's expression was disturbed. "Corinne, what are you—"

"But often, in the din of strife,
There rises an unspeakable desire
After the knowledge of our buried life;
A thirst to spend our fire and restless force
In tracking out our true, original course. . . ."

For a couple of seconds her mother only stared at her in confusion. Then a cow appeared in the middle of the road. Phillip cursed and threw on the brake. As soon as the car stopped, Corinne threw open the door and ran. She ducked through the side streets and alleys so that they couldn't follow, angling her way in the direction of the Cast Iron.

She could hear her mother's shouting, but it was soon drowned out by the rush of cold wind in her ears. She ran all the way to the club, sliding on the icy sidewalk at every corner. She fell only once, a block away, but picked herself up before her knees and palms could even start stinging. Her chest was heaving when the red front door finally came into sight. She ducked down the narrow passage between the Cast Iron and the empty store next door. She slowed her run when she saw Gabriel in the back alley, leaning against the brick wall beside the door. His left hand was shoved into his coat pocket, and he held a lit cigarette in his right.

When he saw her, he straightened up. His features were as cool and inscrutable as always, but she couldn't stop thinking about his face the last time she had seen him, just before they took him away. Vulnerability wasn't something she'd ever expected to see in Gabriel Stone.

"Is Saint downstairs?" she asked him, resting her hands on her knees to gasp in a few breaths.

He nodded, taking in her disheveled appearance without any clear indication of what he thought about it. "He's asleep, I think. Are you okay?"

"Well, I'm not dead," she said.

"Where's Ada?"

"Being a noble idiot. You get out early for good behavior?"

"Turns out it's not actually illegal to be in the wrong place at the wrong time. They released everyone they took to the station. I'm guessing Haversham wasn't so forgiving?"

Corinne's mind flitted past the wooden door, down the dark steps, and across the iron floor. So many people dead and already forgotten. She wouldn't let that happen to Ada.

"Ada's still there," she said. "The HPA agents are coming. We have to get Saint and get out of here."

"Wait." Gabriel grabbed her wrist before she could open the

door. "I should have told you sooner that I knew the Witchers. I'm sorry."

Corinne looked at him, unsure what to do with the sudden apology. He hadn't changed out of his tuxedo yet, though he had unbuttoned his coat enough to loosen his tie. Corinne could see that the shoes and the cuffs of the trousers were ruined from Silas's sorry excuse for an escape route.

"It doesn't matter now," she said.

She expected him to protest with another apology, but she should have known better.

"I suppose it doesn't," he said. "How did you get out of the asylum?"

"Apparently my brother's marrying into the Haversham family grants me some privileges."

"So what makes you think they're coming here?"

"It's a long story."

His hand was still around her wrist, and she wondered if he could feel the unsteady rhythm of her pulse. The chandeliers and champagne of the rehearsal dinner felt faraway now. The world had shrunken into this dark alleyway, crowded on all sides by the terror of the asylum and the ache of missing Ada already and the feeling that maybe she should say something more to Gabriel Stone, but she couldn't think of what.

"Your hand is bleeding," Gabriel said. His brow furrowed as he turned her hand over.

Corinne looked down at the blood from the scrape on her palm. "I'll live."

"Cor, I didn't think I'd ever see you again," he murmured.

Corinne's head was ducked, but she could feel him looking down at her. The last time he had been this close, they had been in the car, and she had felt his warm breath on her lips. Corinne wasn't sure why, in this moment of all moments, she was remembering how that felt. Or why she couldn't shake the thought that if she lifted her face and stood on tiptoe, her lips would meet his without any trouble at all.

Corinne was positive that if she kissed Gabriel at that moment, he would kiss her back.

But the smell of sewage reached her nostrils, and the steel in his gun was intruding on her consciousness as a bare twinge of pain. Miles away, in the depths of Haversham Asylum, Ada was sitting in handcuffs, alone.

"I have to wake up Saint," she said.

There was a sound at the end of the alley. When a lurching figure turned the corner at the edge of the building, Corinne was so relieved that it wasn't Wilkey or Pierce that she almost didn't react. He was hunched under an oversized coat, and his steps dipped and swayed with the roiling of an invisible sea.

It was Harry.

Corinne swore under her breath right as he saw them. He stumbled faster toward them, arms outstretched in pleading.

"You're here," he said. "Everything is dark, and I can't see straight. Corinne, you gotta help me. I just need some blue skies and sunshine. Just need to shake the ghosts loose."

He looked worse than the last time she had seen him. The skin was sagging around his emaciated face, and his eyes were cavernous in his skull. Corinne felt that she was in Haversham again, staring into the dying man's face as his blood trickled away, but it was the hemopath clubs that had drained the life from Harry. She shuddered when his grimy fingers touched her sleeve. It was a light touch—spectral, as if he already had one foot in the grave.

"I can't help you," she told him.

"You won't help me."

His fingers curled around her arm, but there was no strength in them. To her right, Gabriel moved, as if to push Harry away, but she pressed her free hand against his elbow to stop him. She peeled Harry's fingers away from her sleeve. She used to think that edgers were weak, but now she was thinking about that moment in Silas Witcher's office, when he had laid down a few words and twisted her brain into darkness. And the way Ada's song had climbed into her head and forced her to leave her best friend behind. Their gifts were a double-edged sword.

The Cast Iron and the Red Cat had given Harry blue skies and sunshine, without warning him of the ghosts that crept through the cracks. Without warning him that every song and poem he chased led him closer to the edge.

What must it be like, to crave your own destruction?

"I'm sorry," she whispered.

Stooped as he was, his eyes were close to hers. Once they might have been a clear gray, but now they were bloodshot and murky.

"Where's Ada?" he asked.

She was still holding his quivering fingers in her hand.

"She's in trouble," Corinne said. "I can't help you because I have to help her."

Harry dragged his hands across his face. His fingernails were torn and bleeding. She couldn't tell if the dampness on his cheeks was sweat or tears.

"Ghosts in my head," he murmured. "God help me, I don't know what to do."

Neither did Corinne. She reached out, tentatively, but let her hand fall short. He would find no comfort in her touch. For the first time, she wondered if they were wrong trying to put every-thing back to the way it was before. She wondered if they were any better than Dr. Knox.

"Corinne," Gabriel said.

He didn't have to say more. Corinne remembered why they had come, how much they had to lose. She nodded, and he opened the door. She made it two steps into the storage room before she turned and walked out again, brushing past Gabriel.

Harry was on the ground with his head between his knees. His shoulders were shuddering, though he made no noise. Corinne crouched beside him and quoted into his ear.

> "Who shall hear of us
> in the time to come?
> Let him say there was
> a burst of fragrance
> from black branches."

The shuddering stopped, and he breathed deeply and released. A rich, rushing sound. Corinne left him with a head full of blue skies and sunshine and went back to the open doorway. Gabriel was standing there, watching her with an expression she didn't understand.

"What?" she asked.

For a couple of seconds, he just kept staring. Then he shook his head. "Nothing," he said.

He stepped aside to let her enter first, and Corinne went inside without looking back at Harry. She didn't want to think about the double-edged sword right now. There wasn't time.

· · · · · ◆ · · · · ·

Ada's solitude lasted only a few minutes before Dr. Knox returned. He blinked in confusion at the new placement of her chair but didn't address it. He took his seat again and flipped to a clean page in his notepad. Ada still couldn't reconcile his brisk, professional demeanor with the dank horror of their surroundings.

"Now," he said, "I believe my files on you and Wells are sufficient, but there are some items missing from Sebastian Temple's. Tell me about his affliction."

Ada stared at him, trying to fumble her way through her own confusion and weariness to a reply. "His affliction?" she echoed.

"His hemopathy," Dr. Knox said with an impatient wave of his hand. "His talent. I don't know the slang you people use for it."

Ada swallowed and shifted her stare to the floor. She didn't speak.

"Remember the rule, Ada," Dr. Knox said, pulling a second iron coin from his pocket and setting it on the table. "I'm afraid I can't make any exceptions."

Ada's stomach turned so violently that she thought she might be sick. She wished, for the fifteenth time in so many minutes, that Corinne were still beside her. Then she berated herself for wanting that. Corinne was free so that she could help Saint. It was the only way.

"We know about the Cast Iron's secret basement," Dr. Knox said in response to her silence. "Agent Wilkey and Agent Pierce are on their way now to pick up Temple. There's nothing you can tell me that I won't find out for myself in a couple of hours. I just want to speed up the process. Now tell me about his affliction."

Ada hesitated, unable to pull her eyes away from the iron coin. Such a simple, unobtrusive object to hold such a consuming threat of agony.

Surely there was nothing wrong with telling Knox things that were already common knowledge.

"He's an artist," she said. "He can pull objects from his paintings."

Dr. Knox's hand fluttered again. "Yes, yes, I know all that," he said. "But I've been told that he can do more."

"Who?" The question burst from her before she could think twice. "Who is telling you all these things?"

"That's not relevant," Dr. Knox said. "Let's stay on task, shall we?"

Ada rested her head back against the wall, frustrated.

"I don't even know what you're talking about," she said. "He can pull anything from a painting that will fit through the canvas. I've never seen him do anything else."

"This is getting tiring," Dr. Knox said, setting down his notepad and picking up the coin. "I would have expected as much from the Wells girl, but I was hoping *you* would be more sensible than to lie to me."

"I'm not lying," Ada said, unable to keep a tremor from her voice. She was trying to remain strong and silent and unaffected, but with Corinne gone, she felt like she was missing that half of herself. With Corinne gone, she couldn't pretend this was just a game to be won. It was so much more than that. So much worse. "I've never seen him do anything else, I swear."

Dr. Knox tapped the edge of the coin on the table and regarded her with a crease between his eyebrows. Ada could hear her own heartbeat slamming against her chest. She was desperately relieved that she didn't know anything else. If she did, she knew she would tell him everything. That realization was an acrid taste in the back of her throat.

"All right," Dr. Knox said at last. He set down the coin and put away his notepad. "I'll get the rest once Temple and Wells are here."

He was getting up to leave, but Ada knew she had to at least try to find out more.

"Don't you think that the Wellses are going to notice when their daughter goes missing again?" she asked. She didn't even try to mute her panic. "Don't you think this will be the first place they'll look?"

The lightbulb flickered, casting Dr. Knox's thoughtful expression in and out of focus.

"Mr. Wells's intervention was a regrettable complication, but it won't make a difference," he said. "When the law against hemopathic activity passed, I was assured by Councilman Turner that I would be given every consideration for my work here."

"Ned Turner?" Ada knew that his embarrassment on the Harvard Bridge had driven the councilman to throw his full support behind the bill to outlaw hemopathy, and that he had been the chief reason it had passed, but she had never guessed his hatred for hemopaths would extend this far.

"I suggest you try to get some rest," Dr. Knox said, opening the door. "We'll start the next round of experiments soon, and I'll need you in fighting form."

Ada wanted to ask him how he expected her to get any rest in this hellhole, with steel around her wrists and the suffering on the other side of wall, but before she could open her mouth, the door had been shut and latched.

She was once again alone.

The basement of the Cast Iron was quiet and dark. Corinne hated seeing it like this. In the past there had always been a light burning somewhere, even in the middle of the night. She maneuvered her way through the common room by touch. She managed to avoid the armchair but bashed her shin on the edge of the coffee table, rattling the glass bottles. She cursed right as the light came on.

"You okay?" Gabriel asked from the light switch. There was a hint of amusement in his voice that Corinne opted to ignore.

"Never better," she said.

She went into Saint's room without knocking and was surprised to find the light on, bathing his paintings in a dingy yellow. Before she could speak, Saint's arms were around her in a fierce embrace.

"I thought you were dead," he told her.

Corinne coughed into his shoulder, and he released her.

"Where were you? Why didn't you call?" And then, when he'd had a chance to take in her bedraggled state: "What happened to you?"

"There's not enough time for the long or the short version," Corinne said. "We have to get out of here. The HPA is—"

When the door shut behind her, her first thought was that Gabriel had come into the room. She turned, but he wasn't there. There was a soft click, and her heart leapt into her throat before her mind had even registered what the sound was.

A key turning in the lock.

She tried the handle, because she didn't want to believe it, because she *couldn't* believe it.

"What's going on?" Saint asked behind her.

"Gabriel," Corinne said, pressing her cheek against the wood. "What are you doing?"

There was a moment of quiet, a moment when she still had hope, but then his voice came through the door.

"I'm so sorry, Cor."

Her disbelief was eclipsed almost instantly by a searing, blinding panic. She yanked at the handle, ignoring the blood coating her palm, and when that didn't work, she threw her weight into the door. It shuddered but didn't budge. Her breaths were stabbing pains in her chest. She couldn't stop thinking of that iron corridor, of the woman's screams echoing in her ears, and of Wilkey's sunny, stomach-turning smile.

You'll be back soon.

"They're going to take us both back there," she cried into the unyielding wood. "Gabriel, the things they're doing to hemopaths—it's—you can't—please."

"I don't have a choice." His voice was softer now, barely audible over the pounding of her pulse.

"Gabriel," she screamed, throwing her weight against the door again and again. "Gabriel!"

But there was no reply.

CHAPTER FIFTEEN

CORINNE DIDN'T GIVE UP HER ASSAULT ON THE DOOR UNTIL HER shoulder ached so badly she was afraid she had broken something. She turned to find Saint kneeling on the floor, putting final touches on a large canvas that leaned against the opposite wall. It was the outside of the Mythic Theatre at night, the marquee glowing orange and red, the sidewalk dark and slick with recent rain.

"If you're not too busy, you might consider helping me escape our doom," Corinne said.

Saint dabbed his brush on the palette. "Even if you did manage to knock down the door with a hundred and twenty pounds of raw obstinacy, how were you planning on dealing with Gabriel and his gun on the other side?"

He smudged the orange around the letter M to give it a bleary look in the misty air.

"I was leaning toward strangling him with my bare hands," Corinne said, dropping onto Saint's cot. "I'm open to suggestions, though."

"The door opens inward," he said. "All you're doing is exhausting yourself."

He was very matter-of-fact about it. His attention seemed to be mostly on his work. There were flecks of black paint in his auburn hair and a smudge of orange on his chin.

"So you just want to sit quietly and finish up your magnum opus until it's time for us to be dragged to the asylum?" Corinne asked.

Saint snorted. "It's hardly my magnum opus. At least I hope it's not." He frowned at it, considering. "A little derivative of Van Gogh, actually, but it'll do the trick."

"You mean trip up the HPA when they come through the door?"

Saint stood up, dusted off his trousers, and put the paintbrush into a cup. He sat down next to her on the cot and took her bleeding hand in his. He pulled a rag from his pocket and pressed it against her palm.

"I'm sorry about Gabriel," he said. "Really."

"He doesn't matter," Corinne said.

But she couldn't find any conviction to inject in her words. There were voices outside the door. Footsteps. Corinne thought of Agents Pierce and Wilkey sauntering arrogantly through the life they had built, and her pulse roared in her ears. Saint jumped to his feet and faced her.

"Come here," he said, offering her his hand.

"Why, Sebastian, are you going to propose?"

"You will literally be making sarcastic comments as they pour dirt in your grave, won't you?"

"Probably." She took his hand and stood up, keeping the rag gripped in her right palm.

"I've never done this before," Saint said. "Not with a person." His eyes were bright in the dim light. She could see that he was anxious, but there was also excitement there.

"If you're thinking about kissing me," Corinne said, "I'm not sure how to break this to you, but you're half in love with someone else, who happens to be a man."

He blushed at that but otherwise ignored her words.

"If this doesn't work, I'm sorry," he said.

"Saint, what the hell are you—"

He moved backward quickly, dragging her along. She saw that he was about to back straight into his wet painting and tried to pull him to a stop, but he kept tugging, until he was falling backward and Corinne was falling into him.

When she opened her eyes and rolled off him, she was lying on damp concrete. She looked up and saw the marquee lights of the Mythic Theatre, glaring red and orange.

"Saint," she said, struggling to her feet. "Saint, what did you do?"

She turned in a circle. Her shoulder was aching in rhythm with her heartbeat, radiating through her fingertips, but she ignored it. This part of town was mostly dark at this time of night, but there was no denying that they were in front of the Mythic Theatre, in all its shabby grandeur.

Saint was still lying on the ground. He was laughing.

"It worked," he said. "I've been doing cups and spoons and eggs for months, but it only works once for each painting, and I can't paint that fast."

"I can't believe this. The eggs—you should have told me." Corinne was still turning slowly, trying to get her bearings. Of course she knew exactly where they were, but it was hard to wrap her head around it. Only seconds ago they had been ten blocks away.

Saint climbed to his feet. "It never seemed important before."

"Are you joking? This is incredible, Saint. I can't believe this."

"You said that already." In the dimly glittering lights of the marquee, she could see that he was blushing again.

They went around the back of the theater, and Corinne banged again on the stage door. For a while there was no answer, but Corinne kept knocking, and eventually the panel slid open. James's face appeared, midyawn. His eyes were bleary and his hair rumpled.

"What?" he said, banging his forehead against the wood of the door. "What in the name of all things sacred are you doing here?"

"I brought Saint with me," Corinne said helpfully. "Let us in."

"Hello, Sebastian," James said, managing to sound vaguely cordial. He looked back at Corinne. "It's three in the morning. I'm going back to bed, and you can come back tomorrow. Or never. Not you, Sebastian, of course. You can come back whenever. But not at three in the morning. That is the point I'm trying to make here."

He started to slide the panel closed.

"There are HPA agents at the Cast Iron," Saint said quickly.

James hesitated but still didn't open the door.

"So? They were bound to raid it eventually."

"Gabriel is a rat," Corinne said. "He told them—I don't know—probably everything. And if he told them about the Cast Iron, you can bet he told them about you and Madeline."

James stared at her for a few seconds. He swore softly. Finally the door opened.

"Come on," he said, looking past them nervously, as if he half expected the agents to be on their heels.

They congregated in the dressing room, and James woke up Madeline.

"Maybe you're blowing this out of proportion," she said, once she had been brought up to speed. She was slumped on the couch in a black silk dressing gown, her dark hair in tangled disarray.

"Johnny's dead," Corinne said. "Luke Carson was run out of town for selling off his people as lab rats, and Silas Witcher is probably still at the asylum. There aren't any safe havens left for hemopaths in Boston."

"Well, I don't know what you expect us to do about it," Madeline said with a yawn. "James and I have always avoided Johnny and all the rest. We don't have anything to do with it."

"She's right," James said. "You're the ones who mixed us up in this. Maybe it's best if you both leave."

"James, listen to me," Saint said. His voice was taut but even. "Things are only going to get worse."

"We don't have anything to do with this," James said, echoing his wife's sentiment. "We just want to run our theater."

"We're past that now," Corinne snapped. "Gabriel saw everything. He knows everything. You don't get it, do you? What they're doing to hemopaths. Dr. Knox is a madman, and he won't be happy until he's sliced us all open and figured out what makes us tick."

James pursed his lips.

Madeline had sat up a little straighter. "You're exaggerating," she said, not as a statement but more as a probative question. "They can't get away with that. We have rights."

"They *are* getting away with it," Corinne said. "I've been there. I've seen it."

The iron corridors, the glistening white tile, the draining blood—she didn't think she would ever be able to *stop* seeing it.

"What are you suggesting, then?" James asked.

"We save Ada," Corinne said. "And then . . . I don't know. I really don't."

"We have to get her out of Haversham tonight," Saint said. "And I don't think we can pull it off without you two."

Madeline and James looked at each other, their conversation a silent one.

"I've always wanted to play a doctor," James said.

"The Mythic is in the red anyway," Madeline said. "I don't suppose some light felonies will do us any harm."

"Thank you," Corinne said. She had never meant those two words so much. She glanced at Saint. "Thank you."

"Please tell me there is an actual plan in place," Madeline said. "Or are we expected to come up with that as well?"

"I think I have an idea," Corinne said. "But we need a songsmith."

"Everyone who worked at the Cast Iron is gone," Saint said. "I don't know where to find them."

"Actually, I have someone else in mind," Corinne said. "We need to make a stop at the Red Cat."

CHAPTER SIXTEEN

THEY STAYED AT THE MYTHIC LONG ENOUGH FOR MADELINE AND James to get dressed and for Corinne to talk them through her plan. Then Corinne and Madeline set off for the Red Cat on foot, while James and Saint gathered the rest of what they needed from the theater.

"Meet us with the car in two hours," Madeline said as she and Corinne slipped into the alley. "Don't be late."

"We'll be there," James said.

"I'm serious. You two had better not waste any time canoodling. You're a married man, James."

James shut the door on her, and Madeline laughed.

The Red Cat was less than a mile away from the theater. The sky was heavy with the promise of more snow, and they both shivered in their coats as they walked.

"You think this will work?" Madeline asked when they were almost there.

"I've gotten into the Red Cat before," Corinne said. "Their security isn't as tight as they like to pretend."

"No, I mean everything. The whole plan."

"I don't know," Corinne said. "But I don't see what other choice we have."

"And then what?" Madeline asked softly. "Are we even going to be able to stay in Boston?"

Corinne was quiet for half a block. A taxi revved past them, its headlights momentarily blinding and then fading into the distance.

"I don't know, Maddy," she said at last. "I guess I don't really know anything right now."

"I gave up everything for that stupid theater," Madeline said. "Everyone thought I was mad. My family barely acknowledges me anymore. You know what my father's last words to me were? He told me he wished I had turned out better. Who says that on their deathbed?"

"Someone who was disappointed in his own life and wants to take it out on you," Corinne said.

"No," Madeline said. Her voice was faint, and Corinne could see her puffs of white breath as they passed under a streetlight. "Someone who really means it."

The Red Cat came into view. Its glittering sign still lit up the street, reflecting red and gold off the slick sidewalk. The doorman in his navy-blue uniform and cap was still standing watch, though there was no sound of music.

"Now's a good time for your brilliant plan," Madeline said, giving no evidence of her fragility moments before.

"You ever seen Eva Carson?"

"A couple of times. The Carsons show up at the Mythic occasionally."

"Think you can pull her off?"

Madeline considered, then nodded.

"Perfect," Corinne said. "Then we'll just walk in like you own the place."

Madeline closed her eyes for a few seconds, tilting her head to the left, then the right. She chewed on her lips, shook her shoulders loose, and cleared her throat. It wasn't an instant transformation. It was more like the pieces of Madeline that were most like Eva Carson—the big eyes, the puckered lower lip—became more like

Eva. The parts of Madeline that were nothing like Eva became less and less important, gradually eclipsed until suddenly the exact image of Eva was standing in front of Corinne. She picked at one of her red manicured nails and looked over Corinne with a haughty eye.

"Are we going to stand here all night then?" she asked. The voice wasn't exactly right, but it was close enough.

Corinne couldn't help but smile.

They went straight to the front door.

"Excuse you," Madeline said to the doorman, who blocked their way.

"Mrs. Carson?" he said, blinking. "I didn't see you go out."

"I was stealing a smoke," Madeline said, patting his lapel in a dismissive gesture. "I found this little vagabond while I was out there. We're going to have a chat inside."

The man looked between her and Corinne, his mouth gaping. "Mrs. Carson, if you want, I could—"

"I'm bored with you now," Madeline announced. She brushed past him, and Corinne followed, keeping her head low so that her smile wouldn't be so obvious.

They edged around the tables with the last sleepy patrons and ducked backstage. Somewhere along the way, Eva had vanished, and when they stood blinking in the dim backstage area, Madeline was standing beside Corinne again.

"Do we even know if he's here?" she whispered to Corinne.

"They would have just finished their last set. He's around here somewhere," Corinne said, though she wasn't as certain as she tried to sound.

After opening a few doors to empty rooms, supply closets, and one couple passionately necking in the dark, they finally found the back room where the band gathered, cleaning their instruments. Charlie was just tucking his French horn into its case when he saw them. He jumped up.

"What are you doing here?" he demanded in a low voice, crossing the room.

"Damn, Charlie, my man," said one of the musicians. "You get around, don't you?"

"Introduce us to your friends, Charlie," said another.

Madeline waved cheerily at them as Charlie herded them out of the room and slammed the door.

"We're not here to cause trouble," Corinne told him.

"Little late for that," he said, glancing around them nervously. They were alone for now.

"Ada's been taken to Haversham," Corinne said.

He started at that. "How did—"

"Listen to me, Charlie," Corinne said. She was so desperate that her words spilled out almost faster than she could think them. "I know the only illegal thing you've ever done is play these shows for the Red Cat, but we need your help. I've got a plan to save Ada, and honestly there's only a snowball's chance in hell that it will work—"

"That's the first *I'm* hearing of those odds," Madeline interjected.

"—and Ada is going to murder me when she finds out I dragged you into this," Corinne continued. "But I can't think of any other way, and there's no one else I can ask. Please—"

"Corinne," Charlie started.

"Just listen to me," Corinne insisted. "I know you haven't even known her a year, but she's my best friend in the entire world, and it's her own fault she's there alone right now, but I have to get her out. I'll do anything."

"Corinne—"

"Dammit, Charlie. Can't you at least consider it for a few seconds before you say no?"

Charlie raised his eyes heavenward and rubbed his finger across the bridge of his nose. "As soon as you're done yammering, maybe we can leave," he said.

Corinne blinked, caught off guard. "What?"

"If Ada's in trouble, of course I'm going to help her. I'll meet you out back in five minutes," he said. "Don't be seen."

Eva Carson was waiting for Madeline and Corinne outside the stage door. Beneath her fur-lined coat she wore a green silk dress and black gloves. Her golden hair was twisted atop her head, with an impeccable curl falling on either side of her face. Her arms were crossed.

"Damn," Madeline said. "I didn't do you justice, did I?"

Corinne elbowed her. Eva smirked at them. In the shadows of the alley, without her thick-necked husband beside her, she looked sharper. More dangerous.

"I never smoke after midnight," she said. "I also don't hire idiots."

"Good to know," Corinne said. "We were just leaving."

"Charlie Lewis is a good boy," Eva said, as if Corinne hadn't spoken. "He's been with us a long time."

Corinne waited for a threat, but it never came.

"He's got a shiner from one of the HPA agents your husband is in bed with," Corinne said.

Eva tossed her head and snorted. Somehow, she made it look like an elegant gesture. "Luke is no choirboy, but he would never work with the agency."

"I saw him take the bribe," Corinne said. "Last night when I was here."

Madeline had grabbed her wrist, but Corinne refused to back down. Someone had to answer for Luke Carson's crimes. It might as well be Eva. She was probably behind them all anyway.

"What you saw was my husband trying to pay them to leave our boys alone," Eva said. "But the HPA wouldn't take the money. If I had to guess, I'd say they have a better arrangement with someone else."

"The bulls?"

"Johnny Dervish."

Eva said it like a challenge. She was facing Corinne head-on. No more pouting smiles or tinkling laughs. Eva Carson was all business.

"Why would Johnny have anything to do with the HPA?" Corinne asked.

Eva shrugged without uncrossing her arms. "Maybe he was bargaining to keep the HPA away from the Cast Iron. Or maybe he knew that when enough of our crew disappeared, it would be Luke's head on the chopping block. Or maybe he just needed the money."

"I'm going to get to the bottom of this," Corinne said. "If you help me, then Luke will be able to come home."

For a moment she thought Eva was going to laugh. Instead, she let out a long sigh.

"Luke was a good husband," Eva said. "But he's done all he can for me, and he knows it. The Red Cat is my club."

"Cold," Madeline said.

Eva shrugged again. "He knew the deal when we got married,"

she said. "He's got enough money for a new life. Maybe one day he'll make his way back here. Until then, I've got bigger fish to fry."

She pushed between Corinne and Madeline to open the stage door.

"That's it?" Corinne asked. "No burly men with guns to take us for a ride?"

Eva did laugh this time. It was different than Corinne remembered—rich and full instead of twittering.

"I meant it when I said I liked you, Corinne. Stay out of my way, and I'll stay out of yours. And you'd better take care of Charlie."

The door clicked shut behind her, and Corinne exchanged a glance with Madeline.

"I changed my mind about being an actress," Madeline said. "I want to be her when I grow up."

CHAPTER SEVENTEEN

ADA WASN'T SURE IF HOURS OR MINUTES HAD PASSED SINCE Dr. Knox left. Her headache had faded—or rather, it had melted into her bloodstream so that her body held nothing but pain. The nausea came in waves, and she only barely managed to keep the contents of her stomach where they belonged.

She wondered if the agents had arrived at the Cast Iron yet, and if Corinne had made it in time. She wondered how badly it would hurt to die, and if her mother would ever know what had happened to her.

She wondered who at the Cast Iron had betrayed them.

She couldn't do anything but wonder, and that was worse than the steel on her skin.

When the latch on the door slid open, Ada struggled to sit up straight, to effect some semblance of fortitude, but in the end she was too exhausted. She slouched back down as the door opened to admit Agent Wilkey, who looked much more composed than when she'd last seen him. He smiled at her and picked up the metal gag from the table.

"Dr. Knox asked me to prep you for the second phase," he said almost casually. "He doesn't trust the nurses down here. Weak stomachs, you know."

Ada had thought that she was well past panic by now, but it reared in her throat again. Before she could attempt a desperate melody, Wilkey had fastened the gag in her mouth. Her headache flared again with renewed vigor, draining the little strength she had left. Wilkey half dragged, half carried her into the other room, past the rows of beds with white sheets covering the atrocities that had been committed underneath. The woman hooked up to the machine wasn't screaming anymore. Her breath came in crackling, irregular gasps. Someone had pulled a sheet over the man in the bed beside her. *Failed subjects,* Dr. Knox had called them.

At the far end of the room, near the door to the corridor, there was a wooden chair with dangling leather straps beside a table of metal instruments that blurred in Ada's vision. She realized with distant mortification that she was crying, but she couldn't stop the welling tears. Wilkey uncuffed her hands and pushed her into the chair.

She tried to rise, more from instinct than from any real thought of escape, but her arms and legs felt disconnected from her body. She was nothing but her pulsing headache and her hot tears. Without her violin or her voice, what power did she have?

Wilkey worked quickly, buckling the straps across her chest, arms, and ankles. Ada tried to remember the devastation she had wreaked on him, but it didn't make her feel any better. She had never wanted to use her talent to hurt people. She wanted to be like Charlie, playing hope and joy into places where there had been none before. Now she would never get the chance.

The thought of Charlie softened her headache somewhat but made the tears flow faster. He had told her that he loved her, and she'd given him nothing in return. Another chance lost.

Wilkey pulled something off the table, cradling it with both hands. It was a brass cagelike apparatus, a dizzying conglomeration of rods, screws, and knobs.

"I'll confess I'm not entirely sure how this thing works," Wilkey said conversationally. "Dr. Knox tells me that once it's tightened over your head, it will guide in those metal spikes I mentioned earlier. Of course, we'll have to drill the holes in your skull first."

He smiled at her again, an almost cherubic expression in his doughy features.

Ada fought back her surging nausea and broke from his gaze. The door to the corridor opened, and Ada clamped her fingers around the arms of the chair, expecting Dr. Knox. Would they give her anesthesia first? Maybe she would just go to sleep and never wake up.

When she first saw Johnny, she thought they must have already injected her with something. Johnny Dervish was dead. He couldn't be striding through Haversham's basement with the same confidence he'd once had in the Cast Iron.

When he spoke, his voice was so real that Ada realized she must be dead too.

"Wilkey, what the hell is going on here?" he asked, taking in the sight of Ada with a disturbed frown.

"You're not supposed to be down here," Wilkey replied. He set the apparatus back on the table with the utmost care.

"Dr. Knox owes me money." Johnny glanced at Ada. "And an explanation as to why he's taking my people."

"You're dead, remember?" Wilkey said. "They aren't your people anymore. And none of the other hemos you've given us survived the tests."

"That's not my problem. I delivered on my end of the deal, and I want my money. Where's Knox?"

"Busy."

Ada's head was pounding with every word they spoke. She thought about Stuart Delaney and the other Red Cat musicians Charlie said had gone missing. Her heart was stuttering as she looked down the length of the room at all the silent beds. Johnny had been selling hemos to the HPA? He'd been selling them into this hell?

She was misunderstanding. She had to be. She coughed around the gag, desperate to speak.

Johnny leaned over and loosened the straps behind her head, ignoring Wilkey's objections. The gag fell into her lap, and she sucked in a breath.

"Johnny"—but that was all she could manage. Her eyes were burning with tears again.

"Are you okay?" he asked her. "Don't worry. I'm going to get you out of here."

Wilkey laughed shortly. "As amusing as your selective compassion is, Dervish, you're not taking her anywhere. Dr. Knox has big plans for this one, and the other two you've been keeping all to yourself."

"They're just kids," Johnny snapped.

"So were a lot of the others," Wilkey said, gesturing toward the long line of beds. "And none of them were half as potent as this one. Dr. Knox isn't going to—"

The door flew open again. It was Dr. Knox this time, dragging Corinne by the arm. Ada wasn't sure if she was relieved or furious to see her down here again. They both stopped in their tracks when they saw Johnny.

"Johnny, you— I thought you were—" Corinne sputtered. She looked at Dr. Knox, then at Ada, but no explanation seemed forthcoming.

"Knox, just what do you think you're doing?" Johnny asked. His voice was low, dangerous.

Dr. Knox licked his lips, opened his mouth, shut it again. He had dropped Corinne's arm, but she didn't move. She was still staring at Johnny, her features balled up in confusion.

"My job," Dr. Knox said at last.

"We had a deal," Johnny said. "I want my money."

"Right, right," Dr. Knox said, bobbing his head. There was something wrong with him. He seemed bewildered. "Agent Wilkey, if you would be so kind as to—"

But he cut himself off and frowned.

Wilkey was shaking his head and chuckling. "Slagger bastard," he said, drawing his gun. "You almost had me."

"What are you talking about?" Knox demanded. He threw out an arm to shove Corinne back as she tried to move forward, which was the moment when Ada put it together.

"Knox's eyes aren't blue," Wilkey said, raising the gun.

Before his finger made it to the trigger, Johnny whirled on him, something glinting in his hand. Ada saw that it was his pocketknife half a second before he sliced it across Wilkey's throat. For a moment everything was still. Wilkey coughed once. It was a wet, horrible sound. The gun fell to the floor, and he pressed his hands against his neck. They were immediately rimmed with blood. He staggered, and Johnny gave him a shove. Johnny's expression was one of pure disgust as he watched Wilkey fall.

"I never liked you much," he said to the twitching form. Then he cast an appraising glance over Dr. Knox, who seemed to be sagging around the edges. "Let me guess. James Gretsky?"

"We all thought you were dead," James said, becoming himself again in less than the time it took for Ada to blink.

"How did you even get in here?" Johnny asked. He knelt down and started unbuckling Ada's ankles.

"We called ahead," Corinne said. "James imitated Mr. Haversham so that the nurse would have the gate open."

"And she bought that?"

"There may have been a very persuasive French horn in the background," James said.

"Where have you been?" Corinne asked.

"I'm sorry," Johnny said. He pushed his hands through his greasy hair. "I had to take care of some things, but it's over now."

He met Ada's eyes, and she felt him searching her. Trying to guess how much she had figured out. How much she was going to tell the others.

"Johnny, why?" she whispered.

She could see in his expression that his mind was racing, but she couldn't tell what choices he was weighing. She did know the moment he made his decision. She saw it in the set of his jaw, in the flash of regret in his eyes. He stopped his work, having freed only her left ankle, and sat back on his heels.

"You were never supposed to know," he said softly. "I tried to keep you both out of it."

"What are you talking about?" Corinne asked.

"Johnny, all those people." Ada's gaze was drawn over his shoulder, toward the rows and rows of unmoving bodies. They'd been snatched off the street and murdered by a madman's experiments. And Johnny had been the one to give them up.

"Can we talk about this later?" Corinne looked between the two of them, frowning. "We've got to get out of here."

She moved to help Ada but hesitated when Johnny stood. He turned his knife over once in his hands. Wilkey's blood still gleamed red along its edge.

"I can't let you leave," he said. "No one else can know."

He spoke so frankly, so simply. Then he drove his blade into Corinne's belly, aiming upward for her heart.

Ada's vision slanted, but in that moment her nausea and headache deserted her. She was left with nothing but the clarity of Johnny Dervish with a bloody knife in his hand, and Ada knew he was coming for her next. She closed her eyes and told herself to sing, but the music had deserted her too. A hot, aching sob was building in her chest. She couldn't breathe.

In a faraway and foggy part of her mind, she had the thought that maybe she couldn't live without Corinne. Maybe her lungs knew that. Maybe her heart would stop next.

When she heard Corinne's voice, echoing around her in a cloud of static, she almost couldn't comprehend the words.

"This is a public service announcement, brought to you by Gerard Manley Hopkins, who gave a lot more thought to the meaning of life than is strictly healthy."

The cavalier tone was entirely Corinne's. Ada opened her eyes to the impossibility before her and immediately felt sick again. James was kneeling on the floor, and the girl in his arms was Madeline, her long hair tangled around her face as she gasped for breath.

Johnny was staring down at them, knife in hand. He looked wildly around the room; then realization dawned on his face. Ada followed his eyes to the loudspeaker mounted over the door. Johnny swore and fumbled for his earplugs. He ran into the corridor.

"Maddy, come on," James was saying, his voice breaking. "Maddy, please."

Ada struggled against her restraints, but of course it was useless.

"James, you have to untie me," she said.

He didn't look up. Over the PA system, Corinne was flying through the poem at a breathless rhythm. Underneath her voice Ada could hear a sonorous tune, churning out persuasion so powerful that Ada almost lost herself in it. It was a French horn. She shook her head to break away from the music and whatever illusion Corinne's poem would conjure.

"James!" Ada cried. "Look at me. He might come back. We have to go."

At last he tore his gaze away from Madeline and laid her gently on the floor. He fumbled at the buckles with shaking hands but finally managed to free Ada's right wrist. She helped him with the other straps and jumped up. Together they dragged Madeline to her feet. She screamed through gritted teeth but stayed upright between them, her arms over their shoulders. Ada had never seen so much blood on a person. Madeline's pale pink dress was drenched in crimson.

They staggered through the iron-paved corridors. Ada kept looking over her shoulder, certain that someone would be following them. The hall remained empty. The loudspeakers were silent now, but the uneasy quiet was short-lived. A bell started ringing from the upper floor—the fire bell, Ada realized. Corinne's poem must have fabricated flames for everyone in earshot. Under the dual spell of her words and Charlie's horn, no reg without earplugs would have been able to resist.

She made sure that James had a good hold on Madeline and started to open the door.

"Wait," James said. His voice was hoarse. "Corinne said to wait."

"Wait for what?" Ada whispered.

"She said we'd know."

There were nurses running past, as well as a few men in suits who must have been HPA. None of them noticed that the basement door was cracked. Ada watched the flashes of color until there was no one left in the hall. Another few interminable seconds passed, and Ada itched with the impulse to throw open the door and run for freedom. She waited.

The speakers crackled again, and Corinne's voice filled the hall.

"That's all for tonight, ladies and gents. Don't forget to tip the band."

Ada pushed open the door and helped James and Madeline up the last few steps. The three of them weaved through the corridors toward the lobby. Madeline was gasping in her ear, and Ada's hand was so slick with blood that she could barely keep a grip on her.

Corinne and Charlie ran to meet them as they stumbled into the lobby. The fire bell was still clanging with deafening fervor. Looking over Corinne's shoulder, Ada saw that the desk nurse was slumped over her paperwork, snoring loudly.

"Go!" Corinne shouted.

Charlie wrenched open the front door. Corinne pushed at Ada and James from behind. They barely managed to keep Madeline supported between them. The cold air assaulted Ada as Charlie yanked the door shut behind them. He was saying something, but Ada couldn't hear him over Madeline's cries and the ringing echo of the fire bell in her ears.

Someone grabbed her arm, and Ada whipped her head around. It was Saint.

The world was cacophony and blood. Haversham's night-shift employees were scattered across the edges of her vision, watching them with numb confusion. Charlie's playing would only just be wearing off. Any second now they would start to realize what had happened. Saint pulled her across the gravel drive, away from the people. Ada couldn't focus on anything but Madeline's weight. She squeezed Madeline's wrist so hard that she couldn't tell if the erratic pulse she felt was Madeline's or her own. The doors to the asylum opened again, and Dr. Knox emerged, flanked by three HPA agents.

Ada realized that even if the gate was still open, they had nowhere to go.

She had the thought, brief but piercing, that they weren't going to make it. They were going to die in the basement of Haversham, strapped into chairs while Dr. Knox recorded the time in his little notebook.

Saint was still pulling on her arm. He wasn't leading her toward the car that was parked near the gate but onto the grassy lawn to the left of the drive. There was a blanket spread across the ground—no, it was a giant painted canvas, like a backdrop for a play. Ada recognized it from a recent production at the Mythic Theatre. That was all she had time to register before Saint stepped through the canvas, dragging her with him.

Corinne was last in the chain that Saint pulled through the backdrop. She felt someone's fingers—she didn't know if it was Dr. Knox or one of the agents—brush across her coat sleeve just before the painting swallowed her. She fell downward, feetfirst, but almost as soon as the asylum's lawn and iron gate disappeared, the world shifted and suddenly she was stepping forward. She closed her eyes against the twisting sensation, willing herself not to be sick. Charlie's hand fell from hers, and for a split second she was utterly alone, with only the solid ground beneath her feet to reassure her that she had made it to the other side.

When she opened her eyes, Corinne was staring across a body of water. The sun was starting to rise, inching over the horizon to her right. Boats bobbed on the choppy waves, their tiny lights twinkling in the hazy distance. Through the early-morning fog she could see the smokestacks and masts of the Navy Yard across the harbor. They were in the North End.

The clanging of the fire bell was gone, replaced by a faint buzzing in her ears.

She looked down to see James on his knees, clutching Madeline. There were angry streaks of red across his cheek and in his blond hair. Ada had pulled off her coat and was pressing it into the wound, but Corinne could already see that there was too much blood.

She knelt down on Madeline's other side and took her hand. She brushed the dark hair out of her face so that Madeline could see dawn blossoming in the sky overhead. James was sobbing in short, shallow bursts, gripping Madeline's arm as if he could somehow pull her back. Corinne looked pointedly at Saint, who knelt down beside James and put his arm around his shoulders.

"Guess I'm pretty good at being you," Madeline said to Corinne, her voice weak and slurred. She started to cough. More blood.

"It's my fault," Corinne said. She wasn't crying. It wasn't a lamentation or a plea for forgiveness. Just a statement of fact. There were a dozen different ways of sneaking into the asylum. Using Madeline and James as a distraction was the one she had chosen, and now Madeline was going to die.

Madeline shook her head, still coughing. "God, Cor, it's not all about you," she said. She made a wheezing sound like a laugh, then winced. "It hurts—really bad."

Corinne looked at Ada, who nodded and began to hum. After

a few seconds, Charlie joined in beside her. The song settled over them slowly, gently.

The pain in Madeline's expression began to fade. "James," she said. She had started to cry. "James, you'll be all right. Say you'll be all right." She gripped at the front of his shirt.

"Maddy," he said, taking her hand. "Maddy, hold on."

"Thank you for the Mythic," she said.

"You did that. It was all you, Maddy."

She smiled through her tears. "You are the best thing that ever happened to me," she told him. "And I'm not just saying that because I'm—I'm—"

She squeezed her eyes shut.

"Corinne," she said, her voice barely a whisper. "Cor, I always wanted to see Paris again. Just one last time."

Corinne gripped her hand more tightly and swallowed at the lump in her throat. She leaned forward to put her lips near Madeline's ear. She didn't have her grandfather's watch, but it didn't matter somehow with Madeline's limp hand pressed so tightly in her own. Her focus had never been so absolute. She whispered:

"Demain, dès l'aube, à l'heure où blanchit la campagne..."

It was a French poem about trudging alone through forests and mountains, about a bouquet of holly and heather and a grave to lay it on.

As she quoted, Madeline's eyes glazed over with the sights of Paris. By the time Corinne finished the last stanza, Madeline was gone. James buried his face in Saint's chest, his shoulders shaking. Corinne found her feet and walked closer to the water's edge.

The sun had almost broken free from the horizon, and the water reflected its light in blinding white.

For a long time she stared at the rippling waves, cresting toward the light, then falling back into the blue-black of the harbor. Eventually, Ada joined her.

"It wasn't your fault," Ada said.

Her voice was thick, and when Corinne glanced at her, she could see that Ada had been crying.

"I dragged them out of their beds," Corinne said. "I told them this was the only way, that if we did nothing, we'd all be human science experiments. I didn't give them any choice but to help me."

"You weren't lying," Ada said.

"I guess not," Corinne said. "Probably the first time in my whole damn life that I told the honest-to-God truth, and now Madeline's dead."

They stood without talking for several minutes, just letting the daylight wash over them. The day was going to be warm for this time of year. Corinne had the distant, irrelevant thought that her brother was getting married today.

"Where's Gabriel?" Ada asked.

The way she asked it was like she already knew the answer. Corinne bit her lip. She didn't want to think about her hand in his, or the lipstick on his cheek at the Lenox, or his mother calling him *myshka*.

She made herself think about the room in the basement of Haversham, the glossy tile floors so white beneath so much death. She thought about the woman screaming, the scratching of Dr. Knox's pencil, and the look in Ada's eyes as she sang Corinne into submission.

If Gabriel had told the HPA about the secret passage at Down

Street, then he was the reason that Ada and Corinne had been caught in the first place. He was the reason that Madeline was dead.

"He's been helping the HPA this whole time," Corinne said. "He was just going to let them take me and Saint back to the asylum."

She felt like there was more to say. There was so much more inside her, pushing to be free. She closed her eyes.

"Cor, we can't stay here," Ada said. "They're going to figure out where we are. Knox or Johnny or—"

"Johnny?" Corinne's eyes flew open, and she looked at Ada, whose lips were twisted with uncertainty.

"He was in the basement," she said. "He—"

"That's impossible," Corinne said.

She backed away from Ada and stalked toward the group. There was a sudden cluster of pain behind her eyes that made her feel ill.

"Just listen to me," Ada said, chasing after her.

"Johnny can't be alive," Corinne said. He would never have abandoned them to the HPA like that. He would never have let the Cast Iron go dark.

"Who else do you think stabbed Maddy?" James was climbing to his feet. He was covered in her blood.

"What did you just say?" Corinne demanded, her fingers clenching into fists.

"You heard me," James said, shaking off Saint when he tried to put a hand on his arm. "Your precious Johnny Dervish gutted Madeline with a knife when he still thought she was *you*."

Corinne fell back a step.

"He wouldn't do that," she said. Her vision was swimming with her headache. "It had to be someone else."

"You think I wouldn't know another thespian if I saw one?"

James asked. There was a terrible sneer on his face, birthed of all his rage and bitterness. "I'm sure it was in his best interest to play dead while Boston fell to pieces."

"You're wrong!" Corinne was dimly aware that she was shouting. "Johnny would never do this to us."

Ada's touch on her arm was whisper soft, and Corinne's tight fists loosened just the slightest bit.

"If it had been a thespian, he would have seen through Madeline's disguise," Ada said. "Johnny's been selling names of hemopaths to the HPA. He was there to collect his money. I think—I think he wanted to kill us so that we wouldn't tell anyone the truth."

The implications of Ada's words swarmed Corinne, adding to the anger and grief that had nowhere to go. She felt like the world was falling in on itself. Like something nameless had splintered inside her. She felt like she had when Gabriel had locked that door, when the first few notes of Ada's song had wrapped around her mind.

She felt broken.

CHAPTER EIGHTEEN

WITHIN HALF AN HOUR, THE SHORE WAS EMPTY ONCE AGAIN, with only a dark stain seeping into the winter ground to tell of the morning's tragedy. James had refused to leave Madeline, and so it was decided that he would take her to the hospital with a story of a mugging. He promised to meet up with them later, but Ada wasn't sure when that would be, and if he would even be able to find them.

Ada had led the others into the safety of the city, keeping to the empty side streets. She was ahead of the others, with Charlie a few steps behind her, and Saint trailing even farther back with Corinne, who hadn't said a word since they'd left the shore. She had that same fatalistic look in her eye that she'd had outside Down Street and in the basement of Haversham, only now it was tinged with defeat instead of determination. Ada had never felt so far away from her before, even when they were miles apart.

There was a knot of grief and guilt and fury balled up so tightly in Ada's chest that she could barely breathe. When she'd shaken hands with Johnny Dervish four years ago, on the day she'd first decided to help Corinne on a con, she had never dreamed it would end like this. All she had wanted was enough money to give her mother a good life, and maybe the chance to take back some of the power that had been stripped from her because of the color of her skin, the affliction in her blood.

Now everything she'd worked for was falling to pieces, and Madeline Gretsky was dead.

Ada jumped when she felt a touch on her arm. It was Charlie. His fingertips were warm.

"Take my coat," he said.

Ada shook her head, but he had already slid out of it and was dropping it on her shoulders.

"Thank you," she said.

She didn't know what else to say. He was so close to her, the backs of their hands brushing with every step. In the clear sunlight, the bruising around his eye was a myriad of purples and greens, subtle shades in the brown of his skin. She wanted to ask him if it hurt, to caress every inch of his face that wasn't bruised. She wanted to tell him she was sorry, even though she didn't know what she was sorry for, exactly.

All of Boston felt faraway and irrelevant in the face of the night's events. Ada was adrift in a vast ocean, and Charlie was the distant shore. He was so tall and imperturbable, with his horn dangling from his left hand, with a soothing tune in the back of his throat.

"I'm sorry you got caught up in this," she said.

"I'm not."

She knew that should make her happy. Instead, her aching chest tightened further. She sucked in a breath of the morning air and swiped the back of her hand across her eyes before the tears could form.

"You remember when you said you felt like there were things I wasn't telling you?" she asked. She kept her voice quiet, so that only Charlie could hear. Saint and Corinne were still half a block behind them.

"Yes."

"That's because there are," she said. "If you even knew half of the things I've done for money—twisting people up inside, stealing their memories, forcing them to remember what they would rather forget—then I'd lose you. I know I would. And I can't stand the thought of it, but it's not fair for you, Charlie. You've never done anything but give people hope and joy, and I don't think I've ever done anything but take it away from them."

Charlie was quiet for a while, his eyes fixed steadily ahead.

"I think you're being too hard on yourself," he said at last.

The city was coming to life around them. Ada could hear the revving of cars and the blare of work whistles from the direction of the docks. Even from the narrow side street they were walking, she could smell the bread from a bakery a few blocks over.

Ada's breath escaped her like a sigh. "Tonight I used a man's worst memories to crush him, because I thought he deserved it. And even when I could see that he'd had enough, I kept going."

She could feel Charlie's gaze on her profile, but she didn't look at him. She didn't want to read his thoughts on his face. From the corner of her eye, she could see him rolling up his sleeve.

"Did I ever tell you why I got this?" he asked.

Ada glanced over to see the leafless tree inked on his forearm, its branches black and twisting. She shook her head.

"When I was a little boy, I used to climb a tree just like this every day of the week." He rubbed his thumb absently along the trunk. There was a single line etched between his eyebrows at the memory. "Then one morning I went out to climb, and they'd hanged a man from the branches. After that, I never went near it. I started having nightmares so bad that I woke the neighbors. Finally, months later, my mother made me pick a bunch of wildflowers from the yard. Then she took me by the hand and led me straight down the road to that old tree. There were budding leaves on it and a bird's nest right where the rope had been tied. And my mother said to me, 'Charles, sometimes there's more bad in this world than good, and sometimes it's the other way round. But nature ain't good or bad, and it can't help that some people get so mixed up that they can't tell one from the other.'"

They passed briefly into the sunlight. Charlie's eyes flashed golden, while the bruising on his face shone in ugly contrast.

"She told me that because of people like that, I wasn't going to have a lot of choices in this life," he said. "But one thing I could always choose was to do more good than bad. Then she climbed up to sit on the lowest branch, and I sat beside her, and we dropped the flowers one by one in remembrance, until the wind took them all away. The day she got sick, I got this tattoo, so that I would never forget what she told me."

There was a hitch in his voice at the last, and his Adam's apple lurched with a swallow.

"Ada, there's nothing you can say or do to convince me that you're a bad person," he said. "I just think you get so caught up in the choices you don't have that you forget the one you do."

Ada had a memory of her own mother pulling Ada's hair into braids and telling her that if everyone would just give more than they took, then the world would be a better place. Maybe there was still a chance for her to do more good than bad in her life. On impulse, Ada reached out to take Charlie's forearm in her hands. She ran her fingertips along the tree, tracing the branches, then entwined her fingers with his.

If she was honest with herself, she'd known a long time ago that she and Charlie had left "simple" behind. But maybe it was better this way. Maybe it was worth it.

Now that the painful knot in her chest had started to loosen,

Ada realized that she had no idea where they were going right now. They couldn't go back to the Cast Iron, or anyplace else where Johnny might think to look for them. With the HPA on their trail too, there might not be a safe place in all of Boston.

Ada glanced over her shoulder at Corinne, to see if she had shaken off the despondency that had claimed her at the waterfront. In the past, Corinne had always met her gaze with instinctual accuracy, but this morning Corinne's eyes were locked on her feet. Ada looked ahead again with a pang. When she and Corinne weren't in step, the whole world was off balance. Corinne was always the one with the plans and the drive to set them in motion. Ada was more comfortable pointing out the flaws in the plan and then salvaging it whenever Corinne decided to go ahead anyway. But they'd been walking for fifteen minutes now, and she still had not heard a word from Corinne.

What if their escape was just delaying the inevitable? What if Madeline's death was for nothing?

"I don't know what to do next," Ada said, not loud enough for Corinne or Saint to hear. Barely loud enough for Charlie to hear.

He squeezed her hand a little tighter.

"I think I know where we can go," he said.

Eva Carson lived above the Red Cat, behind a black door with a permanent sign reading: PRIVATE. Charlie didn't seem concerned about it when he knocked, despite the ungodly hour of the morning. The staircase was at the back of the club, blending in with the mahogany-paneled walls. Corinne waited at the bottom of the steps with Ada and Saint, thinking about how eerie the club was in the empty daytime. The tables were all stacked with chairs, and the bar was polished and bare. There was an abandoned mop and bucket onstage.

Eva answered the door in a violet silk robe, her hair a tangled mess around her shoulders. She said something sharp to Charlie, then glared down the stairs at them. Finally she snapped something else and disappeared back inside. The door slammed shut.

"That didn't sound good," Ada said.

"It's all jake," Charlie said. "She said we could crash in the wine cellar for a few hours."

"And then what?" Corinne asked.

They couldn't hide in the Red Cat indefinitely. Corinne hadn't even wanted to come here in the first place. Eva had told her to stay out of her way, and Corinne was inclined to take that seriously.

The wine cellar was the size of the common room in the Cast Iron, and Corinne was momentarily impressed by the rows upon rows of corked bottles tilted on the shelves. In the dim light, the bottles reminded Corinne of the handful of sea glass her brother had shown her one summer on Martha's Vineyard, all dusky greens and oceanic blues.

Charlie had rustled up some blankets from somewhere and was laying them on the floor. Saint had already flopped down on one, burying his head in his arms. Corinne slipped down another tight aisle of shelves, running her fingers along the glass. She pulled out a bottle and tried to read the label, but it was in German, accompanied by a sketch of a castle.

"*Liebfraumilch,*" said a voice behind her.

Corinne turned to face Eva Carson. She was still in her robe, with her hair now pulled into a loose braid.

"Not my favorite," Eva said. "I prefer a good brandy."

Corinne slid the bottle back into place. There was still some blood crusted under her fingernails, and she felt momentarily nauseated. She squeezed her hands into fists at her sides.

"Thanks for putting us up," she said to Eva.

"It's only for a few hours." Eva examined her own nails, picking at a cuticle. "I still might change my mind if I don't like your explanation as to why you've shown up at my doorstep at six in the morning."

"Ask Charlie." Corinne had no desire to talk about the night before, much less with Eva Carson.

"I'm asking you."

"Madeline Gretsky's dead," Corinne snapped. "Johnny killed her while he was trying to kill us."

A wrinkle formed in Eva's brow, but she wasn't shaken. "Why?"

Corinne tried to move past her, but Eva grabbed her wrist. Her nails dug into Corinne's skin.

"Why?" she asked again. Her voice had a barbed edge.

"You were right about him," Corinne said, jerking her arm away. She stumbled back into the shelf. Glass rattled, but nothing fell. "He was trading hemopaths to Haversham for money, like we're goddamn baseball cards."

Fury, restrained but undeniable, flashed across Eva's face. Most of the victims had been Carson's crew. Corinne wondered how many had been Eva's friends, or if a woman like Eva even had friends.

"Why did he fake his death?" Eva asked. "What else is he planning?"

"I don't know," Corinne said.

"You're lying."

"Do you think if we knew *anything*, we'd be crawling to you for help?" Corinne demanded.

"I think you know more than you're telling me, and if it's something that puts my business in danger, I have a right to know."

Eva was much taller than Corinne, and the shadows cutting across her face transformed her graceful features into a portrait of severity. Corinne had the uncomfortable thought that if Eva was a hemopath, she had no idea what kind. If she didn't know what to expect, she couldn't guard herself against it.

"Cor, come on." Ada was at the other end of the aisle. She had shed Charlie's coat, revealing the rust-colored blotches all over her dress.

Corinne watched Eva take in Ada's appearance, watched the twinge of horror in her expression when she realized it was blood. That made her feel better somehow. She went to stand by Ada.

"Is Madeline really dead?" Eva asked. The severity was muted now. She hadn't taken her eyes off the stains on Ada's dress.

Corinne nodded.

"And Silas Witcher was taken to Haversham?" Eva said.

"Yes," said Corinne.

Without her lipstick, Eva's lips were a pale pink. She pressed them together and shook her head.

"I don't like admitting when I'm wrong," she said. "I never trusted Dervish further than I could throw him, but even that was too much apparently. I should have helped you two when you came to the Red Cat that night to talk to Luke. If the HPA got to Witcher, then they can get to any of us."

"They already have," Corinne said. She was thinking about Gabriel again, about how much he knew, about how much she had *told* him.

"So what can I do?" Eva asked. She had recovered from her temporary distress and stood as regal as ever. She might as well have been wearing a coronation gown. Corinne couldn't fathom how she had ever thought that Luke Carson was in charge.

"Nothing yet," Corinne said, exchanging a glance with Ada.

"Just let us stay for a couple of hours," Ada said.

"And what are you planning on doing after that?" Eva asked, her left eyebrow cocking.

"Something daring and stupid, I'm sure," Corinne said, locking her arm with Ada's.

"Our specialty," Ada said.

Eva's eyes, canny and calculating, scrutinized each of them in turn.

"You're both really quite young, aren't you?" she said, and shook her head. "The liquor truck only delivers on Thursdays, so you can stay until five, when the club opens."

She lifted her hand in what was ostensibly a wave but felt more like a dismissal. Then she left.

Corinne and Ada stayed behind the shelf, listening to her footsteps creaking on the stairs.

"Did the most powerful woman in Boston just offer to be our ally?" Corinne asked, once the door had shut.

"Seems like it."

"I feel like we should celebrate. There should be cake or something."

"There's plenty of champagne," Ada said, dragging her fingers across the bottles. "But honestly, sleep sounds like a better reward right now."

Corinne laughed. It felt strange, like the mirth was seeping through the cracks in her anger and grief. Ada smiled, but there was something sad behind her eyes. The moment was suddenly heavy, as if they had both just remembered what still hung between them.

"I wish there had been another way," Ada said.

In her quietest moments, Corinne could still feel Ada's melody in her head, sliding through the edges of her consciousness. She wondered if it would ever truly leave her. She wondered if all the people they had ever entertained or conned were carrying around pieces of poems and songs deep inside them, maybe never to be remembered, but certainly never to be forgotten.

Gabriel had asked, *How can you realize what it's like for the rest of us?*

Maybe for the first time, she knew.

Wordlessly, she lifted her hand, palm up. Ada smiled again, and this time it was genuine. She tapped her fingertips against Corinne's, then threw her arms around her in a fierce embrace. Corinne coughed a little at the impact, though she didn't try to pull away. There was more she wanted to say, like that she didn't think she would be able to sleep because she could still feel Madeline's hand in hers, or that a small part of her believed that this was all a mistake and Johnny was innocent, or that when she thought about Gabriel, her stomach cinched into knots, and she couldn't breathe. She didn't say any of those things right now. She knew she would, in time.

When Ada finally pulled away, they went to lie down on their makeshift pallets. The boys were already asleep. Charlie was on his back, an arm flung over his face. Saint was curled into a ball, snoring softly. As she'd predicted, Corinne couldn't sleep. Her mind raced through the day before, skipping over everything she wanted to focus on and instead lingering horribly on the worst parts, on Madeline in the dead grass, on James sobbing like a child, on Gabriel in the Cast Iron, and on Eva Carson asking the question that Corinne couldn't answer and couldn't escape.

What else is he planning?

"The liquor truck only comes on Thursdays," Corinne said out loud. She sat up so quickly that her head spun.

Charlie rolled over. Saint jolted a little but didn't wake up.

"What?" Ada mumbled.

"Charlie," Corinne said, and when he didn't respond, she shouted: "Charlie!"

He jerked upright and looked around in bewilderment. "What's wrong?" he asked.

Ada had propped herself onto her elbows and was staring at her.

"How many bottles of liquor does the delivery truck bring here every week?" Corinne asked Charlie.

He stared at her for several seconds, his mind clearly trying to catch up to her words.

"I don't know," he said. "A truckload."

"Saint," Corinne said, turning to him. "Saint . . . *Sebastian.*"

Saint made an exasperated noise and stretched out flat. "What?" he demanded of the ceiling, his voice hoarse.

"You're around the Cast Iron the most. How often did Johnny take deliveries?"

"Why would I pay attention to that?"

"Think!"

"Once a week, I guess. Or twice."

"What about at the warehouse? The one on the wharf?"

"Almost every night," Saint said. He sat up and ran his hands down his face.

"What is it, Cor?" Ada asked.

"The Red Cat has just as many customers as the Cast Iron, and they only go through one delivery of liquor a week. Why is Johnny taking deliveries at the warehouse every night?"

"How do you know it's alcohol being delivered?" Charlie asked.

"I've been there before," Saint said. "I helped them unload a couple times a few years ago, before Johnny hired Tom Glenn."

"I've never been there," Corinne said. "How big is it?"

"Takes up almost a whole block. It was mostly empty back then, though."

"I bet it's full now," Corinne said.

Ada sat up and crossed her legs, tugging the blanket over her lap.

"The Eighteenth Amendment," she said. "If one more state ratifies it, Prohibition will go into effect next year."

"And Johnny thinks the law will pass," Corinne said.

"So he's been hoarding liquor?" Charlie asked.

"Ever since the law banning public hemopathy passed, the Cast Iron has been struggling," Ada said. "The warehouse must have been his ace in the hole."

"He kept it a secret so that none of his competitors would catch on," Corinne said. "He's probably been using the money from the HPA to stay afloat, trying to buy himself time to finish stocking the warehouse."

"But that doesn't explain why he faked his death," Saint said.

Corinne swallowed hard. Her head was pounding again. She looked at Ada, who was twisting her blanket between her fists, her expression dark.

"We're dead weight," Ada said. "He knows he can't keep the club open anymore, not with a ban on both hemopathy and alcohol."

"He probably thought we'd all scatter once he was gone," Corinne said.

"Most of the crew did," Ada said. "When Prohibition takes effect, Johnny will have the largest stock of liquor in Boston— probably in the whole Northeast. He'll be rich."

"And he won't have to split the profits with anyone," Corinne said.

"What a piece of shit," Charlie said, dropping back onto the floor.

"We've been wrong this whole time," Ada said. She lay down too. Her voice was soft with weariness. "All those cons we pulled, all those people we robbed—we thought we were doing it for the Cast Iron, so that we would be safe. But we were just propping up Johnny on his throne."

"As a particularly pretentious ass once told me," Corinne said, "kingdoms always crumble."

"So what are we going to do?" Charlie asked.

"I don't know." Corinne flopped down and crossed both arms over her face. She didn't want to think about Johnny, about how easy it had been for him to use them—and how eager she had been to be used. She had spent her whole life trying to always be the cleverest person in the room, and it was just now occurring to her how boundless her own stupidity was. "We should lie low, I guess, for now."

"Doesn't sound like you," Saint said.

"Maddy's dead," Corinne said, a little sharply. "None of us is going to be next."

"She's right," Ada said. "Besides, she's got a wedding to attend this afternoon."

Corinne groaned.

CHAPTER NINETEEN

By the time they had all woken and washed up as best they could, it was nearly two o'clock in the afternoon. Ada spent a full fifteen minutes convincing Corinne that she had to attend her brother's wedding.

"You won't exactly be able to keep a low profile if your mother calls the National Guard to search for you," Ada argued. "Besides, the president himself wouldn't dare interrupt that wedding. You'll be safe there."

"What do you mean, me?" Corinne demanded. She looked up from the spot of dried blood on her dress that she was scrubbing at furiously with a damp cloth. "You're coming too."

"Look at me, Cor. I could play a whole sonata and still not convince your family to let me through the doors of that church," Ada said. "Besides, I don't want to go."

Corinne made a face at her but didn't have a ready response. Ada decided that now was as good a time as any to break the news.

"I'm going to see my mother."

Corinne's gaze snapped back to her.

"You can't. The HPA knows where she lives."

"Surely we caused enough of a ruckus at the asylum to divert them for a while."

"You don't know that." Corinne waved the rag with more dramatics than was strictly necessary.

"I'll take Charlie with me."

"And what exactly is Charlie going to do?"

"I don't know." Ada shrugged. "Safety in numbers, I suppose."

Corinne snorted in a way that would make her mother weep. "If that's what you want to call it."

"I'm sure I don't know what you mean," Ada said, fanning herself with mock indignation. But she was relieved that Corinne didn't seem inclined to press the matter further.

Charlie turned out to be even more against the idea than Corinne. It took Ada threatening to go by herself to convince him to come along. Their walk across town—which involved mostly side streets and back alleys—was more silent than Ada would have liked, but she couldn't think of anything worthwhile to say. After their dawn conversation and the revelations about Johnny, everything else seemed trite in comparison. It did occur to Ada, when they neared her mother's street, that Charlie might be afraid. He'd had a close brush with the HPA and could have ended up with a lot worse than a black eye.

She wanted to ask him, but it seemed an unfair question somehow.

Ada wasn't afraid. She knew she should be, but last night had wrung her out. She didn't have the capacity for fear anymore. She just wanted to make sure her mother was safe.

They approached the street cautiously. The agents' car was nowhere to be seen, but Ada knew that didn't mean anything. They could very well be inside the front lobby waiting. They might have already taken her mother into custody, someplace where Ada would never find her.

Ada ignored the gnawing uncertainty and crossed the street. She considered asking Charlie to wait outside, but that seemed too ungenerous considering the circumstances. Her mother answered the door on Ada's second knock. She must have seen them through the kitchen window. She was wearing a simple brown dress and a vibrant blue head scarf with green flowers. She didn't say anything to them, just opened the door wide.

The silence continued as Nyah served them coffee in the living room. Ada didn't touch hers. Charlie drank his in three gulps, and Ada pushed her cup over to him as well.

"Well," her mother said, "do I get to know his name?"

"Charlie Lewis, ma'am," he said, reaching over to shake her hand.

"I am Nyah. It is nice to meet you, Charlie Lewis."

Ada couldn't stand the pleasantries. She went to the window and opened it, suddenly desperate for the fresh air. Her mother clicked her tongue with a disapproving sound but didn't say anything. Ada breathed in the chill. She didn't want to do this. She wanted to be anywhere but here. The familiar feeling of powerlessness swept over her, but she fought it. She told herself that she did have a choice, and she was choosing to protect what she loved.

"Mama," she said, turning around to face her, "it's not safe here anymore."

She was sure her voice would break, but it stayed strong. Her mother was watching her, jaw set, hands folded primly in her lap.

"I know," Nyah said.

The words were like hammered nails. Ada knew they couldn't go back.

"I've been hiding cash in the hatbox under your bed," Ada told her. "There's enough for a train ticket and a place to stay for a while. Pick a town at random. Somewhere in Ohio or Illinois."

"What about your father?" her mother asked. "I am supposed to leave him behind in that prison?"

"He'll understand," Ada said. "He would want you to be safe."

Her mother's hands clenched more tightly, and she pressed her lips together. Ada could feel Charlie's eyes on her, and she avoided them. She went to the kitchen counter, found a pencil and a piece of paper, and wrote out the Wellses' address.

"Here." She handed it to her mother, who didn't reach to take it. Ada set it in her lap. "Write to that address when you're settled, but put Corinne's name on it. She'll make sure I get it."

Ada stood in front of her mother, helpless to say or do anything further. It was a plan she had thought up years ago, when she'd first gotten involved with the Cast Iron's illegal activities, right after her father was convicted. The idea had been more of an exercise back then. A puzzle to figure out. It had never occurred to her that one day she would have to follow through.

"Thank you, Ada," her mother said. "You have always taken good care of me."

Ada glanced at Charlie, who had already stood up, wiping his hands nervously on his trousers.

"We have to go, Mama," she said. "You should leave as soon as possible. Today."

Her mother nodded gravely. When she was like this, so solemn and regal, Ada could imagine that the bedtime stories were true. That she really was a queen with a palace atop a mountain, who kept wise counsel with bold lions and clever snakes, who had all the treasures of Africa at her fingertips.

But this wasn't how that story ended.

Ada and Charlie left. As they went down the stairs, it was all Ada could do to keep her eyes dry. There was a white-hot flame at the base of her throat that would not be quenched. Charlie was ahead of her, and when he reached the bottom step, he turned and looked up at her. She loved the way he looked in the plain light, so honest and open. Like his face had never hidden a secret, had never held a private shame.

"Are you sure you're ready to leave?" he asked.

The tears in her eyes spilled out the corners, and she whirled to run back up the stairs. She pounded on the locked door until it opened, then threw herself into her mother's arms.

"I'm sorry, Mama," she managed through her burning throat. "I'm so sorry it has to be like this. It's my fault."

"A turn in the tale is not the end," her mother whispered, squeezing her tightly.

"It feels like it, though."

Her mother rocked back on her heels to look Ada full in the face. Ada tried to memorize every graceful line of her mother's features, the light of her eyes, the scent of bread and grape-seed oil and coffee.

"You must always give more than you take," her mother said. "You will remember that, won't you?"

"I'll remember," Ada said. "I love you, Mama."

Her mother kissed her forehead, sealing the memory there. For a glorious moment, the flame inside her was quiet, and Ada felt at peace.

"I know," her mother whispered. *"Nakupenda sana."*

"I know."

Phillip and Angela's wedding was at three o'clock in the afternoon, just before the setting sun cast a glow over the white steeple of the Old North Church. Corinne arrived at fifteen till with Saint in tow.

"Just sit somewhere in the back," Corinne told Saint. "And try not to look conspicuous."

"And when someone inevitably tries to kick me out?" he asked.

"Tell them you're Phillip's uncle Ambrose's son."

"Who is Uncle Ambrose?"

"Someone whose son they wouldn't want to kick out."

Corinne went around the back of the church to find her mother, who had a predictable reaction to her daughter's state of dress and overall appearance of having been to hell and back.

"I can't believe you ran off like that. I didn't sleep a wink," Mrs. Wells told her, as she buttoned her into the dress that had been ordered specially for the wedding. It was a respectable navy blue, with quarter-length sleeves and a hemline that made Corinne feel like a spinster aunt. Angela had probably picked it out.

"Mother, if I'm being perfectly honest with you, it's probably going to happen again," Corinne said.

"I wish you would talk to me," Mrs. Wells murmured, fussing over Corinne's hair with a brush. "I don't see you all year, and even when you're home you're somewhere else. And then that horrible incident last night."

"It's all a big misunderstanding," Corinne said. If only that were the truth. "It will all be straightened out by the time I go back to school."

Mrs. Wells made a noncommittal sound and handed Corinne her powder compact.

"Hold this. Those dark circles are dreadful."

Corinne had thought the compact was silver, but as soon as it touched her skin, she realized it was steel and dropped it.

"Sorry," she said immediately.

"No, I'm sorry, honey. I always forget," her mother said, scooping it up and putting it on the table.

"It's all right, I— Wait. Forget what?"

319

Her mother was silent, patting at Corinne's face with the powder puff.

"Stop it," Corinne said, pushing her hand away. "Forget what?"

Mrs. Wells sighed and sat down at the table. She put away the compact and fiddled with the hairbrush.

"Mother," Corinne said.

"I've known since the first time I saw you after you—you got sick," said her mother. "Your aunt—my older sister—was the same way. She used to write stories, beautiful stories. I was the only person who ever knew how she could bring the stories to life. We had an old iron tub in the house, and she used to cry until she was sick whenever my mother made her bathe in it."

"You never told me you had a sister," Corinne said.

"Her name was Alice. When she was a little older than you are now, she—she hurt herself." Her mother squeezed the brush in a trembling grip. Her voice was thin and tight like a string. "The doctor couldn't bring her back."

Alice the lion tamer. Alice the pirate. Alice the opera singer.

Alice the wordsmith. Alice who couldn't be saved.

Corinne swallowed hard and knelt down beside her mother, wrapping her mother's hands in her own. The loss of her grandfather's pocket watch was more real than it had been before. She felt somehow heavier without the familiar weight in her pocket.

"I'm sorry," she said.

"That was a long time ago," Mrs. Wells said, smiling though her eyes were damp. "Stand up, Corinne. You'll wrinkle your dress."

Corinne obeyed, shaking out the hideously long skirt. For the first time, she considered the significance of her mother's not calling the police the night before. She'd been lying to her family for years, assuming that her mother was too dense to figure it out. But maybe Mrs. Wells knew more about Corinne's life than she let on. Corinne thought about her mother's refurbishment of the house, of all those iron fixtures replaced with brass, under the pretense that *Garden & Home Builder* had declared it the height of style. Maybe her mother, who stowed the ideals of Down Street so deep in her heart, understood that some secrets should be kept.

"Does Father know?" Corinne asked.

She almost didn't want the answer. She was remembering all the dinner parties throughout the years where her father had expounded on his views on hemopaths, all the years of unfeeling, offhand comments, each one a burr under her skin that she could never quite be rid of.

Her mother seemed to understand what she wasn't saying. She reached out and took Corinne's hand in both of hers. The gold of her wedding rings was cool against Corinne's wrist.

"I thought maybe you would tell him, when you were ready," she said. "I hoped that you would tell all of us, in time."

The words weren't a reprimand, and they held no disappointment. Instead they were extended like an olive branch, or a promise. Corinne didn't know what to say. She'd been fighting against her family and her name for so long that she'd forgotten what it felt like to have even one of them on her side.

"Mother, have you seen my—" Phillip appeared in the doorway, cutting himself short when he saw his sister.

"Hello," Corinne said.

"Where have you been?" he demanded. "Are you okay?"

He came into the room, and Corinne wasn't sure if he was going to throw something or shake her by the shoulders. Instead he pulled her into a hug. The sensation of being trapped inside her brother's bearlike grip was not entirely unpleasant. She hadn't hugged him since she was eleven years old, the day she left for boarding school.

"We looked for you all night. God, Corinne, we thought—" Phillip choked up, which was something else that hadn't happened in years.

"I'm okay," she said. "Mostly."

Phillip held her at arm's length and examined her with a stitch in his brow. His bow tie was off-kilter, and Corinne straightened it.

"I'm sorry," she told him. "I never meant for things to go this far."

"And is it over?" he asked. "Whatever it is?"

Corinne shook her head. "Not yet."

Mrs. Wells stood up. With swift, practiced motions, she dusted off Phillip's lapel and smoothed down Corinne's hair. She let her touch linger, looking between them. There was an emotion in her eyes that Corinne couldn't identify or understand, and it made her wonder why she'd ever thought her mother was anything but fathomless.

"Phillip, you're going to be late to your own wedding," Mrs. Wells said. "We'll sort this all out later."

Corinne knew that none of this would be sorted out as easily as her mother made it sound, but she decided to let herself believe for a few precious seconds that it could be. That brief respite gave her the strength she needed to follow them into the chapel.

The interior of the Old North Church was painted all white, but it bloomed pink in the sunlight that streamed through the windows. There was a display of white roses every two feet along the aisle, and someone had draped garlands along the upper balconies. Corinne sat beside her mother in the first pew on the groom's side. The whole ordeal seemed to drag on for hours. By the time Angela actually made it to Phillip's side at the altar, Corinne was certain that half the congregation was asleep. The minister's smile shone benevolently upon them, and then he started into a speech that had all the indicators of being everlasting.

Corinne sank down a little in her seat and stole a look over her shoulder to furtively scan the crowd. She finally found Saint in the last row, being blessedly unobtrusive. The church wasn't full—which the marital couple would no doubt take as a personal offense—and there was only one other person on Saint's row. He seemed familiar somehow, with a round face, overlarge nose, and long ears. Corinne racked her mind. He was familiar in the way politicians were familiar, not because she'd ever met them but because she had seen their faces plastered across the newspaper headlines.

Saint's drawing. The one of the man who had shot Gabriel.

She craned her head to look back again, no longer caring how subtle she was being. One of the doors of the cathedral had opened slightly, and a latecomer slipped in. She had never seen Johnny in a suit before. She didn't know how it was possible, but he caught her eye immediately, as if he knew right where to find her. He smiled and slid in on the other side of Saint. When Saint saw him, he blanched a ghostly white. He started to stand up, but the man on his other side clamped a hand on his shoulder. Suddenly the man was different. His face had melted into one that Corinne knew very well. It was Guy Jackson.

Johnny leaned over, his eyes still on Corinne, and whispered something in Saint's ear. Saint closed his eyes and locked his jaw. He nodded.

The three of them stood up and left quietly, with Saint between the two men. Corinne strained to see, earning a swat from her mother and a glare from Aunt Maude, who was behind her.

Corinne crawled over her mother and father and the various great-aunts and cousins in her row and made a beeline for the side door. She didn't dare look back for fear her mother's glare would actually turn her to stone. Touching family moment aside, disturbing the Wells-Haversham wedding was treachery that could not be borne.

The street in front of the cathedral was empty by the time Corinne reached it.

"Dammit," Corinne screamed, heedless of the twittering of two old ladies walking past.

Panic reared inside her, and she ran to one side of the church and then the other. She screamed another profanity, not caring who heard her.

"Cor?"

Corinne spun around to see Ada and Charlie coming down the street.

"He took Saint," she cried. "Johnny was right here in the church, and he took Saint, and now they're gone."

They stared at her in shocked silence for a few moments, until Charlie finally blinked.

"Where could they have gone?" he asked. "The Cast Iron?"

"I don't know," Corinne said. She started to pace. "I don't know. Jackson was with him. We assumed the gunman at the docks was a thespian pretending to be Jackson, but Jackson was just disguising himself."

She remembered James pointing out how much the sketch looked like Babe Ruth and for a split second felt the awful surge of a laugh. Jackson must be a baseball fan. She should have known. She should have figured it out in time to stop any of this from happening.

"The warehouse," Ada said suddenly. "Think about it."

"I'm a little too stressed right now to think about things, Ada," Corinne said. "So if you could just explain yourself, that would be grand."

"If Jackson shot Tom Glenn and Gabriel, it must have been because Johnny told him to."

"But why?" Corinne asked. "Glenn just helped at the docks. He hardly ever came around the Cast Iron."

"That's what I'm saying. Glenn and Gabriel both knew where the warehouse was and what he was storing there."

"That explains why he came for Saint," Charlie said. "Saint said he'd been there before."

"This is all about that damn liquor," Corinne said. "We have to find that warehouse."

"We don't even know if that's where they're going," Charlie said.

"It's our best option," Ada said. "We have to try."

"There are miles of wharves and hundreds of warehouses," Corinne said. "Saint doesn't have that kind of time."

"He might be able to help with that," Charlie said, pointing.

Corinne whirled to follow his finger across the street. Gabriel was standing there, his hands in his pockets, unmoving.

"Excuse me," Corinne said. "I need to go perform a ritual disemboweling. I'll be right back."

She marched across the street, ignoring the honking car that almost mowed her down. She tried to think of something scathing to say, but for the first time in her life she had no words. So instead when she reached him, she punched him in the face.

Gabriel stumbled back, clutching his mouth. Corinne shook out her hand and swore, surprised at how badly it hurt. She had a feeling she might have hurt herself worse than Gabriel, which only infuriated her more. Her chest was tight and aching, and she couldn't seem to catch her breath. When Gabriel lowered his hand, there was blood on his fingers. He stared at it for a second, eyebrows drawn in bewilderment.

"Corinne, please just listen to me," he said, taking a step toward her.

"No, you listen to me," Corinne shouted. She shoved him back again with as much force as she could muster, though even then he barely faltered. "I can't believe you ever had the nerve to ask me if I felt guilty. Here's a question for you, Gabriel Stone. Do *you* feel guilty? Because Maddy is dead, and it's your fault."

He swallowed and wiped his mouth with the back of his hand, smearing bright red across his lower lip.

"I'm sorry," he said. "I really am."

Even knowing his secret, Corinne still couldn't read his expression. Whatever he was feeling remained as guarded as ever.

"I was an idiot to have trusted you," Corinne said. "You're not even that good a liar."

"Someone once told me that the smartest person in the room is the easiest to fool."

There was a quirk right at the corner of his lips. Almost a smile, but not quite. Corinne refused to be sidetracked by the veiled compliment.

"And someone once told me that high stakes are the key to a good bluff," she said. "So let me guess—Johnny promised you a fortune beyond your wildest imagining."

"I was never working for Johnny. I'm guessing that's why he tried to kill me."

"So just the HPA, then." In her vehemence, she had forgotten all about Agent Pierce. She glanced around, half expecting the

HPA to be closing in. There were a few pedestrians on the sidewalks, but no one was paying her and Gabriel any special attention.

"They don't know I'm here," Gabriel said, gleaning her thoughts with an ease that made her want to punch him again.

"Are you some kind of initiate?" Corinne asked. "Were we just a way to earn your badge?"

It wasn't the question she really wanted to ask. Judging from the look in his eye, Gabriel could see that too, but he just shook his head. He retrieved something from his pocket and pushed it into her hands.

Corinne stared down at her grandfather's pocket watch, once again speechless.

"Do you really want explanations?" Gabriel asked. "Or do you want to help Saint? I saw Johnny and Jackson take him. I know where the warehouse is. I've got the Ford around the corner."

She wrapped her finger around the brass, which was still warm from Gabriel's coat.

"Did you know that Saint would be able to get us out of the Cast Iron?" Her voice felt ragged.

"Not for sure. But I hoped."

Corinne managed, with some difficulty, to meet his eyes again. "And how do we know it's not some kind of trap?" she asked.

"Number twelve, Belvidere Street," he said.

"What?"

"That's my mother's address."

"So?"

"So if I'm lying, then you can give it to the police. She doesn't speak any English. They'll be more than happy to deport her, I'm sure."

Corinne frowned at him. He hadn't broken her gaze. She was

struck again by how dark his eyes were, with the pupils almost indistinguishable from the irises.

"I would never do that," she said.

"I know," he said. "I trust you."

And he wanted her to trust him. She didn't know if that was possible, but they had to help Saint, and there didn't seem to be any other way. Even if she couldn't trust Gabriel Stone, she could use him. She shoved her grandfather's watch into her pocket, where it belonged.

"Let's go," she said.

CHAPTER TWENTY

THE SUN HAD SET BY THE TIME THEY ARRIVED AT THE WARE-
house. The water glimmered darkly in the moonlight, and the air
whispered with the sound of ships rocking gently against the docks.
Gabriel parked a few blocks away, and they walked to the wharves.
When he pointed out the warehouse, Ada had to grab Corinne's
arm to slow her down.

"Wait," she said. "If we run in there without thinking, we're all
going to be killed."

Corinne's breaths were coming in quick gasps, but she seemed
to understand the wisdom in Ada's concern.

"You and Charlie have your instruments," she said.

It had been Charlie's idea to stop at the Red Cat on the way.
He had retrieved his horn and a violin for Ada that he claimed to
have borrowed and not stolen. It wasn't as nice as hers, which was
still probably tucked away in the basement of the Cast Iron, but it
would serve.

"There's got to be a back door to this place," Corinne went on.
"I'll go in the front and distract Johnny, and you two find a place to
hide. Try to put them to sleep, or at least make them listen to me."

"That's a terrible plan, assuming they're even in there," Gabriel
said. "And you're not going by yourself."

"Excuse me," Corinne said, not quite looking at him. "But who
is the only person here who doesn't have the ability to control people's minds? You're a liability, Stone."

"He's right," Ada said, absorbing the glare of betrayal that

Corinne shot her. "Don't be an idiot, Cor. You're not just going to walk in there by yourself. Gabriel, I'm assuming you're still armed?"

He nodded.

"Let's go then. Be careful."

Ada was pleased to find that everyone listened to her. She might be developing a taste for being in charge, because she could see why Corinne enjoyed it so much. They stayed together until they were one building away from the warehouse. There was a single streetlight ahead, but it flickered on and off. Charlie broke away for the gap between the two buildings, but Ada hesitated.

"Cor, wait," she whispered.

Corinne turned around, her expression one of determined irritation. Ada held out her hand for their handshake, and Corinne softened. She pulled Ada into a sudden, desperate embrace.

"Don't die," she said into her ear. "And for cripes' sake, tell Charlie you love him already."

They parted smiling, and Ada ran to catch up with Charlie. They crept through the narrow alley, stepping around broken glass and murky puddles that were covered in fine swaths of lacy ice. The back of the warehouse was lined with grimy windows. Ada tried to peer through one, but the window was too dirty to make out anything. They ducked below them just in case and found the back door. There was a rusted latch on it that was padlocked.

For a few seconds, they just stared at it.

"We probably should have seen this coming," Ada whispered.

"This whole breaking and entering thing is pretty new to me," Charlie replied.

"What do we do? If we break a window, they'll hear us."

"Maybe there's a crowbar in the car. Or we could use the hand crank."

"You won't be able to break the padlock with a hand crank."

"No, but it looks like we only need a little leverage to break off the latch from the other end."

Ada stared at the latch doubtfully. "I guess we have to try," she said.

"That's the spirit," he said cheerfully. "Stay here. I'll be right back."

"Charlie, wait."

She grabbed his shirt as he turned and pulled him back. His lips met hers so fast that he must have been reading her mind. His mouth still had the brassy taste from tuning his French horn. His hands were around her waist, and she savored the way she fit right into his arms. It felt better than easy. It felt right.

She pulled back until there was a hairbreadth between their lips, their foreheads touching. "I love you," she whispered.

He grinned and met her mouth for one more kiss.

"I'll be right back," he said.

Ada nodded, breathless, and he jogged off. She could hear him humming as he ran. She pressed her hand to her lips and tried not to smile.

The warehouse was cavernous, and when Corinne and Gabriel entered, it was eerily quiet. There was a row of electric bulbs hanging from the ceiling, buzzing with a golden glow. The knot in Corinne's chest tightened. Someone was definitely here.

They edged along the inside wall, using the stacks upon stacks of wooden crates as cover. There was a low voice that she was positive was Johnny's. For a while, as they crept through the maze of crates, she couldn't make out the other sound. Then she caught a glimpse through a gap in two crates and realized it was Saint, sobbing.

She sank to her knees, pressing both hands over her mouth to smother a cry. Saint was dangling by his wrists with his toes barely brushing the ground. The chain around his wrists was also lashed around his bare torso three or four times. Corinne knew without looking a second time that it was pure iron. Gabriel's hand was on her back, and she realized he had crouched down beside her. She looked at his face illuminated by the sliver of light between the crates. The disgust and anger she saw there bolstered her somehow. If he could face it, so could she. She peered back through the gap.

Jackson was slouched in a chair off to the left, checking the bullets in his gun. Johnny was standing in front of Saint, speaking in earnest tones that were completely at odds with the scene.

"I just need to know who else you told," he said. "I wish we could have handled this in a more civilized manner, but I have to be sure. My sources assure me that the Eighteenth Amendment is going to be ratified. A year from now, when Prohibition goes into effect, this warehouse is going to be worth more than all of Boston."

Saint was shaking too hard to speak, tears streaming down his cheeks.

"I'll just shoot him," said Jackson. "Sniveling little shit didn't tell anyone."

"Is that true?" Johnny said to Saint, catching his chin in his hand. "If you think you're protecting your friends, don't worry—I'll be taking care of them in short order."

Saint jerked his head, succeeding only in swaying his entire body in the chains.

"You said if I came with you—" But he couldn't finish.

Corinne could see his teeth were stained scarlet with blood. Someone must have hit him. She balled her hands into fists, trying to gain control over the fury that was building in her veins.

"I lied," Johnny said. "To be honest, I just wanted to see if you were made of stronger stuff than your old man. After you left Ada high and dry, it didn't seem likely. At least now you can die knowing you've redeemed yourself. It's more than your father managed."

"This is taking too long," Jackson said.

"I thought a thespian of all people would appreciate the theatrics of it," Johnny said, more to Saint than to his cohort. "This is how the ironmongers do it, you know. String the slagger up with iron, then slit the calves open, here and here." He drew lines with his finger across Saint's calves. "Chain 'em and drain 'em."

Saint whimpered. Blood was dripping from his mouth, bright and angry against his pale skin.

"It's not *my* fault," Johnny said. "This would have been so much easier if you'd just kept your mouth shut at the station last month. I had a nice, quick death arranged for you in lockup. Shiv to the neck. You would have bled out before you realized what was happening."

There was a sound near the back of the warehouse.

"Jackson, go," Johnny said.

Jackson had jumped out of his chair, clicking the chamber of his gun closed. It was a strange model that Corinne had seen a few times before. Johnny had had them specially made somewhere overseas. Pistols and bullets made entirely without iron. Still just as deadly though.

She realized that the sound had to be Ada and Charlie at the back door. Without thinking, she stood up and rounded the crates.

"Johnny!" she yelled.

Both men's attention snapped to her.

"Corinne," Johnny said. She could tell he was surprised but not necessarily alarmed, which she would have preferred.

"You're a hard man to track down," she said. She was pleased to find that her voice wasn't shaking.

"I guess this means that Ada is around here somewhere," Johnny said. "Jackson, put your gun on Miss Wells, and if she says another word, shoot her."

"Don't."

Corinne heard Gabriel's voice behind her. She glanced back and saw that he had his gun trained on Jackson. He moved up slowly to stand beside her.

"Now, you're the last person I expected to see here, Stone," said Johnny.

"Please tell me you have perfect aim," Corinne said to Gabriel.

"Better than him," Gabriel said, nodding toward Jackson. "He was only a few yards away when he missed me."

"Won't happen again," Jackson growled.

Corinne held her breath for a few seconds, hoping to hear the first strains of music, but there was nothing yet.

"Take Saint down," Corinne said, lifting her hands slightly, palms up. "We can work something out."

"I think we're past that now," Johnny said quietly.

To Corinne's chagrin, he had stepped partially behind Saint, where Gabriel no longer had a clear shot if it came to that.

"You didn't have to do this," she said. There was a quiver in her voice now. She hoped he couldn't hear it. "We've always had your back, Johnny."

"That's true," he said. His eyebrows tilted downward in the barest frown. "I didn't plan any of this, you know. But you just had to pull the Bengali banker. How am I supposed to run a business when the cops are sniffing outside the doors every night? And when they pass that amendment, the Cast Iron will be finished. I even tried to give you an out. I sent Jackson as Gordon to make sure you thought I was dead. I figured Ada would leave town and you would run back home. It should have been a clean break—except neither of you could leave well enough alone."

"Told you they wouldn't," Jackson said, earning a cutting look from his employer.

"We'll leave it alone now," Corinne said, "if you let us take Saint."

Johnny shook his head. He was pulling something from his pocket—earplugs. Jackson had a pair around his neck and used one hand to shove them into place, keeping his gun hand ready. Corinne realized it didn't matter where Charlie and Ada were now. It was over.

"Sorry, Corinne. It can't be helped," Johnny said. "Jackson, kill them."

Gabriel grabbed Corinne's arm and yanked her behind him. She closed her eyes waiting for the shots, waiting for the end of everything.

But there weren't any.

Just a loud thump, followed by a softer one. She opened her eyes and looked past Gabriel and saw Charlie standing over Jackson's prone body, gripping his French horn.

"Who would've thought these things could be so versatile?" he asked.

From behind Saint, Johnny spat out a curse. Corinne saw the knife glinting in his hand and ran forward, her warning caught in her throat. Saint let out a gasping cry and kicked both legs backward. His heels caught Johnny in the chest, and Johnny stumbled backward, right into the steel bar that Ada was swinging at his head.

He crumpled to the ground without a sound, and Ada flung the hand crank away, wiping her hands on her dress to alleviate the burn. Corinne and Gabriel ran forward to help Saint. They managed to get some of the chains loose from his chest, but even standing on the chair, Gabriel couldn't loosen the chains from his wrists.

"We have to lower him," he said. "Up there."

They could see that the chain was looped over a ceiling brace above and secured on the railing of the warehouse's mezzanine.

"I'll get it," Charlie said, taking off.

"Dammit," said Gabriel. "Where's Jackson?"

As soon as he spoke, the warehouse went dark. At first all was silent. Then there was a gunshot, and the world became chaos. Someone knocked Corinne over, and she crawled for the crates she knew were to her right, calling out for Ada and Gabriel as she went. She felt the wooden crates with her hands and tried to move to where she would be covered, but she didn't actually know where the gunshot had come from.

She shouted for Ada and Gabriel again, and then jumped at Gabriel's voice in her ear.

"He's across the room. We need to move farther back."

She nodded, though he couldn't see her, and tried to follow his lead. Her heart was skipping every other beat, and her head pounded with adrenaline. She reached out to touch Gabriel, desperate for an anchor in the darkness. Her fingers brushed what must have been his gun hand, because she could feel the cool metal.

Except it didn't sting, the way that steel should.

She stumbled backward, her mind reeling to catch up. From the corner of her eye, in the distance, she saw a glint of orange light in the black. Gabriel was lighting a match.

Before she could scream, Jackson had lunged on top of her and clamped a hand onto her face. She kicked blindly, feeling the barrel of his gun pressed into her stomach. She managed to bring up one of her knees for leverage and rolled hard to the right, slamming his shoulder into a crate. She heard the clunk of the gun hitting the floor and tried to pull up her other knee so she could push away from him. He moved both his hands to her neck, and she choked on her last breath as his grip tightened around her windpipe.

Her vision exploded into red and violet. She clawed at his hands, digging her fingernails into skin, but his hold was a vise. She could hear music through the rushing in her ears. She wondered if instead of seeing her life flash before her eyes, she was going to relive one of her most cherished, most private memories. Huddled on her bed in the Cast Iron, still in the black dress from her grand-father's funeral, and Ada sitting beside her, coaxing everything bright and beautiful in the world back to life with only the strings on her violin.

Somewhere in the recesses of her mind she realized that the music was real. With her last reserve of strength she lifted her right hand and raked her fingernails across Jackson's face until she found his ear. She yanked the earplug away and then stopped struggling, because she was just too damn tired.

As she slipped into unconsciousness, she thought his grip was loosening. But that might have just been wishful thinking.

Ada played the violin until Gabriel switched the lights back on. At first she didn't even notice when they plunged back into light. Her eyes were shut tightly with focus. She was trying to aim the music directly toward Jackson, which was something she had never attempted without actually being able to see the person. But Jackson was the one with the gun, and she couldn't risk putting everyone else to sleep if he still had the earplugs in. She was hoping that Jackson had removed them to hear better in the dark.

When her eyes had adjusted to the light, she surveyed the warehouse, spinning in a tight circle. She could see Charlie above at the railing, and Gabriel was behind her, coming back from the light switch, but Corinne was nowhere to be seen.

"Cor," she shouted, running down the length of the warehouse, scanning the rows of crates.

Then she saw Jackson, slumped on the ground, and Corinne beside him. She screamed.

She ran to them, not caring if he would wake up, not caring if he still had the gun. She could hear Gabriel behind her as she threw herself down beside Corinne, who was lying unmoving on her back. Jackson's hands were loose around her neck, and Ada pushed him off.

"Cor," she said, sliding her hands underneath her head to cradle it. "Corinne, wake up."

"She's breathing," Gabriel said, the relief evident in his voice.

Ada saw that he had taken one of Corinne's hands in his own. When Ada caught his eye, he dropped her hand and grabbed Jackson's gun from the ground.

"Here," he said, flicking on the safety and giving it to her. "Just in case."

Ada stared at the unfamiliar weight in her hands. It was relatively small and would fit easily in her coat pocket. That was where she tucked it, for now.

"How long will Jackson stay asleep?" Gabriel asked.

"Not long," Ada said.

"Stay with Corinne," he said. "I'm going to help Charlie get Saint down so we can reuse those chains for Sleeping Beauty."

Gabriel took both of Jackson's wrists and dragged him out of the aisle and toward the center of the warehouse. Ada maneuvered to rest Corinne's head on her knees. She hummed a low tune, willing the melody to follow Corinne into her dreams, to bring her back soon.

CHAPTER TWENTY-ONE

W<small>HEN</small> C<small>ORINNE REGAINED CONSCIOUSNESS, IT WAS LIKE WAKING</small> from an afternoon nap. Ada's music was inside her, filling her up with a serenity she had never found anywhere else. It wasn't until she had opened her eyes that her head began to split and her throat began to burn. She coughed and sucked in ragged breaths.

"You're all right, you're all right," Ada kept repeating, though Corinne couldn't help but feel it was more for Ada's benefit than her own.

She sat up with Ada's help.

"Can you walk?" Ada asked. "We've got Saint in the car. We didn't want to move you until you woke up."

"Where's Johnny?" Corinne pressed her palms to her eyes, trying to edge out her agonizing headache.

"Gone. Who knows where. He must've slipped out while the lights were off."

Corinne nodded slowly, relieved that she didn't have to face him again. She accepted Ada's help in standing. They walked outside together, with Corinne leaning on Ada's shoulder. Saint was in the backseat of the car, head resting against the window. Charlie stood a few feet away, watching the street nervously. Gabriel was leaning against the driver's side door, smoking a cigarette. On the ground beside him was Jackson, who was fettered well with iron and apparently unconscious.

"What are we going to do with him?" Corinne asked.

"Drop him off at the police station, I guess," Ada said. "They probably know he's one of Johnny's crew."

Corinne would have much preferred to drop Jackson into the bay, but maybe Haversham would be an equally fitting fate. She straightened up and was relieved when her knees supported her. She went to Gabriel.

"Can I talk to you for a second?" she asked.

He nodded and ground out the cigarette under his heel. Corinne grabbed his wrist and led him away from the car, back inside the threshold of the warehouse, where they could be alone.

"Corinne," he started.

"Thank you," she said. "I mean, I'm not saying I forgive you, because most of this is your fault anyway."

"I'm—"

"You never made it a secret how you feel about what I do for a living, so I suppose I should have seen it coming."

"Corinne—"

"It's not like you redeemed yourself or anything, but at least you're not a psychopath like Johnny. And I—"

Gabriel leaned down and kissed her, sliding his hand around the nape of her neck, his touch so light she could barely feel it. For a split second the press of his lips, slightly chapped, felt like something she wanted—then her mind caught up. She pushed him back.

"No," she said.

There was more she wanted to say, but she couldn't remember any of it.

"I'm sorry," he said. He took a small step away from her. "This is the second time in so many nights I've thought you were dead."

It was easier for her to think, now that he had moved back. As always, the steel of his gun was nudging at her consciousness, pulling her focus. Her headache was getting worse.

"You'll have to excuse me if I'm not sympathetic," Corinne said. "Especially since you were the one who sold me out the first time."

"I'm sorry," he said again, his voice softer.

In the dull light of the warehouse, the angles of his face were less severe. Corinne could see a glimpse of the vulnerability she'd seen outside Down Street.

"That doesn't mean anything," she said.

Gabriel broke her gaze. He stared to his right, where half an hour ago Saint had been dangling from iron chains. He released a slow breath.

"My father was a Bolshevik activist in Russia," he said, dropping his eyes. "Eleven years ago, before the *Bolsheviki* took power, he was in a protest that got out of control. Several police were killed, and my father was executed in the street. Some of his comrades helped my mother and me flee the country. I knew I shouldn't attend those meetings at Down Street, but I couldn't stay away. Those ideas felt like the only thing my father had ever given me."

He hesitated, staring down at her hand in his.

"Then my name was put on a list, and one night they dragged me into the police station, and Pierce and Wilkey told me that if I didn't help them, they would put me on the next ship to Russia and leave my mother to fend for herself."

Corinne bit her lip. She remembered the way his mother had clutched him so desperately, calling him *myshka*.

"They're going to know you helped us now," Corinne said. "They'll probably even think you helped us escape Haversham."

"I know. My mother and I will have to leave. I'll find work somewhere else. New York, maybe."

His eyes were still downcast. He pushed his hands into his coat pockets.

"It was the hardest thing I've ever done, Cor—you have to know that. When you told me you weren't a nice person, I tried to believe it. I hoped it would be easier if I thought the worst of you. If you were just a privileged, arrogant thief without a morsel of empathy." He met her eyes suddenly. "But you're more than that," he said. "And I can't tell if you really don't think so or if for some reason you're determined that no one but Ada will ever find out."

"I wasn't lying when I said I wasn't a nice person," Corinne said.

He smiled ruefully. "You're definitely not a nice person, but there's more to it than that. I tried not to see it, but it's impossible to ignore. You're best friends with Ada and Saint, and you love the Cast Iron for what it could be and not necessarily what it is, and that night in the alley, you gave Harry a poem when he needed it most. You're not nice, but you're *good*."

Corinne couldn't catch her breath. The sincerity in his eyes was iron on her skin.

"You should have told us about the HPA," she managed finally. "Ada and I would have found a way to help you."

"I don't doubt it," he said, his eyes lowering again. "I wish . . . a lot of things had been different."

Corinne studied his expression for a few moments, considering. "I wish things had been different too," she said. "Especially the part where Madeline died choking on her own blood."

Gabriel flinched, and for a heartbeat she could read the sorrow in his face as clearly as if it had been written there.

"I never—"

"I know," Corinne said. "But that doesn't change what happened."

"I know."

They were both quiet for a long while. Corinne could hear the mechanical sputtering and coughs of the car as it was cranked to life outside. If there was more to say, she couldn't think of what it might possibly be. She had the thought that she might not ever see Gabriel Stone again after tonight. She couldn't decide how she felt about that. She couldn't decide how she felt about anything right now. Her head hurt so badly.

She massaged her temples and sighed. "You and Charlie drop Jackson off at the station and take Saint to the Red Cat," she told Gabriel. "Ada and I will be there later."

The lines in his forehead deepened, and he took a step forward.

"You two can't just go off alone," he said. "The HPA is still looking for you."

"Let's get something straight," Corinne said. The flaring anger in her chest was easier than her other conflicted feelings, and she latched onto it. "You don't get a say in how we conduct our affairs. Normally I would tell you that New York is a pit of despair where dreams go to die, but maybe it's for the best if you take your mother and go."

She didn't relish the hurt that registered in his features, and she hated herself for the words as soon as they left her mouth, but she didn't take them back. It didn't matter how sorry he was. Madeline was gone. Nothing would ever be the same again. She turned away before she could reconsider and walked out of the warehouse.

Ada followed Corinne without hesitation. Corinne didn't say where they were going, but it didn't seem to matter anymore. They were in step again, in the way that drew everything into sharp relief, in the way that balanced the world. The night was still clear, with a raw wind blowing from the east, howling through the streets. Their skirts blew about their knees as they walked. They didn't pass many pedestrians on their way, and the farther into the financial district they went, the more deserted the streets became.

"We've made a balled-up mess of things, haven't we?" Corinne hugged herself and pressed her chin against her chest.

"Johnny used us," Ada said. "We couldn't have known that all he cared about was the money."

"We could have seen it," Corinne said. "If we'd wanted to."

The bitterness in her voice was impossible to miss. Ada had to listen harder to catch the wounded strains underneath. Ada thought about her mother's last admonition and nodded.

"You're right."

Corinne stopped walking and squinted up at the buildings around them.

"It was right here," she said.

"What was?"

"Our first con together."

Corinne dropped down to sit on the curb, mindless of the freezing concrete and the remnants of snow packed in the gutter. After a few seconds Ada sat down beside her. They were across the street from the Oriental Tea Company, with its giant teakettle sign over the front door. Steam drifted from the spout in ghostly whorls.

"You jumbled the lines to 'Song of the Moon' and lost the illusion halfway through," Ada said.

"Only because I was distracted by your pitiful attempt at Beethoven."

"Tchaikovsky, actually."

"My point."

Ada laughed. She nudged her shoulder against Corinne's, and Corinne nudged her back.

"Damn, we were good, though, by the end," Corinne said.

The way she said it made Ada realize where the conversation was really headed. Corinne had rested her head on Ada's shoulder. She was picking at a loose thread on her navy-blue dress, unraveling the seam stitch by stitch.

"Do you remember what it felt like, when it actually worked that first time?" Corinne asked.

Ada watched a light in an upstairs window across the street flicker off. She listened to the sound of distant motors revving, carrying people to their homes. One block over, a trolley whirred its way down the icy tracks.

"Not really," she said. She remembered the pride that had welled inside her when Johnny had handed her that first stack of cash. She remembered the look on her mother's face when she'd seen her new apartment for the first time. She spent every day of her life trying to forget all the rest.

"I do," Corinne said, in a distant voice. "It was like we were invincible. I guess Johnny probably knew that."

Looking back, knowing what she knew about Johnny, Ada could see the patterns now. The way he'd used their dependence on the Cast Iron against them, how he had made sure the danger of the HPA was close but not too close, how he had whittled away their ties to their old lives until they'd felt they had no choice but to trust him. No choice but to lose themselves in the thrill and glamour of the Cast Iron's underworld.

It wasn't all Johnny's doing, though. Ada knew that after her father was arrested, a part of her wanted to be lost. Pretending she didn't have a choice was easier than admitting that she had made the wrong one.

"I don't know if we can do better," she said, resting her cheek against Corinne's head. "But I think we should try."

"How?" Corinne asked. "Even if we could somehow set the Cast Iron to rights, we still have the HPA after us. And what about Haversham? We can't just abandon those people to Dr. Knox and his sick experiments."

Before Ada could remind Corinne that she was always the one with the brilliant plans, an idea came to her. She stood up and pulled Corinne to her feet.

"I know something we can try," Ada said. "You're going to hate it, though."

"Try me."

"How did you leave things with your brother?"

Corinne groaned. "You're right. I hate it."

Ada laughed and wrapped an arm around her shoulder. They headed south, in the direction of the Red Cat, leaving the sleepy quiet of the financial district behind them.

CHAPTER TWENTY-TWO

THE DAY AFTER THE WELLS-HAVERSHAM WEDDING, WHICH WAS the headline of all the society pages and the talk of all the country clubs, Phillip Wells followed the handwritten directions his sister had given him to a building between the South End and the theater district. Corinne met him at the door and let him inside. He didn't say much, just stood in the empty club and stared at the lonely microphone on the stage.

"What did you tell Angela?" Corinne asked.

She moved behind the bar, still watching her brother as he walked the length of the Cast Iron, his hands shoved into his pockets. It was strange, having him here. Two parts of her life that were never supposed to meet had collided.

"I told her that my sister left me a mysterious urgent note to meet her at one of the most notorious hemopath clubs in town," Phillip said. He had stepped between two tables to examine one of the framed photos hanging on the wall—Johnny shaking hands with his predecessor.

Corinne thought he was joking at first, but then he turned and she saw the frank expression on his features.

"Wait, you told her the truth?"

"Of course I did."

"Did you tell her about going to Haversham too?"

"She's my wife," Phillip said, speaking slowly, as if Corinne might not understand otherwise. "I love her, and I trust her. So yes, I told her about the asylum."

It had never occurred to Corinne before that her brother might love Angela. She had always guessed that the entire arrangement was some kind of political agenda. She felt the sudden need to apologize for thinking of him in such ungenerous terms. That urge confused her even more, so finally she gave up thinking about it and dug out the bottle of cognac to fix them each a sidecar.

"So what is it?" Phillip asked once he had come to sit across from her at the bar. He accepted the drink but eyed it doubtfully, swirling the amber liquid in the glass.

Corinne had considered a hundred different ways of approaching the subject with Phillip. She had talked through all of them with Ada the night before, weighing each argument, trying to decide which would convince him to help. In the end, Corinne knew that she just had to say it.

"I need you to talk to Mr. Haversham and get him to stop the experiments at the asylum."

It sounded so simple leaving her lips. As if all it would take was a memo from Mr. Haversham, and Dr. Knox would pack up his work and give all his victims proper burials.

Corinne wasn't a fool. She knew it wouldn't be that easy. But she also recognized, possibly for the first time, that she and Ada couldn't do it by themselves.

"I don't think I can do that," Phillip said.

He finally took a sip of his cocktail. Corinne could read all over his face that his brief foray into the basement had left him scarred. Yet still he wouldn't help.

"I know you hate hemopaths," Corinne said. "But what he's doing down there—"

"I don't hate hemopaths," Phillip said, looking at her sharply. "Why would you say that?"

"Father always says your campaign platform is going to be—"

"Father says that," Phillip said, interrupting her a second time. "I never have. Is that really what you've been thinking all these years?"

"You married into the family that's made its fortune torturing hemopaths, so it's not that much of a stretch." Corinne slammed her glass down on the bar. Liquid sloshed onto her knuckles.

"I didn't know any of that was happening," Phillip said. "Neither did Angela."

He grabbed a towel from farther down the bar and handed it to her. Corinne accepted it, keeping her eyes on her brother.

"And now that you do?" she asked.

Phillip tapped his finger against the glass. He was quiet for a long while.

"I want to help you," he said. "I just don't know what I can do. Angela's father is a businessman, not a humanitarian. If I go to him about this, he'll just tell me I have a bleeding heart."

"What a lovely family you've hitched yourself to."

Phillip shrugged. "Angela didn't choose her family."

"I guess none of us did."

Phillip's mouth curved into a bare smile, but there was sadness in it. "You remember the summers on Martha's Vineyard?" he asked. "You used to follow me around like a puppy. We'd search for sea glass together."

Corinne's first impulse was a sarcastic reply, but it died in her throat. She could almost smell the salt spray again, feel the hot sand sticking to her skin as she knelt beside him at the edge of the surf. He was using a stick to gently nudge a starfish back into the oncoming tide. She'd thought for sure it was dead, but he assured her it wasn't.

"Chin up, young man," he'd said to the pale-yellow star, sounding so much like their father that she'd wanted to giggle. "You've got a second chance to get it right."

The cool water had rushed over their hands and knees, and when it rushed back into the sea, the starfish was gone. Phillip had laughed and put his heavy hand on her shoulder. Farther up the beach, their mother was calling them back for lunch, radiant in a blue dress and a white sun hat. For just that moment, Corinne had thought her life was perfect.

"I remember," she said quietly.

Phillip absently rotated his glass in his hands, letting the liquor swirl almost to the lip.

"Then your second year at the Academy you stopped spending any time at home."

"That's when I manifested and moved here," Corinne said. "I haven't been back to school since then."

Phillip surveyed the club's interior again with new dubiety. Then he took a long drink.

"I thought you'd hate me if you ever found out," Corinne said. It cost her more than she would've thought to say those words, but she was glad that she had.

"I guess we don't really know each other that well, do we?" Phillip said.

"Guess not."

Phillip rested his arms on the bar and looked at her.

"I know you've been on your own for a while now," he said. "But we can be in this together, if you want to be. You're my sister, no matter what else you are."

A slow smile spread across Corinne's face. "I think maybe you just found your campaign platform," she said.

"What?"

"Mr. Haversham wants you to run for office, doesn't he? You leak to the press the story of me being taken to the asylum, of you coming to get me and seeing what's really going on there. You and Mr. Haversham can clean house, and you'll run on the platform of making Boston safe for everyone, even hemopaths."

Phillip stared at her. "That sounds like a wonderful way to lose an election," he said finally.

"You'll get the hemopath vote," she said. "And once I give a few speeches to the reporters about how scared I was when they dragged me off the street without even charging me with a crime, and how happy I was when my big brother came to my rescue, then you'll get the vote of every half-decent family man in the city."

Phillip set down his glass and rubbed the bridge of his nose as he weighed the possibilities.

"Everyone would know about you," he said. "Couldn't they arrest you again?"

"It's only illegal to perform hemopathy, not to be one," Corinne said. "They'd have a hard time proving anything."

"Even so, you'd be hounded day and night by every journalist trying to earn his stripes. You'd really do that for me?"

"I'll do anything to stop what's happening in Haversham," she said. She paused. "I mean, I'd do it for you too."

Phillip cracked a smile and shook his head with what could only be termed ruefulness.

"I don't know," he said. "Maybe."

"You know how much I hate to be the voice of reason," Corinne said, eager to prove her argument, now that she actually had one. "It's not as if you have enough political experience to inspire confidence in the population otherwise. You were at a cushy outpost for barely a year of the war, and you don't have a medal or a commendation to your name. Ned Turner's already got the anti-hemopath agenda all wrapped up, so this is really your only option."

He stared hard into his drink, then downed the rest in a gulp.

"You're a real pain in the ass sometimes, you know?" he said, swiping his sleeve across his mouth.

"So I've been told."

"This will probably end up being a terrible mistake, but I'm in."

Phillip stuck out his hand, and she shook it. Trying to conceal her elation, she poured them each a finger of cognac and lifted her glass.

"Here's to us and a successful partnership," she said.

"I wasn't aware that we were going into business together," Phillip said wryly.

"I suspect we may have an easier time being business partners than siblings."

He laughed at that and clinked his glass against hers. "To my little sister," he said. "Who's better at politics than she ever was at dinner parties."

The mention of dinner parties jarred something in Corinne's memory. A flash of invaluable information that might just be the final piece of the puzzle.

"And here's some free campaign advice for you," she said. "Ned Turner's seat is going to be vulnerable this term."

Phillip raised an eyebrow. "And what makes you say that?"

"Sorry, secrets of the trade." She swallowed the rest of her drink. "You should get back to your blushing bride. I just remembered I have to ruin someone's day, and I don't want to be late."

"Corinne, wait." Phillip stood up when she rounded the bar. "When are you going to come home?"

It was a question she'd spent the past four years trying to ignore. Corinne cast a glance around the Cast Iron, which even in its stillness made her feel more alive than she ever had at the Wells estate. Johnny Dervish had taken a lot from her, but he had given her at least one thing.

"I'm always here for you," she said. "And for Mother and Father. But I'm not coming home."

Phillip followed her gaze around the club but didn't seem to find what he was looking for. He shook his head.

"I suppose if the Wells family was going to have a black sheep, we could have done worse than you."

He reached out to ruffle her hair in the way she hated, but she dodged away and led him out the front door. The sun was bright today, casting a sheen on the last vestiges of ice from the night before.

"Give Angela my regards," Corinne said, which she thought might be the nicest thing she'd ever said to her brother.

Phillip seemed to agree. He pulled her into a hug that caught her off guard, but after a second she relaxed into it.

"Angela and I are thinking about renting a house on Martha's Vineyard this summer," he told her. "If you won't come home, maybe you can find your way there, for a little while."

Corinne smiled against his shoulder. "Maybe I will," she said. And she meant it.

Phillip released her and crossed the street to his car.

"I liked your wedding, by the way," she called after him.

"A little bird told me you ran out like a madwoman before we'd even said our vows," he called back.

"Vile slander, I assure you."

Phillip was laughing as he cranked the car, and he waved out the window as he drove away. Corinne waved back, unable to bite back a smile. She stood in the shadow of the Cast Iron for several minutes after he had left. She didn't know how they would keep the club open, but she knew they had to try. Funds might run low without a steady stream of cash conned from unsuspecting regs to replenish the coffers, but Corinne wasn't worried. She and Ada would find a way. A helpful start was the rather large warehouse full of liquor they had recently inherited, due to Johnny's disappearance. Corinne didn't think he would dare come back for it, now that Eva Carson and the Witchers knew of his treachery. Boston had no safe haven for Johnny Dervish anymore.

She locked the door to the Cast Iron and started down the street. The last threads of a plan were coming together in her mind—a daring and stupid plan, to be sure. But she didn't know how to live any other way.

The cigar club where Councilman Ned Turner went to unwind was one of the most exclusive clubs in Boston. Members only, no guests. There were six separate lounges, each complete with its own bar and wait staff. Most days, like today, the councilman's status earned him a private room.

He was in a leather wingback chair in front of the fireplace, rolling a fat cigar between his fingertips. His eyes were closed as he blew out a redolent cloud of smoke.

Corinne coughed politely, to let him know they were there. The councilman's eyes sprang open, and he jerked forward in his chair. Neither Corinne nor Ada blinked.

"Who are you? How did you get in here?" he demanded, craning his neck to survey the otherwise empty room. The wait staff was conspicuously absent. Heavy drapes covered the windows, and the flames in the fireplace behind the girls crackled and leapt, casting their distorted shadows across the wall and ceiling.

"I think you'll find that we never have any trouble getting into places we want to be," Ada said. She stared pointedly at the cigar that he had dropped onto the rug.

"What do you want?" Turner scooped up the cigar and rammed the lit end into the ashtray.

"I'm a little hurt that you don't recognize us, Councilman," said Corinne.

"Don't take it personally," Ada told her. "I'm very good at what I do."

"True, true."

Councilman Turner was staring at them with a growing expression of horror. He might not remember the incident on the Harvard Bridge well enough to recognize the culprits, but he had no doubt heard about their capture and subsequent escape. He put the pieces together while they watched; then he swore at them.

"Rude," Ada said.

Corinne clicked her tongue. "And to think my father voted for you."

Turner jabbed the cigar toward Ada. "You're a wanted fugitive, and you—" He shot a glare at Corinne. "Your family name might give you a reprieve this time, but you'd do best to go back to boarding school and hope your parents find someone desperate enough to marry you."

"Now, see, that doesn't work for me," Corinne said evenly. "Does it work for you, Ada?"

"No, Corinne, it doesn't."

"Here's our counteroffer," Corinne said, crossing her arms. "You release Silas Witcher and drop all charges against him and Ada."

Councilman Turner's eyes narrowed, and he relaxed marginally into his chair. "You two think you're really clever, don't you?"

"We think quite a lot of things about ourselves, as a matter of fact," Corinne said. "Chief among them being that we're both a lot smarter than you."

"And we have better things to do than stand around here proving it," Ada said.

The councilman snorted and reignited his cigar with the table lighter.

"I'm not going to negotiate with a couple of slaggers," he said, puffing a thick cloud of smoke in their direction.

"Oh, you must be confused," said Corinne.

"This isn't a negotiation," said Ada.

"It's blackmail."

The councilman snorted again, blowing smoke through his flared nostrils. "You don't have anything on me."

"We took two thousand dollars from you on the bridge," Corinne said.

"Allegedly," Ada corrected.

"Right, allegedly. And I happen to know for a fact that you requisitioned twenty-five hundred from the city to buy those elephants."

Turner's cigar looked perilously close to being dropped a second time. He was trying in vain to rearrange his features and hide his surprise. Corinne smiled.

"Now," she said, "I wonder if you, being the honest civil servant you are, gave back that extra five hundred?"

A bright red flush was creeping from the councilman's jowls to his ears.

"We just want what's best for the city," Ada told him.

"And you think what's best for Boston is letting criminals loose on the streets?" he demanded.

"Trust me, Silas Witcher and Ada here are not the worst criminals you have to deal with," Corinne said.

"We can keep the Witchers and Eva Carson in line," Ada said. "Hemopaths can give more to Boston than they take. You just have to give us the chance."

"And while you're at it, you can tell your HPA lapdogs to lay off Gabriel Stone," Corinne said, ignoring the sideways glance that Ada gave her. "He's under the Cast Iron's protection now."

Councilman Turner put out his cigar again and dropped it in the ashtray. His hand was trembling a little in the firelight. No doubt he was thinking about his hard-won reputation going up in smoke if even one reporter decided to pay attention to what these two girls had to say.

"Fine," he said. "It doesn't matter anyway. When Prohibition takes effect, you'll all be shut down for good."

"Have a nice day, Councilman," Corinne said. "You know, if politics is too stressful, you can always take your own advice and try to find someone desperate enough to marry you. I hear the quiet family life isn't all bad."

Before the councilman could manage a reply, they were both gone.

It was only Thursday night, but the club at the corner of Clarendon and Appleton Streets had a dance floor that was packed before the show had even begun. If the neighboring buildings hadn't been deserted, there would have been noise complaints. Despite the two extra bartenders under his command, Danny was swamped, doling out cocktails almost faster than he could keep track of the tabs.

Corinne felt like every drop of her blood was singing with the magic of it. The lights in the Cast Iron blazed so brightly that her vision blurred at the edges. They had pulled out the best tablecloths and polished the dance floor until it sparkled. Corinne had ripped the photograph of Johnny off the wall and replaced it with one of Saint's paintings. The bucolic scene that he'd given to Ada, with the sprawling tree shading emerald grass and wildflowers, wasn't the Cast Iron's usual aesthetic, but it was the only one of Saint's paintings that the HPA agents had left alone, and it felt right for it to be hanging in a place of honor.

Corinne circulated through the room, glad-handing the patrons like she'd watched Johnny do a thousand times before. James had returned and was sitting at a corner table with Saint, nursing a drink. He even managed a halfhearted smile as Corinne passed. Eva Carson was here, sharing a table with the Witcher brothers. George, who was bearded and pudgy, in a simple brown suit with elbow patches, did not look at all pleased to be there. He glowered when he caught sight of her, but beside him Silas gave her a courteous nod, albeit begrudgingly. Eva was halfway through a Manhattan and wearing a gold dress that was probably designed solely to make men like George Witcher uncomfortable. She winked at Corinne when their eyes met.

Corinne smiled broadly at them, blew a kiss to George, and headed for the stage. Ada was already there, doing a last tune-up on her violin and laughing while Charlie whispered something in her ear. She was still using the violin that he had "borrowed" from the Red Cat. Corinne knew that Ada's violin, the one Johnny had given her, was sitting in the basement. She hadn't asked Ada about it, and Ada hadn't brought it up.

Corinne took the steps two at a time and stole a gulp from one of the musician's drinks. She went to the microphone and reveled in the way the room fell silent at her approach. Prohibition had been ratified. In a year, the iron-free clubs would be shut down, no longer a refuge for hemopaths trying to escape a world of iron, or for regs trying to lay their worries aside for a single night. Corinne didn't want to think about that. She felt so alive right now. She felt like she'd been born to stand here.

"Welcome to the Cast Iron," she said.

It was all that needed to be said. They couldn't go back to the way things had been, but they could do better. Tonight was that promise.

Corinne glanced at Ada and nodded.

Ada pressed her bow to a string and sent a single, crystalline note into the air. No loss or nostalgia tonight. Only hope. Only paradise.

Corinne leaned into the microphone and began to recite.

CHAPTER TWENTY-THREE

THE DAY WAS DAWNING WHEN THE LAST OF THE PATRONS FINALLY weaved their way out of the Cast Iron. Corinne left Ada backstage, where she was trying to convince Charlie to go home and get some sleep. Corinne figured the kind of convincing that Ada really wanted to do warranted some privacy. She made her way to the back of the bar and through the storage room. Gordon's chair was still there, in the corner. The police had found him dead in his apartment, his cat curled up next to him. As far as Corinne knew, they were charging Jackson with the murder. On the chair, the vigil candle that Charlie had lit the day before had gone out.

Corinne went out the back door, hoping to cool down. When she found Gabriel leaning against the wall and smoking a cigarette, she couldn't even manage to be surprised. If she didn't think about it too hard, she could pretend it was still a week ago, when there had been nothing but possibilities between them.

She pressed her shoulder blades against the wall beside him, letting her fingertips rest against the icy brick. Wordlessly, he offered her the cigarette. She shook her head.

"You catch the show?" she asked when she could no longer stand the silence.

"No."

"Still got a problem with what we do here?"

"My mother bought a new table. She needed help moving it up the stairs."

A laugh escaped Corinne at the absurd simplicity of the

statement. She jammed her knuckles against her lips and glanced sideways at Gabriel. He was smiling. She liked the way it softened the angular planes of his face. She found herself wishing he smiled more often.

"Ada invited me," he said, staring hard at the cigarette between his fingers. A thin rivulet of smoke drifted skyward, melting into the sunlight above the alley.

"Ada thinks she's awfully clever."

"She also told me what you did for me—what you told the councilman."

Corinne swallowed. She could feel him looking at her now, and even though she steeled herself, the dark of his eyes still made her heart skip a beat when she met his gaze.

"You helped us save Saint," she said. "I thought that was worth a token effort on my part. If they deport you anyway, don't expect me to do anything about it."

She was pleased at how resolved she sounded. She almost believed herself.

Gabriel looked straight ahead again and took a pull from his cigarette. When he released the smoke, it sounded like a sigh. Corinne drove her fingertips into the wall, letting the brick abrade her skin. She told herself to go back inside, but of course she didn't listen.

"Can I ask you something?" she said.

As usual, Gabriel didn't reply, with assent or otherwise. He did look at her again.

"That first show you attended," she said. "What memory did you have while Ada was playing? What made you leave?"

He had told her it was the happiness. When Ada played childhood bliss, Corinne remembered the hot summer days on the beach on Martha's Vineyard and the cold winter nights in her grandfather's study, listening to him tell the stories of his travels.

A frown etched itself between Gabriel's eyebrows. "My seventh birthday," he said. "My mother made an apple cake. My father brought home *petushok* candies—lollipops shaped like roosters. They were my favorite when I was a kid."

Gabriel seemed to have forgotten about the lit cigarette, which was burning perilously close to his fingers. He was staring ahead, his eyes locked on the middle distance.

"It was a couple of weeks before my father was killed, but in my head it all blurs together. Somehow while my mother is lighting the candles, she's sobbing about my father's death. And while my father and I eat the candy, the kitchen is filled with the mourners from his funeral."

His hand jerked, and he dropped the cigarette. He closed his eyes and leaned his head back against the wall, turning his face upward to catch a ray of the sun. Corinne looked down to see that their little fingers were almost touching on the wall. She lifted her hand, hesitated, then fit her fingers between his. His knuckles were cool and chapped beneath her palm. When she looked up again, his eyes were on her.

"I'm sorry," she said. "I could show you how to resist hemopaths—if you decided to stay, that is."

"Do I look like I'm going anywhere?" he asked.

"Did you mean what you said at the warehouse?" The question escaped her before she could second-guess it. "About me?"

His lips quirked.

"Shouldn't you know? You're the one who told me I was a bad liar."

"I lied."

"I meant what I said."

More than anything, she wanted to kiss him. He was so bright and beautiful and vulnerable in the daylight. But she couldn't let herself. No matter the reasons, he had sold them out to the HPA and now Madeline was dead. She couldn't forgive that, not yet. Maybe not ever.

"I'm sorry," she said again, though she wasn't sure why. She pulled her hand away from his. "You should go home. It's getting late—or early, I guess."

He kept her gaze for a long second, then nodded and straightened. "If you need me—"

"I know where you live now," Corinne said.

Gabriel smiled barely and nodded.

"Hold on," Corinne said. She reached into the breast pocket of his coat, where she knew he kept his matchbook. "I do need these."

For the space of a breath, while they were inches apart and her hand was so close to his heart she could feel it beating, she thought about forgetting everything that was between them and telling him the truth. That she couldn't remember what her life was like before he had come into it, and she was having a hard time imagining what it would be like if he were gone.

She curled her fingers around the matchbook and stepped back.

"You're not armed," she said, trying to clear her head.

"I am, actually. Switched to an iron-free piece."

"Damn, you're getting more inconspicuous."

"Thanks."

Corinne closed her fist over the matches and opened the back door. The familiar scent of old wood and alcohol reached her nose. She breathed it in with relish.

"Cor, wait," said Gabriel.

She turned to face him. His hands were shoved into his pockets, and the frown line had reappeared between his eyebrows.

"I know I might not ever make things right." His eyes dropped briefly, and he sucked in a short breath before looking up again. "But I hope you'll let me try."

Corinne tried to think of something to say, something witty or honest or *anything*. But words wouldn't come, and Gabriel left the alley. She watched him go. When he stepped out from between the two buildings, the sunlight turned him briefly golden. Then he turned the corner and was gone.

Ada was waiting for Corinne in the storage room. She'd finally managed to send Charlie home, after one last kiss in the dazzling sunlight, just outside the front door. His years playing French horn translated to a host of other skills involving his mouth—French and otherwise. It still barely distracted her from the letter that was folded in her pocket. She'd found it shoved under the Cast Iron's front door the morning before. The script was her mother's handwriting, and at first she thought Nyah had left it on her way to the train station, but it wasn't a farewell letter.

In Portuguese, her mother told her again how much she loved her, and how much she wanted her to be safe. Then she wrote that she was staying in a hotel for now, but she was not buying a train ticket to the Midwest. She wasn't leaving at all.

I will not leave my family behind, she wrote. *I said nothing when you were here before, because I knew you would be too stubborn to listen. It is my own fault. You are your mother's daughter.*

Ada had cried through the rest of the letter, her tears spotting the ink. She couldn't stop thinking about the story of the beautiful queen and her prince from a faraway land. Maybe her mother was right. A turn in the tale wasn't the end.

Ada had wanted to see her mother right away, but she needed to wait until they'd closed everything up. Corinne looked small and worn when she came in from the alley—a far cry from the force of nature she had been all night, sailing through Dante and Rossetti and Tennyson without dropping a single syllable. Her hair had lost its curl, and some of the jet beads on her champagne-colored dress were missing.

"Is everyone gone?" she asked, locking the door behind her.

Ada nodded. "Saint's still at the bar. James is sleeping in the basement."

"Good." Corinne gave her a once-over and smiled. "Your lipstick's smudged."

"Can't imagine how that happened," Ada said airily.

Corinne laughed, but the sound was forced. She opened her hand to reveal a book of matches. Ada watched as she lit the candle on Gordon's chair. They stood in silence for almost a minute, watching the bright flame sway. Finally Corinne pocketed the matchbook, and they went upstairs together.

Ada had told Danny not to bother cleaning up that morning, and the tables were covered with glasses and plates and cigarette butts. The hardwood floor was spotted with spilled drinks and dropped appetizers. Saint was behind the bar, wetting a rag. He glanced up at them when they entered but said nothing.

Corinne sat on a stool at the corner of the bar, nearest the back door, and laid her head down on her arms. Ada picked absently at the buttons on her coat. Exhaustion crept over her, but she didn't want to sit down. "We should probably go downstairs and get some sleep," she said.

Corinne didn't move. Saint, who was wiping down the bar at the opposite end, looked at her again but didn't reply. She couldn't blame them. They had gone to the basement only once, two nights before. Knowing that Pierce and Wilkey had been down there, sifting through the lives they had built, was a violation that Ada couldn't stand to think about. Johnny's office had been mostly emptied out. The entire contents of her and Corinne's bedroom were in a heap on the floor, and all the decorations on their walls—the newspaper clippings and swatches of wallpaper and silken scarves—had been torn down. She'd seen her violin on top of the pile. The case had been opened and one of the strings had snapped, but otherwise, it appeared unharmed. It was still the most beautiful object she had ever touched. The only companion more constant than Corinne. But Johnny had given it to her. It was a remnant of a life she hadn't meant to live. She left it where it was.

Ada had peeked into Saint's room, where he was sitting on his cot, arms on his knees. He had raised his soft gray eyes to her, and the bleakness there wrenched Ada's heart. All his paintings were gone. She had gathered blankets from a storage closet, and the three of them had slept on the stage, spending half the night in whispers.

Ada turned around, taking in the Cast Iron's disarray. Even though hours ago it had been packed with laughter and clinking glasses and swinging music, it felt emptier than it ever had before. She tried not to think about what had been lost, about Madeline by the waterfront, about Johnny in the warehouse.

"It feels smaller than it used to," Saint said. He wasn't looking at either of them, or at the scattered tables and chairs, or at the last of his paintings mounted on the wall. He just kept pushing the rag across the bar in methodical motion.

Ada glanced back at Corinne, who had straightened up on her stool. She seemed to know exactly what Ada was thinking. As always.

"For each age is a dream that is dying,
Or one that is coming to birth."

Instantly the lights dimmed and changed—no longer strings of electric bulbs but flaming sconces along the walls and glimmering candles on the tables. The tablecloths were gone, the furniture rearranged. Instead of a dance floor there were more tables, spaced between oaken pillars. Ada could see the first-ever patrons of the Cast Iron like faded ghosts in the candlelight, men in waistcoats and knee breeches, some with powdered wigs and polished buckles on their shoes. They leaned close over their mugs of ale, eyes bright with the talk of revolution. Ada moved forward into the scene, transfixed by the intricacy of the illusion all around her. The years passed by like a rushing wind, and the patrons flashed in and out of focus, a parade of changing fashions and evolving ideals.

Revolutionaries and poets. Intellectuals and industrialists. Soldiers and politicians. The Cast Iron had hosted them all throughout the decades, reg and hemopath alike.

Seeing all that had come before made Ada realize how far the Cast Iron had fallen.

"Touching." Johnny's voice, somehow both achingly familiar and terrifyingly strange in the midst of the shifting apparitions, made Ada whirl.

The illusion fell away, and she saw Johnny standing in the doorway of the storage room. Corinne saw him too, but before she could move, he lunged forward and dragged her off the stool.

Ada ran forward, and Corinne cried out in pain, but she quieted abruptly. Johnny held her tight in front of him, his knife against her neck. Ada froze.

"If you even think about singing, I'll cut her throat," Johnny said.

He was in the same clothes he'd worn in the warehouse, unkempt, eyes bloodshot. Corinne made a cursory attempt at struggling but winced as Johnny pressed the blade harder against her skin. In her gauzy party dress, with her gold headache band askew, she looked like a porcelain doll in his hands. She looked helpless.

Ada tried to breathe. After Haversham and the sunrise by the waterfront, drenched in Madeline's blood, Ada had thought that nothing could scare her. But as she stared at the knife against Corinne's neck, there was terror burning in her veins. For a few moments the only sounds in the club were Johnny's jagged breathing and Corinne's short gasps.

"If you kill her," Ada said slowly, "you'll be unconscious before she hits the ground. I only need a few bars. You know that."

She spoke with as much force as she could muster, but really she was just figuring it out. Of course Johnny knew what she could do. That was the reason Corinne was still alive. The second he lost his leverage, he was at Ada's mercy. But she couldn't risk anything while he had Corinne.

Movement in the corner of her eye. Ada looked to see that Saint had taken a few steps backward, closer to the front door. His eyes were wide, and she could see that he was trembling. She jerked her gaze toward the door, willing him to leave. For a split second she thought he would obey. But then he shook his head, his anxious eyes angling back toward Corinne.

"You could have just left," Ada said to Johnny, fighting to keep her voice steady, fighting for more time to think. She was keenly

369

aware of a weight in her coat pocket that she had forgotten until now. "No one would have been able to find you."

"I've been stockpiling my fortune in that warehouse for years," Johnny said. "I'm not going to walk away and let a bunch of slagger kids take *my* club."

Ada flinched at the slur from Johnny's lips. She couldn't stop thinking about Corinne, curled up on her bed, weeping because he was gone. All that thundering rage and pain, and for what?

"You should have left it alone," Johnny went on, his grip on the knife tightening. "You two wouldn't be able to keep it open during Prohibition anyway. The Cast Iron will never be what it was."

Corinne squeezed her eyes shut, and Ada saw a thin trickle of red running down her neck.

"We have to try," Ada said.

"No," Johnny said simply. "It's over now."

In that moment she believed him. They'd dodged the Hemopath Protection Agency, survived Haversham Asylum, and outsmarted a councilman. And now the end had come, at the hand of someone she had once trusted with her life. With her mother's life. With everything.

The storage room door flew open behind Johnny. He spun around, jerking Corinne with him. The newcomer was Guy Jackson, looking worse for wear and beyond furious.

"You lying son of a bitch," he shouted at Johnny. "I'm going to kill you!"

He stormed into the room, and even though he didn't appear to be armed, Johnny took a few steps back. Corinne clutched at his arm and stumbled back with him, still trapped in his grip.

"What are you doing here?" Johnny asked, suspicion rising in his voice.

"I know it's a real shock," Jackson spat. "You figured I'd just rot quietly in prison—well, I'm not taking the fall for you, Dervish. I'm getting every penny you owe me, even if I have to take it off your corpse."

With Johnny's back still turned, Ada slipped her hand into her coat pocket. Jackson's gun from the warehouse was still there. It was a sliver of a chance. She gripped it, her finger questing for the safety. She flicked it off and lifted the gun, aiming it at Johnny's back. She had the power to end this. All she had to do was pull the trigger. She didn't have a choice.

In her mind's eye, she could see the tree from Charlie's childhood and the wildflowers swirling in the breeze. She was a liar and a thief, but she had never killed anyone. She'd thought that the day she shook hands with Johnny Dervish was the day that everything had been irrevocably lost, but maybe there was more to lose. She still had one choice she could make.

She didn't pull the trigger.

Jackson had seen the gun, and at his expression Johnny spun back to face Ada. He stared at the raised gun in her hands, confusion melting away. He smiled thinly.

"You always were too hesitant," he told her.

"Shoot him," Corinne said.

"Go ahead," Johnny said, giving Corinne a shake. "I hope your aim is good."

Ada met Corinne's eyes, saw the fatalistic determination there. She really wanted her to do it. She was ready to die if it meant taking Johnny with her. Ada shook her head.

"I can't," she said, dropping her arm.

"Jackson, get the gun," Johnny said.

Jackson's gaze darted between Johnny and Ada, weighing his

options. Finally he stepped forward, his blue eyes glinting in the dim light of the electric bulbs. He reached for the gun, and with Johnny's knife still at Corinne's throat, Ada didn't know what else to do. She let him take it.

She had the distant thought that she hadn't replied to her mother's letter. Her parents would wonder what had happened to her. They would probably never know.

Instead of just shooting her, Jackson backed toward the front door, training the gun on Johnny.

"I'm not doing your dirty work for you anymore," he said. "I want my money."

Johnny glowered at him, but the wheels in his head were obviously turning. "Help me clean up this mess," he said, jerking his head toward Ada, "and I'll pay you double what I owe."

Jackson paused, considering. Almost faster than Ada could follow, Saint rounded the corner of the bar, charging Jackson. For the space of a breath, they struggled over the gun. Then Jackson yanked it free, shoved him to the floor behind the bar, took aim, and fired.

There was a scream, mingled with the deafening gunshot. When she felt the raw pain in her throat, Ada realized it was her own. She ran forward, too intent on Saint to think about the fact that Jackson was in her path. When he leveled the gun at her, Ada stopped. Her chest heaved as she stared down the barrel. She couldn't see Saint over the bar. She couldn't feel anything but her own hammering heart.

"Shoot her," Johnny said, "before she tries anything."

"No!" Corinne struggled against Johnny, heedless of the blade breaking skin.

Ada stumbled backward on numb legs, unable to tear her eyes away from the gun. Jackson moved with her, kicking stools aside, aim never wavering. But he didn't pull the trigger. Ada stopped when she hit the edge of a table. She reached back, pressing her palms against the satin tablecloth, trying in vain to steady herself.

"Do it now," Johnny said.

But Jackson still hesitated, glancing toward Johnny with an unreadable expression on his face. Ada's eyes found Corinne's, and she knew what Corinne wanted her to do. It was their last chance. She had to sing.

Ada's mouth was bone dry, and she trembled uncontrollably. She needed only a few notes to trap Johnny and Jackson under her will, but Johnny needed fewer than that to slit Corinne's throat. Ada licked her lips, mind fumbling for the right melody.

"Useless," Johnny snapped. "Give it to me."

He shoved Corinne forward, and Ada's song caught in her throat as Corinne careened into her. Johnny moved to take the gun from Jackson, but Jackson spun on him immediately and rammed the barrel against Johnny's chest, right at his heart.

"Madeline loved a good revenge story," Jackson said.

Johnny's eyes widened in realization, but it was too late. Guy Jackson had aimed the gun, but it was James Gretsky who pulled the trigger.

A gunshot echoed around them, seeming to fill up the world. For a moment, the Cast Iron was perfectly, completely still.

Then Johnny crumpled to the ground. Ada's heart skipped a beat. She couldn't seem to catch her breath, and her ears rang from the shot. She clutched at Corinne's elbows, still trying to steady her. Behind the bar, Saint came into view, dragging himself upright. He was paler than usual but otherwise unharmed. Corinne took a step forward, then another, but she didn't seem to know where she was going exactly. James still had the gun trained on the lifeless heap that had once been the indomitable Johnny Dervish. His expression was somewhere between horror and relief, and there were silent tears streaming down his face. The gun was trembling in his grip.

No one moved. No one spoke.

Finally, with careful steps, Saint came around the bar. He went to James's side and gently closed a hand around his wrist. James relaxed as Saint lowered the gun and pried it from his fingers. A few interminable seconds passed; then James let out a single, strangled sob and threw his arms around Saint.

Corinne turned to look at Ada. Crimson spilled from the cuts on her neck, pooling at her collarbone. Ada could see in her eyes what had to be done. She nodded once and picked her way around the scattered chairs to where Saint's wildflower painting hung on the wall. She lifted it free and crossed the room to him and James.

"It's time to leave," she told them.

James pulled back from Saint and looked at her, disoriented. Ada pressed the painting into Saint's hands, and he stared down at it as if he were seeing it for the first time. It was the only one of his paintings that had survived. And soon it would be the only thing left of the Cast Iron.

"Head toward the Red Cat," Ada said, pleased to find that her voice wobbled only slightly. "Charlie will be there."

Saint looked between her and Corinne uncertainly.

"But what about—"

"Go," Ada said, giving both him and James a little shove toward the door.

"We'll catch up," Corinne said.

Saint looked like he had more to say, but he only nodded and took a few steps backward, hugging his painting against his chest.

James hesitated where he stood. He couldn't seem to pull his eyes from the blood on the floor. Finally Saint took his hand, and he turned away. They left through the front door.

Corinne had leaned against the table beside Ada, squeezing the sides of her skirt in white-knuckled fists. She had lost more of the jet beads from her dress, and her dark hair was slick with sweat. For a long time, neither of them spoke. Ada let her gaze drift around the Cast Iron, avoiding Johnny's body. She wished they could've known it at the height of its glory, before it had been tainted by greed and hate.

"It wasn't all bad," Corinne said at last.

Ada nodded.

Some of it was perfect, Corinne thought. The problem was that there was no way to separate the perfect from the polluted. No way to carve out Johnny's avaricious legacy and separate it from all the things the Cast Iron had been built to represent. Even now his blood was seeping into the floorboards, staining them forever with his death.

Corinne stumbled around Johnny to the bar, ignoring the stinging, bloody cuts on her neck. She dug through the cabinets until she found the clear, unmarked bottle that Danny kept hidden for special occasions and particularly stressful nights. They'd hosted last night's party as a celebration, but now it would be a send-off. A grand farewell to all that had come before.

They could do better.

Ada was coming across the floor toward her. She moved like a memory, gliding past the tables that hours ago had held patrons with stars in their eyes. Corinne popped the cork from the bottle and dumped the contents onto the bar, from one end to the other.

Ada watched her without questioning. Corinne knew that she understood what they had to do. They couldn't perform on that stage anymore, pretending they were untouchable. Danny couldn't serve up drinks to the judges and politicians, while Johnny traded favors and secrets at his corner table. The line of patrons, dressed to the nines in silk and furs, couldn't slip through the mirrored corridor with the watchword on their lips. For better or worse, Prohibition had passed, and everything was going to change. Johnny had been right about one thing—the club couldn't be as it was. Maybe it was better this way.

The Cast Iron would be his funeral pyre.

Corinne rounded the bar to stand beside Ada several feet away, pulling Gabriel's matches from her pocket. She lit the entire book. For a split second she didn't move. Just held it there between them. Her eyes met Ada's over the flames.

Ada gave one quick nod. Corinne flung the matches to the counter, and it came alive with heat, roaring orange and yellow, blinding them momentarily. It was simultaneously the most beautiful and most terrifying thing Corinne had ever seen.

They left through the front door. Corinne stopped at the fire alarm box at the street corner and pulled the handle. She and Ada kept walking, their heads ducked against the wind. The city of Boston stretched before them like a second chance. They said nothing, but Corinne lifted her hand, palm up, and Ada tapped her fingertips twice.

Soon the flames behind them would tear free, straining for cool oxygen to devour. Until then the Cast Iron remained quiet, its red door radiant in the January dawn.